Praise for *Kiss of Steel*

"Exquisitely imagined… McMaster's wildly inventive plot deftly blends elements of steampunk and vampire romance with brilliantly successful results. Darkly atmospheric and delectably sexy, *Kiss of Steel* is an extraordinary debut."

—*Booklist* Starred Review

"Dark, intense, and sexy… A stunning new series."

—*Library Journal*

"An enthralling debut… A leading man as wicked as he is irresistible… Heart-wrenching, redemptive, and stirringly passionate… A series opener to be read and savored."

—*RT Book Reviews*, 4.5 Stars

"An interesting twist on the vampire mythos and the brutal side of London high society."

—*Publishers Weekly*

"A stellar steampunk novel with an amazing world, complex characters, and action-packed plot. Steampunk fans will gobble this book up…an excellent example of how great steampunk can be."

—*The Romance Reviews*, 5 stars

"Unique, spellbinding, thrilling. and complex… a must-read for paranormal fans and steampunk fans alike."

—*Night Owl Reviews* Reviewer Top Pick, 5 Stars

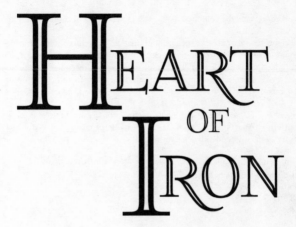

HEART OF IRON

BEC McMASTER

sourcebooks
casablanca

*To my Mum and Dad. For teaching
me to chase my dreams.*

One

London, 1879

FOG CLUNG TO THE THAMES LIKE A LIGHTSKIRT TO A rich patron. Here and there, gaslight gleamed, flashing will-o'-the-wisp in the shrouding pea soup mist. It was the perfect night not to be seen.

Will Carver loped across rooftops and gables, leaping across an alley and coming to a halt behind a chimney near Brickbank.

A man landed lightly on the tiles beside him, breathing hard from the exertion. He wore black leather from head to toe, and the only weapons he carried were a pair of razors, tucked in his belt. "Bloody 'ell. You tryin' to run me to death?" Blade muttered.

The words were quiet, but the sound carried in the still night. Will's lip curled, and he glared at his master.

"They won't be listenin' for *us*, bucko." Blade straightened, staring at the ruddy pillar of smoke ahead of them. "Not with that burnin'. And none of 'em 'as your hearin'."

A column of red glowed against the night sky

ahead, barely muted by the fog. Every time Will breathed he could taste the ash in the air. Ahead, a massive brick gate and wall blocked the way into the city. A company of metaljackets paced in front of the gate, gaslight gleaming off the shining steel plates of their armored chests. With the flamethrower append-ages in place of their left arms they looked formidable enough to keep the general rabble at bay. They were, however, automatons and not human.

He'd long since learned they didn't look up.

"Over?" he asked.

"I got me pardon now," Blade said. "Could waltz right on through them gates and they'd not say a word." The devilish light in his eyes said he wanted to try. There was nothing Blade liked better than thumbing his nose at the blue bloods who ruled the city.

"Yeah, well, we ain't all that lucky," Will reminded him. "I've still got a price on me head."

Blade sighed, eyeing the massive edifice. "Over it is, then."

"You're gettin' lazy."

"I should be at 'ome, tucked up with me cheroot and a nice glass of mulled blud-wein." What he didn't add was the fact that he most likely wouldn't have been doing either of those things. If the fire hadn't called them out, Blade'd be in bed with his wife, Honoria.

Will took a few steps back. No point him being at home. The flat he rented these days was cold and uninviting. There was nothing for him to go back to.

A wide leap took him sailing across the street and onto a rooftop beside the gate. Taking a running start, he bounded up and over the wall before the guard on top had finished shaking out the flame on his match. Human eyes were sometimes just as bad as the automatons.

Bootsteps echoed him on the rooftops as he flitted lightly through the night. Fog parted around him, drifting in his wake, but he was moving too fast for anyone watching to see.

Here in the city the streets were a touch wider, the buildings not as jammed together as they were in the Whitechapel rookery he called home. Blood flushed through his veins as he leaped from rooftop to rooftop. He'd been cooped up for too long; he needed this.

Screams caught his ear along with the organized shouts of people trying to marshal water pumps. Little snowflakes of ash floated through the air, almost thick enough to choke a man. Will paused in the crook of a chimney.

Ahead, the world looked like it was on fire. Billowing gouts of orange flame licked at the skies, and a thick dark pall of smoke hung over the river. Lines of people manned water pumps, desperately trying to stop the flames from spreading.

"Jaysus," Blade cursed as he knelt at Will's side.

"The draining factories," Will said. "Someone's fired the draining factories."

It was unthinkable. The line of factories down by the river were owned by the ruling Echelon to filter and store the blood gathered in the blood taxes. This would be a huge blow to them.

Blade's eyes narrowed. "You and I ought to get out of 'ere, quick-smart." His nostrils flared. "The place'll be swarmin' in metaljackets before we know it."

Will backed up a step. He knew what Blade wasn't saying. Two more perfect scapegoats couldn't be found. Most of the aristocratic Echelon had been furious with the queen's pardon and knighthood of Blade three years ago. And Will was just a slave-without-a-collar to their eyes.

A clink of metal caught his ears. Iron-booted feet on distant cobbles. A legion of metaljackets by the sound of it. "Go," he snapped, shoving Blade in the back.

Blade needed no urging. He scrambled up the tiles on the roof, a break in the clouds bathing him in moonlight. Once, a few years ago, his hair would have lit up like a beacon. Now it had dulled to a light brown, and his skin was no longer as pale as marble.

Will followed at his heels in an easy lope, his ears alert to the slightest sound behind them. They'd seen what they came to see. No doubt word of it'd be all over the streets by morning.

Movement ahead caught his eye. A swirl of a black cloak stirring the fog. Will leaped forward and shoved Blade flat, covering him with his body.

"Ooof," Blade wheezed. He lifted his head. "Thanks, but I've already got a wife—"

"Shut up." Will pressed his hand between the other man's shoulder blades, coming to a crouch. His gaze raked the fog. There. A metallic chink. Voices in the shadows.

From Blade's stillness, he'd heard them too.

"Stay here," Will breathed, close to his ear. "Keep your bloody head down and I'll check it out."

"Do I look like I need a friggin' nursemaid?"

Will shot him a look. Three years ago, no. Blade'd

been the most dangerous thing to stalk the night. But his hair and skin color weren't the only changes in him since he'd started drinking Honoria's blood.

"You go left," he finally murmured. Short of tying Blade to the chimney with his belt, there wasn't much chance of leaving him here.

Both of them faded into the fog. The voices ahead were getting farther away. Will moved like a wraith through the night, the movement rippling his dark wool coat around his hips. Beneath it he wore a heavy leather waistcoat that had been modified with steel inserts, as well as steel caps over his knees. You couldn't be too careful in a world where a man's main weapon might be a shiv or a heavy wrench. His loupe virus could heal almost anything, but being knifed still hurt.

Metal clanged and a pair of curses littered the air. Then silence, as though both people froze to see if they'd been heard. Will slowed, creeping across the tiles with one foot placed carefully in front of the other. He knelt low, easing on hands and feet around the edge of a chimney. There was no sign of Blade, but then Blade was even better at this sort of thing than he was.

"You drop that again and Mercury'll have your head," someone snapped.

Two figures. Both dressed in black and moving with a footpad's efficiency. The shorter one picked up something heavy. A hollow metal tube, like the flamethrowers that the Spitfires used.

"Mercury ain't here, is he?" asked the shorter man, hefting the flamethrower over his shoulder. "And when he hears how well we done, then he'll be burying us in ale and whores."

"That's if the Echelon don't rip your guts out first," Blade said pleasantly, materializing out of nowhere.

Shit.

Will leaped forward, even as the two men turned on his master. Despite their bickering, they moved with military efficiency. The shorter one snapped the flame-thrower up, just as the other drew his blade. The tube coughed and then bright orange flame spewed through the fog, highlighting the roof and everyone on it.

Blade spun low, sweeping the knife-wielder's feet out from under him. Will grabbed the barrel of the flamethrower and elbowed the man in the face. There was a satisfying crunch, then his mind registered just how hot the tube was. He dropped it and it rolled toward the edge of the roof, catching in the gutter.

"Just the two of you boys?" Blade taunted, not even bothering to draw a knife. He bent backward, avoiding the swipe of the knife with a gravity-defying movement, before snapping upright.

The man he was facing stiffened. "Frigging bleeders!" He reached into his pocket to press some-thing and then agony screamed through Will's head.

The sound was like an ice pick to the brain, wiping out all sense of time and place and even connection to his body. He hit the tiles, scrabbling blindly for purchase as he started to slide.

Something hit him hard under the chin, snapping his head back with resounding force. Words sounded, distorting the high-pitched scream, but he couldn't make any of them out. Then movement blurred at the edge of his vision. Another smashing blow against his cheekbone. Blood splashed over his face, wet and hot.

Will clapped his hands over his ears, collapsing back on the tiles. That sound! Like razors in his head.

In…his pocket. Something in the man's pocket. A device of sorts, making the noise.

Grinding his teeth together, he saw the shorter man lifting the flamethrower high. No time to think. He kicked out, aiming for the man's knee.

A heavy weight landed on him and they both grunted. The throbbing squeal of noise pounded in time to his heartbeat. Will clawed to his feet and staggered forward, searching for Blade.

There. On the roof. The other man knelt over him and Will realized he had a knife buried deep in Blade's chest. Trying to cut out his heart.

"No!" he roared, seeing red.

Anger rushed over him, swallowing him whole and burning him in its wake. He grabbed the man by the collar and flung him away. Blade gasped, clapping a hand to the knife hilt, but his reactions were still slow, disorientated.

The noise.

Will slammed the man down and yanked at his pocket. A small, vibrating device came free. He crushed it in his fist and the world fell silent.

Will staggered, throwing aside the crushed pieces. His ears were still ringing, but at least he could think. Breathe. Move.

The scent of hot, coppery blood washed over him.

"Blade," he growled, leaping over the gasping man on the roof and sliding to his knees beside his master.

Blade lifted his head, then collapsed back down. "Bloody… Get it out…'s silver." He lifted his fingers and flinched as they brushed against the knife hilt.

"Hold still," Will snapped. A cold ring of sweat beaded on his forehead. The knife was buried to the hilt. He had no idea of the damage it had done, or what would happen if he removed it.

Behind him, the two men helped each other to their feet. Will spared them a glance, but they were trying to get away, now that the advantage had shifted once more to him and Blade.

"Gutted by a human." Blade laughed incredulously. "Always thought…it'd be one of the Echelon. In the end."

"Stop your whinin'." Will wrenched his shirt off, a frisson of icy cold trailing down his spine. Blue bloods were notoriously difficult to kill. That was one reason the French revolution had guillotined their aristocrats. The only other way to stop them was to cut out their heart or cause severe damage to it. He swallowed hard and shoved his shirt around the wound to stop the bleeding. "Nothin' more'n a scratch. We'll have you hale in no time."

Blade met his gaze. His fingers were surprisingly strong when they closed around Will's. "Swear you'll look after 'er," he snarled. "If…if I don't…"

Will dropped his gaze. "Aye. You know I'll do it." He owed Blade his life, no matter what he personally thought of Honoria. "Hold still. You need blood."

Darkness slithered through Blade's pale eyes. His head rolled to the side. "Feels…numb…" he murmured.

Panic speared through Will's gut. "Don't you

dare!" Ripping at the heavy hunting knife he carried, he cradled his friend's head in his hands. "Here. Have me blood. It'll help."

It was short work to slash the vein in his wrist open. He cupped the back of his head and held Blade's mouth to his wrist.

A moment of hesitation that never used to be there. He knew what Blade was thinking. He'd stopped taking directly from any of his thrall's veins when Honoria came into his life. Now he drank his blood either from her or cold, out of the icebox.

"Don't be a fool. She won't mind," Will snarled.

That hint of darkness swept through Blade's irises again. Will's chest caught. Not in fear. Gods, not that. Anticipation swept through his veins, lighting them on fire. It'd been a long time since he'd been one of Blade's thralls. He'd not realized how much he missed it.

As Blade's mouth closed over his wrist, his tongue sliding over the ragged wound, Will collapsed forward onto his hands. A gasp tore from his lips. Feeling flooded through him that he hadn't felt in years. It had confused him when Blade first took him as a thrall, but it was nothing more than his body's reaction to the chemicals in his master's saliva.

But the moment of closeness…

This was all he'd ever have of that.

He ground his teeth and tried to deny the pull. Twice as harsh after three years of abstinence. And just as confusing.

He didn't feel this way with females.

Or he never had. Until Lena walked into his life.

And I'm not *thinkin' of her.* Will bit his lip, trying to ignore the flush of pleasure that thought brought. Dark hair, dark eyes, that flirtatious little smile that drove him insane… His groin tightened and he growled, head bowed as the sensation against his wrist increased.

It was over all too quickly. Will collapsed onto his backside, clutching his wrist against his chest. The skin throbbed, still feeling the imprint of Blade's mouth. Heat flushed through the ragged edges of the knife cut—his loupe virus, rapidly healing the wound. It would be gone by the end of the hour, barely a pink pucker against his swarthy skin.

Blade gasped, drawing his feet up. His eyes blazed with black fire, and he grabbed the handle of the hilt and ground his teeth together. Crying out, he drew it out of his chest and collapsed back on the roof, panting for breath.

The wound was still bleeding, but sluggishly now. With his blood flushing through Blade's system, there was a strong chance he'd pull through. Verwulfen blood was thrice as potent as a human's.

"Honoria'll…kill me…" Blade gasped.

That's if he survived. Will took one look at the ashen color of his face and looked away swiftly. Damage to the heart was always dangerous. He had to get him back to the warren, where Honoria, with her medical background, might be able to help.

Rigging up a makeshift bandage, he held his coat in place to suppress the bleeding and then tied the ends of his shirt off. "There. That'll hold until we get you home." Sliding his arm under Blade's shoulder, he helped him to sit.

Blade gasped, clutching at his chest. The sight tore another shaft of ice through Will's gut. Followed by a hot stab of anger. Three years ago Blade would've laughed this off. He was no longer standing on the edge of the Fade—when the craving virus finally overtook a blue blood and he turned into something else, something worse—but for a moment, Will didn't know if that was any better.

"Can you stand?"

Blade struggled to his feet, his eyes glassy with pain.

"You have to hold on," Will warned, bending and easing the other man over his shoulder. "I'm goin' to get you home. To Honoria. She'll know what to do. Just you hold on."

❧

Honoria eased the blankets higher and then turned the knob on the gas lamp lower. Light muted, casting a variety of shadows across the room as Blade slept. Will paced in front of the fire, his wrist tingling as the skin healed.

Honoria washed her hands, moving away from the bed. Her face was composed, but deep shadows lingered in the hollows beneath her reddened eyes. As she turned, the light caught her profile and for a moment Will stopped breathing, seeing another's face in the shadows. Then she looked up, arching a brow at him and the image was gone. She shared the same dark eyes and rich mahogany hair as her sister, but Lena's face was prettier and she was a good inch or two shorter than Honoria.

Just the ghost of her image lingered, haunting him.

A quick jerk of the head meant Honoria wanted to talk to him. Outside.

Shooting Blade one last look, he strode to the door. An old shirt of Blade's hung loosely over his chest. He couldn't quite button it, and the sleeves stretched taut over his arms. Foolishness. But he wasn't knocking on Rip's door—Blade's other lieutenant—and asking for a shirt that might have a better chance at fitting him.

Honoria eased the door closed. "I think he'll be fine. The bleeding's stopped and I'll get some more blood into him. Thank you for bringing him home to me."

Will nodded. He never had much to say to her. They'd tried, after she first married Blade, to find some common ground between them. But he knew what she thought of him—had overheard it in quite explicit detail the night before he moved out of the warren.

Dangerous.

Unpredictable.

A threat to her sister.

Sometimes he wasn't sure if she hadn't been half right.

Her gaze dropped to his wrist. "Do you need tending—?"

"It'll heal."

"Something to eat then? There's stew…in the kitchen. I'll just—"

"Ain't hungry." He nodded his leave of her, then turned on his heel. The back of his neck was itching.

"Will. Please."

He stopped moving and glanced back over his shoulder.

"You know you can come home now. It breaks

his heart that you're living on your own. And you know…she's not here anymore either."

Honoria would never understand. He shook his head. "She weren't the reason I left," he growled. *Not the only one anyway.*

Then he turned and stalked out into the darkness, feeling her eyes on his back the entire way.

～∞～

No point going home.

Will stared at the fire in the distance, still raging out of control. Something bothered him about the attack. The mysterious device. The flamethrower. The silver knife. Those men had been prepared to face a blue blood and incapacitate them.

He breathed deeply through his nose. It was hard to pick up a scent trail with the overwhelming cling of ash in the air but not impossible. Moving east, he loped across the rooftops, his unease growing as the men circled back toward the north. Toward Whitechapel.

Just before the wall that circled the rookery, they dropped off the rooftops and disappeared into an alley. Will knew the area well. It was a dead end.

He followed them in and stared at the brick wall at the back of it. The ripe scents of the rookery spilled over into the surrounding streets. He wrinkled up his nose and looked around. There was a grate in the cobbles, but surely they wouldn't have gone down. That led to the sewers and from there into the notorious sprawl of Undertown. Weren't nothing living there now, only ghosts and whispers. People had tried to move back in once the vampire that had slaughtered its residents was killed, but something drove them back out.

If they came back at all.

All that space, the caverns and homes carved into the old underground tunnel scheme. Empty. Or was it?

Will hauled the grate out of the cobbles and dropped down into the dark, landing lightly on the pads of his feet. His nose told him there was nothing there. Nothing but refuse and the odd rat skittering away.

Without the ash or a breeze, it was easier to follow the trail. The men weren't moving fast, probably thinking they were safe from the Echelon and their metal army down here. Will shook his head. Dead men walking. The Echelon didn't just rely on the metaljackets. Give them an hour and the tunnels would be full of Nighthawks, the infamous guild of trackers that did most of the thief-taking in the city. Rogue blue bloods who could smell almost as well as he could and track a shadow over stone, or so it was said.

He'd have to hurry if he wanted to get his hands on them first.

He waded into the sluggish stream, his nose almost shutting down. He'd smelled worse things—the vampire sprang to mind—but right now they were only a distant memory. It was the curse of heightened senses. He could smell everything, from a woman's natural musk to the slight hint of poison in a cup; he could see for miles and if he listened, he could hear things people didn't want him to hear.

Like stealthy footsteps, a few hundred yards in front of him.

Will made no sound as he stalked them. Whispers echoed and then a light appeared. A shuttered smuggler's lantern by the look of it.

"Got him," the short, fat one crowed. "Right in the chest. Won't be so high-and-mighty now, will he?"

Will's eyes narrowed.

"Shut up," the taller shadow snarled. The acrid scent of fear-sweat washed off him. "Didn't you see his bloody face?"

A shrug. The short man sloshed through the water carelessly. "All looks the same to me. Pasty-faced vultures."

"It was him," the other man replied with a shudder. "The devil himself!"

"The Devil of Whitechapel?" The shorter man's face stretched in a delighted grin. "Cor, Freddie! All them years and the Echelon themselves ain't been able to get near him! And you done him in! You're famous now!"

"I'm bloody dead, is what I am," Freddie snapped back. "If that were the devil, then you know who the other one was!"

Will took another step forward, drawing the blade at his side. He smiled. *That's right, you son of a bitch. You're in trouble now.*

"Who?"

"The Beast," Will hissed, his voice echoing out of the darkness.

Freddie screamed and swung the lantern.

Will smashed it aside and it hit the water and hissed out. Darkness fell like a theatre curtain, but he was already moving, driving his fist up under the whistling swing of an arm and connecting with a pair of ribs. Bone snapped and then Freddie was down with a gurgling cry, splashing under the water.

Will stilled, listening to the frantic sound of breathing.

"Freddie?" the fat man whispered. He fumbled for the sides of the sewer, his breath high-pitched and panting.

Will took a slow step forward, water sloshing around his knees.

"Oh, God." The fat man tried to run. "Oh, God, no! I didn't have naught to do with it! It were Freddie! Leave me alone!"

Will grabbed his cloak and hauled him back. He landed with a splash, his legs kicking in the sewer water as he squealed like a downed pig. Fisting the cloak, Will wrapped it around the fat's man throat and then hauled him up in a choking grip.

"Who are you? Who do you work for?"

The fat man kicked, making strangled sounds. Will held him long enough for the kicking to falter, then dropped him in the water.

Movement behind him. He lashed out, catching the heavy metal tube as Freddie swung it and followed through with a punch. Blood sprayed as his fist connected with Freddie's nose. The coppery tang of it flavored the air, and Freddie screamed and fell back into the water.

"Jaysus." The fat man sobbed, his throat hoarse.

Will caught him up by the coat and slammed him back against the slimy walls. He slid his hand into the man's coat, rifling his pockets. A switchblade the idiot was too dumb to draw, a piece of waxed paper, and an odd, finger-shaped device. Another one of those noisemakers. He pocketed both it and the piece of paper.

"Consider yourself lucky he ain't dead." The thought set off the red-hot flare of rage in his head, and he slammed the fat man against the wall. Then again.

"Please, please don't kill me!"

Careful, a little voice warned. *Don't lose control.*

Will growled, the sound echoing inhumanly through his throat. They already thought him a beast. Why the hell shouldn't he rip them apart? They'd put a knife in Blade. Nobody touched his adopted family and lived to tell of it.

Shouts echoed through the tunnels. Will's head shot up and he clenched his fist. Nighthawks. On the trail already, damn it.

He leaned closer and sniffed the air beside the man's ear. "Got your scent now," he whispered. "You ever come near Whitechapel again and I'll come for you. I'll rip you apart, one piece at a time…and feed it to you. You don't want that, do you?"

The stench of urine filled the air and the man sobbed his agreement. Will dropped him with a splash then turned on his heel.

The Nighthawks would smell him, but they wouldn't catch him. This was Will's turf here, and they wouldn't dare cross the wall circling Whitechapel to hunt him. Time to get the hell out of here. He gave Freddie and his fat friend one last hungry look, then turned and fled into the darkness.

They'd remember his threat. That was all that mattered.

❧

Will tossed the shirt away with a wet slap and then started on the buttons of his breeches. Both stunk from the tunnels, but he felt a damned sight better. The tension between his shoulders eased with every blow he'd dealt.

He'd wanted blood. Wanted to kill. But sometimes it was best to leave them alive. Witnesses. Men who'd spread the stories in hushed tones in local alehouses, warning others not to risk the wrath of Whitechapel's Beast. It was all part of the legend he was carefully cultivating. A lesson he'd learned from Blade.

Fear was often the best defense.

The air was chilly as he kicked off the rest of his clothes and strode for the washbasin. He usually didn't notice the cold, but he'd been wet for hours and his stomach was empty. Scrubbing the stink off himself, he draped a blanket around his hips and then turned toward the kitchen. There was bread and cheese left over, and a jug of clean water.

Resting his backside against the table, he bit into his meal and stared at his shirt. There was something sticking out of it. A piece of paper. The note the fat man had carried.

He padded across the room and knelt, chewing slowly. The paper was thick with wax. Whoever had written it had wanted it to stay dry, which meant he thought the recipient of it would get wet at some stage. Will frowned. Just where had those two been heading—in the sewers? The water this time of year was barely knee high.

There were whispers that it was deeper down below, though. In some parts of Undertown.

Fishing it open, he tilted it toward the single lamp. Lines of symbols crisscrossed the parchment—letters, numbers, and odd slashing marks. An incomprehensible mess.

What the hell had he stumbled upon? Will took another bite of his bread and cheese and stood, crossing closer to the lamp. The better light made no sense of the symbols, not that he'd expected them to.

Will flipped the paper over, but there was nothing on the back. No scent but the odd waxy substance. He frowned. Burning down the draining factories, coded letters, strange devices that had obviously been made to incapacitate blue bloods... Somebody was looking to start a war.

Two

"HOW SPECTACULARLY...GAUDY."

Lena glanced away from the curtained platform, her attention drawn by the dripping malice in her friend's tone. "Whatever do you mean, Adele?"

Adele Hamilton—a former diamond of society—leaned closer and turned her lip up. "They've got puppets. I'm surprised Miss Bishop hasn't invited an entire menagerie to perform for us this evening. Or a circus troupe."

"You're just jealous because she signed a thrall contract with Lord Macy and you thought he was going to offer for you." Lena turned her head to the balcony where Miss Bishop was sipping champagne and glowing with happiness. Having signed a thrall contract with Lord Macy, Miss Bishop was now set for life. It was the highest ambition of any debutante. To be protected. Showered in diamonds and fancy golden steam carriages. Dripping in pearls.

All it cost was a little something in return.

Blood.

Lena shivered and looked down into her half-empty glass.

"As if I'd accept someone like Macy." Adele sniffed and drained her glass. Yet her pretty almond-shaped eyes watched the pair on the balcony like a hawk.

Macy rested his hand on Miss Bishop's gloved one and slowly stroked her fingers. Even from the gardens below, Lena could see her breathing quicken and Macy's eyes darken with desire. He seemed so much older than Miss Bishop in that moment. So much more powerful. It made Lena feel sick to her stomach.

Stop it, she told herself sharply. *Don't think about it.* It was Miss Bishop's choice. She wasn't being forced into this.

Except by circumstances.

"I can't believe they're carrying on so in public," Adele continued. "He might as well throw her down now and have her."

Caught in her own discomfort, Lena's voice was sharper than she intended. "Sheathe your claws before you cut yourself."

Adele shot her a devastating smile, one that had won half the hearts in the Echelon. And then broken them. "Miaow," she purred.

Despite her unease, Lena couldn't stop an answering smile from tugging at her lips. Adele was the kind of friend you certainly couldn't trust, but after the debacle last year where she was caught in the gardens with Lord Fenwick—who later refused to contract her—Adele was also an outcast of sorts. She'd clawed her way back into society via an icy heart and an unwavering smile, but her time, like Lena's, was running out. And unlike Lena, who was here for a purpose, Adele had no other options in life.

A crowd was gathering in front of the curtained stage. Service drones hovered, the silver platters fitted on their heads offering an array of beverages. Lena slipped another pair of champagne flutes from the tray, avoiding the drone's steam vent. They were highly practical, rolling quietly through the crowds, but more than one young lady's dress had been ruined and Lena was wearing crushed violet silk.

She kept an ear open as she moved through the crowd, idly listening—and then discarding—conversations. Being a debutante was the perfect disguise. In a way, she was almost invisible. People said things in front of her that they would otherwise have kept quiet.

It was a most convenient way to spy. She barely had to *do* anything at all.

"Puppets." Adele shook her head. Yet, she too gathered in front of the stage, desperate not to miss a thing.

The night was mild, stars glittering overhead. Lena looked up, her vision adjusting to the light. A thousand diamonds, her mother used to say when she was a little girl. "All for me," Lena would cry, and her mother would laugh and kiss her good night.

Now the stars seemed to have lost some of their luster, and the diamonds too. The world around her was too bright, too shiny, all silk and gold and malicious laughter. The world of the Echelon had once been the only thing she'd ever wanted, and now that she danced along its verge, she couldn't help wondering if there was something more out there for her.

Not that she would ever admit that.

She'd begged her sister, Honoria, for this chance

when it became clear that there was nothing left in Whitechapel for her. Pleaded for weeks to be allowed back to her former life, and the possibility of making a thrall contract.

Strangely enough, an ally had come from an unexpected source: Leo Barrons, her half brother. As heir to the Duke of Caine, Leo could never reveal the truth of their connection—and his own illegitimacy—but he'd offered to take her as his ward and Lena had gratefully accepted. When her father had been alive, she'd hovered on the edge of the Echelon. Now, with a man as powerful as Leo as her guardian, she was embraced completely.

And she'd never felt more alone.

An uneasy feeling lifted the hairs on the back of her neck. The sharp, horrible sensation of being watched. Lena looked around but there was no one there. Something hissed and she flinched. It sounded like a kettle giving vent to its rage. The crowd pressed closer and conversation dimmed. On stage, the tinny sound of an organ grinder began to play.

It struck a chord in her memory; the raucous sounds and laughter of Whitechapel, the press of unwashed bodies, and the bawdy language that she'd pretended not to memorize. Music on the streets, in the penny gaff houses. A sound best forgotten. She'd left Whitechapel behind a year ago. It felt longer. In that time, she'd lost all of her youthful pretensions and realized exactly what type of world she lived in—and the fact that there was very little she could do about it.

But what she could do about it, she would. There was a movement brewing to restore humans to equal status as blue bloods—no more blood taxes, no more martial law, no more involuntary thralls—and she was in an ideal position to help them. Lena had access to a host of the Echelon's secrets…if she kept her ears open.

"It seems Miss Bishop has a monkey after all," Adele whispered.

"Shush," Lena said, rising on her toes to see. As she did, she ran her gaze across the crowd, relaxing only when she realized there was no one watching her.

Just nerves… She was safe here, with the crowd and Adele at her side.

The curtains parted with a melodramatic jerk. On the terrace, the gas lamps suddenly faded, the muted flames casting a surreal blue light across the gathering. Steam curled out, obscuring a figure on the center of the stage. Its arms jerked into the air, the strings clearly visible against the gaslight.

"Marionettes," Adele dismissed.

The Contract Ball of Miss Bishop had been talked about for the last month as *the* event of the Season. Gossip had promised delights and curios far beyond anything ever seen, but so far the night had been disappointing. Lena relaxed down onto her heels just as the crowd gave an appreciative gasp.

"Oh my," Adele said. "Look, the strings have fallen!"

And so they had. The marionette gave a feeble jerk, its arms collapsing to its sides. And then slowly, with the mysterious steam curling around its feet, it began to straighten.

"It's an automaton," Lena said.

The metal creature began to move, his hands coming

up as though he held someone in his arms. Against the tinny organ-grinder music, he began to waltz.

Lena's mouth dropped open. She'd seen numerous service drones and dozens of the armored metaljackets that protected the streets and imposed the Echelon's will, but she'd never seen anything like this. Why, the joints were streamlined, and the movement of the automaton was peculiarly fluid, almost human.

The performance came to an end, the organ-grinder winding down slowly. The automaton's pace slowed and it began to falter in time to the music. Whoever the handler was, he was a man of great skill.

Lena clapped enthusiastically. She wanted a closer look. She was talented with her steel clockworks, but this was artistry on a level she could barely comprehend.

Unfortunately, most of the crowd wanted a closer look too. Lena found herself separated from Adele and eddied to the side, like a piece of flotsam in a raging current.

Dashing a feather out of her vision, she looked for Adele.

And that was when she saw him.

The warmth drained from her face. Alaric Colchester, the Duke of Lannister, watched her from across the crowd, a predatory smile on his thin lips as he sipped a flute of blud-wein. Her heart skipped a beat. Against the pale, powdered skin of his face, his red-stained lips flashed through her mind, reminiscent of a time long ago. But that time, the blood had not been watered with wine.

He wasn't supposed to be here. She made certain of that before she accepted any invitations these days.

With a meeting called in the Ivory Tower between the Council of Dukes that ruled the city, she'd been sure she'd be safe.

It must have finished early.

Lena tore her gaze away, her heart thundering in her ears. *Don't run.* If she'd learned anything over the years, it was that fear roused a blue blood to uncontrollable hungers.

A swift glance showed movement through the crowd. The pale, shining blond of his hair as he stalked her. Lena strained on her toes. Where had Adele gone? There was sometimes safety in numbers.

If Colchester felt like playing by the rules.

He was a duke, after all. Head of one of the seven great Houses that ruled the city. If he wanted to take her here, right now, then he could drag her off and no one would dare say a thing. Her guardian, Leo, the only man with the strength to counter Colchester, had been at the Ivory Tower meeting, standing in for his father, the Duke of Caine.

Lena moved into the crowd, a smile pasted on her face. The patch of bare skin at the back of her neck tingled. Lifting her glass, she tried to catch a hint of his reflection, but the crowd was too dense.

Damn him. She shot a look over her shoulder.

Too many people, pressed together and laughing at the mechanized puppetry. No sign of Colchester.

Music and laughter assaulted her ears. The crowd was a riot of bright colors as she whipped her head around, a fist clenched in her skirts. *Don't run. God, don't run.* But where the devil had he gone?

A large pink ostrich feather floated through her

vision. Adele. Lena pushed toward her. A pair of ladies gossiped behind their fans and Lena staggered between them, straight into a firm chest. Gloved hands caught her shoulders, as if to steady her.

"So sorry," she murmured, then froze as she saw the ink-black velvet coat, with its gold epaulets and a tassel draped from his right shoulder.

"You look pale, my dear." Colchester smiled his shark's smile and his hands tightened as she instinctively tried to draw back. "Like you need some air."

His grip urged her to the side, toward the garden. Lena dug her slippers in and shook her head, a desperate smile pasted on her face. She couldn't let anyone see her distress. It would only start rumors she couldn't afford. A lady's reputation was all that kept her from being claimed by any blue blood as his blood whore for the night.

Somehow she forced a laugh. It was her only defense. "Au contraire, Your Grace." A swift gesture at the gardens around them. "I have nothing *but* air, it seems."

His eyes glittered with dark enjoyment. The hairs along her spine rose, but somehow she managed an insouciant shrug. Colchester would scent the rising spike of fear, acrid on her skin. A delicate sauce, he'd once told her, to flavor the meal...

"Thank you for catching me, Your Grace. But I'm afraid I must find my friend, Adele. She was feeling poorly. I was supposed to fetch her some water."

"A pity," he soothed, his hand dropping to hers. He stroked her fingers through the silk of her gloves. "I was hoping you would save a dance for me. The *assah*, if you will."

A dance designed to tempt, to best display a potential

thrall's assets to a blue blood. The smoky eroticism of it was something she'd never surrendered to in public, but to witness it... Oh, to witness it was something else. "I'm afraid I—"

"I wasn't asking."

Lena tugged at her hand, but his iron fingers curled around her wrist, a hint of shadow darkening his pale eyes.

"Don't tempt me, my dear. I'm trying to be courteous, but I'm afraid your beauty quite drives me... out of my mind." A smile, then he brushed the back of one hand against her cheek.

Laughter surged through the crowd, making her jump. They were so close and yet they might as well be in the Orient for all the good they would do her.

"Have you thought any more on my offer?" he asked.

"I'm afraid I've been terribly occupied—"

"It's been a month."

Not long enough. She would never be his thrall. Lena tipped her chin up and stared him directly in the eye. "It's been a *busy* month, Your Grace."

"Colchester. I told you to call me Colchester. After all," a smirk, "we are rather well-acquainted, are we not?"

She wanted to smash the glass bulb from her champagne flute and stab him in the eye with the stem. The thought of Colchester with his mouth on her body made her stomach twist.

Never again.

"Must I wait another month for an answer?"

"Let me go, Your Grace. This is unseemly."

"Answer the question."

"Lena!" Adele's cry came out of nowhere. "There you are!"

A burst of perfume washed over them, then Adele was there, the feathers in her hair tickling Colchester's nose. He flinched away, his face tightening with fury. Adele clapped a hand to her mouth and giggled, seemingly overcome by champagne. "Oh, Your Grace! I didn't see you there. My apologies."

The crowd pressed upon them. He had no choice but to let her go.

Lena tugged her hand close to her body, as if he'd done her some injury. Fingers brushed against hers and then Adele squeezed her other hand.

Colchester gave her a curt nod. "Until next time. I will demand an answer." Then he turned and strode through the crowd.

All of a sudden Lena couldn't breathe. Adele took one look at her face and hustled her away, into the edges of the garden.

"Here," Adele said, snatching a glass of champagne off a service drone's platter. "Drink this."

"I...I can't..." The only thing holding her upright was Adele's hand.

A small folly appeared, shadowed from the rest of the garden party. Adele spun her around, forcing her to put her hands on the railing and lean forward. Tearing apart Lena's buttons, she loosened the strings on her corset.

Lena collapsed forward, sucking in a lungful of air. Her body was trembling from top to toe. She didn't know what had happened. Only that she hadn't been able to draw breath. Still couldn't, really.

Warmth splashed down her cheeks and she dashed at them with her gloved hands. Adele rubbed small circles on her back.

"Thank you." She'd never have expected Adele, of all people, to come to her rescue.

Adele's hand paused. "I just wish there'd been someone there…for me."

Lena looked up and met her gaze, her breath shuddering through her. "I thought you went willingly with Lord Fenwick?"

"That was the rumor he put about. They all know, of course." Adele's lips thinned. "It's become sport amongst the younger circles. They think taking a woman as thrall is old-fashioned. Why support her for life when you can take what you want from her then cast her aside?"

"But…that's appalling!"

"One step removed from a blood slave." Adele shrugged a slim shoulder. "The reason I was chasing Lord Macy is because he's a traditionalist. He believes in protecting his thralls. If I were you, Lena, I would look to someone older. And don't settle for anything less than a thrall contract. It's the only protection you or I have these days."

"Why doesn't anybody say something?"

"Who would dare?" Adele laughed, but there was no humor in it. Her expression hardened. "And why should any of the Echelon stir a finger to help us? We're food, Lena. The only interest they have in keeping us alive or taking us as thralls is because it's easier for them. We're like penned livestock."

Anger flared. "They're not all like that. My guardian, Leo—"

"Knows what's going on as surely as we do. And has he said a single word about it?"

Lena opened her mouth. And said nothing. Everything she saw on Adele's face was but an echo of how she herself felt. Trapped. Prey.

No. Not prey. She took a deep shuddering breath. Prey didn't fight back; they didn't find a way in which they could make a difference, and that's what she was doing.

"Take my advice," Adele continued. "I saw the look on Colchester's face. You need protection. Your guardian isn't enough—he's not even here, is he? If I were you, I would find some old decrepit lord with enough power to stand up to Colchester and beguile him into taking you as his thrall."

"That shouldn't be the only option I have."

"Unfortunately, for girls like you and me, there isn't any choice. The sooner you open your eyes to the world you truly live in, the better. Otherwise you're nothing but a fool—and fools don't survive very long here."

❦

"What's wrong with you this morning?"

Lena opened her eyes, her head resting against the carriage's window. Her companion, Mrs. Wade, peered at her over the top of her crochet. There was no sign of the attack of the megrims that had plagued her last night, keeping her from Lord Macy's ball.

Rubbing at her aching eyes, Lena sat up. "Nothing. I didn't sleep very well last night, is all."

"Perhaps we should return to Waverly Place."

Concern rounded Mrs. Wade's eyes. "You could do with some more rest."

Lena's eyes narrowed. "Your motivations are utterly transparent." Leaning forward, she peered through the velvet curtains of the steam carriage's window, her fingers tapping on the box in her hand. She hadn't dared let it out of her sight.

Mrs. Wade had the good grace to blush. She had her own feelings on what constituted as appropriate recreational pursuits for ladies. Designing clockwork toys was not one of them. "I'm simply concerned about your reputation. If anyone saw us at that *shop*…"

"Who would see us here? And if they did, I'm only purchasing a new clock."

The steam carriage rattled to a halt outside Mandeville's Clockwork Emporium. Her eye skipped over the dirty ragamuffins playing tumbler in the alleys and the coal lasses slipping through the crowd with their pails balanced on their shoulders. She'd seen all too much of it during her sojourn in the rookeries of Whitechapel, after her father's death. Indeed, that had once *been* her, before Mr. Mandeville took her on as his apprentice.

Sympathy choked her. No matter the dangers of her own life at court, they were nothing to what the coal lasses risked, walking the streets unprotected. At least in society she would never be left to die bleeding in the gutters, her life worthless to the blue bloods. Her position saw to that. She was potential prey—but she was also protected prey.

The door opened and a footman appeared. "Miss."

"Thank you, Henry." Lena accepted his hand

and stepped down onto the cobbles. Mr. Mandeville saw her coming and opened the door for her. With the curled ends of his waxed moustache, the pair of magnifying glassicals perched upon his windswept gray hair, and a distinct patchwork quality to his waistcoat, he would never be received within the great houses. Yet he was one of the finest clockmakers she'd ever seen.

And so much more.

He'd also been her savior, dragging her out of the gutters—when she'd *been* that bleeding, discarded coal lass—and tending her in his shop. Offering her respectable work. Then later, giving her some sense of hope when she had first begun to realize that her life at court wasn't the safe world she'd been searching for.

She could remember only too well the day she'd returned for her cloak and overheard him discussing secrets that could get a man hanged. The shock had nearly floored her. Mr. Mandeville, a humanist? She'd kept the secret to herself for days, tossing and turning at night as questions started to gnaw at her. Excitement. Finally she'd confronted him and demanded to join the cause.

"Miss Todd," Mr. Mandeville greeted, though he'd once called her "Lena" and threatened to rap her knuckles if she knocked over any of his clocks.

"Mr. Mandeville," she replied, proffering the box. "You're looking well. The summer air must be agreeing with you."

"Is this it?" His eyes lit up as he saw the box.

A warm spark of something sinfully proud reared itself in her chest. There were very few things she'd ever been good at. "It is," she breathed. "Oh, you should see it. It works exactly as I'd planned."

"May I?"

At her nod, he ushered her toward the counter. The walls seemed to encroach the farther one went into the shop due to dozens of hanging, ticking clocks that loomed off the plaster. As his apprentice, Lena had grown used to the sight of them. Mrs. Wade, however, hovered near the windows, glaring at the swinging pendulums from the safe depths of her bonnet.

Mr. Mandeville placed the box on the counter and slid a glance toward Mrs. Wade. "Old Dragon-Breath is still in the dark?"

"She thinks I've come to see if you've any orders for me." The work was steady enough to keep her occupied, though she had to do so under her brother's name. A Charlie Todd original clockwork toy went for a rather generous price. They weren't always for children either, though Lena took the most pleasure from those commissions.

"Hmm." Mandeville opened the box and slid his long fingers under the foot-high clockwork. He lifted it reverently and set it on the counter. "Oh, my. Oh, Lena, this is your finest work. He's utterly magnificent. Wherever did you come by the inspiration for such a thing? I assume it walks?"

Steel overlapping plates drew the eye, burnished to a polished gleam. The clockwork sculpture was a man, a burly figure carved from iron sheeting and seething with an interior of springs and coils. It stood on a metal plate, with a windup key at the back. Heat crept into her cheeks. The last thing she could admit was her inspiration. She'd never before dared take this image from the sheets of paper she sketched upon to work in iron sheeting. "It does more than that. Here, let me show you."

The key grew tighter and tighter to turn. The figure trembled, his rough-hewn face jerking almost with violence. *How apt*, she thought, then let the key go.

For a moment nothing happened. The virile iron man quivered, and then slowly the gears started turning. The plates slid back upon each other, revealing a swift glimpse of the cogs within. Then a creature began to form, just as wild and fierce as the iron man had been.

Mandeville sucked in a breath. Lena watched his face as he tugged his magnifying glassicals up and peered closer. "My goodness, Lena! It's incredible. Look at it transform! One moment a man, the next a wolf."

She put her hand on his. "Wait."

Breathlessly they both watched as the wolf slid back into the man, the clockwork gears grinding slower and slower, until finally it stopped, caught in transition, the man's face scowling out over a hint of the wolf's jaws.

"Well? What do you think?"

Mandeville let out his breath and cleaned his glassicals. "You truly have a gift, my dear. This is beyond compare. Beyond!" Her heart swelled, until she saw him shake his head. "However, you'll never sell it. What on earth possessed you to create such a thing? The Echelon will have you thrown in the dungeons of the Ivory Tower!"

"Maybe a year ago," she replied, glancing over her

shoulder at Mrs. Wade. Her voice dropped. "Times are changing, Mr. Mandeville. There's talk of the Scandinavian Empire sending an embassy to London."

Mr. Mandeville stilled. "Where did you hear that?"

"There's a loose grate…in the ceiling of my guardian's study," she admitted. "I often do some of my work in the solar above."

A conspiratorial smile. As though her ingenuity had surprised him.

"Leo was entertaining the dukes of Malloryn and Goethe yesterday morning. It's not common knowledge yet, but the Council is concerned."

Mandeville leaned closer, peering at the clockwork transformational through his glassicals. His attention, however, was all upon her. "I still don't see how this changes matters. The Echelon exterminated the Scottish verwulfen clans at Culloden. This…this piece stirs dangerous sentiments toward an ancient enemy."

He picked the clockwork back up and began to nestle it safely in its box, where it might never again see the light of day.

"The Duke of Malloryn said that the Echelon were considering a peace treaty with the Scandinavian clans," she blurted.

Mr. Mandeville froze. Both his eyebrows slowly vanished into his hairline. "That's unheard of. The Scandinavian verwulfen have been at odds with Britain since Culloden. There's no chance they would agree to a treaty."

"That's all I know. Mrs. Wade discovered me and I was forced to go look at bonnets."

"Goodness," Mandeville whispered. "I shall have to pass this information on. At once."

Lena glanced at Mrs. Wade, who was tapping her reticule impatiently. "Do you think I should meet with Mercury? To tell him what I know? Firsthand?"

For months Mercury had been only a dashing figment of her imagination. As the mysterious head of the secret humanist movement working right here in London, he was little more than cloaks and shadows. Rumor had it that the Council of Dukes had posted an extravagant reward with the infamous Nighthawks for his capture.

"No. No, I'll pass the information on. It wouldn't do at all to have you involved any further. The fewer people who know of Mercury's identity the safer he is."

"I would never tell a soul."

"Oh, Lena, you're so terribly innocent still." He gave her a sad smile. "There are ways for a blue blood to make a young woman tell them everything they want to know. Especially those rotten bastards in the Ivory Tower." He patted her hand. "I'll pass the message on. Hopefully we can use this information. If this alliance between the Echelon and verwulfen clans goes ahead, there'll be little chance for the humanists to defeat the Echelon. They'll be too powerful."

He slid a folded envelope toward her, beneath a sheaf of orders. "The usual spot, if you will?"

Lena palmed it, pretending to rifle through the orders. Her voice rose. "Of course. Thank you for the commissions. I shall select which ones I deem appropriate."

"Let me know if you hear more." A frown crossed

his face. "I am most curious about why they're talking of peace."

"I will."

Lena picked up the box with the snubbed clockwork inside and turned her back on him. Pasting a smile on her face, she ignored the curiosity that lit Mrs. Wade's face and gestured toward the carriage. She was about to make her companion's day much worse.

"Oh look, we've time to visit my brother and sister," she said lightly, though in fact she'd planned on it.

Mrs. Wade paled. "Not the rookeries, Lena. If anyone sees—"

"We'll be discreet. And they're my family, after all—even if they are considered *persona non grata* to the Echelon." She stepped through the shop door into the warm sunshine. "I've a mind to gift Charlie with this toy. Mr. Mandeville doesn't want it." And she couldn't bear to let it go to waste. It was the finest thing she'd ever created, even if it bore striking familiarity to a certain hulking brute that she knew.

Not that she'd be seeing him this time of day. She'd lived at the warren long enough to know the times that Will came and went. Midday usually found him asleep after his nightly sojourn guarding the rookery.

Which suited her perfectly.

She wouldn't care if she never saw him again.

❧

If Honoria was surprised to see him so early, she gave little sign of it. Will growled a greeting and strode past. Sunlight spilled through the attic window, dust motes swirling through its beams. The stink of chemical took his breath, with the faint, underlying tang of blood and chamomile tea.

"Blade's still in bed," Honoria said, brushing a lock of dark hair behind her ear. "He's recovering well, though not as quickly as I'd like—"

Nor as quickly as he once had. Will nodded brusquely. "I seen him."

"Of course."

It was the first place he would have gone.

Tugging off her magnifying glassicals, she began to remove her apron. The attic had been sectioned into two rooms, one for Honoria's laboratory and the other for Blade's boxing saloon. Will'd never been in here before. It was solely Honoria's domain, and while he'd expected sterile benches and equipment, he was surprised by the pair of cozy, overstuffed armchairs by the hearth and the mounds of paperwork. Honoria struck him as someone who was obsessively organized.

"Can I help you with anything?" No doubt she was almost as surprised to see him here as he was.

Will dragged the letter from his pocket. He couldn't make heads or tails of it, but Honoria's inquisitive little mind took to codes like a duck to water. "Can you decipher this?"

She took it, scratching her thumbnail through the waxy substance that coated it. "Hmm. I can try. It might take a while. Is it important?"

"Could be."

She shot him a look.

"Found it on the men as stabbed Blade."

The color drained from her face and she glared

down at the letter. "I'll do my best then. When did you retrieve this?"

"This morning," he muttered. "Tracked 'em into the sewers."

"Are they still breathing?"

"Aye."

Surprise widened her eyes—then they narrowed with an expression that was quite bloodthirsty. "May I ask why?"

"The Nighthawks were on me heels. They've got 'em in custody, no doubt."

"That's not like you, leaving an enemy behind." Crossing to the bench, she tapped the letter against her lips.

His cue to leave.

As if sensing it, she glanced over her shoulder, eyelashes shuttering her luminous eyes. It felt like a punch to the gut, the gesture so reminiscent of Lena that he swallowed hard. Definitely time to get out of here.

But as he turned, he heard a set of footsteps on the stairs.

"May I ask a favor of you, Will?"

His hand hovered over the doorknob, nostrils flaring. The scent of leather and blud-wein assaulted his nose. Blade. Which meant Honoria had him neatly trapped. He couldn't be rude and make his escape. "What?"

"Blade suggested I should take a sample of your blood."

Of course he did. She'd spent the last three years sticking holes in her husband. No doubt Blade thought it high time she turned that obsessive little mind toward someone else. A chill ran down his spine. Needles. Frigging needles.

Seeing the look on his face, she hurried on. "To see if there's any chance of finding a cure. Or vaccination." With a sigh, she added, "My work here has stalled. Charlie's not responding to the vaccinated blood the same way as Blade did. And Blade's results have reached a plateau for the moment. His CV levels are sitting as low as forty-eight and have been for six months, thank goodness."

The door opened. Honoria's gaze shot straight past Will. For once, he was grateful not to be the recipient of that diamond stare. "What the devil do you think you're doing out of bed?"

Blade kicked the door shut with his heel. White as parchment and moving stiffer than an eighty-year-old man, he struggled to catch his breath. "Good to see you too, luv."

"I gave strict instructions that you were to remain bedridden for the next three days. Then we would renegotiate."

"Which means she'll decide if I can or can't get up." Blade winked at Will. "I couldn't stand to be without you another moment, luv. Me 'eart were breakin'."

Honoria pointed. "Chair. Now."

Handing Will his bottle of blud-wein, he settled into one of the armchairs by the fireplace whilst Honoria clucked and scolded him. Blade bore it with goodwill, but his eyes sparkled whenever her back was turned.

Will shifted on his feet, but Honoria saw the movement and looked up from where she was tucking a footstool under her husband's feet. One delicate eyebrow arched in question.

"What's up, luv?" Blade asked, catching the look.

"I asked Will if he'd consent to having some of his blood examined."

"You don't 'ave to," Blade hastened to assure him.

That was the thing he hated the most now. The hesitant way they spoke around him, as if fearing he'd walk out the door and never come back.

Folding his arms over his chest, he glared at Blade. As if he'd ever abandon him. Without Blade he'd probably still be trapped in a cage, reduced to little more than an animal.

A hot little coal flared to life inside him. If only he hadn't bloody been there that night. If only he hadn't heard Honoria ask if he was dangerous, if he could be trusted around Lena...

And then the hesitation.

He'd never doubted himself before. Never doubted his control. Years in the cage had taught him to leash the anger, the beast within. He choked it down, trapped it in solid iron bars—a manifestation of the cage he'd spent ten years in. Nobody could reach in there.

Until Lena came along.

She'd driven him near insane. It was nothing but a game to her, a flirtation, a tease. A way to test her burgeoning womanhood on someone she thought was safe. But he wasn't safe. And he didn't play games. After two years of living with it, the edges of the cage had started to grow ragged. If Blade had noticed the restless prowl of the beast within him, if Honoria had... Then how close had he been to losing control?

How long had they watched him? Not trusted him?

"Will?" Honoria asked.

"Do it," he snapped, somewhat harsher than he'd intended. "But hurry up. I've got things to do today."

Three

"BE BRAVE, WILL," BLADE CALLED. "AIN'T NAUGHT TO it. Just a little prick, much like your own. You don't 'ear the lasses down on Petticoat Lane complainin', do you?"

Will swore at him and stared ferociously at the wall as Honoria slid the needle in. The silver began burning immediately. Cold iron healed in seconds, but silver kept the wound open long enough for her to take her sample. Sweat dripped into his eyes, and a chill ran down his face. Bile churned in his stomach.

"There we go. Nearly done," Honoria crooned, patting his shoulder. "It's a nice red sample, Will. I'd grown used to Blade's blue blood."

The sound of light footsteps in the hall caught his ear. His head swam as he turned his face that way, cold spiraling through him. A warm, floral scent curled through his nose. Honeysuckle. *Oh no. Not her. Not now…* Somewhere in the distance he thought he heard Blade asking if he was all right. As the room buzzed, he glanced toward the needle and the vial thick with his blood.

A mistake.

The next thing he knew, he was lying flat on his back on the floor and shoving at the vile smelling salts someone waved under his nose. His fingers grazed a lady's breast, and his eyes shot open as Lena tumbled backward, the smelling salts spilling everywhere.

Months since he'd seen her. Months where the image of her had faded until the memory was almost a blur. Now here she was, as vibrant and beautiful as ever, her dashing red skirts spilled across the floor like a pool of blood. The hunger in him, the raging warmth, bubbled up, flooding through his vision until he knew his eyes were wolf-gold. Vision sharpened, picking out every single strand of hair that tumbled over her shoulders, the dew on her lips, the light reflecting off the bleached tips of her lashes.

Mine, something inside him snarled. For a moment the world blurred and when he wrenched back his control, his hand was half lifted toward her.

"What the hell are you doin' here?" he snapped, still disorientated. Cold sweat ringed his neckline.

Blade caught his hand. "Easy there." The words were light, but Will knew them for the warning they were.

Control it. Rein it in.

The effort left him breathless. As his vision faded back to normal, he realized they were all staring at him in various states of wariness.

"I'm fine," he muttered.

Blade knelt back on his heels. "Good. Don't think I could take you on just yet."

Lena sat up, her face pale. The coffee-dark color of

her hair was the same precise shade of her sister's, but her brown eyes were warmer, more almond shaped. Smiling eyes, meant to tempt and tease.

They weren't smiling now.

Lena's lips curved, but it didn't light up her face the way it could. "Goodness," she said in a falsely bright tone. "How much blood did you take, Honor?"

"I had no idea you had a fear of needles," Honoria said, glancing at the tiny vial.

"Thought I could handle it." It had been a long time since he'd fainted.

"The exhibition?" Blade asked.

Where he'd found Will as a boy. Chained up on stage in London's East End and forced to exhibit his monstrous strength and healing capabilities to the gasping crowd. The showman, Tom Sturrett, cut him with iron blades. Despite the presence of the loupe virus, the poor conditions and lack of food meant he didn't always heal as quickly as they wanted. Then Mrs. Sturrett would stitch him up with her coarse needle.

It wasn't long before just the sight of it was enough to make the blood rush out of his head.

Lena clasped her gloved hands in her lap, tendrils of soft brown hair escaping from her chignon. She must have been in a rush, for her hat was still cocked jauntily across her brow, a scarlet feather trailing over one cheek. His gaze lingered on the feather.

"The exhibition? What exhibition?" she asked.

Blade met his gaze. "When—"

"Nothin'," he snapped.

They all looked at him again and Will cursed his bluntness. Nothing would fire Lena's imagination more than a brusque denial. He could already see the curiosity forming in her eyes. She'd be after his secrets now like a ferret.

Maybe it was best to give them the condensed version. "Used to be displayed in the penny gaff shops as a curio. Or up on stage in Covent Garden." Pitching his voice louder, he mimicked Sturrett's showman cry. "Come and see the ferocious Beast! Witness London's last remaining verwulfen in chains!" He could almost smell the cheap shag tobacco the audience smoked and the reek of stale, unwashed bodies. "After the singin' and flash dancin' I were the main event. They'd drag me out in a cage and the audience'd throw rotten food at me. Or sometimes they'd dress me in wolf furs and have some of the actors play at blue bloods. It'd usually end when they attacked me with swords."

Lena's eyes went round. "They didn't really stab you?"

"With iron." His voice was hard. "Heals right quick. Unless it's silver-alloy."

"A similarity you share with Blade," Honoria mused.

"Honestly, Honoria. How can you think about the disease after hearing something so dreadful!" Lena snapped at her sister. Then looked back at him. "I thought you were fifteen when Blade brought you home?"

"I were. Or nearabouts. Didn't keep much track o' time, in the cage."

Lena's eyes softened with distress.

Will hadn't expected her to defend him or sympathize. Most of the crowd had been costermongers and the like, but sometimes one of the Echelon paid Sturrett to display him in their grand homes in

Mayfair. The ladies wore fine silks and toyed with the extravagant diamonds and pearls around their necks—fancy women dressed like Lena—but at least they didn't throw nothing at him. Instead they'd eye him with their hot little eyes, whispering and smirking behind their fans.

The gentlemen hadn't liked that at all. Will hadn't the heart to tell them he shared their sentiments. It wouldn't have mattered anyway. Nobody listened to him when he was in the cage. He'd become little more than an animal to them. In the end, he'd stopped speaking, growling and snapping at them when they came near him. That was the worst of the degradation. If Blade hadn't been in the audience one night and forced Sturrett to free him, he shuddered to think what he might have ended up like.

"Both diseases dislike the presence of silver," Honoria mused. "Which suggests a common... ancestor, so to speak? The more we know, the more likely I could find a cure. I'll examine the sample under the microscope and begin tests. Perhaps it were best if you weren't here, Will?"

It wasn't the sight of blood as did him in, so much as the needles. But he had to get out of here. His skin was itching.

"Aye. I'll be off."

"Not home," Honoria said. "You're not fit to leave just yet. I want to check on you before you go. Lena?"

Lena's head lifted like a startled doe. "Yes?" she asked warily.

Honoria took a shallow breath, as though considering her words. "Can you see Will to the kitchen and sit with him awhile? Make sure he gets something into his stomach. You know how he gets after some excitement."

"That ain't necessary," he said.

Lena exchanged glances with him. "I was hoping to speak to you, Honoria."

Even Blade stared at her, a silent question in his gaze. Honoria's eyes met his and somehow the question was answered. Blade growled under his breath and nodded. "Best to get somethin' into you, Will. We'll be down shortly."

No help for it. He was stuck with her and the room was suddenly far too small. Will opened the door and stalked through. Lena hurried behind him in a swish of skirts with a muttered curse about gentlemen allowing ladies to go first.

"I ain't no gentleman."

"Well, everyone knows that," she murmured. "They don't call you the Beast for nothing."

The words shouldn't have stung. He'd been called worse for years. Indeed, he'd taken the name on, molding himself into it. Using it to keep curious humans at bay and predators on their toes.

But for some reason, hearing it from her lips felt like a knife to the chest.

Following his nose to the kitchen, he found it empty. Lady Luck wasn't with him today. Though a bubbling pot of soup on the stove bore evidence of Blade's housekeeper, Esme, there was no sign of the actual woman.

A light touch fumbled at his wrist. The smooth silk of her elbow-length gloves. "Here," Lena said, tugging his hand toward one of the low stools by the hearth. "Sit. I'll fetch you some soup."

She let him go, but the feel of her touch remained, like phantom fingerprints. Will sank slowly onto the stool, watching as she bustled about the kitchen.

Lena looked out of place. The hearth dominated the room and emitted a constant blanket of heat. Soot stained the ceiling, and the workbenches were heavy and scarred from frequent use. Strings of onions and herbs dangled over the main bench, along with a row of copper pots strung from metal hooks. It was homey and inviting. Precisely everything that Lena was not.

Her red velvet skirts were hooked up just enough to reveal a flirtatious froth of underskirt, and her corset narrowed an already slender waist to a size he could span with his hands. Black bands of lace decorated her bodice and the panels of her skirts. As she reached up to try and fetch a bowl, the creamy mounds of her breasts threatened to tumble from her bodice. A hint of black lace edged against her creamy skin.

Will's fingers *itched*.

He could remember the first time he'd ever seen her, bustling along Petticoat Lane with her gray Serge skirts swishing around her ankles and her battered bonnet barely protecting her from the rain. Clutching a sodden newspaper over her head, she'd slipped on the edge of the gutter and the newspaper had torn in two, disintegrating in Lena's hands. With a helpless laugh at a pair of street urchins, she'd given a shrug, then tossed the newspaper aside. The sound of her laughter went straight through him; it was the type of sound that always made Will feel like an outsider looking in. Joy radiated off her, like warmth from the fire on a cold winter's night, and Will felt an almost envious stirring, as if he wanted to stretch his hands out and catch some of her effervescent happiness. Dragging her bonnet off her head, she'd tilted her face up to the rain as it wet her lips, her eyelashes fluttering against her pale cheeks, and Will had almost fallen off the roof as he strained to look.

Women made him uncomfortable at the best of times. His own mother had sold him once it became clear he was verwulfen, and the only other woman in his life had been Esme. After a year or so of her presence at the warren, he'd started to relax around her, but everything about Lena set his hackles on edge. A curious, uncomfortable feeling that he didn't understand. With a vampire stalking the rookeries, he'd been in charge of keeping an eye on the younger Todd siblings and protecting the house at night. Every day he'd followed Lena to work and then home again, without her even knowing. He complained about it to everyone he knew, but the truth of it was that he began to relish the moments when she'd appear at the door of the clockmaker's, giving a cheery little wave back into the shop. In the grim reality of Will's life, Lena became the one bright spark, a yearning for something he'd never had or felt before.

It was safe for him to feel that way. She was a stranger still, no threat to him, nor he to her. It wasn't until he came face to face with her that he'd realized how different reality might be. Stepping out onto the roof one night in her nightgown, of all things, Lena had stared at him as if he were some hulking brute, darting a swift glance at the window she'd come through.

With his palms sweating and his throat tight, Will had been unable to speak. Then suddenly the words had come, blunt and awkward. "*You wouldn't make it in time,*" he'd said. "*And if you couldn't avoid me, then you couldn't avoid it either. Are you stupid, girl, to come out here with the creature on the loose? Or just wantin' to die?*"

The worst thing he could have said, for her eyes had narrowed and she'd drawn herself up as if she were a queen and he the lowest of street scum.

She made him feel like the small, helpless boy that nobody had wanted—nobody but Sturrett, who'd seen a way to make coin off him. Will had sworn he'd never feel that helpless again, but seeing her always threw him into a maelstrom of emotion, and even now the hungry, angry part of him was restless. His beast, prowling like a caged wolf inside his chest.

Can't let it out.

Can't ever let it out.

"You don't need to do this," he said bluntly, as she bustled around the kitchen. "I can manage by meself."

Lena unpinned her hat and tossed it carelessly on the bench, followed by her gloves. The hint of smooth skin and manicured nails drew his eye. She'd touched him once with those hands and he'd never forget it.

"You always need food after one of your episodes." Humming under her breath, she began to ladle soup into a bowl.

"It weren't an episode." His tone was far sharper than he'd intended and she stilled. Cursing himself, he continued, "I only get shaky when I've exerted meself, or lost too much blood. It's just the virus, healin' me. This is different."

"Honoria told me to feed you." Despite her studied nonchalance, she was nervous. Of him. He could smell it. "You can argue with her if you want. I'm not going to waste my breath."

When he said nothing, she went back to ladling the soup.

"Didn't know you knew your way around a kitchen," he said, simply to chase the uneasy silence from the room. "They teach that in them fancy drawin' rooms?"

Dark eyes looked up over the bowl. She seemed genuinely surprised he'd asked a question. After spending the last three years trying to ignore her, there was little doubt why.

"I used to prepare most of the meals after Father died and we first came to Whitechapel," she replied, her lashes lowering again as she concentrated on the bowl. "Honoria was always home from work later than I."

"*You* cooked?" He took the bowl from her and reached for the spoon. Her hand was tiny next to his, and very pale. Different worlds, the pair of them.

"Badly." She shot him a sudden smile that lit her whole face.

Bloody hell. He stared at the soup. Six months since he'd seen her last—a deliberate act on his behalf—and he'd almost forgotten the way she could heat his blood with a smile, a look.

A careless kiss.

"And now you go to balls." He put the sneer in his

voice, but the effort felt hollow. Taking refuge in the soup, he almost burned the roof of his mouth.

"I like dancing." Her eyes narrowed dangerously. "And balls. The men there behave like gentlemen. It's a pleasant surprise."

"You ain't got a thrall contract yet." He'd been waiting to hear word of it. Imagining one of those blue blood bastards with his mouth and hands all over her as he drank her sweet blood.

Color flooded her cheeks. "No. I haven't made my mind up. And there's no rush."

"No rush? Ain't you gettin' perilously close to bein' on the shelf?"

"I'm barely twenty," she snapped.

"I see. You'd prefer to keep 'em danglin'?"

"That's not what I meant."

"Seems like the sort of games you'd play."

A dangerous look in those eyes. Lena swished on her heel, snatching at her gloves. "I hope you choke on your soup, you big, hairy lummox. You don't know anything about me. Anything!"

A piece of paper tumbled from her sleeve as she turned, fluttering to the floor like a dying moth.

"Ah, we're back to that, are we?" he asked, putting the soup aside to cool. Stooping, he plucked up the piece of paper. "You dropped something."

Lena froze in the doorway. Her hand went immediately to her sleeve, and then she spun around, her eyes widening. "Give it to me!"

Will stood, breaking the seal and unrolling the small furl of paper. He caught just a glimpse of thick black letters before Lena tried to tug it out of his grip.

"A love letter, I'll bet." He turned around and pretended to read it.

A whoosh of scent enveloped him, her skirts swishing against his legs. She clutched at his shoulder, trying to drag his arm lower, her breasts crushed against the broad expanse of his back. Any attempt at reading went straight out of his head.

"What would you know of love letters?" She climbed on the stool and reached for the piece of paper. The step put her on eye level with him. Dangerously intimate. "The type of woman as would have *you* isn't the type to be writing poems."

"Don't be so sure," he shot back. "You'd be surprised at the type of poems they whisper in me ear."

"Urgh. You're despicable."

The stool teetered and their gazes clashed. Lena shrieked and clutched at him as she fell. Will found himself with an armful of soft velvet and warm flesh, and the sound of two racing hearts.

The world slowed down. Became nothing more than the feel of her in his arms. Will stared into her eyes, then his gaze dropped, unbidden, to her lips.

Lena's eyes widened and she made a choking noise. "Put me down."

He could barely breathe. The hunger inside him was suddenly choking him, desperate to get out and rule his body. He knew the burning amber of his gaze was intensifying; he could almost feel the molten heat of it run through his irises as the color changed.

"Will," she whispered. "Your eyes."

Her breath was warm on his lips. She'd been chewing something with apple and cinnamon in it. He could scent it on her breath and suddenly he wanted to taste it.

Don't.

Shoving her away, he turned, the paper crumpling in his fist. He had to get out of here. Away from the scent of her. Away from the temptation to do something she'd never forgive him for.

Maybe Blade and Honoria were right. Maybe he couldn't be trusted?

"Will," she whispered. "You're shaking."

He looked down at his hands. The tremble started there, swept all the way through him. "You were right," he said hoarsely. "Maybe I did exert meself."

"Perhaps I'd best go?"

It seemed some sense of self-preservation had come over her.

He nodded, struggling to hold onto himself. What the hell was wrong with him? What did it matter if she'd found…someone? Instantly the anger was back, thick and choking, a red haze threatening his vision.

"You shouldn't have come. This ain't your world now." The words were harsh and he'd meant them to be.

Silence. "I know. I thought you wouldn't be here. You're never here at midday."

Which was why she only visited at those times.

"Then why don't you go?"

"My letter?"

Soft footsteps shuffled behind him. Her skirts brushed against his legs and then her hand slid down his arm, closing over the letter in his grip. A letter she was so desperate to regain.

There was only one reason she wouldn't want him to see it.

Suddenly he couldn't stop himself. He had to know, even if the answer was one he wouldn't particularly like. Lena cried out, fighting him for it.

It tore in half and both of them staggered apart, left with a piece each. Will unrolled it, his gaze darting over the piece of paper. Not letters. Not writing. His gaze sharpened. He'd seen this before. The same bloody cipher he'd found on the men who'd fired the draining factories.

His stomach dropped. "What the hell are you doin' with this?" he whispered, his voice filled with a cold, inexplicable dread.

Lena gave a strangled cry and darted for the door. Will grabbed her skirts almost as an aside, shock running its icy fingers down his spine. "Don't think you're goin' anywhere. Not until you tell me where the bloody hell you found this!"

"I picked it up," she lied, the bitter smell of it all over her.

Will grabbed her by the shoulder and spun her toward the stool she'd almost toppled. "Sit," he growled, shoving her into the seat. "And explain. And if I were you, I wouldn't dare tell me another lie."

Four

WILL TOWERED OVER HER WITH A GLOWER. ALL nearly seven feet of him.

"Explain," he demanded.

His eyes glowed that eerie amber color that showed he wasn't quite human. Lena fell back, holding onto the bench to keep herself upright. She didn't dare move, even as the stool teetered beneath her.

But she didn't dare tell him.

"Or?" she asked, tipping her chin up and meeting his furious gaze. Her heartbeat pounded in her ears. He wouldn't hurt her. Yet her gaze dropped to the quiver in his hands. Maybe it was exertion. Maybe not. She'd never seen him like this before.

His nostrils flared and he turned and slammed both hands on the bench. Head bowed, he sucked in a deep breath. Then another.

"I—"

"Don't speak." A gravely rasp. "Give me a moment."

Lena swallowed. What was wrong with him? She eased herself upright, setting all four legs of the stool on the ground. The clock on the wall ticked out the seconds. Each tick seemed to stretch out, time slowing as the tension settled in the room. She could hardly stand it.

As suddenly as he'd turned, Will lifted his head and pushed away from the bench. His golden-brown hair was long enough now to touch his collar, and he raked it out of his eyes with a sharp gesture.

"No lies," he warned, pointing a finger at her. The piece of letter was still crushed in his other fist. "Where did you get this?"

"I can't tell you."

Will put both hands on the bench behind her and leaned closer. Trapping her. "Don't make me tell Blade."

If Will talked to Blade, he would talk to Honoria and then Honoria…well, she would probably scream at Lena about how stupid she'd been, getting involved in such a thing.

"You'd run along and tattle on me?" She ignored the angry flare of molten-gold in his eyes. Will would never understand what she was trying to do, and she was very well aware of the dangers of involving other people.

Will caught her chin in his fingers. His lip curled back off his teeth. "This ain't a game. I'd tell Blade because it's clear you're in over your 'ead. I seen somewhat like this before. On a man who burned the drainin' factories down. Lena, they're government owned! The Echelon will destroy whoever did this." He waved the letter at her. "If it kept you from gettin' your head cut off, then I'll take a bloody full page out in the *Times*!"

"That almost sounds as if you gave a damn."

Thought flickered through his hooded gaze. Indecipherable. She found she was holding her breath, which was ridiculous.

"I don't want to see you hurt," he said finally. "And your sister'd skin me alive if anythin' happened to you and I'd known about it."

Foolish, to think that he might have cared, even a little. Her shoulders slumped. "I promised a friend I'd deliver it for him. I had no idea what was inside it. I still don't. That could be a laundry list, for all you know."

"Let's pretend I can't smell it every time you lie to me."

"That is the truth!" This was the hardest part of her cause—lying to her friends and family. But if she involved them now, who knew what might happen? Will was right. The Echelon would kill anyone they even suspected of being involved in this. She glanced uneasily at the letter. Mandeville had told her she was only dropping off meeting points and times to one of the other spies who worked within the Echelon.

She sent the letters by crow to some mysterious conspirator and received them for Mr. Mandeville. What if one of those letters had been instructions to burn the factories? She desperately needed to be alone, to think.

Suddenly, the world had become a far more dangerous place.

"Lena." The growl that came out of his throat was almost primordial. The kind of sound you expected to hear in a snowy forest, late at night, alone. The kind of growl that sent shivers down her spine because she knew it meant she was the prey.

Run, a little voice whispered.

"I—I—"

No longer content to play games, he gripped her chin and stared at her, his amber eyes burning right through her. Lena stopped breathing. She had nothing to fear—this was Will—but something in her, some unconscious part of her body, recognized danger when she saw it. The little hairs along her arms rose, her stomach turning to lead.

"I'm not—"

Laughter sounded on the stairs. Lena looked toward the door in relief as Blade's housekeeper Esme and her husband Rip came through it.

Instantly Will straightened, his fingers slipping from her chin. He glanced away in order to hide his eyes from the newcomers and give himself a chance to leash the beast inside him. It rode close to the surface of his skin today, a predator beneath all those sleek muscles and powerful brawn.

"Lena!" Esme greeted, her black hair knotted back into a simple chignon. She took Lena's hands and kissed her on the cheek. "I didn't know you were visiting today."

"It was a momentary decision," Lena replied quickly. "You look well. Married life suits you."

Esme smiled over her shoulder at Rip. The menacing giant had frightened Lena in the beginning, with his heavy mechanical arm and dark expression. In the first few months she'd lived at the warren with her sister and Blade, Rip had been suffering through the initial stirrings of the craving virus. She could remember his screams and the way he tore through his room in a rage. Not even Blade had been able to manage him and only Esme could calm him.

"And Will," Esme said, with a faint note of scold in her voice. "I see you've been at my soup."

"Honoria's suggestion, I'm afraid," Lena replied. She smiled sweetly as Will turned around. "He had an episode involving a fit of the vapors."

If looks could kill...

But she was safe now, with witnesses in the room. When he got her alone—and he would, she knew—he might do anything to her.

Rip barked a laugh. "You fainted, boy-o?"

"I had to use my smelling salts," she replied, sneaking her hat and gloves off the bench. Will's eyes watched the movement, though his body and face never moved.

"Lena," he said gruffly. "You'll take a walk with me?"

Not a chance. She shot him a charming smile. "I'm afraid I have to go. I have an appointment at the milliners. It was nice to visit, though. I'll have to come more often." Another blatant lie. She wouldn't be coming back here unless absolutely certain Will wasn't there.

He took a step toward her, but Esme was in the way. Will pulled up short, frustration flickering across his face. But he didn't dare push past. Not with Rip standing guard over his wife and still overly protective.

"Until next time," she said, staring him baldly in the face.

He was a long time replying. And when he did, she almost stepped back at the menace in his tone.

"It'll be sooner than you think."

Will slammed the door, his gaze raking the small apartment. It was where he lived, but it wasn't home. It lacked the warmth and laughter of the warren. He tossed his coat aside and lit a candle, his breath steaming in the evening air. Despite a full afternoon dealing with Blade's business in the rookery, the scent of honeysuckle still clung to his clothes.

He scowled and found a piece of leftover pie in the icebox. He didn't want to be thinking of that. Lena thought she'd gotten away from him today, but she had forgotten one thing.

Will always got his prey. In the end.

What the hell was the fool girl up to? Carrying around such a potentially devastating document? If anyone in the Echelon found her with that on her person, there'd be questions. If they knew what it meant, then she'd be executed.

Cold punched through him at the thought. Her laughter and teasing, forever cut short. Though her presence made him uneasy, he never wanted to see her harmed. In fact, the very thought made his hackles rise and the berserker rage threaten to spill out over him.

He'd never felt this way before. One glimpse of her and every primitive need rushed to claim him, threatening to overwhelm his careful defenses.

The mere thought of her in danger…

He stopped. Put his fork down. The vein in his temple throbbed as he sucked in a deep breath. Then another. *Don't think about it.* Not until he had himself under control.

Whenever that might be. With a gruff laugh, he

picked up the fork again and stabbed it into the pie. As he bit into the flavorsome meat, a sound caught his attention from the stairs outside.

Someone sneaking up to his door.

Someone preternaturally quiet.

Sliding the fork into a stronger grip, he held it low against his thigh and crossed silently to the door. Leather flavored the air, but no personal scent. A blue blood then. They lost their distinctive smell when they became infected with the craving.

Will ripped the door open and stepped forward, grabbing the intruder by the throat and slamming him up against the wall.

A hand caught his wrist, the thumb digging into the tendons just hard enough to ease his grip. "Truce," Blade said hoarsely. "If I wanted you dead you wouldn't a 'eard me comin'."

Will let him go with a scowl of disgust. "Bloody hell. You should be in bed." He stepped back. "Does Honoria know where you are?"

"Of course. Can't you 'ear the argument ringin' still?" Blade loosened his collar. "I'm not a feeble ole man. And I can't afford to be trapped in bed for the next half week."

"You're puffin' like a bellows."

"I'll catch me breath." Blade peered past him. "You're a mite skittish there, Will. Got somethin' on your mind?"

He gestured Blade inside, then closed the door behind them. This whole thing with Lena had him on edge, expecting blue bloods in every shadow. "What's the problem? You're not one for social visits."

Blade cocked his hip on the table and crossed his arms. "Ain't I welcome?" The words were quiet, but the glint in Blade's eyes spoke of a whole lot of other things.

Will slammed into his chair and picked at the pie. He'd lost his appetite. "Don't be a fool," he muttered. "You're always welcome."

A steady gaze, watching him. Then Blade sighed. "What do you make o' this?" He withdrew a scroll from his pocket and tossed it toward Will.

Who snatched it out of the air. Unrolling it, he held the parchment up to the light. The letters were slanted and looping. And written in gold.

"'The Council of Dukes requests your presence at Lord Harker's ball tomorrow night at eight,'" he read slowly, fumbling with the words. "'The house will be considered neu-neutral territory for the evenin'. Bring the Beast. He shall receive safe passage for the night.'"

Lowering it, he met Blade's gaze. "A trap?"

Blade scratched at his jaw. "Don't think so. But it's a game play of some sort. Damned if I can work it out." Their eyes met. "Or why they're involving you."

"Well." Will crushed the parchment in his fist. "I don't owe 'em nothin'. And neither do you."

"Aye. But what do they want?" Blade scowled. "I 'ate these bloody games. Dare I ignore it? It could be anythin'." With a sigh, he eased away from the table. "I ain't expectin' you to come. It's dangerous for you, that world—"

A thought struck him. Lena was certain to be in attendance. This was precisely her sort of thing. And the last place she'd be expecting to see him.

Thought you could run, did you?

"It's dangerous for both of us," Will corrected slowly. "You go, I go." He was Blade's bodyguard in all matters. "And I've other business to see to there. Might as well take up their kindly offer of safe passage and see what the bastards want."

"Wouldn't 'appen to be business of the petticoat variety?"

Will shot him a dark look.

"You need a woman," Blade added bluntly.

The words conjured an image: dark hair, dark eyes, a wicked little smile. His cock clenched. "The last thing I need's a woman."

"You need somethin' then." Blade's gaze roamed his meager surroundings. "You ought to come 'ome, Will. It's a cold, lonely place. You don't belong 'ere."

I don't belong anywhere. Not really. He looked away, his shoulders stiffening. "We've had this discussion. The answer's no."

A long, drawn out sigh met his ears. "Aye. I'll leave you to it then. Just you and the mice. Be ready then, tomorrow at six. Oh, and Will?"

"Aye?"

"Wouldn't 'urt to 'ave a shave."

Five

"I NEED SOME AIR," LENA SAID, FANNING HER FLUSHED face. The peacock feathers brushed against her lips, but she ignored them, her gaze following the handsome young Duke of Malloryn as he escorted the Duchess of Casavian out of the ballroom.

Both were heads of their Houses and members of the ruling Council of Dukes. And since the Duke of Goethe had retired barely five minutes ago, she could only presume that they were meeting to discuss something important.

Hopefully the Scandinavian matter.

Adele downed a glass of iced lemonade. "Is that wise?"

Green eyes met hers, the hard look in them turning wary for a moment. Lena squeezed her hand. "He's not here. I checked."

"Don't blind yourself, Lena. Colchester's not the only danger."

Lena nodded. The room swept around her in a riot of color as the crowd danced. Around the walls loomed a dozen blue bloods, sipping at their blud-wein and watching the dance floor with predatory eyes. "You'll be safe?"

"They're not the only ones hunting." Adele smiled, but it didn't touch her eyes. "I told you I need a patron."

"Be careful." Lena squeezed her gloved hand. The duke and duchess had disappeared. Giving Adele one last smile, she hurried after them.

The duchess had been wearing a deep aubergine gown that set off the color of her coppery hair. Lena exited the ballroom. Peering over the balustrade of the second floor, she raked her gaze across the white tiled entry below. An enormous staircase took up most of the foyer. Over a dozen men and women lined the stairs and the entry, gowned in a variety of brilliant colors. From the warmth of their skin and the dark, raven locks on a pair of them, they were most likely human, none of them high enough in rank to receive the gift of infected blood. Only those of good bloodlines and standing went through the blood rites at the age of fifteen. It was a sign of status, of prestige.

It took more than being a blue blood to be considered part of the Echelon. Any other unfortunate who was accidentally infected was considered little more than a rogue. Such blue bloods were either drafted into the Nighthawks, offered a place in the Coldrush Guards that protected the Ivory Tower and the Council, or were killed.

Humans could navigate the shadowy edges of the Echelon—like her—but they were never truly a part of it. They had their place, either as thralls or potential consorts, if their bloodlines were good.

Avoiding the soaring marble statue of an angel,

she peered down the hallway. Two dozen of Lord Harker's distinguished relatives glared down at her from the walls. Lena swept across the top of the stairs, her peacock green skirts rustling. There was another hallway on the other side.

She was just passing the enormous grandfather clock that held pride of place at the top of the stairs when a hush fell over the foyer.

Two footmen held each of the main doors open, their faces impassive. Blade strolled in, swinging an ebony-tipped cane. He tossed his top hat to a waiting footman and saluted the gaping group on the stairs. Another footman swept past with a tray of blud-wein, and Blade stole one, examining the foyer with interest.

Will stalked in at his heels, his shoulders straining the black coat he'd obviously borrowed. He wore a gray waistcoat, carefully brushed, and his boots had been scrubbed. Candlelight gleamed off the coppery highlights in his hair, and he towered over the hovering servants. Despite their training, two of them bolted out of his path like frightened rabbits. Will's hungry gaze followed them as if he were considering giving chase.

Lena's breath caught, the heat draining from her face. "Will," she whispered. *What the devil was he doing here?*

Will stopped in his tracks, his head lifting like a lion scenting gazelle, the brilliant, burning amber of his gaze locking on hers. His lips curled in a threatening smile, and Lena took a step back.

"*Later*," he mouthed.

She tore her gaze away, her heart pounding madly in her chest. For a moment she'd thought he was here for her, but that was foolishness. Not with the price on his head. What was he doing in the heart of Echelon territory? They considered his kind fit only to be caged or chained. If he'd gotten himself in trouble…

"Sir…Blade," the butler recovered himself well. "Master Will. This way, if you care. Lord Barrons is waiting for you."

Leo. Her half brother had something to do with this. Lena's hands unclenched from her skirts. Why would Leo invite them here, when he could just as easily have visited Whitechapel? He was one of the few members of the Echelon Blade trusted enough to grant passage to Whitechapel.

The butler led them across the foyer and into one of the lower hallways. Just before he disappeared, Will looked up, shooting her one more blazing look. It scorched all the way through her, igniting a mixture of fear and nervous anticipation that she couldn't quite name.

Heavens. She let out the breath she'd been holding and backed toward the second hallway. She had to get out of here before he found her.

But first, she had a little reconnaissance to finish. Find out what was going on between the Council members, if she could.

Then she was going to plead an attack of the vapors, which, considering how rapidly her heart was beating, shouldn't be that difficult at all.

❧

"Be ready for anythin'," Blade murmured as they strode through the halls of Lord Harker's mansion.

Will rolled his shoulders, his eyes darting through the shadows. Blade had no need to warn him. He'd been on edge ever since they got out of the cursed carriage. Coming here, into the very heart of society, was dangerous. He had to be ready for anything; no more surprises.

He'd already had his first surprise for the evening. Lena. Though he'd been expecting her, even relishing the opportunity, the sight of her temporarily struck him dumb. She'd always been well-dressed but wreathed in shadows, the gaslight picking out the soft curves and mysterious depths of her body… She'd been breath-catching.

Her hair tumbled over her shoulder in an elaborate cascade of curls, an elegant comb holding it up. Emeralds dripped into the deep vee of her green dress, drawing his gaze lower. He couldn't wait to get her alone. Anticipation thrummed through his veins, alerting all of his senses.

He just didn't know yet whether he wanted to throttle her—or kiss her.

A door opened and a swathe of golden light cut through the shadows. Will reined in his thoughts swiftly. No time for distraction. Best way to get his throat slit.

A man appeared, wearing crisp black from head to toe. He moved with the dangerous grace of a swordsman, his body lean and hard and his dark eyes cautious as he surveyed the darkened hallway. A diamond stud winked in his ear, and though he wore no weapons, an aura of dark violence hung over him.

Leo Barrons. Lena's guardian and possibly the only blue blood Will could tolerate besides Blade.

"Blade." Barrons offered his hand. His gaze examined the scene swiftly but Will knew he'd noted everything around them, from the pattern in the red carpets, to the fall of their coats. "Excellent timing. The prince consort should be arriving any moment."

"The consort?" Blade arched a brow. "My, my, they must want somethin' from me badly, if they're bringin' out 'is Royal Pastiness."

Barrons's lips quirked slyly, but he shook his head in warning. "The others are inside." A cue for Blade to shut his mouth. Barrons stepped forward with a hand offered. "Will. You look like a mountain, as always."

"Near eats me out of 'earth and 'ome," Blade muttered.

Will eyed him coolly. "Got me own set of rooms now."

"Aye, and yet you're still in me bloody kitchens every time I turn 'round." A wary smile; Blade was playing it up for Barrons's sake—and the others inside—but he hadn't forgotten where they were.

"Come in," Barrons said, gesturing to the door. "I'll send for some blud-wein. Will, do you want anything? Ale? Wine?"

Will gave him a long look. No chance in hell he'd be eating or drinking anything as come from this house. "Prefer to keep me wits about me."

"Ah, the stoic bodyguard."

"Somebody's gotta watch Blade's back."

Both Barrons and Blade exchanged a look. Blade strode toward the door. "They won't knife me 'ere. Ain't the done thing. It'd be in an alley one night, when I'd least expect it. This is just games. Come on, Will. Let's see what the Council wants."

When Blade'd least expect it...like in the drawing

room of a manor whilst a party was in full swing. Will stalked behind the pair of them, prepared to leap forward at a second's notice. They'd taken his weapons at the door, but that was no matter. His body *was* a weapon.

Firelight spilled through the room, the shadows flickering. Will glanced up, his eyes drawn by the carved panels that lined the walls and the ornate ceilings. He'd never seen so much gilt in all his life.

And silk curtains. What a bloody joke. Half the people of London could barely pay the Echelon's exorbitant taxes and yet here sat one of their lords, in a house that could probably feed Whitechapel for a year. Or five.

He wasn't here to gawk at the furnishings. Will lowered his gaze, even as Blade turned on his heel, staring up. "Gor, will you look at that," Blade said. "Ain't the ceilin' a sight to see? All them cherubs and clouds."

"Thank you," a cool voice said. "The manor's been in my family for eight generations."

Will's gaze narrowed on the speaker. Lord Harker, he presumed. Standing by the fire, with his hands clasped behind him.

The others sat in a half circle around him. He knew who the woman must be. There was only one female blue blood in England, the Lady Aramina, Duchess of Casavian. Met her once, didn't much trust the look in her eyes. Yet when the Council had held Blade's life in its hands, she'd been the final vote, her choice sealing his fate. For whatever reason—whim or politics—she'd chosen to let him live.

One of the other men was tall, with a hawkish nose and neatly trimmed beard. Touches of gray flecked his hair, signs of a distinguished air, rather than age and feebleness. Manderlay, the Duke of Goethe. Another who had cast his vote in Blade's favor.

Which left the last little lordling, who sat back in his Louis XIII chair, examining the play of light in his blud-wein. Rings glittered on his fingers and his collar had been left rakishly open. A half-empty bottle rested beside his booted feet. Will didn't recognize him, but the griffin signet on his finger said that this was Auvry Cavill, the young Duke of Malloryn. The least likely threat, Will thought, turning his gaze back to Goethe. He knew who the most dangerous man in the room was.

All of them had voted in Blade's favor. Will smelled politics in the air, stale as a moth-eaten coat. The prince consort must want something badly.

"How is your wife?" the Duke of Goethe asked.

"Curious. Stubborn. Same as ever." A genuine smile softened Blade's face.

"And how goes her experiments?" the duchess asked.

The only way she could have known of them was if she were having the warren watched. Will's eyes narrowed. None of the three had shown any sign of surprise. Which meant the Council likely knew everything that went in and out of the warren.

Something Will'd have to see to when they got out of here.

"She likes to tinker," Blade replied with a shrug. He played this game far better than Will ever could. "Thinks she'll cure me one day."

"Do you think she will?" The duchess sipped at her blud-wein. The firelight turned her coppery hair into a flaming corona around her head, but despite the brandy brown eyes and hint of color in her cheeks, her manner was as cool as winter. A little clockwork spider crawled across her shoulder, tethered by a fine steel chain to a pin at her breast. The glass dome of its body showed the exquisite brass cogs of its clockwork interior. He'd seen the type before. Flip them over and the belly was a watch.

"Keeps 'er amused and outta me 'air." Blade's smile held a knife-edge. "Everybody knows there ain't no cure for the cravin'."

"Yes, but her father was Sir Artemus Todd. Wasn't he the genius who discovered all those weapons for Vickers, before you killed the duke? I hear Todd was close to discovering a cure even then. Perhaps your wife knew something of his work?"

Blade could be quite reasonable at times. But not when Honoria was concerned. He bared his teeth— some people might have called it a smile—but Will knew it was just the expression he wore before he cut someone's throat. "Maybe she does. Like poisons that actually work on a blue blood, or a gun with bullets as explode on impact. But nothin' of cures, princess."

To her credit, the lady never even flinched. Instead, she picked up the clockwork spider, letting it crawl over and under her fingers. "I see your knighthood has taken none of the savagery from you."

"Did you expect it ought?"

"Fifty years ago you were dangerous, Blade. Times change. Our resources have changed. If we wanted to get rid of you, we'd simply send the Spitfires in and burn the rookery to the ground." The duchess poured more blud-wein into her glass and stirred it like tea. As if she weren't speaking of war. "Right now, you're… an inconvenience. Out of sight and out of mind. Like someone's embarrassing, black sheep cousin who keeps showing up to balls."

"If you're tryin' to grease me up for this favor you want o' me, you ain't doin' much of a bang-up job, princess."

The duchess stopped stirring, tapped the spoon against her goblet three times, then set it aside. Her almond-shaped eyes lifted, thick dark lashes fluttering against her smooth, pale cheeks. "Who said the favor we wished was from you?"

All eyes turned toward Will.

Leo grimaced. "I thought to warn you—"

The hair on the back of Will's neck rose. He crossed his arms over his chest and glared back. "No."

"You haven't heard what it is yet," the young Duke of Malloryn murmured.

"I don't like you no more 'n Blade does. And I don't trust you as far as I could throw you." He eyed the handsome young peacock and bared his teeth. "A struttin' tom like you? Why, I figure I could throw you a fair way too."

Malloryn raised lazy eyes toward him. A quick flick of his wrist and a knife appeared, balancing on point on his finger. "You'd have to get close enough."

"Auvry, that's enough," Barrons murmured. Their eyes met and Barrons straightened, his posture screaming out the silent challenge in the air between them.

Malloryn shrugged—and the knife disappeared. "You're no fun anymore, Barrons."

"Let's at least remain civilized long enough to give some credence to our claim of being gentlemen." Barrons eased gracefully into a chair by the fire, hooking his ankle up on his knee. Despite the appearance of relaxing, his lazy-lidded eyes examined the room.

"And you're the ones as want somewhat," Blade replied, sinking into one of the other chairs. He tested it, impressed with the padding. "Never treat with a man as 'olds a blade to your throat. That's what I always says."

Will stayed on guard. A sound in the hallway alerted him. Three separate footfalls, all moving with purpose toward the room.

The door opened and a pair of the elite Coldrush Guards entered first. As part of the prince consort's retinue and custodians of the Ivory Tower, they were taken from their families when it became clear they'd been infected, put into the strict tower camps, and trained to kill. Will sized the pair of them up. One of them returned his stare with a wary surveillance. Not fear. But marking him as a potential adversary.

The man who followed them towered over the guards. With thick brown hair and glassy, almost-colorless eyes, he strode into the room as if he owned it. His long red coat swirled around his hips, and a gleaming metal breastplate protected his chest.

Will had always thought the prince consort was an older man. He was surprised to find that he was perhaps younger than Blade. Ascending to the

Regency nearly thirty years ago, he'd steered the young human princess through the treacherous waters of the Echelon after her father had been overthrown. To consolidate his power, he'd then married her when she came of age, ten years ago.

The fact that he'd been the one who'd overthrown the human king wasn't something that was generally mentioned in polite company.

"Your Highness." The men stood and bowed.

The prince consort strode to the fire, holding out his hands to warm them. He looked up, his icy blue eyes examining Will. "So this is the Beast of Whitechapel?"

A growl sounded low in Will's throat. Both the Coldrush Guards straightened, hands resting on their pistols.

The prince consort's lips crooked up, just slightly, and Will forced himself to relax. Bloody games. Testing him to see what manner of man—or monster—he was.

The prince consort examined the room. "Have they told you why you're here?"

"You want somewhat from me," Will replied. No wonder they'd wanted him and Blade to come here. A meeting could have been set up anywhere in the city for them if it had involved only the Council. But the prince consort was another matter.

"I have a proposition. An…opportunity for yourself."

"How very kind of you," Will drawled. "Lookin' out for me interests like that."

Another oily smile. "Well, yes, also an opportunity for us. But I'll state it plainly. I don't intend to use you without your knowledge. And you will be ably compensated."

Like he'd ever given a damn about money.

The duchess spoke up. "There's talk that the French are in discussions with the Illuminist fanatics from New Catalan. It's an uneasy concept, to say the least."

Verwulfen were a blue blood's natural enemy, the only creature dangerous enough to kill a blue blood and do it easily. But in the eyes of the Illumination, any supernatural creature was an abomination that needed to be eliminated. The tales of New Catalan's Inquisition was enough to make even the bravest shudder.

"And how am I to help?" Will asked.

"We're not the only country with an interest in the proceedings across the Channel," Barrons replied. "If the Illumination gains a foothold in France, they'll have access to the northern waters, plus all France's airships. We're considering an alliance with the Scandinavians to prevent that. We have ships—the dreadnoughts—and the Scandinavians have their dragon-ships and air fleet."

Bloody hell. A husky bark of laughter erupted from his throat. "You think the Scandinavian clans would ally with *you*? The Butchers of Culloden? Let's not forget what's been done since. All them verwulfen trapped in cages and bought and sold like fuckin' slaves."

Blade caught his arm as he took a half step forward. A caution. Will shook it off, trying to focus through the red-hot flare of rage. The beat of it thundered in his blood, echoing dully in his ears.

"Culloden was a long time ago," the prince consort replied coolly. His guards had stepped forward as if fearing an attack, but he settled into a chair and flicked a piece of lint from his sleeve.

"It weren't that long ago to some of us."

"Culloden was a mistake." The words came from behind, from Barrons. All heads turned in his direction and he shrugged, as if admitting a truth they were too embarrassed to claim. "You cannot slaughter an entire race without consequences. Wiping out the Scottish verwulfen clans was only ever going to incite anger. But it was done by our forefathers and there is nothing we can do about it, Will."

"And the Manchester Pits? Where they throw us in with wild dogs and bears to bait? Or pit us against each other for blood sport?"

"They are private enterprises," the prince consort replied, his fingers slowly drumming on the armrest. "Most of them owned by humans, actually."

Which meant he didn't give a damn. Will knew what it was like to be trapped behind bars, or cut open for the pleasure of a crowd. And yet there was nothing to be done… Verwulfen were outlawed in Britain and capturing them and using them as slaves was not only legal, but encouraged.

Staring at the prince consort with his pale bloodless face, Will could barely control the surge of anger that boiled in his gut. "What do the Scandinavian clans think o' your policies?"

The prince consort's fingers stopped tapping. "Do you know what they do to blue bloods in Scandinavia?" A tight little smile eased over his mouth. "As I am willing to overlook certain things for the greater good, so are they. This threat from the Continent is of far greater concern than a few individuals."

Will shot a look of pure hatred toward the man.

"Then I ain't inclined to be obligin'. You'll have to use someone else."

Turning on his heel, the heat of fury burning in his cheeks, he jerked his head toward Blade. As far as he was concerned, this audience was over.

"Not even for ten thousand pounds?" The prince consort barely raised his voice, but Will heard it.

He laughed darkly. The Echelon. Thinking they could buy a man for his weight in gold.

He had one hand on the door handle when Barrons spoke up. "What if the terms were ones that interested you?"

"You can't buy me. Not even you, Barrons."

"What if the price was a change in the law?"

Will froze, hand on the doorknob.

As if encouraged, Barrons stepped closer, his boots sinking into the plush carpets. "If you help us sign this treaty with Scandinavia, then we would be willing to make certain changes to the law. No more cages or headhunters, Will. We would outlaw pit-fighting if you wished it."

His breath caught in his chest, and he turned on his heel. The five blue bloods stared at him without expression. The sight gave him the impression that this had been the trap all along. "Why do you need me so much? Sounds like you've almost got it signed."

"There are opposing factions in each camp," Barrons replied with a grimace. "The Norwegian clans are furiously adamant that they don't need us, and there are one or two Council members of our own who oppose this."

Will took another look around. Not only councilors

who'd voted for Blade to live then, but the ones who wanted this treaty to succeed. "And I'm to woo the Norwegian clans?"

"They're old-fashioned," the prince consort replied. "And crude. But they're also a loud voice in the Riksdag. We would like to show that our two species can live amicably." His smile widened. "And you are a perfect representative. You would appeal to them immensely."

"I think 'e just called you crude," Blade muttered.

Will ignored him. "If I can win the Norwegian clans over and see the treaty signed, then you'll revoke the law that outlaws verwulfen?"

The prince consort nodded.

"I'll want that in writin'," Will said. "And witnessed."

A slight narrowing of the prince consort's eyes. "Agreed."

"That ain't all. I want the pits outlawed. All verwulfen that are caged or slaved are to be set free and given equal rights as humans...or blue bloods."

Another nod.

"And the price on me head is lifted, you understand? I come and go as I please." No more skulking about the city, running the rooftops at night. Free to go where he wanted. Free to walk the city streets without people trying to kill him—or cage him.

The prince consort waved a negligent hand. "Would you like that in writing too?"

Will bared his teeth. "Absolutely."

❦

"That were well done," Blade said, hauling himself up into the steam carriage with a grunt.

Will nodded past him to Rip, who wore a coachman's livery and heavy cloak. Beneath that cloak lurked an armory of weapons, as well as the heavy, mech arm that would damn him in this company. At the back of the carriage hovered Tin Man, another of Blade's men. Light gleamed off the metal cap that was meshed to his scalp. He couldn't speak, but he was damn good with a blade.

"Take 'im home," Will said, clapping Tin Man on the shoulder. "Make sure he gets there."

Blade poked his head through the window. "Where're you goin'?"

"Takin' care of a promise I made."

"Alone?"

"I've got safe passage," he retorted. "Might as well use it for the night."

A long pause. "Be careful."

"Always." He turned on his heel and strode back toward the ball. Despite the overwhelming presence of blue bloods, a small smile played about his lips.

This time Lena was his.

Six

No sign of the duke or duchess anywhere.

Lena growled under her breath and retreated down the hallway. It wouldn't do to be caught here alone. As much as she wanted to discover more about the Scandinavian treaty, she wasn't foolish enough to start searching rooms by herself at a ball full of predators.

Noise washed over her as she returned to the entry. Keeping an eye open for a certain verwulfen she wished to avoid, she ducked into the ballroom.

Time to leave. She just had to find Adele and her mother—who was chaperoning her tonight—and plead a case of nerves. Pasting a wan smile on her face, she slipped around the edges of the ballroom, searching for them.

A full circuit took her back to the main doors. Adele was wearing white, as befitted a woman actively searching for a protector, but none of the white-gowned debutantes were her. A little tick of fear started in Lena's chest. She wouldn't have left the ballroom, would she? Adele knew the consequences of that as well as she did. Here, they both had an illusion of safety.

Unless…she'd left with someone on purpose. Perhaps she'd found someone willing to take her as thrall?

Lena scurried along the windows, peering out into the shadowed gardens. Adele—cunning, smart Adele—would never place such a risk to her reputation again. Not without an ironclad thrall contract in hand.

Smiling at Adele's mother, who stood gossiping with another matron, Lena pushed through the crowd and staggered into the entry. The grandfather clock ticked slowly in the middle of the staircase, but the room was empty.

The powder room. Maybe she was there?

Pushing open the small room, she ran into the Duchess of Casavian.

The woman caught her with strong, pale hands. Years ago, her father had infected her with the craving so that when he died, his House would not fade into obscurity. Aramina should have been considered a rogue, but her House was one of the Great Houses. After numerous assassination attempts she'd somehow survived, some said she'd blackmailed her way to power, forcing the Echelon to accept her.

"I'm sorry," Lena said. "I was looking for my friend."

Aramina's eyes narrowed. "You're Barrons's ward, aren't you?"

And too late, Lena remembered the blood feud between her half brother and this woman. "Yes."

"A girl like you shouldn't be out here alone. It's dangerous."

"I know. I couldn't find my friend… And I won't go back without her."

Consideration lit those brandy-brown eyes. Then the duchess's ruby-tinted lips thinned. "I'll look for her. What's her name?"

"Adele Hamilton," Lena said, collapsing against the wall in relief. "She's wearing white."

The duchess paused with her hand on the door handle. "The name is not unknown to me. Wasn't she the girl caught with Lord Fenwick last year?"

"Not by choice," Lena admitted, wondering whether the duchess would care.

They all knew about it, after all.

After a long stare, the duchess slipped through the door. "I'll find her. Stay here; it should be safe."

Lena fanned herself furiously. Of all the things to happen, she would never have imagined that the Duchess of Casavian would help her. She was notorious for her cool demeanor and frigid temper.

And her hatred of all things of the House of Caine, Leo included.

Why help the ward of her enemy?

Unless she wasn't really going to search for Adele… Lena's black lace fan slowed. The duchess had told her to stay here, not return to the ball, where she might be safe. It was highly unlikely a blue blood lord would stumble into the powder room, but it was also the perfect place for an ambush. Dark, secluded… Far enough away that nobody would hear her screaming over the music.

All the duchess had to do was find one of the more dangerous young bucks and whisper in his ear. Then Lena would be ruined—just another pawn lost in the game between the duchess and Leo.

She couldn't stay here.

Bolting for the door, she slipped out into the darkened corridor. Was it her imagination, or had the gaslights been turned down? Heart thumping in her chest, she hurried toward the ballroom.

Too late, she saw shadows shifting in the corner of her eye. Someone moved from behind the statue of an angel and a large bronzed hand clapped over her mouth. *No!* Lena's eyes shot wide as she was dragged back into a man's solid chest. Then, feet kicking uselessly, he dragged her into the darkness of one of the many rooms.

⁓

Lena screamed against the flesh of his hand, her slippered feet kicking at his shins. Will's predatory smile slipped. He'd meant to startle her, but the terror emanating off her roused all his dangerous instincts.

"Hush," he whispered against her ear and she shivered. "Lena, it's me. It's Will."

The tension drained out of her so absolutely he had to catch her up against him. With a sob, she turned toward him, tucking her face against his chest. Each small gasp strained her corset, and her fingers fisted in his shirt, dangerously close to the area over his heart. Will froze, his hand hovering over her hair.

What had frightened her so badly? Somehow he didn't think it was his own actions; from the way she'd relaxed into his grip, she'd been expecting someone else. The thought raced through his mind, bringing with it a wave of red. The hair along the back of his neck rose, a growl consuming his vocal cords.

"Lena?"

"I'm fine," she snapped. Balling her other fist, she punched him in the arm. "Were you trying to frighten ten years off my life?"

He barely felt the blow. "What's got you so scared? Who's huntin' you?"

Lena froze. Her other fist unclenched from his shirt and she took a step back, her skirts rustling loudly. "Nobody's hunting me."

Lie.

"Nobody except you." Her eyes narrowed. "What are you doing here? Are you insane? They'll tear you apart!"

"I've safe passage for the night."

"Why?" A look of concern crossed her face and she took his arm, her gloved fingers resting on his sleeve. "Don't trust them. Don't let them mix you up in their schemes. If there's a way around whatever they've promised, they'll find it."

Curious words from a woman who had dreamed of living amongst the Echelon for years.

He looked at the small hand resting on his arm. And realized that they were alone, in a darkened room together.

Will's gaze slid to the low scoop of her neckline and the full curve of her breasts. Moonlight glimmered through the curtains, casting a silvery sheen across her flesh. She was beautiful. A goddess of the night, limned by silvery light. Each curve of shadow beckoned him mysteriously, dared him to put his hands on her, to trace the dips and curves that filled out her gown. *Christ.* His cock hardened, straining against the fabric of his breeches. He could almost taste the warm perfume of her skin.

Taking a step back, he shook her hand off. "You owe me some answers."

"I don't have time. Not at the moment."

He grabbed her wrist, stroked his thumb across the sensitive skin. "Then make it."

She staggered into him, her other hand resting lightly against his chest. Something must have shown on his face, for she sucked in a deep breath. "Please, Will. Not now. There's something I must take care of."

"Course there is."

"You don't understand. I have to find my friend. I think she might be in trouble."

Her scent changed. Something bitter and sharp. Fear. Will let her go, staring down into that heart-shaped face. "What kind of trouble?"

"There's a…a game the blue blood's play. If they get a girl alone." She rubbed at her wrist unconsciously.

"Go on."

"Adele would never have left willingly. She knows the consequences. Please, I have to find her. Before it's too late."

"You're not goin' alone."

"If anyone sees me with you—"

She'd be ruined. He was half tempted for a moment. She'd never be able to return to this world with the stigma of being caught alone with a verwulfen.

But she'd made her choices. This was the world she wanted. There was nothing for her in Whitechapel; she'd said so herself.

He leaned closer, let his voice whisper over her ear. "Then they won't see me. But I'll be there."

It might have been his imagination, but he thought, for a moment, that she shivered.

⁂

The strains of a waltz floated from the ballroom as Barrons climbed the stairs. He'd hoped to catch a chance to talk to Will before he left, but the man had vanished.

Glancing down one of the hallways as he crossed it, he saw the sweep of aubergine skirts and the beguiling hint of coppery hair vanishing into a room.

He stopped in his tracks.

Interesting.

The waltz beckoned. Laughter loomed. But somehow his feet turned down the corridor.

Slipping silently through the door, Leo found himself in a shadowed parlor. Moonlight streamed through the windows, highlighting the Duchess of Casavian's gleaming hair. She peered through a connecting doorway, her head cocked as if listening.

"Looking for something?"

The words tore a gasp from her lips. She spun, eyes glittering coldly.

"Or is it *someone*?" He leaned against the closed door and crossed his arms over his chest.

"It's none of your business, Barrons." She glided sinuously toward him, the creamy flesh of her décolletage displayed invitingly. A ploy, of course, meant to draw men's eyes, make them forget to watch her hands.

He'd never been that foolish. The woman was dangerous and Leo knew it. She'd like nothing better than to see him and the Duke of Caine dead, their House nothing but a memory. Still…the view was tempting.

"Get out of my way," she commanded. Another step brought her closer, her full skirts sweeping against his ankles. As if she thought he'd obey.

"Why would I?" Leo took a step closer. Her skirts brushed his thighs, and her chin tilted up. "It's a beautiful night and you're a beautiful woman." He held a hand out, gesturing to the room with a mocking smile. "And we're all alone."

A quick movement. He caught her wrist, moonlight flashing off the bejeweled hilt of a dagger. Their eyes met. There was no sign of her discomposure. Nothing but the quirk of her brow.

An ice princess.

Suddenly he wanted to melt her cool mask.

Spinning her back against the door, he forced her wrist—and the dagger—high. Her other hand moved in a chopping motion but he caught that too. Slammed it back against the hard wood.

Pinned.

Aramina's breath caught. "Don't think this makes me any less dangerous."

"I wouldn't dream of it," he murmured. The scent of her perfume curled through his nose. Spicy cinnamon. Alluring. Almost enough to make his grip soften, his body lean into hers.

Almost.

"A knee to the balls?" he asked.

She smiled. There was no warmth in it. "A knife would be preferable."

Leo winced. "You're merciless, my dear."

"I can be." Aramina's gaze lowered. Examined his mouth.

Leo froze. The softening of her expression drew him in, a moth to the flame. The woman was his enemy, her House and his at blood feud with each other. And yet he couldn't deny that she fascinated him.

"I can be merciless too," he whispered, his face lowering to hers. "But you'd like that, wouldn't you?"

She wet her lips. Turned her face away. Leo's breath stirred the curls at her ear. His heart pounded as his lips brushed against her jaw. The sweet kick of her carotid proved she wasn't as immune to him as she pretended. He slid his lips over it, felt the pulse through her veins. Heat flared, his cock grinding against her. Somehow his hands were on her hips.

"You should look to your House," she whispered.

He traced the curve of her throat with his tongue, teeth grazing the vein. God, how he wanted her blood. "What do you mean by that?"

A soft laugh. Aramina's face turned to his, her lips brushing his cheek as she whispered in his ear. "Where's your ward, Barrons?"

Something sharp dug into his groin. The knife.

He hissed. "What have you done with her?"

"Me? Nothing." Aramina lifted on her toes, her breasts brushing against his chest. "That," she said, "was almost too easy."

The blade forced him away from her. Aramina opened the door, glancing casually over her shoulder.

The dagger had vanished. "I was actually trying to do the girl a good deed. I like her." A swift smile. "And she has her uses." Slipping through the door, she threw over her shoulder, "You'll find her in the powder room."

❧

Lena strode down the hallway, checking room after room. The skin on her arms and neck prickled, knowing that Will watched. She couldn't see him anywhere, yet his presence gave her the kind of confidence she'd not felt in a long time.

Easing the door to Lord Harker's study closed, she froze. What was that? A soft cry in the dark? Taking a quiet step toward the library, she kept her head cocked.

There it came again. "*No. Please.*"

Adele. In the library.

Anger burned through her, white-hot. She slammed open the door. A single candle flickered, highlighting the daybed by the cold fireplace. Adele was wilted over it like a fading flower, blood dripping down the smooth column of her throat. Her bodice was soaked, the bright scarlet vivid against the white silk.

A man looked up, his lips painted red and the black of his eyes reflecting the candlelight. Benjamin Cavendish, the eldest son of Baron Rackham, and one of the younger pack.

He wiped his mouth with the back of his sleeve, an insolent smile on his face. "Ah, the main course arrives."

"Get off her."

"I was done anyway." His gaze slid over her sinuously. "It's Miss Todd, isn't it?"

Adele whimpered, her hands on her throat. Her frightened eyes met Lena's. "*Run.*"

Lena's fists clenched. The bastard thought he had her cornered. Will's silent presence gave her strength she hadn't realized she'd had. She snatched a poker from the fire set and faced him. "You get away from her now."

"A feisty one. It's much more fun when they put up a struggle." He laughed.

Lena hefted the poker as he took a stealthy step toward her. "You're a coward. Stalking young ladies at balls… It's all you're good for. You're not a man; you're just a little bully who's grown up."

Cavendish's eyes narrowed. "*You* are going to regret those words."

He made a snatch at her skirts. Lena brought the poker down with relish. *Take that, you slimy little cretin.* "Get your hands off me!"

The next few seconds happened too quickly for her to keep track of. One moment Cavendish was hissing at her, clutching his injured hand. The next he was slammed up against the fireplace, Will's hand wrapped around his throat.

"Will! You're not supposed to show yourself!"

"He put his hands on you."

The depth of his voice sent shivers through her. Dangerous. Brutal. A voice that had no give in it, no means of reckoning with it. She had to stop him before he killed someone.

"He barely touched me. Will! Let him go." She dropped the poker and grabbed his arm. It was useless. Her slight weight didn't so much as shift him. "Will! If you hurt him, they'll kill you."

"You!" Cavendish gasped, his eyes full of malevolence. They shifted to her. "Little verwulfen slut. I'll—"

Whatever he'd been about to say was choked off as Will's fingers tightened.

"Look at me," he said, the predator within him riding just under the surface. Cavendish was helpless to disobey. "You ever come near her again I'll kill you. And it won't be quick." He smiled and Lena shivered. There was a wealth of viciousness in that smile. "Don't think there's anywhere you can hide. I can get to you, no matter how many guards you think you have. Do you understand?"

Cavendish's fingers tore at Will's hand. His face was rapidly turning purple, but somehow he managed to nod.

Will let him go and Cavendish staggered back, slumping against the fireplace.

"If there's even a whisper about tonight—about Lena—I'll come for you," Will promised. "Now get the hell outta here before I change me mind."

Cavendish scrambled for the door.

The ease with which Will did it... Lena felt a brief stab of jealousy. Oh, to be a man, to be strong, to be feared...

A strangled cough came from the daybed and she turned, her skirts swirling around her ankles as she ran to Adele.

"What happened?" Lena knelt, turning her friend's face to the side to look at the damage. He'd cut her deep, using one of the elegant little blades the Echelon preferred. Some of the crueler blue bloods filed their teeth into points, but the majority used blades.

At least he'd had the presence of mind to lick the wound afterward. Whatever was in a blue blood's saliva, it promoted swift healing.

"Here," she murmured, tearing a strip off her petticoat. Rolling it into a pad, she tore another strip and bandaged the pad to the wound.

"Came looking for you," Adele whispered.

"I was only going to the powder room."

"Colchester...arrived."

Lena's hands stilled. Then she continued cleaning away the blood. "You still shouldn't have come alone."

"Saw Colchester talking to Cavendish." Adele swallowed. "He left the room and I thought—"

"They set you up." Damn Colchester. He'd deliberately sent one of his cronies out to ambush Adele. Her actions the other night must have drawn his ire.

"Who's Colchester?"

Lena froze. She'd forgotten all about Will. Her skirts rustled as she turned to look at him, her mind racing. She'd seen the look on his face when he'd choked Cavendish. If she told him about the duke, then there was a chance he'd go after him.

"The Duke of Lannister," she replied carefully. "He has some grievance against Leo."

Adele shifted and Lena squeezed her hand in warning. *Don't say a word.*

Will stared at her, his face expressionless.

Beside her, Adele cleared her throat. "Who... is this?"

"He's Blade's man," she replied, turning her attention back to her wounded friend. The bandage slowed the bleeding. There was no saving the dress, however. They'd have to get her out of here without anyone seeing.

"Cavendish said he was…" Adele trailed off.

Lena had never seen her look frightened before. World-weary and cynical, yes, but not truly frightened. She looked up and then paused, realizing how it would seem to Adele. Will hovered in the shadows, but everything about him was intimidating to someone who didn't know him. And even then…

Adele would have heard stories—blue blood stories—about verwulfen and their violent, unrestrained passions. To the Echelon, Will was dangerous and nothing more than a monster.

"Verwulfen? Yes," she replied, helping her to sit up. She smiled at Adele and leaned closer to whisper, "Don't be frightened by the scowl. He thinks it's impressive. But he's a soft-heart beneath the grim exterior." Lena couldn't help smiling. "Some boys were drowning a bag of kittens once and he rescued them. For months they followed him around the warren. I'm afraid it's quite ruined his carefully cultivated reputation in my eyes. All I can see is Mother Hen and his little charges." Her smile faded. "The only monsters here are Colchester and his little friends."

Will's eyes were sleepy looking. A dangerous sign. It meant he was thinking and she didn't want that. Meeting his gaze, she tipped her chin up. "We have to get her out of here without anyone seeing. If they do, she's ruined."

Will shrugged out of his coat and offered it. Adele flinched but took a slow breath and let Lena drape it around her shoulders. It was deliciously warm and she breathed in, filling her nose with his scent.

Will rolled the sleeves of his shirt up and candlelight gleamed on his bronzed forearms. Not for the first time, she wondered if his skin was that same molten gold all over.

Dangerous thoughts. She looked away quickly.

"Here," he said, trying in his own way to be polite. "I can carry you."

Adele's eyes widened, but she nodded and let him slip his arms around her. Will straightened, lifting Adele easily. His gaze sought Lena's. "Where to?"

With Will at her side, negotiating the dark hallways was easy. His superior senses saved them from discovery several times over. Slipping out through the servant's entrance and the garden, they hastened toward the Hamilton's steam carriage.

Weak from the loss of blood, Adele settled into the carriage sleepily. Lena tucked the lap rug over her and checked her makeshift bandage, then turned to murmur to one of the waiting footmen. "Will you fetch Mrs. Hamilton?"

There was one last matter to attend to. Stepping up onto the carriage's step, she turned to face Will reluctantly. "Thank you. For helping me with Adele."

He stood with his back to the gaslight, his face cast in shadows. A thin gleam of amber indicated his mood. "You and I need to talk."

"There's nothing to talk about." She turned, intending to settle inside the carriage, but he caught a fistful of her skirts.

"I ain't goin' away, Lena."

A glimpse over her shoulder revealed the aggressive truth of that on his face.

"Why won't you let it be? It's none of your business." It wasn't even as though he cared. He was only doing this for Blade's sake.

Turning around on the step brought her face to face with him. Though she'd always felt at a disadvantage with her lack of height, it was suddenly far too intimate. The heat of his large body protected her from the cool evening breeze, and her skirts pressed against his thighs. She searched his gaze for something, anything, to tell her that she was wrong. That he was here for her.

"Why?"

His gaze flickered away, thoughtful. "Found the same code on a man as stabbed Blade inna heart. Something's stirrin', Lena. I'm not about to let him—or the rookery—get caught up in it." His smoldering gaze caught hers. "And I think you know more'n you're sayin'."

Her lips thinned. Of course. Blade. And the rookery. "Do you really think I would be involved in anything that might hurt Blade—and through him, my sister and brother?"

"I don't know," he said quietly.

In that moment she hated him. No matter her many flaws, she would never risk Honoria or Charlie's life. Reaching for the carriage door, she shot him one last glare. "Go home, Will. You don't belong here, nor are you wanted. Just go home and patrol your little part of London. I won't visit and I won't expect to see you in the city."

She gave his hand an icy look and he slowly released her, tension riding through his shoulders.

"I didn't mean it like that," he said. "I know you love your brother and sister."

"One of the few things you seem to know about me." Sweeping her skirts inside the carriage, she went to shut the door.

Will caught it, leaning closer. The sleeves of his shirt strained over his arms. "Lena, damn it—"

"I say… Is this chap bothering you?"

With Will so close, she hadn't realized anyone else was there. Neither had he, by the shock that shuddered through him.

Giving him one last spearing look, she glanced over his shoulder at the slightly inebriated young lord and smiled. Saved by a blue blood. How ironic. "He was just leaving. Thank you."

"My pleasure." The young buck shot her a wink and a salute. She'd seen him before, though his name momentarily escaped her.

Will lowered his hand from the door. "I'll leave you be. This time."

Lena shut the door and smiled through the glass at him. With a growl, he turned and shot the young lord a look that made his face pale. Then, hands in his pockets, he stalked into the shadows, fog swirling around his ankles.

※

"So," Adele murmured, resting her head against the carriage seat. She was still snuggled in the black coat. "Tell me about this Will."

"Hmm?" Lena looked up from where she'd been smoothing her skirts. "What about him?"

Adele's eyes narrowed. A hint of her old spark was starting to warm her cheeks. "He looks like he wants to eat you up, Lena. And not in a scary manner."

"Will? He does nothing of the sort! He's made it quite—" And then she stopped, aware of what she was about to reveal.

"Quite…?" Adele prompted. When Lena said nothing, a weary smile stretched over her face. "You do realize I'm not going to leave it there, my dear."

Staring out the window, Lena watched the lights glittering in the windows of Lord Harker's mansion. It wouldn't be long before the footman would bring Adele's mother. Then she would be safe from prying questions.

Yet…a sudden urge welled up. The need to confide in someone, even Adele. She'd been holding so much inside her for months that she felt almost fit to bursting.

"I kissed him," she blurted. "I don't know why. It was always just a game I played with him. A flirtation. I never meant anything by it." *Hadn't she?* Lena frowned. She couldn't, in truth, answer that question. "It was awful. He didn't even kiss me back. And when I stopped…" Her cheeks were burning now. "He told me that he would tolerate my childish little games for Blade's sake, but that he would prefer it if I didn't throw myself at him. Especially since we were living beneath one roof." The very memory of it turned her stomach. He'd been so angry with her he was shaking. Then he'd turned and walked away without another word.

Somehow she managed a lighthearted shrug for Adele's sake. "The next day he moved out of the warren. And I decided it was time to return to society. There was nothing left for me in Whitechapel."

"He never kissed you back?"

"Not even slightly."

Adele's eyebrows drew together. "How unusual. For I would have suspected quite the opposite, my dear. He couldn't take his eyes off you. And when Cavendish tried to grab you, I thought he was going to kill him."

"His loyalty is to Blade. If he allowed me to come to any harm he'd have to explain it to him. And Honoria."

"Hmm." Adele settled back on the seat, snuggling in wearily. "I'll stake a hundred pounds that you're wrong."

"And how do we prove that?" she asked tartly. "I'm not about to ask him."

Adele's eyes closed. A little smile played around her lips. "Because next time, I'm certain that he'll kiss *you*."

❧

The door to Lord Harker's private study slammed open.

Colchester looked up over the rim of his glass. His gaze raked Cavendish, from the rumpled collar of his coat to the seething fury in his eyes. If he wasn't mistaken, there was a large bruise forming against the other man's throat.

"What the devil happened? Surely she didn't put up that much of a fight?"

Cavendish shot him a filthy look and crossed to the liquor decanter. "You forgot to mention she had protection." He splashed a liberal dash of blud-wein into a glass and drained it.

"Protection?" Colchester asked silkily. His eyes lifted again to that bruise. "What manner of protection?"

Cavendish lowered the glass and muttered, "Nothing."

Colchester eased to his feet, tossing aside the newspaper he'd been reading. Below, the ball was still in full swing by the sound of it, yet he had little intention of joining the swirling throng. No, he had other plans.

Plans that Cavendish just might have ruined.

"I thought you were a blue blood, Cavendish. Not a puling human. I asked you to ruin the girl and you couldn't even handle that." He sneered, circling the other man. "Did she beat you with her reticule? Or was there more than one of them? A whole flock of debutantes to frighten you—"

An angry gleam turned Cavendish's eyes to shadows. "I'd like to see you take on the Beast. Seems your little bitch has gone and got herself a filthy verwulfen to watch her back."

"What do you mean by that?"

Cavendish sneered. "Probably plundering the girl right now, as we speak. Seems you're not going to get your hands on that one after all."

Colchester had him by the throat before he realized it. "Whitechapel's Beast?"

Cavendish struggled to nod.

Shock sliced through him. The little bitch. Thought she could find a protector, did she? As Cavendish made a strangled sound, Colchester dropped him and stepped away, raking the glasses off the tray. Glass smashed across the floor, littering the carpets. Lena was his. But if she'd polluted herself with one of those filthy creatures then she was no longer fit to be his thrall. By God he'd make her regret this act.

Cavendish slumped against the table, watching him warily. "What are you going to do?" he asked, and Colchester realized he'd spoken out loud.

Bad enough that the rest of the Council sought to ally themselves with these creatures. Now one of them moved to steal his thrall right out from underneath his nose. That, if nothing else, made him want her even more.

He smiled. Darkly. "Let me deal with it. I'll make her regret it." Flicking glass off his sleeve, he turned toward the door. "I'll make them both regret it."

Seven

"COME IN."

Will shot a look down the hall, his booted heels muffled on the Turkish runner. He could sense Lena in the house somewhere, but not nearby. Which suited him perfectly for the moment.

Slipping inside the study, he closed the door behind him. Morning light spilled through the windows. An ungodly hour of the morning, in fact. He'd barely slept, his mind replaying every scene from the night before. As soon as he grew close to the edge of sleep, the memory of Lena's fear scent would sweep through him and his eyes would jerk open again. He needed to know more. Especially about the one name that frightened her.

Barrons looked up from his desk, his dark eyes widening slightly. "Will." He leaned back in his chair, his progress marked by the shifting of well-oiled leather. Dressed in a black velvet coat, the only sign of color was the spill of white lace at his wrists and throat. A little ruby pin winked against the lace. "You do realize the price on your head isn't lifted until you sign the prince consort's document?" He lifted a sheaf of papers, frowning. "Which is right here, I believe."

Will crossed his arms over his chest. "What d'you know about a man named Colchester?"

"Colchester?" Barrons's hands stilled on the paper. "He used to be a friend, until I orchestrated the duel between his cousin Vickers and Blade. Why do you ask?"

"Why would Lena be afraid of him?"

Barrons straightened, a dangerous look coming into his obsidian eyes. "What do you mean?"

"Had business with her last night. When I found her she were terrified. O' him."

Barrons leaned back in his chair. "Tell me."

Will relayed the story, omitting any mention of the code or the letter. "Don't know 'im. Ain't never heard much about him." He scratched at the stubble on his jaw. "Is he dangerous?"

"All blue bloods are dangerous."

Will met his stare. "Can he get to her?"

For once, Barrons's cool composure vanished. Uncertainty shadowed his brow. "I don't know. She has a companion and she only ever attends events with a chaperone or myself. But there are ways to get around that for a man like Colchester."

"What does he want with her?"

"I can only presume," Barrons replied. "Vengeance against me. Or perhaps some interest in Lena herself. Rumor has it he's hunting for another thrall."

"You wouldn't let that happen?"

Barrons leveled an intense look upon him. "What's your interest in the matter?"

"Blade protects his own," he replied promptly.

"And I protect him. He wouldn't survive goin' up against another duke. I want this stopped before it gets to that."

"I see." Barrons gestured toward the chair facing him. "How do you propose to stop it?"

Will sank into the chair. "Thought of a way to protect Lena and help with the prince consort's task. Killin' two birds with one stone, so to speak."

Barrons gestured for him to continue.

"This ruse of the prince consort's—me, dressed up like a court jester and bobbin' to his tune—it ain't gonna work. I don't know nothin' of court ways."

"And?"

"Who better to teach me than Lena? Keep me from makin' too big a fool of meself, or steppin' on the wrong toes."

"Unless they happen to be Colchester's…upon whom you wish to step quite firmly, if I may guess where this is going?" Barrons leaned forward. "He's a dangerous man, Will."

"So am I."

Barrons examined him for a long moment. Then nodded. "A verwulfen bodyguard. It would certainly give most sane men pause. Done. I'll inform her that she's to help present you to the court and squire you about."

"If she's with me, then he can't make a move."

"Don't do anything untoward," Barrons warned. "Remember your cause—if you kill Colchester, you can wave good-bye to any assistance or goodwill from the prince consort. Including this reform of the laws that you are so anxious to establish."

Will bared his teeth in an anticipatory smile. "Would you like to let Lena know about her new duties, or can I?"

&

"Hike in blood taxes!" the headlines screamed.

Lena dipped her spoon into the crater of her boiled egg, her gaze darting over the article. "Mrs. Wade, have you seen this?" she asked, gesturing with the spoon. Runny yolk dripped over the paper and she hastily put it down. "They're raising the blood taxes! From two pints a year to three. Anyone who hasn't donated in the last month must attend a mandatory bloodletting in the next two months."

"A young lady doesn't speak of such things. Especially over the breakfast table." Meticulously carving her sausage, Mrs. Wade's lips thinned. "Have you read the society pages? What did you think of the description of Miss Hambley's gown?"

"A withered daffodil? Rather accurate, if I do say so," she replied distantly. "It must be in response to the draining factories burning down. The Echelon must be dangerously short of blood supplies."

Though they kept thralls for fresh blood, they also needed a supply of chilled blood on hand. It was dangerous to take too much from a thrall, and draining one to death was in utter poor taste. The only lords who could afford to keep and maintain enough thralls to survive off of were the great dukes who ruled the city. The rest of the Echelon were forced to buy blood from the government-owned draining factories or keep blood slaves.

"The working class won't be very happy about this." There'd already been three riots this year, twice about automaton factory workers taking jobs and then again when a young woman was found drained to death in an alley.

Mrs. Wade made a disapproving sound and stabbed a piece of sausage.

A knock sounded and Leo appeared in the doorway of the dining room, dressed in his usual strict black. "Ladies," he greeted.

Mrs. Wade snatched her napkin to her lips. "Good morning, my lord. You are joining us for breakfast?"

"I'm afraid not." He glanced toward her and Lena stilled. From the look in his eyes, Leo was up to something.

"Yes?" she asked, her heart starting to pound. Had he heard of what happened to Adele? Or Cavendish?

"I've a favor to ask," he said, resting his hip against the edge of the dining table.

"Of course. What is it?"

Movement shifted at the edge of her vision. Will. Stepping into the room, his hands shoved into his pockets and satisfaction burning in his eyes.

Lena stared. His collar was open, revealing a healthy slice of tanned flesh, and he hadn't bothered to shave. With his burning amber eyes and the stubble on his jaw, he looked eminently dangerous. A silver claw hung from the leather thong at his throat.

His mouth curved with a rusty smile, sending her pulse into a frenetic tempo. Oh Lord! She'd rarely seen him smile. And certainly not at her. The result was rather devastating.

Leo cleared his throat and Lena tore her gaze away. "Absolutely not," she snapped.

"You haven't heard the proposition yet."

"I don't need to."

"Carver's received a commission from the Crown," Leo continued.

The words jerked her attention away from Will. "A commission?" What could the prince consort possibly want of him? For that was where the commission had to have come from. The queen might sit on the throne, but she was the prince consort's puppet-on-a-string. She barely dared speak without his permission.

"There's a delegation arriving from Scandinavia in a week."

"There is?" she asked breathlessly.

"Just some political business for the Council and the prince consort," Leo said. "Nothing interesting, I'm afraid. But you know how feelings run between our two countries. It was felt that Will's presence might be some sort of soothing factor."

Lena nodded slowly, her mind scalded with shock. Will was involved in this?

"He needs tidying up," Leo continued. "Both in manners and appearance. And he also needs someone to guide him through the dangerous waters at court. Unfortunately, I don't have the time…"

Oh, yes. She saw where this was going.

"You want me to escort him." Her eyes narrowed on Will. "I wonder whose idea *that* was?"

He didn't even have the grace to appear guilty. Leaning against the door, he smiled his cat-got-the-cream smile.

The one that did so much damage to her insides.

"Your skill in navigating the Echelon would serve your country in good stead," Leo replied.

"My, it's so terribly well thought out." Inside she was boiling. How dare he? And yet this was precisely what Mr. Mandeville had warned her about when she first agreed to spy for the humanists. She couldn't allow her feelings to disrupt such an opportunity.

Finding out about the Scandinavian treaty was more important than braining Will Carver with the soup tureen.

"You'll help us then?" Leo asked.

"I could hardly refuse such a gracious offer. We'll start tomorrow." She ran her gaze over Will's unkempt hair, the glorious honey-brown strands that tangled about his shoulders. "Though heaven knows where I'm going to begin."

"He doesn't need to be perfect," Leo said. "Just polished. And taught what to say."

"Or rather, what not to." Her eyes narrowed. "He'll have to look like a gentleman at least. A haircut, a shave...possibly delousing." A smile blossomed. "A complete new wardrobe. Dancing lessons."

Will arched a brow. "I ain't dancin'."

"You'll dance if I tell you to dance. You'll bow when I tell you, and you'll keep a civil tongue." A part of her almost couldn't wait. "Otherwise I'll wash my hands of this whole affair and you don't want that, do you?"

Oh no, he wanted to be nice and close. To keep an eye on her.

His eyes narrowed, the message in them perfectly

clear. This would be war. But he had no choice but to accept her terms.

Leo looked between them. "Is there anything that I should be aware of?"

"No," both she and Will retorted.

"Nothing at all," she added, glaring at him to make sure he didn't mention anything to Leo.

∽

"I suppose you think this is amusing," Lena said, pulling on her gloves with a sharp jerk.

Will leaned against the wall, lazily watching her. Her cheeks were pale but her eyes spat fire. He wanted to kiss her, wanted to press her back against the Chinese wallpaper and lick his way down her throat.

Dangerous.

He could control this urge, this desire. He had to.

Flexing his fingers, he glanced down the hallway. The chaperone was hovering like a service drone, her eyes flaring wide every time she saw him looking, as though she half suspected he'd pounce on her. Will was tempted to snarl at her. See if she had an attack of the vapors.

"Would it bother you if I admitted I were enjoyin' every minute of this?"

Lena paused, her top hat resting rakishly on her head. Her fingers tangled in the purple ribbons and their eyes met in the mirror.

"I warned you," he whispered, leaning closer so that his image came into the polished glass too. With his dark coat, he looked like an enormous shadow behind her slender purple figure. The big, bad wolf, ready to devour her.

Her scent enveloped him, tempting him to do just that. He wanted to press his face into her neck and breathe her in, let his hands run down over the corseted curve of her hips…

Lena looked up at him helplessly. Some hint of his hunger must have shown on his face for her lips parted with a soft exhalation.

"I will find out what you're up to," he warned.

She broke the spell, tugging sharply at her ribbons as she tied them. "Enjoy the moment, Will. It shall be the last time you get the better of me." With a sweet little smile, she added, "And consider this my warning."

"What d'you mean?"

She turned in a froth of skirts. "This is my world now and you've got no idea what the rules are. You're not going to learn a thing and I…I am going to take great pleasure in this."

She tried to step past him and he refused to back away and give her room. Lena's breathing hastened, but there was no sign of it on her face as she squeezed past, her hips brushing against his thigh.

"What do you—?"

"Tomorrow. At noon," she said, fetching her parasol, some lacy bit of fabric that would do naught to stave off the weather. "It wouldn't do to have you come here too often. People might start to wonder. So I'll come to you. At the warren. I can claim to be visiting my sister or helping her with some project." She ran one last glance over him. "Do try to be clean and appropriately dressed. Tidying you up for society is going to be a rather monumental task as it is."

Eight

WILL PACED THE EDGE OF THE ROOF, STARING OUT OVER the wall that encircled Whitechapel. Chanting and shouts echoed from the north, near the exit of Bishopsgate. It sounded like the low rumble of thunder, and every hour built the intensity of the storm until even Charlie and Lark could hear it.

"What's going on?" Charlie asked, sitting on a chimney and kicking his heels against the brickwork.

At his feet, Lark sat cross-legged at the base of the chimney, chewing on a strand of her long brown hair. Ever since Honoria had moved into the warren with Lena and their younger brother Charlie, the pair had been inseparable.

"It's a riot. Or the starts of one," Will replied.

Charlie's eyes rounded and he grinned. At seventeen, he was still young enough not to understand what was about to happen. "A riot? How smashing! Can we go see?"

"Don't be a nodcock," Lark snapped. Raised in the rookeries, she understood the connotations far better than Charlie ever would. "Nothin' but blood'll come of this."

"All the better." Charlie grinned, a hint of dark shadows swimming through his gaze.

Lark punched him in the thigh and he winced. "You ain't seen a riot dealt with before, you fool. It won't be a sight to see. Nothin' but crushed bodies and broken bones. Men, women, and children." She shook her head. "The Echelon won't stand for it long. They'll unleash the Trojan cavalry to mow 'em down and then there'll be blood in the streets." She shivered. "Not 'ere though. Not near us."

Will stared over the rooftops, his nostrils flaring. "Near Langbourn."

"Oh." Charlie's shoulders slumped. "I was only foolin'. I didn't mean it."

"You didn't think," Lark corrected. Charlie might be a blue blood and three times as strong as her, but the balance of power between them was still weighted in her direction. She had street smarts and a quick cunning—and several older adopted "uncles" to back her up if anyone gave her any lip.

Will ignored their bickering, pacing along the edge of the roof. A quick glance showed him the sun in the sky, battling valiantly behind several fluffy gray clouds. "Charlie, what time is it?"

Charlie tugged out his pocket watch. "Quarter to twelve, sir."

Midday.

A restless edge ran through him. She'd said she'd come here for the lesson. His mind ran through a mental map of the city. If Lena came through Aldgate, she'd most likely avoid the trouble. But if she came out through Bishopsgate, then…

A growl rumbled in his throat.

"Ah… Is everything all right?" Charlie asked. Even he knew to tread carefully around Will's temper.

"Mebbe." He turned and speared them both with a gaze. "Stay here. Keep watch. And *don't*, under any circumstances, leave the rookery. If trouble spills, then you get back to the warren and cry hue."

"Yes, sir!" Charlie snapped to attention. "Where are you going?"

Will strode toward the edge of the wall. "To fetch your fool sister. She said she were comin' here today. Wouldn't surprise me if she gets caught up in that."

⤜⊹⤛

The letter from Mr. Mandeville arrived early that morning.

Lena looked up from her workbench, a variety of cogs and strips of sheet iron strewn across the tabletop. Pushing her magnifying glassicals up on top of her head, she retrieved the letter and slid a screwdriver underneath the envelope to slit it open.

A slow, steady beat began in her chest.

> *Dear Miss Todd,*
>
> *I hope this letter finds you well. I have received a most impressive commission for you, regarding the original clockwork you showed me the other day. I would be delighted to discuss this with you in person, at your convenience.*
>
> *Yours,*
> *Arthur Mandeville.*

Clapping a hand to her chest, she slowly rose. The transforming clockwork! Someone wanted a copy of it!

"Mrs. Wade!" she called, hurrying out of the room to her companion's bedchambers. "Mrs. Wade!"

Within a half hour, she'd hustled her companion into the steam carriage and set out for Mandeville's Clockwork Emporium.

The streets were full and progress was slow. Lena twitched aside the curtains, glancing at the crowds and the omnibus ahead. Passing under Bishopsgate, one of the massive gates that guarded the city proper, she toyed impatiently with her reticule. "Whatever is the crush?"

Mrs. Wade leaned out the window and conferred with the driver. When she sat back down, she was breathless. "A protest. In Langbourn and Lime Street. Those mechanists are at it again."

Lena peered out curiously. She'd heard all about the mechanists—those who bartered years of service to the Echelon in exchange for bio-mech limbs or clockwork organs. Quartered in their steamy enclaves in the city, they were treated as little better than animals. One couldn't trust a man who was half metal. Indeed, many in the Echelon argued that by taking on the metal limbs, they were making themselves less human and therefore did not have the rights of a whole man.

"They should herd them back to their enclaves and lock them in," Mrs. Wade sniffed.

"I don't see what the difference is. Just because someone has a metal arm, it doesn't make him any less a man," Lena replied. Two of Blade's men, Tin Man and Rip, had mech limbs. By rights, both of them should have been imprisoned in the enclaves, but no one dared mention it to Blade.

"You can't trust them," Mrs. Wade replied.

"Why not? The metal does not affect the mind. They are still the same as they were before they received the enhancements."

"It's unnatural, is what it is."

There was no point arguing with someone who had no rational rebuttals. Lena bit her tongue and tried to catch a closer look at the rally.

"Hopefully they'll send the metaljackets in and clear them out," Mrs. Wade added. "Get this traffic moving again."

It wasn't very far to the emporium. She'd walked ten times this distance when she lived in the rookery. "Why don't we walk?"

The suggestion was met with a look of great horror. "With all those mechs running around?"

"We'll take one of the footmen. The carriage can meet us there once this congested traffic starts moving again." Lena reached for the door.

"Wait! Your parasol!" Mrs. Wade huffed after her, bringing her hat, parasol, and the basket of crochet she always carried as Lena hopped down from the carriage. Her eyes darted as if expecting a mech to leap out and attack at any moment.

The crowd thinned the closer they got to Mandeville's. Most people were poor, waving placards and fists, as though the Echelon would even notice. Still, Lena could understand the need to do *something*.

Several streets over, the sound was rather more

intense. Lena steered them in the other direction, even though it took them streets out of their way. She had no intentions of getting caught in the mob.

A burly man with a metal plate curving across his skull staggered into her, reeking of spirits. His hand was mech too, fitted roughly to the flesh of his wrist. From the scarred edges of skin, the work had been done in a hurry, and poorly too. He caught sight of her red skirts and looked up, his gaze raking over the pearls at her throat and the feathers in her bonnet. They were the only adornments she wore and in most circumstances she wouldn't have felt uneasy walking the streets like this.

"'Ere now," he sneered, grabbing her wrist. "A little blue blood whore, all alone."

"I would let me go if I were you," she suggested in her firmest tone. "And I wouldn't assume that I was alone."

Mrs. Wade leveled her parasol at him as though it were a weapon. "Unhand her, you mech brute!"

Lena shot her a glare and shook her head. Precisely the wrong tone and words for the situation. She held up a placating hand. "We have no interest in your—"

"Brute?" he snarled. "A mech brute like me? What, you think you're better 'an us?"

Around them, people were starting to take an interest.

"Let her go or you'll feel the wrath of the Duke of Caine!" Mrs. Wade snapped back, as though that name would hold any weight here.

Lena hastened to diffuse the situation. "We don't think we're any better, or different or—"

"'Ere now, lads!" he roared. "This bit o' fluff's turnin' her nose up at us!"

Mutters and grumbling sprang up. Lena looked around desperately. "No, I don't! I never said that."

"You in the city, you turn your noses up at us. Well, just you wait. Your time's comin'." He leered at her. "We got ways of dealin' with your sort now."

"Unhand her!" the footman insisted, taking the man by the arm. "Miss Lena, are you all right?"

Whistles suddenly screamed through the air and as one the crowd turned with a gasp.

"It's the Trojan cavalry!" someone yelled.

Frightened cries tore through the crowd and they erupted into a panicked mob, streaming for the safety of the square ahead. Lena was swept up in the edges of it, her wrist torn from the man's grasp.

Someone grabbed her around the waist, lifting her off her feet. "Beg pardon, miss," Henry, the footman, said. A strapping lad of nearly six feet, even he had to fight to keep his feet against the horde as he pushed through to the side of the crowd.

Mrs. Wade leaned in a doorway, fanning herself with her hand. "Oh, Lena! Oh, thank goodness!" She dragged her into the safety of the alcove and Henry used his body to shield them from the crowd.

"What's happening?" Lena peered under his outstretched arm.

"The Echelon must have released the cavalry, ma'am," Henry replied, his face pale. "Please don't move. They'll cut down anything in their wake."

"But not everybody is causing trouble," she protested.

"It doesn't matter."

A beat began to ring on the cobbles. Like the sound of a hundred horses marching in perfect unison. A chill ran down her spine. The Trojan cavalry were used to clear most mobs and riots—since the firebombing Spitfires could cause too much damage. There was little that could stand up against the heavily armored metal horses, and she'd heard rumors that they simply rode a man down. Nothing was destroyed that way. Only the man.

Lena looked toward the far end of the street. "What are we going to do?"

"Stay here," Henry said grimly.

The narrow doorway was barely wide enough to fit the three of them. Most of Henry was sticking out into the street. Even now the terrified crowd bumped and knocked him as they streamed past.

"We can't stay here. It's too dangerous." Mr. Mandeville's wasn't far away. They could make it if they hurried. And she knew these streets like the back of her hand.

Mrs. Wade coughed, her face as white as a sheet. Lena's heart sank. Her elderly companion would never make it so far in such a hurry. From the sound of her gasps, she was verging on a hysterical fit.

Unless...

Ducking under Henry's arm, Lena looked up at the gutter overhang. "Henry, when they send the cavalry out, do they send any of the Spitfires or metaljackets?"

"No need for it. There isn't much left once the cavalry rides through."

Most of the crowd had vanished. At the end of the street, sunlight reflected off the burnished armor of a row of metal horses.

"Come, Mrs. Wade," she said gently, taking her companion by the arm. "We have to hurry."

Mrs. Wade shook her head. "No, no, I can't! They'll ride us down."

"Henry, do you think it at all possible to lift her?"

He gave the question some thought, a dubious expression on his face. "I can't say as how far I could carry her."

"Not far at all." She looked up. "We're going across the rooftops."

"Of course! Why didn't I think of that?"

Because he'd never lived in the rookery, where Blade and Will—and most of his men—used the rooftops as their own highway.

Coaxing Mrs. Wade out, she helped Henry lift her. "You're going to have to grab for the gutter!"

"I c-can't!"

"You can and you will," Lena snapped. "I've had enough of these hysterics. If you don't hurry up, then Henry and I shan't have time to follow and then *you* will have to explain to my guardian how you managed to get me trampled!"

That caused a great scurry of activity. Mrs. Wade kicked and puffed, scrabbling for the roof. Henry struggled to lift her above his shoulders, his eyes squeezed tight whilst the voluminous folds of Mrs. Wade's skirts revealed a great deal of her unmentionables to the world.

Steel shod hooves echoed off the cobbles. Lena glanced nervously up the street.

"You next, miss," Henry said.

Lena stepped up onto his bent knee and then shoulder, catching hold of the gutter. She had to hurry. Mrs. Wade had cost them a great deal of time.

Biting her lip, Lena hauled herself up onto the roof, then turned and lay down, peering at Henry.

"Hurry!"

The cavalry was almost upon them. The horses were eight feet high at the withers, with broad, heavily-plated chests and enormous, soup-bowl hooves. Designed like a destrier, steam puffed and snorted from their nostrils. The sight was enough to curdle her stomach.

"Henry!" She extended her arm. His wide blue eyes looked up at her.

"I'll only pull you down," he said, shaking his head.

Lena snatched the parasol off Mrs. Wade and dropped it into his hands. "Hook it into the gutter and use it to help ease your weight! Mrs. Wade!" She looked behind her to where her companion sprawled on the tiles. "Hold my ankles and whatever you do, don't let him pull me off!"

A pair of meaty hands wrapped around her ankles, with the considerable weight of Mrs. Wade to anchor her.

The metal cavalry broke from a trot into a canter and then stretched out into a gallop. A man ran ahead of them and went down beneath the crushing steel hooves. In their midst rode the handlers, each steering a herd of ten with their small, spiked little boxes and the radio signal that controlled them.

"Henry!" Lena screamed, reaching out to clasp his arm as he struggled valiantly to haul himself up.

Behind her, Mrs. Wade cried out and slid a few inches down the roof. Lena shot forward on her stomach, her face and shoulders dangling over the gutters. She wrenched at Henry's arm, but he'd lost the tentative grip he had on the gutter and was dangling by her parasol.

"Don't you dare let me go!" Lena yelled.

Henry tucked his feet up desperately, trying not to get hit as the first line of the metal horses thundered by. Choking dust rose from the street. The inch of sleeve she held slipped even farther through her fingers until—

"*No!*"

Behind her, Mrs. Wade cried out and let go. Lena's eyes shot open and she fell forward, her skirts sliding over the tiles. She caught a glimpse of Henry's wide, horrified eyes as she fell toward the street and then—

Something grabbed her by the skirts.

With a wrench she landed flat on her back on the tiles next to Mrs. Wade, blinking up at Will. His broad shoulders were outlined against the inclement clouds, the muscles in his bare arms bunched as his fists curled. "Ought have known you'd be in bloody trouble."

"Henry!" she gasped, pointing to the edge of the roof.

Will knelt, the leather of his trousers straining over his heavily muscled thighs. He reached down and caught the parasol then straightened as if it were barely any effort at all.

Henry rose in the air, kicking feebly at the end of the parasol. Will snatched his hand and yanked him onto the roof where he collapsed in violent shudders.

"Oh, Lord," he whispered. "Oh, Miss Lena! I thought you were going! You should never have risked yourself."

"Well, I wasn't about to leave you to fall." Kneeling beside him, she checked him over for injuries. Her own hands were starting to shake. *So close. Too close, actually.*

A shadow fell over her. Lena's stomach dropped.

When she looked up, Will wore a murderous scowl. "What the bloody hell were you thinkin'?"

"I—"

"You weren't!" His arms exploded into the air. "You couldn't have been! What idiot gets out of a carriage in the middle of a friggin' mob? Did you not once think about how dangerous it was?"

"I was trying to avoid it. Mr. Mandeville's is two streets over. If we'd—"

"That's two streets too far! Do you have any idea what went through my head when I found the bloody carriage? Turned on its side and abandoned? With your bloody footmen sittin' on a roof, smokin' cheroots!"

Lena stood up, shaking out her skirts. "I didn't think a riot would erupt so quickly. And obviously the carriage was no safer."

"Didn't think? *Didn't think?*" The last came out as a roar that made both Mrs. Wade and Henry flinch.

Heat burned her cheeks. "I made a mistake. But I've been in these kinds of situations before. I wasn't just—"

"What do you mean, been in these situations before?"

Lena took a steady breath. By the look on his face, she was one step away from being shaken like a rag doll. "When I was working at Mr. Mandeville's. There wasn't money enough to catch the tram home, so I had to walk. I got caught in the edges of a riot twice." As his expression darkened, she hastened to assure him. "I climbed up on the roof the first time and hid in a man's home the second. He was terribly nice about it."

Will took a deep breath. Then another. His shoulders were still tense, his eyes wild. "If you *ever* go out into these streets unprotected again, I'll throttle you."

"I spent six months walking home through these streets when I was sixteen," she snapped. "And I had Mrs. Wade and Henry with me this time. That's a lot safer than when we were poor and in hiding from Vickers."

A strangled noise came from his throat. Lena shut her mouth. Not the time to mention all of the horrid things that had happened to her during that awful time after her father's death.

He turned and raked Henry with a gaze that made the lad swallow. "Never again, do you understand me?"

The lad nodded sharply.

"Come," Will snapped. "I'll get you back to the warren. Then we'll see about gettin' you home."

"I have to see Mr. Mandeville first."

He spun on his heel and Lena took a step back.

"He's expecting me," she said. "If I don't arrive, I shouldn't want him to come out into the streets looking for me."

His lips thinned. As he turned back around, she thought he murmured something but she couldn't quite make it out.

She could, however, see the blood rush out of Mrs. Wade's face.

Nine

"THANK GOODNESS YOU'RE ALL RIGHT!"

Mr. Mandeville swept her up into his arms and breathed a sigh of relief.

Lena gave him a swift hug. "Did you see any of the trouble here?"

"Not this time. I could hear them shouting though, streets over." His gaze flickered over her shoulder. Then froze.

"You know Mrs. Wade and Henry." She gestured at the weary pair. Will turned from where he'd been staring out into the streets. The light from the window lit his burning amber irises. "And this is William Carver. A friend of my sister's husband."

The stiffness in Mr. Mandeville's shoulders spoke volumes. He knew exactly what those eyes meant. "A pleasure to meet you," he said, with a sharp jerk of his head.

Lena pasted a smile on her face to cover his rudeness. "Will helped us with some unpleasantness in the riot. He's here to escort me home."

"I see." Mr. Mandeville's gaze shot between her and Will. "Did you get my message?"

"I did. I wanted to discuss the commission further, if you will?"

"The back rooms?"

"I won't be a moment." Seeing Will's glower, she hastened to add. "I promise."

Taking Mr. Mandeville's arm, she steered him toward the back room. As soon as the door closed, he turned on her, but she held up a warning hand and tapped her ear.

"So someone wished to purchase the transformational clockwork?" she asked, picking up one of his spring pens and writing on a piece of paper. *Say nothing you don't want overheard.*

Mr. Mandeville stroked the end of his moustache. "I relayed word of it to a certain friend of mine." *Mercury*, he wrote. "He's interested in presenting it as a gift to the Scandinavian Ambassador once the treaty is signed. He was most impressed with the detail."

For what purpose? The incident with the draining factories was still fresh in her mind, though she could think of no foul use for her transformational clockwork.

He wants to make his own agreements with the Scandinavians. Out loud Mr. Mandeville added, "He's never seen anything like it."

Then, taking a deep breath—and asking how much the commission was likely to pay—she hesitantly wrote. *Do you know anything about the content of these letters? Or about the draining factories burning down?*

Mr. Mandeville stroked his moustache. "I should imagine you could charge a handsome fee. He wants it complete within two weeks."

"Two weeks?" she squealed.

"The Scandinavians arrive next week. I assume there shall be the usual rounds of talks and social entertainments." Taking the pen he wrote, *We're not the only ones working against the Echelon. There is another small faction with rather more drastic notions of how to bring them down. The letters, as far as I know, contain dates and times for meetings.*

He'd barely put the pen down before she snatched it up. *But you don't know that for certain?*

A hesitation. *No. I don't. But I wouldn't condone such outright acts of terror.*

Good. She met his gaze pointedly. *Because I want no part of that either.*

I have another message that needs to be delivered. Will you do it?

Lena stared at the sheet of paper. Doubt was a small, restless tickle. An itch she couldn't scratch. *I want to meet Mercury.*

Mr. Mandeville's head shot up. "That's not possible," he said aloud.

With an angry shake of the head, she picked up the pen. *Then I want nothing more to do with this. I won't be privy to acts that might be killing innocent people. There were guards at those factories. Human guards. I want to talk to someone who knows what is in those letters.*

Mr. Mandeville stared at her, his lips thinned. "I'll pass word along regarding the commission. It shall be up to his discretion to meet with you." Pursing his lips, he held the letter up. *"Will you take it?"* he mouthed.

Lena stared at it. So innocuous. Just a single piece of parchment. Slowly she reached out and accepted it, tucking it in her bodice. Nobody would find it there. *This once,* she wrote. "Thank you. I'll begin work on the transformational." Leaning down, she wrote, *I want to meet with Mercury.*

Mr. Mandeville nodded shortly. "I'll see what I can arrange." He let her get almost to the door before he added, "It was good to meet the source of your inspiration, Lena. But I would urge caution. The blue bloods aren't the only danger to a young woman these days."

Her cheeks heated. "I know what I'm doing, thank you, Mr. Mandeville."

"Aye. I suppose you think you do."

❦

Will strode into the warren with his hands shoved into his pockets. If he had them free he thought he just might throttle her. Two seconds more and she would have fallen, crushed beneath the iron hooves of the Trojan cavalry. Cold caught in his chest. A horrible breathless feeling he didn't recognize. Best not to think of it.

Behind him the footman helped the fat old lady as she huffed and complained up the stairs. Lena suggested quietly that Henry take Mrs. Wade to the kitchen for a good, stiffening drink. From the sounds of the gibberish she'd been uttering for the last half hour, Will suspected she might need most of the bottle.

"Well," Lena sighed, standing beside him at the top of the stairs and watching her companion being led away. "At least she waited until after the mayhem to succumb to hysteria."

The delicious scent of her soap rose off her warm skin. If only she'd use something else for once. He'd come to associate that smell with Lena and even a hint of it in the air made his cock rouse.

Her skirts brushed his shins as she peered down the hallway. "Where would you like to begin the lesson? Blade's parlor?"

The ground floor of the warren was a mess of dust and cobwebs, with creaking floorboards and peeling wallpaper. There was nothing to see down here. Nothing of any value. A deterrent to thieves and anyone who might be reporting back to the Echelon. Upstairs, however, was an entirely different abode. Luxurious carpets and fine paintings, the scent of beeswax in the air and most of the rooms warmed with ornate fireplaces. Very few people were trusted enough to see the upstairs section.

Will nodded gruffly. "It'll do."

"I'll fetch some tea and cakes." She gave him a look. "Are you hungry?"

He was always hungry. The anger and fear in him only burned through more of his body's fuel. "Aye."

"I'll bring something of more substance then."

As she sashayed toward the kitchen, he opened the parlor door. Cool air brushed against his face. The fires hadn't been lit for some time. Blade preferred to sit in Honoria's laboratory upstairs these days.

The cold barely affected him, but Lena liked to sit in front of a good, toasty fire. In various ways she was rather catlike. He'd watched her curl up on the rug many a time, tinkering with the pieces of a broken clock. The inner workings of such gadgets were beyond him, but Lena managed to fit them together as if they were naught more than a child's puzzle.

By the time he had a healthy blaze crackling in the hearth she'd returned. He heard the swish of skirts from down the hall, and the scent of hot roast beef filled the air. Saliva flooded his mouth and he intercepted her at the door, his gaze intent on the heavy tray in her hands.

"Here," he muttered, taking it from her.

Lena's gaze strayed to the fire. She crossed to it, holding out her pale hands. "Mrs. Wade is recovering. She claims she'll be along in a moment." A wry twist of the lips. "I don't think she trusts you alone with my maidenly sensibilities."

Warmth crinkled the edges of her eyes. Will slowly put the tray on a small reading table. A smarter woman than he'd given her credit for, Mrs. Wade.

"Are you hungry?" he asked. The scent of beef drew him to the tray. Will lifted the lid and examined the plate. Esme's roasted beef with gallons of gravy and thick bread and drippings.

"Not particularly."

He balanced the plate on his lap and ate with relish. Far better fare than he was used to these days.

Lena took her seat opposite him, sweeping her skirts to the side. She poured them both tea then fetched a plate of spice cake for herself. Though her soft hum mingled with the comforting chink of silverware, a hint of tension rode the air, heavy as silence. Lena's lashes fluttered against her cheeks as she stole a glance at him, then looked swiftly away.

It had been like this for a year. Ever since that day

she'd crawled onto his lap, fluttered her lashes at him, and then pressed her lips against his.

Right there, on that bloody sofa beside them.

He glared at the embroidered cushions. His first kiss and it had been a bloody fiasco from start to finish. Once the shock of it had pierced his brain, he hadn't been able to get away fast enough. Her lips, like silk against his, wet and lush. Then the dart of her tongue as she licked at him, daring him to kiss her back. Somehow his fist had clenched in her skirts. The other hand was half-lifted, about to capture the back of her neck and tug her closer before he even realized what was happening.

Then he was on his feet, Lena tumbling back onto the cushions, her eyes wide and startled and her green skirts spilling around her. A glimpse of her ankles, the stockinged calves tempting him to explore further. Little hammer-strikes of vision flashing at him. Moments of movement where he wasn't even aware of having done it.

Dangerous. He'd only ever lost control—lost time— once. That she could do it to him so easily frightened him more than an entire army of metaljackets.

If he lost control, if he hurt her, if he infected her... he'd never forgive himself.

"First lesson," she said, her soft voice intruding into his thoughts, "is that a gentleman doesn't stare at a lady quite so...so boldly."

Heat spilled through her cheeks as his vision came into focus. He *had* been staring at her. Like a desperate fool. Remembering that kiss. Remembering the taste of her mouth.

Looking down, he stabbed a piece of beef with his fork. "How's your friend?" he asked. "The blond girl."

Lena broke off a tiny piece of cake with her fork. "Adele? I called on her this morning. Her parents have put about word that's she's taken ill—at least until the mark fades."

A blue blood's saliva hastened the healing process, but he'd seen enough scars in his time to know they didn't always vanish completely. Indeed, if he weren't verwulfen, his own throat would look like a train track.

"D'you think it will?"

"I took her some salve. Something Leo uses for his thralls." Fidgeting with her fork, she asked, "Do you think Cavendish will keep his mouth shut?"

"He will if he wants to keep breathin'."

"You can't simply go around threatening blue bloods, Will. It might work here in the rookery, but you'll be in their world and you must learn to play by their rules."

"Tell me you didn't enjoy it." He put his empty plate aside and leaned back in his chair, sinking into the soft upholstery.

"That's beside the point. Of course I enjoyed seeing him get his just deserts. The man's a bully and a toady. He ambushes young women in secluded corners and forces himself on them. There's no ruin to him or his reputation." Her face darkened. "Only to us."

"*Us?*"

Lena's cheeks paled. "A poor choice of words. I meant the young women of the Echelon. He's never made any overt threat against me before."

"But if he does, you'll tell me?"

Lena looked him directly in the eye. And lied. "Of course."

"Lena," he warned, finding his feet.

She fetched her teacup and nervously put it between them. "I'm not the one he'll retaliate against. You made a fool of him last night, Will. He won't forget that. Promise me you'll be careful."

Leaning down, he rested his hands on the armrest on either side of her. Lena's lips firmed and she rested her teacup in her lap.

"You ain't goin' to distract me," he said, reaching out and capturing her chin between thumb and forefinger.

A mistake. Lena's skin was silky soft, and the slight parting of her lips as she looked up nearly undid him. Her eyes softened, the breath catching in her lungs. For all her devil-may-care attitude, in that moment her expression was oddly guileless. Hesitant. Uncertain of herself.

The hint of vulnerability nearly undid him.

Will jerked his hand back as if scalded and turned away, the breath in him coming hard. "If he threatens you, you'll tell me?"

Lena's gaze dropped to her lap. "Of course."

What the devil was wrong with her now? "You ain't afraid of him?"

"I can handle men like Cavendish." Putting the teacup aside, she muttered, "It's certain other ones that give me a headache."

"Colchester?"

"No." A frown drew her eyebrows together. "Why would you mention him?"

"He scares you," Will admitted, his voice lowering. "Do you want me to kill him for you?"

She surged to her feet. "Are you *insane*? He's a duke! Even if you could get to him, the Echelon would destroy you." Those wide brown eyes met his and then she grabbed his wrist. "Will, promise you won't do anything of the sort! Promise you won't go after Colchester."

The scent of fear was back. But this time she wasn't afraid for herself.

Will rubbed at the back of his neck, eyeing her hand warily. Nobody had ever given a damn about him before. Apart from Blade. "I don't let nobody touch what's mine."

"I can handle Colchester," she stressed.

The tiny hint of doubt in her voice made his hackles rise. "How? By smilin'? By flirtin'?"

"By playing the game! By hiding in plain sight and not letting him get me alone."

"Aye, and what'll you do if he *does* get you alone?"

She had nothing to say to that.

Will drew her up against him. "Well?"

"There are…ways." Her hands rested against his abdomen, trying to restrain him. "Let me go, Will. This is unseemly."

"What kind o' 'ways'?"

Lena glared at him. "I submit. All he wants is blood. It costs me nothing. He can't afford to take too much and have me die. I'm not…not just some poor, unprotected coal lass."

The words pierced him like a knife. White-hot fury seared his brain, the world narrowing in around him until all he saw was Lena's frightened face. "Like hell you will."

Lena flinched as his hands tightened unconsciously. "Stop it, Will. Let me go!"

A gasp from the doorway caught his attention. Mrs. Wade stood there, her black skirts enveloping her like the sail from a ship. "I leave you alone for five minutes and this is what happens! Sir, you will remove your hands at once."

He hadn't even heard her coming.

Whatever expression was on his face, Lena whispered, "Don't you dare."

Her expression turned mulish, completely unafraid of him. It was that that earned Mrs. Wade a reprieve. Few people ever saw a man when they looked at him. Only a monster. He couldn't sully his image in Lena's eyes. Couldn't act like the beast the world thought him.

Eyes shuttering, he opened his hands and she stepped back with a sharp little intake of breath, rubbing at her arms.

Will caught her skirt, leaned close. He wasn't finished by half. "If he makes so much as a single move in your direction I'll kill him, Lena. I'll bury 'im so deep, won't nobody ever find 'im. So either you find a way to stop him. Or I will."

Ten

FIVE DAYS LATER, LENA POPPED A CHERRY IN HER mouth and nibbled on it, watching as Will paced the room. He'd spent the morning being fitted for a new wardrobe with Leo. Though she was in charge of introducing him to the Echelon, there were some events she wasn't allowed to oversee.

A pity, she thought, running her gaze across his broad shoulders.

"Back straight," she called, as she lounged on the daybed in Leo's sitting room. "Do try and walk as if you're out for a stroll, rather than stalking some footpad through the alleys."

She couldn't deny his grace of movement was appealing, but there was something dangerous about the way he moved. Even when he was still, he looked ready to pounce.

Will shot her a dark look. "I ain't gonna mince around like one of them puff-shirted vultures. No matter how many times you make me do this."

Lena sat up. This was the fourth lesson they'd had and he was fighting her at every turn. The problem wasn't that he couldn't do this; the problem was that he didn't give a damn about the rules of etiquette. "Once more," she said, daring him to disobey.

Will crossed his arms over his chest. "I don't see the point."

"You never do. The point is that I told you to do it. And you agreed to obey me. I know this world. You don't. And right now, you look like some rookery bruiser prepared to smash someone's head in."

Visibly grinding his teeth together, he turned and stalked back toward the window.

Lena clapped a hand to her eyes, restraining herself from a sigh. This was going to be a long afternoon. "Tell me, how many sources of power are there in the Echelon?"

"The Council o' Dukes make all the decisions."

"And who sits on the Council?"

"The seven heads o' the great Houses and the prince consort."

"Who can overrule their vote?"

"Technic'ly the queen, through Right of Regency," he retorted, turning on his heel with a flourish that almost reminded her of Blade. "Though she speaks with the prince consort's voice."

The words could have been her own. Despite his lack of education, Will could parrot things back at her verbatim.

"How do you remember all of this?" So far he hadn't missed a single question, though when she lectured him on the power plays of the Echelon she'd been certain he was paying her no mind.

"Blade taught me. We don't write things down

in the warren. So we gotta remember it all. Who owes us some tin, how much, who's paid, street addresses, names, who's been beatin' his moll up…" He shrugged. "Ain't hard."

Will sauntered back toward her. He'd stripped his coat off, as he often did when he was indoors. A gray tweed waistcoat sculpted the broad planes of his chest and he'd rolled his sleeves up again. On the inside of his wrist was a tattoo of a pair of crossed daggers. Blade's mark. A tattoo all of his Reaver's gang wore.

"You'll have to stop doing that," she noted. "Sleeves remain down." *And coat remains on.* But she was enjoying the view enough not to mention it. Taking another cherry, she twirled the stem off it and slid it between her lips.

His gaze lingered on her mouth. "What next? We've covered bowin' and scrapin', mincin' about, who I need to be wary of, who holds the power, who doesn't, what I oughta wear…"

Lena bit through the plump, juicy flesh and swallowed. "Dancing."

"Not more dancin'." He knelt on the edge of the daybed and reached for one of the cherries. "We've already done that."

With Mrs. Wade watching on like a disapproving mama. Now that they were alone… "Definitely more dancing."

Tugging out a pair of cherries, he leaned forward, dangling them over her lips. "You're doin' this to torture me."

Lena bit into one of them and tugged it free with her teeth. "Absolutely."

Lifting the other to his own mouth, he chewed in a considering manner. "Later," he said. "All this prancin' about's borin' me and I ain't been to sleep yet."

"I'm so sorry my company's wearying you."

Leaning back on his hand, he slid her feet up so he could sit properly. He did look tired, the scrape of his stubble shadowing his jaw and his eyes darker than usual. "It ain't your company. Last night someone decided to torch a shop Blade's offered his protection to. Had to find 'em. Some drunk fool who nearly shat himself when he saw us. So gin-soaked he hadn't even seen the pair of crossed daggers carved into the door."

"Fine," she said, sitting up. "Perhaps we'll save the dancing for later."

"No more lecturin' either."

Lena's lips firmed. "No dancing. No instruction. Perhaps you'd find a demonstration better?"

"Definitely."

With a little smile, she shifted to her knees. The door remained open and every so often Mrs. Wade popped her head in, but for the moment they were alone. And she felt like teaching him a lesson about finding her company wearying.

"Tell me," she murmured. "How does a woman demonstrate her availability as a potential thrall?"

"Ain't the foggiest."

Dragging her skirts behind her, Lena stood and crossed to the cherry bowl, adding an extra little swish to her stride. Picking up the gilded bowl, she settled beside him, her emerald skirts brushing his thighs. It was finer than what she usually wore for day dress, but he would never know that.

Will tensed. She'd never before realized how much coiled power his muscular frame held, but it was almost vibrating off him.

"She wears white, to begin with," Lena said, tugging another cherry out of the bowl. "But only during the evening, for it's considered passé during the day. Cherry?"

He stared at her as she lifted it to his lips. For a moment she wasn't sure he would take it from her, but then he reached out and bit into the sweet fruit, vibrant red juice coloring his lips.

"Would you do this?" he asked thickly. "For a blue blood?"

Lena glanced up from beneath her lashes. Then licked the spilled juice from her fingers. "They'd consider me fast. That's a dangerous reputation for a debutante."

His lashes lowered, shuttering those beautiful eyes. "So this is a game you're playin'? With me?"

"It's all games," she replied, giving a little shrug. Watching the color of his eyes change, she lifted another cherry toward his lips. "I'm not putting you to sleep, am I?"

Will caught her wrist. "No."

Taking the cherry from her trapped hand, she bit into it. "Good." Leaning closer, she gestured to her throat, trailing her fingers lightly across the skin there. "There are certain points on a woman's body that she reveals if she's shopping for a patron. Covering them means she's not interested.

"The throat, for example." Arching her neck, she presented the smooth skin to him with languid grace.

"No debutante wears a necklace or choker unless she's in the process of signing a contract."

Will's pupils flared, his gaze dropping over her throat and lower, to her collarbone and the upthrust of her breasts. The gown was daring, even for her. The type of thing she'd only wear for him.

"Where else?" The words were soft, but they buffeted her skin, raised a shiver.

His eyes were a dare.

Leaning closer, she presented the interior of her wrist to him. The soft creamy skin, veins pulsing blue beneath it. "Here." Their eyes met. "Do you remember how you greet a woman?"

He took her hand by reflex, but she kept her wrist presented up, toward him. Will stilled, uncertainty tightening the hard planes of his face.

"You press your lips to the back of her hand," she whispered, lifting her wrist toward him. "For a woman to signify her interest, she presents her wrist instead."

His head lowered, his lips brushing against the delicate inner skin of her wrist. A cool caress. Barely a ghost of sensation. The prickle of his stubble rasped through her, her nipples pressing hard against the stiff black lace of her corset. Lena pressed her tongue against her teeth to stifle a gasp.

"If a blue blood is interested, he lingers," she murmured. "Perhaps a trace of his tongue."

Will lowered his head again, his eyes watching her. Lena's lips parted as his mouth covered her wrist, suckling the soft flesh. The wet rasp of his tongue seemed to touch her deep inside and she pressed her thighs together, feeling it there, feeling the chafe of her drawers.

"That," she whispered, "is rather provocative for a blue blood."

Will's mouth broke from her skin, his warm breath cooling the wetness. Lena's heart thundered behind the constriction of her corset. What was he doing to her? How had he turned the tables so deftly? She couldn't bear it.

His hand was warm on hers, a blaze of welcoming heat. A considering look entered his eyes. "How often do you present *your* wrist?"

"Why?" She shifted.

The amber in his irises flared. "Tell me."

The possessive quality of his voice thrilled her. "What does it matter?"

"*Tell me.*" His grasp on her hand tightened.

"Once," she admitted. "I was young and Lord Ramsay was handsome. I learned my lesson, however. I've not offered it since. Not until now."

"I'm not interested in your blood."

"Then what *are* you interested in?" Lena leaned forward, knowing that her bodice gaped and her curls tumbled around her face.

A long breathless moment. Will leaned toward her unconsciously, as if some invisible force drew him. Reaching out, he brushed the backs of his fingers against her bodice, lightly stroking the silk as if memorizing the texture. The touch sparked through her and she leaned against it, forcing his hand against her aching nipples. That was where she wanted to be touched. There.

Every little hair on her body stiffened. A sudden yearning sprang to life, a desperate need to have his hands on her. Lena leaned forward, her hand sliding over his thigh, feeling the corded power in the bunched muscles, her face tilting toward his…

Opening his mouth, Will tried to say something, but the words died in a harsh growl. "Damn it, Lena." His gaze skittered away. He pushed her firmly away and sat back, arms spread over the back of the daybed. "Learnin' how to do what I'm here for. That's what interests me."

Just like that, she'd lost him. Confusion and frustration yawned like a gaping pit within her. Unfulfilled need. She'd never had any trouble wrapping men around her fingers, but Will constantly defied her.

She could barely breathe. Gave it one last attempt. "Of course, as with the throat, a covered wrist has different meanings also." Gesturing to her gloves on the table. "You'll notice I wear full-length for evening or gloves that cover my wrists quite decently."

"As you should," he muttered.

She shot him a glance, but his expression was flat, unreadable. He leaned his elbows on his knees and glared stonily at her.

"A lady wearing half gloves is another matter. It bares the wrist to a blue blood's lips. A sure sign that she's available, perhaps even a little fast."

"And bare wrists?"

"Never. Only a patron sees a woman with bare wrists. It's considered highly personal."

"Yet you ain't wearin' them now."

"You said yourself you're not interested in my blood."

His expression darkened. Lena leaned against the back of the daybed, her fingers toying with his sleeve. "You might be more interested in the distinction between blood rights and rights of the flesh," she murmured.

The muscles in his arm coiled. "What's that mean?"

"A woman offers her blood rights to her patron when she becomes his thrall in exchange for protection and provision. Her flesh rights are another matter. That's one of the mistakes the middle class makes. They assume a patron may take his thrall to bed as well as drink from her body."

Will's gaze shot to hers.

"Not unless she agrees," she added softly, knowing she was treading dangerous ground. "Her flesh rights are hers to give freely. Perhaps this is more to your area of interest?" Leaning closer, she licked her lips, watched his gaze drop to them. "Do you crave flesh, Will?"

"Are you offerin' it?" His voice was harsh. "'Cause we've a word for that, where I come from." Jerking away from her, he found his feet as if hunted.

"You're confusing the two," she replied. "Flesh rights are given freely. For nothing more than the cost of pleasure."

Hot color burnished Will's cheeks. He shoved his hands into his pockets. "And how does a patron know if they're bein' offered?"

Lena arched a brow. Stroked her finger across the smooth arch of her collarbone. "He finds her naked in his bed."

The bold statement drew a hiss from him. For a

moment she was wondering if he pictured it. The way she was. The thought sent a thrill through her.

"It's not generally spoken of," Lena continued, "but as well as lessons in etiquette and sewing and music, a young woman is often…given hints…in how to please a man, should she decide to offer him her flesh rights."

Not that she'd learned much before her father was murdered and she was dragged to Whitechapel. But he didn't need to know that.

His eyes narrowed. "I'm fairly sure you shouldn't be speakin' o' this with a man who ain't your patron."

"True." Another shrug, displaying the smooth creamy skin of her shoulder. "I'm just teasing."

"More games," he said in disgust. Hands clasped behind him, he paced the small rug in front of her. "Perhaps you need a lesson in what a man'd do in my world, were a women so bold with him."

"You wouldn't dare." It was a statement, not a challenge. She knew how far she could push him. Knew he'd back away the moment she turned the game sexual.

Will turned around. Met her gaze. "Wouldn't I?"

He leaned forward, resting his knuckles on either side of her hips. One knee pressed between her legs, parting her thighs and pinning her skirts. Lena froze as he reached out and captured a lock of the dark hair that tumbled over her shoulder. "All these games you play… I wonder what you'd do if I played 'em back?"

Excitement raced through her veins. He'd never flirted back before. "Don't tell me I'm getting under your skin?" she whispered.

"On me nerves, more like it." His fingers gently rubbed her hair. Then sank into the pile of curls prettily knotted at the base of her nape. It drew a gasp from her lips as he tilted her face toward his. Their breath mingled. Uncomfortably close.

And Lena was aware that she was pinned, trapped neatly beneath him. Catching a handful of his shirt, she stared up at him. His gaze was hard, almost cruel. Suddenly she didn't like this game anymore.

"Let me go," she whispered.

"Why? Ain't this what you want? Me hands on your body? Ain't that what you been playin' at this last hour? Or have I pushed the boundaries? Either say what you mean, Lena. Or I'll take this little game of yours where you don't mean to take it."

One word. *Yes*. One word and he'd do it. But as she met the steely look in those extraordinary eyes, she realized he wasn't playing. When had this become more than a game? More than a light flirtation?

I'll stake a hundred pounds that you're wrong, Adele's voice whispered in her head. *That he'll kiss you next time.*

Yes? Or no? Lena's heart hammered in her chest. She'd kissed him once. A game, nothing more. But his message now was very clear. Will wouldn't stand for any more games. And a part of her was afraid to play for real.

She wasn't that brave. Because if it meant nothing to him, if he used her and then discarded her without a care, she suddenly realized that it would *matter*. To her.

"No," she whispered.

Will's gaze shuttered. "No more of this then. I've had enough games. Enough of these lessons for the day. Most of it's useless anyway." He let her go and straightened.

That drew her ire. She still felt shaky, surreal. As if the world had turned on its axis and she couldn't quite keep up. "It's not useless. I'm trying to help you, yet you don't give a damn about anything I'm saying."

"The Echelon ain't gonna accept me anyway. They want a beast, and I'll give 'em one." A derisive look as he unrolled his sleeves.

Lena struggled to sit up. Her skirts were awry. So too her emotions. Will had taken their little game and turned it on its head. He'd never dared respond before. Years of pricking at him, needling him whilst he ignored her... She'd thought that was the worst he could do—to pretend she didn't exist—but it wasn't. The worst thing he could do was play back, to utterly destroy her defenses and then stand here unrolling his sleeves as though the moment hadn't bothered him half as much as her.

"Then there's no point to these lessons," she found herself saying. Amazing how her voice barely trembled.

Will froze, halfway through one sleeve.

"No point," she whispered, "and therefore no reason for you to continue coming here. Or escorting me in society."

She could see the thought churning in his eyes. "*No,*" he said gruffly. "No. I'll continue with it."

"Why should I waste my time?" She managed to gather herself to her feet, resetting her skirts and smoothing her bodice. A swift glance in the mirror showed her hair tumbling free of its pins. She fixed them ruthlessly, feeling his eyes on her.

Her skin pricked. Damn him.

"You won't listen to anything I say, you deride all of the rules of society and mock my efforts," she continued, trying to ignore the feeling. Her skin still felt too small, itchy. "Do you know the worst thing, Will? The worst thing is that they see you as a beast and you let them." She turned then, met his gaze. "You do everything in your power to live up to the image, the reputation, and then you scorn them for sneering down at you."

Heat flared in his gaze. He took a step toward her. "That reputation might be all as keeps us safe," he snarled. "Besides, I'm verwulfen. They ain't ever gonna see me as anythin' else."

"And neither will you!"

The outburst shocked both of them. Lena let out her breath, staring at him defiantly. "You call yourself a beast, Will, because you believe it. A part of you thinks you're nothing better than what they claim." Taking a shuddery breath, she continued. "You're fighting me at every step of these lessons because you hate the Echelon, but I'm not only trying to help you learn to fit in, I'm trying to show you another way to live."

Silence quivered in the air between them. Will stared at her in shock, instead of anger. Encouraged, Lena took a step toward him.

"Take my lessons," she whispered. "Use them to be who you *want* to be. Force the Echelon to look you in the eye. Dare them to treat you as a man. A dangerous man, if need be, but not…not an animal."

He looked away, as if the truth of her words had

struck him a blow. Then his eyes narrowed. "And what of you?"

"What *of* me?"

"How will you treat me?"

Lena shook her head, her mouth working silently. "I'm not quite sure I—"

His expression hardened. "You know what they'll say. What they'll think when they see you with me. Will you play along? Will you laugh behind your hand with 'em, to assure your own place in their world ain't at risk? Or will you risk their censure? Risk everythin' to prove the worth of your words? For there'll be a cost to this, you mark me words. And you'll be the one as pays it."

She stared up at him, the nearness of his body unnerving her. Not once had she thought of the cost to herself of squiring him about. To be seen with him, with a verwulfen, was tantamount to social suicide.

"Aye," he murmured. "Thought so." Reaching out he cupped her cheek, turning her face up toward his. "You can play games with me, Lena, because here, no one can see. Well, I'm tired of bein' your little toy. Maybe you're right. Maybe I am lettin' others dictate how I see meself. But for all your brave words, so do you."

The words were a blow. For all her hatred of the Echelon, she'd conformed to their rules as surely as he had. She'd let them define who she was. What she thought. What she dared to do.

Her very own cage.

Will let her face go then stepped back. "You never thought of it, did you?" His lips curled in a bitter smile and he grabbed his coat off the table, slinging it over his shoulder. "Guess I'll see you at the official presentation." With a short nod in her direction, he started for the door. "Then we'll see if your words are worth anythin'."

❧

Two days later, Will leaned against a brick wall, examining the enormous white tower that speared halfway to the heavens. The alabaster marble gleamed even in the dismal afternoon rain, an ever-present reminder of the power of the Echelon. Tomorrow night they'd host the official presentation ball there, once the Scandinavian delegate arrived. He'd be required to put on his best manners and charm, try to entice the Scandinavians into signing the treaty. A Herculean task that made his palms wet.

What if he failed?

He'd never realized how much a part of him longed for the respectability of being a free man. No price on his head, able to come and go as he pleased without watching over his shoulder. Able to do anything he wanted…be anything he wanted…without resigning himself to the fact that he was just hired muscle.

He didn't bother to think of it much, but Lena's words the other day were chasing around and around inside his head. He owed Blade the world, but a part of him chafed at the constrictiveness of his life. Something hungry and yearning lurked inside his heart and he didn't know what it was or how to fix it.

His eyes narrowed as a gilded steam carriage pulled up in front of the tower gates, thick coal smoke shooting from its exhaust. He'd tracked it from Mayfair, where he'd been keeping watch over Barrons's mansion all morning. The rain helped hide him and the footmen never looked around. Fools all. It just served to prove how easily Colchester could get at her if he wanted.

A footman opened the door and a slender hand appeared, resting on the footman's. Skirts the color of crushed rose petals swept into view, then Lena alighted, peering up at the tower nervously.

The sight of her never failed to take his breath. Suddenly the unknown need, the hunger within him, had a name and face.

And that troubled him more than the entire Echelon combined.

You can't have her.

She was human and he verwulfen. He could never be in her bed without risking her life, risking infecting her with the loupe. Something he shouldn't have to remind himself of.

With a scowl Will crossed his arms over his chest and settled in to wait. He couldn't guard her within the Ivory Tower and that made the skin on the back of his neck rise. He would just have to trust that Lena would be safe.

The alternative was unthinkable.

※

Lena glanced over her shoulder as she stroked the raven's glossy feather. The rookery at the top of Crowe Tower was full of squawking cages the Echelon had once used to send messages. Now, with the invention of pneumatic tubes and radio frequency, there was no need for them, but the ravens were tradition. To not see them circling the very tip of the tower would seem strange indeed.

And people still used them occasionally. It had become fashionable for blue bloods and young debutantes to send each other secret messages. To get a raven meant considerably more than flowers these days.

Finding the ugly old bird she knew and recognized, she slipped open its cage and coaxed it onto her wrist. Not always as accurate as a homing pigeon, if a crow was trained properly it could find the house it had been bred in. Then a servant would return it to the tower for its next message.

There was no coat of arms bound to this crow's cage; she had no way of knowing who it belonged to.

A steel thong bound its left leg, so she slipped the small leather-bound tube out of her cleavage and secured it tightly. She hadn't had a chance to send the message Mr. Mandeville had given her yet. Too many visits to the rookery might just arouse suspicion and it had taken days of deliberation before she'd decided to send it at all.

This was the last one until she could speak to Mercury.

Glancing over her shoulder, she carried it to the open clock that dominated the room. The heavy bronze clock face at the top of the tower drew all eyes, cold wind streaming in through its open facets. The steady tick of the second hand slid past her face as she lifted the raven and bid it into the air.

The Ivory Tower soared in front of her. Crowe Tower was one of four smaller towers that surrounded the massive keep. Her raven spiraled up, circling the gleaming white tower before vanishing over a nearby abandoned cathedral.

Her duty done, Lena turned for the stairs, gliding between the wooden cages. She'd tried to track the raven once with a spyglass but knew only that it headed west a little distance before spiraling down.

Mayfair or Kensington, she suspected.

Which meant her contact was highly entrenched in the Echelon. A servant perhaps? Even a highly placed thrall? Someone with access to the Echelon's secrets. From the information they passed on, they almost had to be close to the Council of Dukes itself.

In the next day or two an answering raven would scratch at her window with a note to deliver to Mandeville. Leo presumed she had a beau.

Closing the heavy timber door to the rookery, she latched it, then turned. A flash of black silk swept across her vision and someone yanked her back against their body, the sharp edge of a knife pressing lightly against her carotid.

"Don't move," came the hoarse whisper.

Lena froze, her heart leaping into her throat. Had someone followed her? Did they know what she'd just sent?

"What face does death wear?" It could have been male *or* female, she couldn't tell. But she recognized the words. A sign of another humanist.

"A pale one," she whispered.

The knife edge eased. But didn't vanish.

"The Scandinavian delegation arrives tomorrow," the voice said. "I want you to destroy any chance that they'll sign the treaty."

"You're mistaken," she said. "I'm done with this. I've spoken to Mandeville."

The knife edge tightened and Lena arched back, swallowing hard. Whoever held her was taller than her, but not overwhelmingly.

"You're done with this when Mercury says you are." Cold voice, cruel hands.

Lena sucked in a sharp breath. "Are you Mercury?"

There was a long moment of silence. "I pass along Mercury's orders."

"How do I stop the treaty? I don't know—"

"The Beast," the voice whispered. "Use him."

Lena ground her teeth together. "*No.*"

The sharp retort echoed in the stone corridor. The hand around her waist slid away. "Perhaps this will change your mind?"

Something metal and angular was shoved into her hand. Lena lifted it just enough to see, her heart stuttering when she realized what it was.

One of Charlie's clockwork soldiers. She'd made it herself. The last time she'd seen it, it had been on his shelf.

In his bedroom.

"Destroy the treaty." The whisper was harsh. "Or else I'll take more than his toys."

Then the pressure vanished from her throat and she staggered forward as liquid footsteps darted away down the corridor.

The only glimpse she caught of the humanist was of a black, swirling cape. But one thing caught her attention; no human could move that quickly.

It had been a blue blood.

Eleven

THE AIR ALONG THE SOUTHERN DOCKS WAS REDOLENT
with perfume. It couldn't quite disguise the earthy
flavor of the Thames, slightly riper now that it was
summer. Here and there, ladies bought scented
pomander bags to their noses and some had even
stitched them into their fans.

Metaljackets lined the platform that had been
erected along the docks, each standing at strict attention, the blue illumination in their eye slits dulled to
a neutral glow. Gaslight flickered over their burnished
gold breastplates; the Imperial squadron was comprised
of only two hundred automatons, but they were
impressive. Used mainly for ceremonial purposes,
circular throwing blades attached to their arms made
them highly dangerous as well.

Nervousness raced along Lena's skin. The enthusiasm of the crowd was contagious, but Lena couldn't
quite summon a smile. Most of the Echelon was in
attendance, dressed in glittering jewels and bright silks.
Any one of them could have been the blue blood in
the tower.

A hand pressed against her spine, a cool whisper brushing across her ear. "Relax. He's not going to attempt anything here. Not if he wants to keep breathing, anyway." Leo stepped up beside her, his hand warm on the curve of her back.

Colchester. She'd almost forgotten about him.

"I know. Not here. Not in public view, anyway." She glanced to the side. "You've heard nothing of… of Will?"

It had been three days. Leo had had Will's wardrobe delivered, but he'd only sent her a note saying that he was busy with something. Their words the other day had touched a nerve. For both of them. Lena had busied herself with the transformational clockwork, trying not to think of him.

Easier said than done. It didn't matter that she was only dealing with the internal cogs and gears at this stage; sooner or later she would begin to solder the iron sheeting of the exterior into place, forming the roughened physique of her clockwork warrior. Even in clockwork—the one place she'd always been able to switch off her busy mind and simply put together the puzzle pieces—she couldn't escape him.

"He'll be here." A statement, not a question. Leo's dark gaze raked the crowd of gaudily dressed blue bloods. "I'll have to join the Council when the Scandinavians arrive. But I won't leave you unattended."

"I'll be fine."

Leo searched her gaze. Then nodded. "Stay here. I'll keep an eye on you from the platform."

Above the river, the sky suddenly exploded. Gasps flavored the air and people cheered.

A pinwheel of whirling pinks and blues tore through the velvety sky, punctuated by the scream of rockets. An orange fireball bloomed, destroying Lena's night vision.

"Here they come," Leo murmured. "I'd best be off."

As Lena blinked, a hint of a dark outline showed on the river. It glided across the oily waters, as sleek and sure as a serpent. The laughter and cheering died to a hushed whisper as the dragon-ship appeared. The only sound was the whine of the fireworks launching.

Almost two hundred feet long, it faintly resembled the longboats of its ancestors. A sinuous serpent head served as a figurehead, and enormous canvas wings were tucked in tight against its sides. The metal hull gleamed with gold paint, and jeweled shields lined the sides, each gem sparkling in the gaslight.

Two others flanked it, their helium envelopes deflated and stowed away. They could be used both in the air and on water, and were dangerous on each. Tall warriors lined the decks, clad in dark blue regimentals with gold military frogging down the chest, and helmets with tall black feathers. The gaslight on the docks glittered off the amber shine of their eyes.

"Look at them," a woman whispered nearby. "How barbaric."

"I *am* looking," another woman murmured behind her fan and they both laughed.

Fireworks exploded with frenetic enthusiasm. The sky was washed with gold and blue and pink. Lena couldn't help herself. She looked up, her gaze torn from the silent ships on the river.

She felt his gaze long before she saw him.

A tingle on her skin.

The faint, earthy anticipation of her body recognizing danger—even as it thrilled at it.

Will.

Breath catching, her fingers tightening on the fan, she looked down. Blind spots danced in her vision but she hunted for him. The crowd didn't matter. Nor the approaching ships. Not even Colchester.

She'd been in a state of agitation all day, unable to settle. Unable to do more than toy with her food or read a paragraph of the *Times*. His words kept playing through her mind. *Then we'll see if your words are worth anythin'.*

Lena shivered. She could feel him watching her.

Murmurs started behind her. The crowd shifting. A prickle at the back of her neck. As she turned, fanning at herself in agitation, the crowd parted, skirts swishing out of the way like the Red Sea. For a moment she couldn't see him. Only a man dressed in crisp black, who stepped into the wake of the crowd with arrogant disdain, striding as if he belonged there.

She glanced past the elegant cut of his coat, buttoned strictly up the left side of his breast. And then her gaze shot back to him, her eyes widening.

Oh, my God…

Lena actually stopped breathing.

She'd never seen him in anything other than a loose shirt and coat. The sight of him dressed for the evening was utterly devastating. The stark black of his coat drew attention to the dusky gold of his skin, and his hair—the beautiful amber locks that her fingers always itched to touch—was gone.

The fan stopped moving, the ghostly tips of its feathers dancing over her breasts. Will stepped out of the shadows, gaslight highlighting the stark bones of his cheeks and brow, the burnished bronze of his eyes locked on her with an intensity no bystander could mistake for anything other than interest. Pure, predatory interest.

He had to stop looking at her like that.

Lena turned away with a jerk, frantically sucking in a breath. If they saw the intensity of his gaze, her reputation would be ruined.

Which was exactly how he predicted she'd react.

Her shoulders slumped. He'd practically dared her to deny her association with him. And though mockery had laced his tone, there'd been a hint of hurt in his eyes.

As if he knew he'd never be good enough.

Head bowed, she turned toward him, aware of the malicious eyes watching them. If only he wasn't standing there silently, waiting for her to make the decision either to cut him or to forever forsake any chance of joining this glittering world.

But how could the Echelon ever accept him if she didn't?

Will offered her his arm, as smoothly as if they'd practiced it a thousand times and not mere dozens. There was a devilish gleam in his eyes. A dare. "Shall we?"

Despite her gloves, she could feel the unnatural heat of his body through his sleeve as she accepted. Murmurs started as they strolled toward the platform and the smile on Lena's lips died.

"I'm not supposed to be up there," she whispered. Above her, fireworks blazed to life, the shrill scream of the rockets stealing her words.

Will leaned closer. Now that he was in profile, she could see that his hair had been gathered back into a tight queue, the velvet strands of the ribbon brushing against his nape.

"I thought you cut your hair," she blurted.

"You sound relieved. Thought me hair were unfashionable."

Not even a hint that he was as stricken as she. Lena ground her teeth together. "It is."

"Then I'll cut it."

At her shocked look, a smile curled at his lips. Her gaze locked onto it. Dangerous. The little tick of her heartbeat fluttered in warning.

"All of it." He smoothed a hand over his scalp. "Annoys me anyway."

"Do what you want," she lied, "I don't care."

The smile he gave her was answer enough.

"Here we go," he said, staring up at the platform. There was no sign of the prince consort or the queen, but all seven of the Council waited.

Will took a deep breath and for the first time, Lena realized he was nervous. She squeezed his arm. "Have you never met others of your kind before?"

"Never." His gaze swept over the river, lingering on the naval officers that lined the deck of the dragon-ship. "Spent most of me life in that cage, then trapped in Whitechapel by the price on me head."

Something tightened in her chest. Lena slid her hand into his, hiding it against her skirts. All eyes were on the river. She squeezed his fingers and he looked down, considering it for a moment before he squeezed back.

"Truce," she whispered. "Just for tonight?"

"Truce," he agreed.

A breeze stirred her hair as they climbed the stairs, bringing with it the rich, cinnamon scent of Lady Aramina's perfume. Lena stepped into place beside the duchess and tugged her hand from Will's.

Beneath the noise of the fireworks and the murmur of the crowd grew a strange, throbbing hum. A froth of water churned a hundred yards behind the last dragon-ship, and the sleek dark head of something surfaced.

"What is that?" she asked.

"A kraken submergible," the duchess replied, her brandy-colored eyes intently watching the wave. "The stealthy killer of the Scandinavian naval forces. It's the only thing that's ever brought down one of our Dreadnoughts."

Surprised that the woman had answered, Lena dared ask more, "I thought the Dreadnoughts were invincible?"

"You cannot fight what you cannot see," the duchess replied. "And it's only in the last minute that you can feel the throb of their propellers coming. Caught alone, even a Dreadnought can be sunk by their steel tentacles."

The throb echoed through the air, almost humming against Lena's skin. She could only imagine the force needed to create such a disturbance.

"They don't usually venture so far from their waters, however," Aramina mused. "They must be trying to impress us."

"They've succeeded," Lena replied, looking at the awed faces in the crowd as the domed metal and glass head of the submergible surged through the water to present itself.

The first dragon-ship docked. Two of the ship's crews wore the blue regimentals of the Swedish military, with gold tasseled epaulets. Every one of them was as tall as Will. They moved with a militant efficiency and stood sharply to attention as a trio of officers appeared on the foredeck.

The final ship trailed with disdainful ease into the docks, edging just a little away from the Swedish vessels. Scarred and grizzled sailors manned the rails, glaring at the crowd. Thick wolf pelts trailed over their shoulders and most of them were heavily bearded.

The Norwegian clans.

Behind her the sound of metal boots rang on the cobbles. A carriage wheeled into the square, gleaming with mother-of-pearl inlay, coming to a halt directly before the platform. The Imperial metal-jackets created a path, ceremonial rifles slung over their armor-plated shoulders.

The prince consort leaped out in all his elegant glory and the crowd cheered.

Lena didn't know where to look. The world was a conflagration of color as the fireworks went mad. The prince consort opened the carriage door and handed the petite human queen out onto the quay. Behind them the Scandinavians were lining up, an enormous man in a scarlet coat leading them. He stood inches above Will even, and the chiseled contours of his cheeks were softened only by a full mouth.

Will flinched beside her at each explosion above, his nostrils flaring. *Of course.* This was all so new to him.

She tugged at his sleeve. "I assume that man is the leader of the Swedish delegation. Count Stefan Hallestrøm of Skåld. They call him the War Hammer. Even the Norwegian clans step lightly around him and they're not afraid of anything."

Lazy amber eyes considered her. He was relaxing, which was precisely what she'd intended.

"The Norwegians are…tricky," she replied. "Officially, the Storting was disbanded and they bend knee to the Swedish Court now. In the capital, most have adapted to the new ways; however, in the old country they're rather more traditional." She eyed the band of Norwegians scowling on the docks. "The man in front is Magnus Ragnarsson, the Fenrir of the Raven Clan. He might wear an eye patch and be older than you and me combined, but he's considered crafty and his men are murderously loyal. To his right is his son, Eric." Her eyes widened slightly. She'd heard reports he was handsome, but as the blond warrior smiled, half the ladies in attendance stopped breathing. Fans fluttered like an entire swarm of butterflies. "Don't be fooled by his charm. You don't rise through clan ranks without killing someone along the way. The higher they stand, the more blood they've shed. And he's slated to take over his father's role one day."

Silence greeted this statement. She looked up and found Will watching her through dangerously narrowed eyes. "What?"

"I don't think *I* need be concerned 'bout his charm."

Heat rose through her throat and cheeks. She fanned herself rapidly. "I don't know what you mean."

"You sighed."

"I did not."

"It seems you have a dangerous weakness for verwulfen men."

"I assure you I do not." Still, she couldn't stop her curious gaze from sliding back to the golden figure on the docks, with his silver-leaf chain mail and the heavy ax at his belt. She'd once accused Will of being a barbarian, but here was one in the flesh.

A Norse god at the least.

A fanfare sounded and the ranks of Norwegians parted to allow someone through. The verwulfen had won the battle; everyone was craning their necks to see who deserved such a fanfare.

A young woman stepped through the clans.

"Oh," Lena murmured.

A hush fell over the crowd. It was well-deserved. Not only was the woman tall and shapely, with a well-formed bosom, but she had the kind of face that could stun a ballroom to silence. A cascade of loose blond waves fell to her waist and a gold circlet sat upon her brow. She wore nothing more than a simple white dress, with a rakish wolf skin thrown over one shoulder, yet she had no need of more. Gold and gems would only have gone unnoticed in the wake of her pillowy lips and glorious bone structure.

"Jaysus." Will arched a brow.

A hot little spark burned inside her gut. Lena stepped on his foot and put all her minis-cule weight into it. "Shut your mouth before you choke on something," she snapped. "She's not *that* pretty."

Aware that he was still watching her, she looked around. The heat of his gaze lingered on her skin and she found herself fanning rather more rapidly.

"You're jealous? I thought this were only a game?"

The fan slowed. She looked up into the burning intensity of his gaze. The words were lightly said, but the look on his face was anything but. "I'm not. Look at her all you want. I don't care. But my intention is to make you appear somewhat more than a gaping rookery-bred bumpkin, is it not? You want to impress them?"

Whilst she wanted to alienate them.

Her grip on the fan tightened as the bite of guilt filled her. "Don't stare at me," she whispered.

"You're still the most beautiful woman I ever clapped eyes on."

A pitter-patter in her chest. "You shouldn't say such things."

He shrugged. As if it meant nothing to him.

Whilst it meant the world to her.

A thousand meaningless compliments had tumbled from blue blood lips over her time at court. Words meant to charm and seduce. But Will never said anything he didn't mean. Something in her chest warmed.

Then she deflated. If he knew she intended to destroy the treaty, he'd be furious. There would be no more smiles her way, no more compliments. Will would hate her. Lena's fingers curled around the fan, a rash of heat springing into her eyes. She looked away swiftly, swallowing hard. He could never know.

Winning the Scandinavian's support was not as important as Charlie's life.

"You know a great deal about 'em," Will said, as
the prince consort stepped forward and nodded at the
Swedish ambassador. The formal words of greeting
were exchanged, along with rather a lot of edged
smiles and shaken hands.

The ambassador bowed before the queen, the curve
of his back deeper than what he'd offered the prince
consort. He had to know who truly ruled Britain; this
was an insult, one of the first of many, no doubt.

Perhaps her task would not be so difficult after all?

"I was curious." And she'd needed to know who
her targets would be. Again an uneasy churn of guilt
turned her stomach.

"This Magnus," he murmured. "He's in charge of
the Norwegians?"

She wouldn't deny him the information she'd
spent hours gossiping to achieve. "There are only five
remaining clans left in Norway. Magnus rules one,
but for this delegation he speaks with their voices.
The true source of power in Norway is Valdemar
Einarsson, the jarl of all the clans." Another stolen
glance at the young woman bowing to the queen.
"She must be his daughter, the Lady Astrid."

"What happens once they all finish bowin'
and scrapin'?"

"We retire to the Ivory Tower and the welcoming
ball begins."

A slight hint of unease in his eyes.

"Yes, Will. Dancing," she said, relishing the moment.
"Now we see if you've retained any of my lessons."

Light glittered. The official state ballroom walls bore mirror after mirror, the edges scrolled with gilt and interspersed with elegant paintings. Will paused at the top of the red carpeted stairs as his name and Lena's were announced.

Hundreds of faces turned his way. Blue bloods, verwulfen, and human alike. A brief scan of the crowd revealed the Norwegians gathered in the corner, expressions wary and considering. The Fenrir locked gazes with him, his black eye patch distinctly out of odds here in this gleaming paradise. Fur bristled on his shoulders and his iron-gray beard spoke of the weight of years. Will felt as if he'd been weighed and measured by that single eye.

Not a man he'd like to cross.

"Come," Lena whispered, tugging at his sleeve.

Why the devil had he agreed to this? Feeling hunted, he stalked down the stairs beside her.

The next hour was a whirl of teeth-grinding social niceties and false smiles as Lena introduced him to members of the Echelon. Hard looks slapped his back and he saw more than a few blue bloods exchange glances. The looks were easy enough to interpret. What the hell was he doing here? What game was the Council up to?

Lights. Music. Laughter. So bright and glittering, dozens of gaslit chandeliers casting heat across the room. Nostrils flaring, he intercepted a glass of champagne from a drone's tray and handed it to Lena. She served as his only anchor in this world he didn't understand and didn't want to.

It suited her. She laughed and tapped her friends on the shoulders with her folded fan, constantly keeping him involved in the conversation when he'd prefer to have just stood at her shoulder and scowled. This entire evening was effortless for her. Even the blue bloods danced to her tune, kept in place with a coquettish smile and a drawled witticism.

He wanted to smash them in the face for each smile they earned.

"I need air," he growled in her ear.

"Not yet." She took one look at his face and nodded thoughtfully. "Come. Dance with me."

Only for her would he endure such torture.

Taking her by the hand, he led her onto the dance floor and dragged her into his arms. Lena's eyes widened as his hand slid over the small of her back, his thighs brushing against her skirts. But she didn't dare chastise him out loud for holding her too closely.

The music swept them up and Will twirled her in his arms, concentrating hard on counting the steps. It should have looked ridiculous—he was enormous against her delicate stature—but Lena had a grace about her that made it somehow work. It was like holding a spinning top in his hands. She floated, each movement lithe and elegant, with a slight hint of the coquette. If he faltered, she encouraged him with a lowered-lash smile that made all of the steps rush out of his mind.

All of his thoughts, in fact.

"Stop counting," she murmured, a small smile playing about her lips.

He glared at her, twirling her in a pirouette. From

this angle, he could see straight down her dress at the soft swell of creamy flesh she displayed with far too much complacency. Pearls dripped into the deep vee of her gown, drawing his gaze lower. "I thought it were fashion for women searchin' for a protector to leave their throats and neck bare?"

Lena glanced up, over her shoulder, as he guided her through a pirouette. "But I'm not."

"Not what?"

There was a slight hesitation. "Searching for a protector."

His fingers tightened in hers. It shouldn't matter. She could never be his anyway. But the thought still flooded him with a fierce sense of satisfaction. Of possession.

His body curved around hers, drawing her back against his chest as he held her hands up. The movement thrust her chest forward and arched her neck. Each step of the *assah* had been designed to tempt, to show a blue blood a woman's best features. Will had no desire for her blood, but the smooth slope of her neck and shoulder drew his gaze. He wanted to run his lips over her skin, to feel her tremble, to taste her as her skin pebbled and she gasped softly.

His cock roused. Dangerous thoughts. Especially here, in the middle of a ballroom. The swish of her bustle against his groin was a devastating itch, inciting him to harder lengths.

"You're holding me too close," she whispered.

The smile on her face was careless, as if she were not aware of the fact. A charade for anyone watching.

Her breath, however, told another story.

What was he doing? Will dragged in a thick breath and looked away. He spun her in a light circle and she came back into his arms, facing him this time. The look in her eyes devastated him.

Perhaps it had been the other afternoon? Daring her to accept him in public. Challenging her at her own games.

There was no point to this. She wasn't his and never could be. But…it was so tempting to hold her, to torture himself with her nearness when he knew he could never have her.

Just this once.

"Will," she whispered. "Stop it."

He couldn't let her go. Couldn't put the proper distance between them. The music swept through him, a string-and-flute quartet with a slight Middle Eastern hum as exotic counterpoint. Each step came easily now. He wasn't thinking so much. Just following her body through the steps of the sinuous dance. Predator to prey. But this time the prey held all the power, luring him in, drawing him closer.

He didn't speak. And neither did she. Everything that needed to be said was spoken by the entwining of their bodies. Lena surrendered to the inevitable, her cheeks flushed with a becoming pink as she wilted into his touch.

And he claimed her as his; his fingers shackling her wrists as she turned, then sliding down her corseted hips, one hand firm across the small of her back as he drew her back into his embrace. He'd forgotten the steps by now. Created his own. Predator to prey, each movement a prophetic one.

The music trailed to a smoky halt. Clapping erupted and Will stilled, his arms tight around her hips. Lena looked up, her dazed expression fading away as she realized where they were. The pink of her cheeks deepened, her eyes darting past his shoulder.

Far too many interested eyes looked their way. Lena tugged at his grip. He held it for a moment, forcing her gaze to his, then let her go.

With a polite smile, she curtsied. "Thank you," she murmured, knowing every word she now spoke would be heard. "For a wonderful dance."

He bowed his head, a sign of respect he'd give to no other woman here. "I enjoyed it."

A surprise in itself. But her presence had made an excruciating moment a delightful one. He found he wanted to keep going.

Any excuse to keep her in his arms…

Will looked away. He couldn't afford to have thoughts like that. His gaze drifted over the Norwegians in the corner. The reason he was here. Something he shouldn't forget.

"Every woman here wants to dance with you now," Lena murmured.

"I only dance once."

A slight smile. "I think if I asked you, you'd change your mind."

"Are you askin' me?"

Lena looked up from beneath her lashes. "I don't think we should. If I dance with you again, we're going to attract attention."

"We already have."

Lena considered the room. "I need to dance with

someone else," she replied. The light strains of music were starting up again, this time a more traditional dance. A waltz, he suspected.

He grabbed her wrist. "Not the *assah*."

"No?"

"No."

That dance was his.

Her smile bloomed, causing the breath to catch in his chest. "Not the *assah* then. Go. Find your Norwegians. I'll stall the gossip you're no doubt causing." She gave a rueful twist of her lips. "You're going to drive me to bedlam, you know that?"

It was no more than she was doing to him. Thank God he wasn't the only one afflicted by this madness between them.

With one last smoky look over her shoulder, she sauntered into the crowd, crooking a finger at some young lordling in a yellow coat. He swallowed hard and darted to her side, offering a polite hand as he led her into the waltz.

Will turned and strode through the crowd, muttering his apologies as he pushed past. Too many people. The air was too stuffy. And a part of him didn't want to watch her on someone else's arm.

Finding a room with refreshments laid out, he tugged at the collar of his coat. Cool air stirred across his face, and the few people picking at the refreshment table realized who he was and darted back to the main ballroom. Which suited him perfectly.

Taking a plate, he piled it with sweetmeats and pastries and those little cakes Lena seemed to like. Soft footsteps shuffled the carpet behind him and he stilled, catching a hint of a pale shadow reflected in the cut crystal bowl in front of him.

Hadn't taken them long.

Wondering who they'd sent, he turned, eyeing the stranger without surprise.

With a nervous smile for him, the Lady Astrid crossed the room to the refreshment table. Her white gown was cut to move with each step, creating a graceful, sinuous effect that no human woman could ever hope to emulate.

"You are William Carver," she murmured, trailing her fingers over the tablecloth as she stalked toward him. A swift smile. Not so nervous now. If she ever had been. There'd been no hint of it in her scent. "We didn't expect to find one of our own here."

"Didn't expect to be here meself," he replied. There was no point in trying to play word games. He was who he was. No amount of polish could change his nature or make him comfortable with the games the blue bloods enjoyed.

Astrid gave him a sidelong look. "Why not?"

"This ain't my world."

She examined him as if he'd done something unexpected. "You're Scottish, yes?"

"Originally. Were born on a crofter's farm outside o' Edinburgh."

Easing closer, she let her arm brush against his. "How old were you when you received the gift?"

He glanced over her shoulder toward the ball. Through the arch he could just see the glittering skirts of Lena's pink ball gown. Talking to some young pup who hung on her every word. Safe for the moment.

He turned his attention back to the woman in front of him. "I were five. And it weren't no gift."

He could barely recall the stranger who'd ridden in on the back of a cart one day, feverish and sweating, his arms raked with bloody scratches. They'd called for the physician, but the man had gone berserk, throwing men aside as if they weighed nothing. Will had been the only one left standing, staring at the stranger in virulent fear. He couldn't remember what happened next. But they said it took five men to pull the stranger away from his throat.

Nobody expected him to live. The man had torn him apart like a nice, fat rabbit. But somehow his body reknit itself. By the time they realized why, it was too late. He was well into the first transition of the loupe.

"I see." Her eyes softened in sympathy, but her scent was still hard. A lesson in that for him. Trust his nose and not his eyes. "How did you learn to control yourself? Were there others?"

"Me mam sold me to a travelin' showman." An old wound, healed and crusted over, but still scarred. "I were locked in a cage for ten years. If I tried to escape they whipped me until I went down." He took a mouthful of champagne, the bitterness of it bubbling on his tongue. "I learned the hard way not to lose me temper."

Astrid's fingers went to the amulet around her neck and she toyed with it, a troubled look on her face. "How can you stand to be here? Around them? Knowing that their laws locked you away for years?"

"I'm simply doin' a job."

"An attempt to soften our favor? They do not know

us well, do they?" Another brush against his sleeve. Her hand slid over his, gloves rustling. "So how much does this little task of yours cost them?" She took a deep breath, her breasts swelling. "What does it involve?"

He let her stroke his hand. She was beautiful, but she was no Lena. "I get you to sign the treaty."

"And what do you get?"

"I get freedom."

"Worth more than your weight in gold," she murmured.

"For all the verwulfen in the Isles," he added. "No more cages, no more pit-fightin' or prices on our heads. Free men. And women."

Unease prickled her scent. Despite the smile on her face, he'd pricked her conscience.

"A worthy cause." Her finger stroked his knuckle, but her mind was miles away. She frowned. "You should come and meet my uncle. He may be interested in what you speak of."

"Your uncle?"

"Magnus."

Will considered it. Then nodded. He gestured to the plate. "Let me just take this to my companion, Lena."

Twelve

It had taken him all of ten minutes to ingratiate himself with the Norwegians.

Lena bit into a lemon tart, smiling at the young lord in front of her as she surreptitiously glanced over his shoulder. Will clasped hands with the grizzled Fenrir and greeted his son, Eric.

Movement shifted. A hand, sliding over the small of his back. Lena nearly choked on her tart. Her eyes narrowed. That Norwegian witch. She'd known him barely a quarter of an hour and she was already trying to stake a claim.

Stammering a vague reply to something Lord Folsom asked her, she maneuvered herself for a better look. The blond goddess smiled up at him, her hand possessively stroking the smooth tailoring of his coat. Will looked down at her with an amused expression crinkling his eyes.

And Lena's heart twisted in her chest.

"Are you all right, my dear?" Lord Folsom asked. He was only human, his family not deemed important enough to receive the gift of the blood rites.

"Quite fine," she managed to say, passing him her plate. "Just a slight hint of nausea. I believe I might need to escape the crush."

She should have been working against Will instead, but she found she didn't have the heart for it. She needed to clear her head. Gather herself. Before she did something foolish like ask Eric to dance the *assah* with her.

She knew precisely how Will would take that.

Pushing through the crowd, she found herself at the edge of the ballroom. The room was located on the second highest floor of the Ivory Tower, with breathtaking views over the entirety of London. A colonnade circled the outside, a chance for a young lady to stroll within watchful distance of the ballroom.

She pushed through the French doors, the wind whipping her hair out of her face as she leaned against the rail. Hundreds of feet below, the grass beckoned. More than one blue blood had been thrown to his death here. But never when a ball was in progress. Such things weren't done.

Tugging her gloves off, she risked another glance back into the ballroom. With the ballroom lit up so well, everything within was fully visible whilst she would remain hidden in the shadows. She found Will easily enough. His nerves appeared to have settled, for he shared a rare smile with the Norwegian clans as they wooed him.

His own people.

Dress him in furs and let him stop shaving for a day or so and he might have been mistaken for one of them.

Turning around, she balled her gloves in her fist and

leaned on the rail. Foolishness. *You knew he was never for you.* Yet the last week had lulled her into a sense of false hope. A smile here, the brush of his body against hers, their teasing…

If he knew what she was about, he'd never speak to her again.

Lost in her own misery, she barely heard the door open. The wind chilled her skin, but the hairs that rose on the back of her neck had nothing to do with the breeze.

Spinning around, she froze against the rail. Colchester smiled at her, easing the door shut with a soft click. Behind him dancers swept past, their images distorted by the windows. So close and yet so far away.

Lena took a step to the side and Colchester echoed her. A chill ran down her spine.

Tipping her chin up, she tugged her gloves back on. If anyone caught them, there was no need to promote rumors that she'd encouraged him. A bare wrist was tantamount to exposing her breast.

Colchester watched the silk slither over her arms. "That's not going to help, you realize?"

"I'm only observing the proprieties."

He strolled closer, using his body to trap her against the rail. Reaching out with both hands, he caged each side of her waist.

She risked a look toward the ballroom. A man's broad back blocked the doors she'd come through. Cavendish, by the look of it. Preventing anyone from exiting. "I told you I haven't decided," she said, her breath catching as he leaned closer.

His gaze ran smokily down her throat. "Perhaps

the offer's been rescinded anyway. Why would I want soiled goods?"

Fingertips brushed against the curve of her clavicle. She pressed against the rail, but there was nowhere to go. Only empty air and wind behind her. "Soiled goods?"

"Another blue blood I could have forgiven you for. But not one of those filthy beasts." His hand closed over her throat lightly.

Lena couldn't breathe. She looked in those insane eyes and knew he'd do it. "Don't. Not here. People are watching."

His fingers tightened. "Do you think I give a damn?" A bark of laughter. "I'm a duke, Helena. And you…you are nothing."

She grabbed his wrist, trying to ease his choking hold. Her head was swimming. "P-please…"

His grip eased. "I'm sorry? Are you begging for your pathetic little life? You're not doing a very good job, my dear."

Think, damn it.

"You're mistaken. Whatever you think has been happening, you're wrong. Leo asked me to teach Will to move through the Echelon. This is…strictly business, nothing else."

A considering look entered his eyes. He stroked her throat. "Business? After that dance? The beast seems awfully possessive of you, my dear."

She forced a smile. "A crude habit I'm trying to break him of. Really…" She gave a brittle laugh. "Accusing me of such a thing. You know I prefer the finer things in life. Something…sophisticated."

"Mmm." His eyes narrowed. "I'm not entirely certain you've convinced me."

With a sharp move, he grabbed her and spun her toward the rail, pressing her hard against it. Her slippers teetered against the ground, and she clutched at the rail with a scream. The cobbles below seemed miles away.

"Twenty-four people have gone over this rail," he whispered in her ear. "With you sipping champagne all night, it would be terribly easy to convince everyone you'd slipped."

Grabbing her by the bustle, he shoved her inexorably forward. He'd let go of the back of her head for the moment and with an instinct she didn't know she possessed, she slammed her head back.

A deafening crack sounded in her ear and Colchester screamed. The pressure at her back was gone and she tumbled against the rail. So close. Too close... Colchester cupped his face, blood pouring between his fingers. He caught a glimpse of her and murder gleamed in his eyes.

Lena darted for the door. A slashing pain caught her across the upper arm and blood spattered across the glass. He'd drawn his blade, the little one he used for bloodletting. Avoiding his grasping hand, she yanked the door open and shoved into the room.

Cavendish staggered out of her way, surprise widening his eyes. Heads turned and Lena pasted a smile on her lips, her teeth clenched together. The room swam in her panic, gems and faces and dresses leeching into one another. Clapping a hand to her arm, she pushed through the whispering crowd.

He wouldn't dare attack her here. Not with a broken nose. No blue blood would live down the indignity of being outmaneuvered by a simple human girl.

The heartbeat that threatened to choke her began to slow. All she had to do was find Leo or Will. Safe. She was safe now.

But she didn't feel it. Blood dripped between her gloved fingers as she made her way through the crowd of blue bloods. They eyed her with far too much interest for her comfort. The music grated harshly on her nerves.

A gap opened up and suddenly she was staring at Will. His gaze flickered over her, then narrowed on her bleeding arm. The room might as well have gone quiet. No change to his expression, nothing to indicate his mood, but suddenly she realized just how dangerous he was.

Bright copper glowed in his eyes. The woman at his side asked him a question, gently stroking his sleeve. He pushed away from the table he'd been leaning against, ignoring her completely. Lena couldn't make her feet move. All she could do was stare at him and silently will him not to make a scene.

Behind her she heard Cavendish's voice, growing nearer as he looked for her. Will heard it too, his head shooting in that direction with a murderous gleam in his eyes.

"*Don't*," she whispered.

But it was too late. He turned toward Cavendish, his fists tightening. Striding carelessly into the path of a pair of dancers, he stopped the entire waltz.

If she didn't do something he'd kill Cavendish.

Then they'd have no choice but to execute him. Suddenly she could move again. Cutting him off halfway, she grabbed his sleeve.

"Stop," she hissed. "Don't you dare!"

No man looked out at her through those burning coppery eyes. She'd been so certain he'd never, ever hurt her, yet for a moment even she froze at the fury that looked back at her. The wild within.

"Will." There was only one way to stop him in this mood, only one thing that could distract him. "Will, I'm bleeding. I need to go home, to have my arm seen to. I don't feel very well." She made her knees soften, her weight leaning into him.

He caught her, as she knew he would. Blade had once said that Will was the most dangerous man he'd ever met, but his protective instincts overrode his violent ones. A wolf to the core.

As he swept her up in his arms, Lena buried her face against his shoulder. This was it. The end of any chance she had with the Echelon. She might be able to walk its verge, but she would never be a part of it again. Whispers followed them as Will strode from the room.

One last glance over his shoulder as they passed through the doors. The gowns, the jewels, the fancy ladies in all their finery. Gone. Her chance at this was gone the instant she curled into his arms. And strangely enough a weight lifted from her shoulders.

Lena turned her face into his neck, breathing in the masculine scent of his skin. She didn't know what she would do. There was nothing for her in the rookery, nothing for her in the Echelon. Her fingers curled against his collar. Only one thing that she had always wanted and he had not wanted her back.

But did you fight hard enough?

She buried her face in his coat, too afraid to look at the answer to that question. She hadn't fought, hadn't told him how she felt. Too afraid to have her heart dashed to pieces, and so she'd never dared display it.

He would never know how much her games with him were all she would risk.

"Where?" he asked.

She glanced at the enormous circular staircase that spiraled through the heart of the Ivory Tower. A thousand steps, some said, though she'd never bothered to count them.

"The elevation chamber. I want some privacy."

He glanced at the pair of ladies who'd followed them from the ballroom and sent them fleeing with a glare. "Problem solved."

"Don't argue. You can't carry me the entire way down those stairs. We're on the ninth floor."

His face turned to hers, hints of amber burning around his pupil. "What happened?"

She shook her head. She had to get him out of here before he erupted again. "The elevation chamber."

The liveried footman nodded to them as if he saw ladies being carried out of the ballroom every night. The polished brass doors to the elevation chamber slowly opened, revealing the smooth brass panels of the walls.

Will carried her inside and the doors slid shut.

She gestured for him to put her down. A frown drew his eyebrows together, but he complied.

"What the hell happened?" The chamber lurched into movement and he grabbed at the wall, his eyes wild.

"I went for some air on the balcony." There was no getting around the truth. "Colchester came out after me."

Will's gaze dropped to her bloodied glove. His nostrils flared. "He cut you."

The words were a promised threat. She had to diffuse the situation. "I broke his nose. It's an even trade."

"*Lena.*"

"It's barely even a scratch—"

"You were terrified," he snapped. Turning, he swung a fist at the wall and the brass panel caved beneath his fist.

She flinched. "Please. Don't."

Reining himself in with a visible clenching of his will, he slid a hand down the wall. "I wouldn't hurt you. You know that. I'd never hurt you."

She realized she was pressed back against the far wall, her nerves strung too tightly to relax with his temper riding the chamber like a cyclone.

"Yes, I was scared," she said. "But I'm safe now. That's all that matters."

"What did he do to you? What did he say?"

He threatened to kill me. She paled and shook her head.

The steady jolt as the steam engines deep in the Ivory Tower's cellars winched them down became almost hypnotic. Will didn't find them so. He prowled the small room, his hands clasped behind his back and his eyes bright with anger.

"I hate small spaces," he said, too much white showing in his eyes.

And she suddenly realized his temper wasn't only strung so tightly because of Colchester. "Does it—does it remind you of the cage?" She had to clear her throat to get the words out.

His gaze cut to hers and he nodded.

"Here," she said, slipping her hand into his. "I'm here."

Nodding at her, he looked away. But his fingers slid through hers, squeezing hard. "The cage weren't so bad. I could see through the bars." His expression darkened. As if he saw something else, something beyond the smooth walls of the elevation chamber. "When I disobeyed they used to beat me unconscious. But as I grew older the threat of that didn't scare me as it used to." Licking his lips. "There were a cellar. Deep underground. They used to lock me in there. For days. Or weeks. No way o' knowin', it were so dark. Not even a rat down there."

A little boy, lost in the dark. Her heart ached for him. "You're free now."

Will's gaze met hers. "I ain't free, Lena. Not yet. It's just, the cage's bigger now. All o' Whitechapel to roam."

"But you're here now."

An angry twist of his expression. "'Til the treaty's signed. I have to make sure the Norwegians sign it, else I'm back in the 'Chapel and the others, those like me, are still in their chains."

His words took her breath.

"That's what they promised you?" A disaster. An absolute disaster. "They promised you freedom?"

"Me and every verwulfen in the Empire."

She leaned back against the wall, hand to her chest.

Will was more involved in this than she'd expected. By moving against him, working against him, she was threatening to destroy his chances of freedom.

She couldn't do it.

But what about Charlie? Her hand dropped to her side. What was she going to do? Heat ached behind her eyes.

"Lena?"

Will waited for a reply. She couldn't think quickly enough. "The jarl's daughter seemed to take a liking to you," she said automatically, as if her heart didn't feel the blow. "If you charmed her—" She couldn't say anymore. The words shriveled in her mouth.

"I don't know nothin' 'bout charm."

Lena laughed, a miserable little sound. She had to get out of here. The walls felt like they were closing in on her. "That's the truth."

The elevation chamber came to a shuddering halt and she spun around. The bell rang and the doors started to open. Lena stepped through them as soon as they were wide enough to accommodate her.

One more flight of stairs to the ground entrance. She gathered her pink skirts and started dashing down them, but Will leaped in front of her, a frown on his face. "What's wrong?"

"Nothing." She tried to push past, but he blocked her way. Standing two steps below her put his face on a level with hers. "Will, I'm tired. I want to go home. This is not—"

"Your scent changed." He took a step up, his thighs pressing against her skirts. "As soon as I told you what they'd promised."

Did guilt have its own scent? She pressed her fingertips against his chest. Whether to hold him at bay or draw him closer, she didn't know. The superfine of his coat was soft beneath her fingers.

"It changed again," he admitted, little sparks of molten copper flaring in his irises. "When you mentioned Lady Astrid." His head lowered, gaze dropping to her mouth. "Just as it's changed now."

Lena's heart started beating faster. Every emotion, every hope, dream, and despair she thought she'd kept hidden from him was betrayed by her scent. She met his eyes and couldn't read the look in them. Hot amber. Eyes that she could drown in if he let her. The color of them softened, melted, as he leaned closer.

His intentions stole her breath. He meant to kiss her. In the foyer of the Ivory Tower, in front of anyone who walked down the stairs. Exhilaration leaped through every nerve in her body.

"Don't you dare," she whispered.

He paused, his mouth an inch from hers. "I never understand you." His eyes darkened with heat. "Yes or no, Lena?"

Warm breath against her lips. Her hand softened on his chest. She knew the answer before her traitorous mouth could say the words. And so did he.

Will captured the yes on her lips, his hands cupping her face and tilting it up to him. The first taste of him was intoxicating. Lena clutched his lapels and rose on her toes.

The world around them faded. All she could feel was the heat of his hard body, pressed firmly against hers, and the taste of his mouth, of champagne and lemon tarts. Darting her tongue against his, she swallowed his soft moan. As if sensing permission, his own tongue met hers and he devoured her, all hot, male possession.

Will's hand splayed over her bottom and he wrenched her against him. Every burning inch. She could feel the layers of fabric bunching between them, and the hint of his shaft, pressed hard against her hips. Wanting more, needing more, she slid her hands into his hair, abandoning herself to the taste of his mouth. There was no skill involved, no finesse, none of the careful kisses she'd flirted with in the Echelon. Nothing but hunger and the barely contained raw fury she could sense beneath his skin.

Taking him to bed would never be tame. Never safe. And she wanted it more than she'd ever wanted anything in her life.

"Take me home," she whispered, before she dared think about it. "Your home."

Will lifted his head, an iron stillness running through his body. Hot little sparks of copper burned in his gaze and she knew instantly she'd said the wrong thing.

She kissed him again, biting at his bottom lip, but he didn't rise to meet her. Cupping her face in both hands, Will drew back, breathing hard, his forehead pressed to hers.

"Lena." A word full of hunger and denied need. "I can't. We can't."

She slid her hands down his chest, hovering over his abdomen. "Yes, we can. Nobody would know." A shiver ran through her. "I want you, Will. I need you. Need this. It's not a game to me." The last few words were a whisper.

He shuddered, eyes closed, fighting something she didn't understand. "*Can't.*" He tore away from her, red heat flushing his cheeks. The look he shot her was dark, dangerous. Hungry. Slowly he shook his head. "Even this should never have happened."

He might as well have stabbed her in the heart.

"You wanted me," she whispered.

"What I want and what I should do ain't the same." He ran his hands over his head, disheveling the neat queue. Strands of thick honey-gold cascaded around his face, caressing the stark cheekbones.

The denial rocked her. As if in mockery, her pulse raced through her veins, something hot and heavy throbbing between her thighs. Her body had not realized what the rest of her had.

"Why?"

"Because I'm verwulfen, Lena."

"I don't care. You know I don't care—"

Will caught her wrists. "I do."

Everything she'd ever feared. Heat flushed behind her eyes and she turned her face away. This had turned into one of the most horrendous nights she'd ever had.

"Let go of me," she said.

Moments ticked by. Then he let her go and stepped away. Finally some space to breathe. Swallowing hard, she forced her tears back and clutched at her ruined gloves. "You may as well return to the ball," she said. "You have a job to do. I'll find my way to the carriage."

"Lena—"

"I'd rather you went back. I want to go home." Wherever that might be. "To Waverly Place."

Unable to bear his presence anymore, she pushed past in a flurry of skirts and made her escape.

Thirteen

THE SHOP BELL CHIMED.

The man behind the counter looked up, his smile paling somewhat when he saw who stood there. A mercenary gaze raked over Will's workman's shirt and leather trousers. "May I help you, sir?"

The display cases gleamed in the weak sunlight. Row upon row of pistols filled the cases. In the corner was another case with less common forms of weaponry; a gilded crossbow, meant for a lady; a handheld mace; even a pair of leather fingerless gloves, with razors cut into the back of them. One punch and you'd kill a man with them. Will looked at them lingeringly, then pushed toward the pistols. He wasn't here for himself.

"I'm after a pistol," he said. "Somethin' dainty."

The shop owner's eyebrows lifted. "Something like that won't come cheap."

Without looking at him, Will tossed him a purse. It bounced on the counter, heavy coins clinking together. "Weren't expectin' it to."

He leaned on the counter, splaying his hands wide

as he examined the contents. A heavy derringer, a German-made M1879 *Reichsrevolver*, a steam-firing pistol... And there, something small enough to fit Lena's hand.

The inlay was mother-of-pearl, the fittings gilded. A brass eyesight was mounted on the barrel and delicate little etchings lined the handle. "That one," he said, stabbing his finger at the glass.

"A beautiful piece, sir. May I ask its purpose? It was designed for target shooting."

"Protection."

The shop owner unlocked the case and lifted out the mahogany box the pistol rested in. "It's a seventeen caliber. Won't stop much more than a pigeon, or small animal, I'm afraid. Unless you're a damned good shot."

"It will when I'm done with it." He fingered the smooth barrel. A few alterations and Lena would be able to take down a bear—or a blue blood. Her own father had designed a type of bullet that would explode on impact. All he had to do was replicate the chemical mix and refine the bullets to something that would fit the compact pistol.

The shopkeeper fussed about him until his teeth were on edge, now that Will had proven to have good coin.

"And these," he said instinctively, pointing toward the half-gloves before it was too late.

Outside, sunlight danced over the street. Passersby glanced at him in curiosity, but none said a word. A young woman in embroidered yellow cotton grabbed her son's hand and dragged the staring child out of the way. Will was tempted to smile at her with bared teeth, but something about what Lena had said to him rang true. He wasn't a beast. Not truly. No matter what the woman saw when she looked at him. Forcing out a curt nod, he strode past her as if he belonged here.

The night had been long and sleep hard to find. Colchester played on his mind, the adversary he didn't know enough about.

Yet.

If Lena thought her best defense against a blue blood was to lie down and submit, then she had another thing coming. Last night scared him. Even at a gathering of nearly four hundred people, Colchester managed to get near her.

He found his way to a jeweler's and strode in out of the wind. A pair of blue bloods were examining the wares at the counter, clad in velvets and lace. One wore a perfumed, fragrant wig, much in the style of Georgian times, and leaned heavily on a cane. Beneath the perfume lingered a faint rotting smell that made Will's hackles rise.

On the verge of the Fade. The blue blood wouldn't have much time left before someone decided to put him out of his misery—and spare the city another vampire massacre.

The middle-aged man grabbed his arm as the elder turned, leaning heavily on the cane. "Here, Grandfather. Take a seat." He guided him to a chair and gestured at the shopkeeper. "Blud-wein. Now."

Neither of them had smelt him yet. Will prowled the cabinets, fighting the urge to turn and keep them in sight at all times. The scent made his blood chill.

He'd only ever faced one vampire. And one was enough, as the scars across his abdomen would attest. They were the only wounds his virus hadn't been able to heal completely.

In Georgian times, a spate of vampires almost drowned the city in blood. It cost ten thousand lives before the Echelon managed to destroy them all. Now, when the virus finally overtook them and the Fade threatened, a blue blood was closely watched. As soon as his body started paling—his eyes filming over and his teeth sharpening—an ax was sent for.

The shop bell tinkled and a pair of heavy boots strode in. Will caught a glimpse of the newcomer's reflection in the glass of the cabinet.

A long black great cloak wrapped around the man's shoulders, with a spill of lace at his throat. His waist-coat was red velvet, a golden pocket watch gleaming against it. White gloves curled around a golden-handled cane and he glanced at the pair in the corner, his lip curling beneath a battered nose.

"Devil take it, Arsen," the man snapped, tugging out a scented handkerchief. "Haven't you buried that old relic yet?"

Both of the men froze. Whilst the younger stammered, the elder lifted his pale, powdered face, a hint of malice in those dark eyes. "I'm not dead yet, Colchester. Maybe I'll take you with me."

Colchester.

"I should like to see you try, Monkton," Colchester sneered. "Perhaps I can do the job Arsen's evidently been neglecting."

Colchester was younger than he'd imagined, with

the kind of smooth cheeks and rakishly tossed hair that might turn a lady's head. A big, broad-shouldered fellow, he moved with the smooth-limbed grace of a swordsman.

His blue eyes glanced at Will's attire and dismissed him. That was his first mistake. Any true predator would have looked past the clothes to the man within. Obviously years of rank and position had inured him to the dangers of the world. In the Echelon, if a blue blood had grievance with another, they dueled. Will, however, was used to streets where men took what they wanted with a quick knife to the back.

"Please, Your Grace," Arsen stammered. "Grandfather doesn't mean anything by it. We've been watching him closely. We just thought some fresh air would do him good."

"An ax would be better."

Monkton's lip curled up. "Aye. Like the one you forgot to take to the late, unlamented Vickers 'til it was too late?" He laughed, a wheezing sound. "Heard it was a glorious duel with the duke's wig torn off in front of the court and the truth of his condition betrayed. They say it took a week to get the stink of his rot out of the atrium."

Colchester's fist tightened unconsciously. "Don't make a dangerous enemy, Monkton. You're nothing but a minor offshoot of the House of Malloryn. And Auvry's a dear friend of mine. Perhaps I'll whisper in his ear and see the matter dealt with appropriately?"

Both of the men paled. The younger grabbed his grandfather by his velvet-clad arm and hustled him out of the jewelry shop with a steady stream of apologies.

Colchester watched them go with a bored expression on his face. He eased a snuff tin from his pocket and inhaled a pinch of it, wincing through his bruised nose.

Their eyes met in the jeweled mirror on the far wall.

"Aren't you out of your league here?" Colchester asked, tucking his snuff tin back in his pocket.

"You'd be surprised," Will replied. His hands twitched. One moment of violence and Lena would never have to look over her shoulder again… He took a step toward the duke.

The shopkeeper reappeared with a pair of glasses balanced on a tray. He blinked to find the room empty. Colchester snatched a glass of blud-wein as he sauntered past.

"Really, Griffith. The people you allow in here," he muttered, peering at an antique cameo. "I might have to take my business elsewhere."

"Y-Your Grace—" the shopkeeper stammered.

Anger bubbled in Will's chest. The chance was lost. Colchester looked up. "You're still here?"

"I've business 'ere," he replied, stepping out of the shadows. Heat swam behind his eyes and every muscle in his body tightened. This bastard had done something to Lena. He didn't know what, but it was enough to terrify her.

Killing him would be only too sweet. And yet, with it would go any chance he had of freeing himself and his fellows from the cages and arenas.

Instinct demanded he kill the duke. But cold intellect argued against it. He could almost hear Blade and Lena's voices in his ear, trying to explain to him that it would be wrong. Sweat rimed his forehead. This was a world he didn't understand and never completely would. But he trusted them, knew that they would not be pleased if he did this thing.

Colchester would never know how close to death he came as he straightened. "Do you have any idea who I am?"

"Aye. I know exactly who you are."

Colchester's gaze sharpened with interest. Will could feel the heat of his anger burning through him. For once he let it surface just enough to show, the molten gold of it transforming his eyes in the mirror's reflection.

Colchester sucked in a breath and slapped a hand to his belt, as if reaching for a blade.

"Wouldn't if I were you." Will sucked in a breath and looked away. Little gems fractured the sunlight back at him, a thousand different shades and colors. Rings, necklaces, bracelets. An entire corner filled with pearl chokers that were worth more than his life. He focused on them furiously, trying to ignore the duke's perfume.

Colchester's image wavered in the glass, his eyes narrowing at Will's back. "You're the one they call the Beast, aren't you? The one with the price on your head if you step inside the city?"

Will glanced over his shoulder. "Didn't they tell you?"

Colchester's eyes became slits. "Tell me what?"

"Prince consort himself give me pardon."

Colchester crossed toward the window, his hands clasped behind his back. His movements were neat and precise; he was on edge, prepared to fight at a second's notice. Will prowled in the other direction, running his fingertips lightly along the glass counter.

A dangerous dance. The shopkeeper had retreated to the door of the storeroom, uncertain what was going on but aware of the undercurrents in the room.

"I see," Colchester sneered. "This joke of an alliance they're spouting. I wasn't aware of how fully they'd involved you until last night."

"Guess you ain't as important as you think you are."

If looks could kill. "I washed my hands of it weeks ago. It took years to put you savages in your proper places. Why invite you back into our lives with an expression of cordiality?" His gaze ran over Will. "The entire concept is an insult."

The barb went wide of its mark. He didn't give a damn what Colchester thought of him.

As if realizing it, Colchester stepped closer. "I must admit, I'm disappointed. After what Cavendish told me, I was expecting a raving lunatic. They've leashed you well, it seems."

"There's a time. And a place."

"Mmm." Colchester leaned over, examining a pretty butterfly brooch. When wound, the wings would flutter. "Tell me," he said, drawing little circles on the glass with his finger, "has she told you about me yet?"

Silence. "She?"

"Helena," Colchester said, placing intimate emphasis on the name. He looked up. The smile on his lips was as nothing to the one in his eyes when he realized his words had finally drawn blood. "My dear, sweet Helena Todd."

Will held onto himself with the thinnest of leashes. "Why would she?"

"Because she's going to be my next thrall—"

No.

Will had him by the throat before he realized it. His fingers dug into the pallid flesh as Colchester laughed.

"You leave her alone," Will snarled, his voice cold and harsh. "You catch so much as a sniff of her and you turn and walk the other way."

"A sniff?" Colchester managed to gurgle. "I've had more than that, you filth."

"What'd you say?"

"She didn't...tell you?" Delight turned Colchester's pale blue eyes warm. Then they bulged as Will's grip tightened.

He could barely see through the red haze choking him. One twist and he could tear the bastard's head from his shoulders. But movement caught his eye. The shopkeeper, trembling in the doorway as he watched in horror.

Not here. Not now.

But one day, he promised himself.

Forcing his hand open, he shoved Colchester back. The duke staggered into the glass cases, spraying glass across the floor. He was still laughing and the sound of it rode Will's nerves like a saw. He saw red again and turned away, breathing hard.

"She has the sweetest blood, you know?" Colchester called. "Purrs like a little kitten under the touch—"

The next thing he knew, he was slamming Colchester face-first into another case. The shopkeeper cringed, but the laughter finally died. Will dragged the duke out of the mess of glass and jewelry and smashed a fist into his midsection. Colchester bent over like a sack of spilled suet, blood and glass encrusting his face.

A boot hooked behind his and they both went down. Something hot bit into his back but he paid it no mind, riding the edge of the storm within him. Locking his arm around the duke's neck he twisted and slammed him down onto the hard floor, scrambling on top of him with his fist raised—

It never descended.

A hand caught his, iron fingers wrapping around his fist like a manacle. "That's enough," someone barked.

Will looked up, his teeth bared.

"Control yourself," snapped a vaguely familiar voice. The stranger was almost as tall as Will himself, but built lean and hard. His eyes were the same chilling blue as a glacier and he wore black leather from head to toe, the hard carapace of a breastplate covering his chest.

Will blinked, finally noticing the pair of guards behind the stranger. He looked down to find his other hand twisted in Colchester's waistcoat. Blood ran down the duke's pale face, with chips of glass embedded in his cheek.

"Get him off me," Colchester snapped, spitting blood. "I demand this creature be arrested."

And that was when Will realized who the stranger was.

Sir Jasper Lynch, master of the Nighthawks guild of thief-catchers. They'd worked together three years ago to bring down the vampire. Lynch was a hard man, but efficient. Unfortunately he was also a blue blood.

Yanking Will to his feet, Lynch stared down his hawkish nose at the duke. "Your Grace," he said in a voice completely lacking inflection. "On what charges?"

"Assault." Colchester rolled to his feet, brushing glass off his coat. He looked around. "Property damage." A smirk appeared. "Attempted theft."

Will growled and strained forward, but Lynch yanked his arm up behind his back and shoved him face-first into the wall. Even in the grip of the fury, he recognized a man who knew the right pressure points to press to hold him there, despite his superior strength.

"Don't be a fool," Lynch whispered deadly soft. "That's exactly what he wants." Then he gave one last wrench on Will's arm and let him go.

Will shoved free, glaring at Colchester.

"We'll need to have you make a formal complaint at the guild headquarters," Lynch said. "Then we'll have to find a magistrate who'll charge him. And the witness of course," he added, with a nod to the shopkeeper.

Colchester paused in the act of brushing himself off. "What the bloody hell do we need him for? You saw him. He attacked me with no provocation."

"I'm afraid I intervened in an untimely manner," Lynch replied. "I only saw two men fighting."

The pair of them eyed each other. Colchester's eyes narrowed. "You're making a mistake, Lynch. I'll have you replaced before sundown."

"Unlikely, Your Grace," Lynch replied. "The Council commands law enforcement in the city. Not you."

A moment of heavy silence descended before Colchester looked away. "So be it." Colchester's fists clenched at his sides, and he looked past Lynch at Will. His teeth were bloody as he smiled. "Don't think you'll be the first. The little slut's got a taste for it."

It took the three Nighthawks to hold him back this time. Will fought to push past, straining for Colchester. The duke straightened his lapel, brushed the glass shards out of his cheek, and then sauntered out the door.

"Let him go," Lynch snarled. "You'll only get yourself killed and he's not worth it."

Will looked up. They'd pinned him against the wall and he was distantly aware of something warm and wet trickling down his back. Lynch stared at him for a moment then nodded curtly and stepped back.

"Let him go, boys."

They stepped aside, breathing hard.

"You're bleeding." Lynch's nostrils flared.

Will winced. The rage washed out of him, a half-dozen cuts and bruises suddenly springing to attention. The throb in his back intensified as the heat washed out of his head and his vision returned to normal. He glanced over his shoulder, then swore as it pulled through the muscles in his back. There was something sharp there.

Lynch reached out and yanked a glass sliver out of his muscle.

Son of a bitch. Will hissed. "Some warnin' would have been nice."

"You'll heal." Lynch said. "Perhaps it will teach you to keep a cool head." He glanced at one of his comrades. "Take a witness statement, Garrett. And an estimation of the damage."

For the first time Will looked around. Glass littered

the room, precious jewels tumbling from their cases onto the timber floors. Blood dripped from a nasty sliver of glass casing and he had the pleasure of the memory of smashing Colchester's face into it, again and again.

The shopkeeper stared at the damage soundlessly. His eyes were wide and unblinking. "How am I going to tell Martha?" he whispered. "The duke'll blacken my name. He'll destroy me."

Will's fingers curled in shame. He should have held his temper. "I'll pay the damage bill."

Lynch grabbed his arm and gestured toward the front door. The grim crawl of evening darkened the sky outside, thick clouds boiling on the horizon. "I'd suggest it's time for you to leave. It wouldn't surprise me if Colchester returns—with a few friends. He's not likely to take this lying down. And I've done as much as I can."

Will nodded. Christ. What had he been thinking? He hadn't obviously. One mention of Lena and the rage had overtaken him completely. Then his eyes narrowed. "Why?"

"Why what?"

"Why help me?" He could count the number of people who'd ever volunteered to help him on one hand; in his experience, there was always a price.

Lynch paused in the doorway, eyeing the curious crowd that was beginning to form. Tiny lines feathered out from the corners of his eyes, and his dark brows drew together in a frown. "Three years ago Blade saved my life down in the sewers. I owe him. Consider this repayment."

Will eyed the other man's tense shoulders. "And?"

Lynch stroked his smooth jaw. "There is...a certain amount of pressure coming from the Council. I need to locate a revolutionary by the name of Mercury. He leads the humanist movement here in London and he's directly responsible for the firing of the draining factories. I'm not a fool, Carver. Blade has ears in places I could never reach." A direct look into Will's eyes. "And so do you. I could smell your scent in the tunnels when we arrested the pair responsible for the draining factories."

"We had naught to do with that."

"I know. The pair told us everything. They thought they'd killed Blade."

"Only stuck him a bit." No need to spread word that Blade was fallible. His legend had kept the Echelon at bay for fifty years. "You want word o' Mercury then?"

"Anything you know."

A chill feathered down his spine. Lynch was desperate. He could smell the edge on him. No doubt the Council was tightening the noose around his throat. Everybody knew that the Nighthawks were comprised of rogue blue bloods—those created illegally or accidentally. Most rogues were killed when they first became infected with the craving. Those that could control themselves were offered another choice: a grim, solitary life as a Nighthawk, kept on the leash of the Council. They were useful to the Echelon, but they would never be a part of them.

Expendable.

Especially if they didn't perform.

The image of that coded letter he'd found on Lena

sprang to mind. If there was any way she could be connected to the humanists, to this Mercury… The fear grew, gnawing at his gut. What had she gotten herself involved in? First Colchester and now this.

"I'll keep me eyes open," he said, aware that Lynch was watching him intently. "Anythin' I hear I'll pass along."

Lynch searched his gaze. "I wouldn't cross me on this, Carver. If there's anything you know—anything at all—you'd best tell me."

Will nodded. The Nighthawk had picked up on the tension in his body no doubt. "Aye. I'll send word if I hear anythin'."

First *he* had to figure out exactly what was going on.

Fourteen

A COOL BREEZE WHISPERED OVER HER SKIN. LENA looked up from the mess of cogs and gears that covered her small writing desk. Slipping the magnifying glassicals up on top of her head, she put aside her fine pliers and stood. Her nightrobe tumbled around her bare feet, the rose-colored silk caressing her shins.

"Hello?" she called, tugging her robe tight and retying the sash. It was almost midnight. Mrs. Wade had retired hours ago, but she hadn't been able to sleep. Too many things whirling through her mind. She'd decided she might as well use the time to work on the life-size transformational Mercury wanted her to create. Clockworks were easy and they always fit together… Unlike her life. Besides, she had only a week until the treaty's official signing. She'd started the clockwork interior of the piece, but a week was barely time enough to finish it. She'd have to use Mandeville's help for the outer casing.

The door between the sitting room and her bedchamber wheezed, stirring in a breeze that shouldn't have been there. Lena snatched up the poker.

Her heart pounded in her chest as she crept toward the door. Nobody would dare attack her here, would they? The place was well-guarded, even at night, as it wasn't unknown for assassinations to occur in the Echelon. The Duke of Caine was frequently indisposed, and Leo ruled as acting head of the House. No doubt a half-dozen minor offshoots of the House were starting to grow ambitious.

Thunder rumbled in the distance.

The soft glow of a turned-down gas lamp barely lit the shadowed bedroom beyond the door. For a moment Lena was half tempted to wake the household. But if the latch had merely blown open, she'd have woken them for naught.

Her eyes darted around the room as she slipped through the door. Soft gauzy curtains floated in the wind, rain spattering the polished floors. One of the French doors to her balcony had become unlatched, but there was no sign of anyone in the room.

"Damned wind."

Pressing the door shut, she latched it tightly. Lightning flashed and suddenly the floor creaked behind her.

A scream tore from her throat, captured by a man's large hand. He yanked her back against his hard chest and water from his clothes saturated the back of her. Her lips pressed wetly into his hand and his warm breath brushed against her ear.

"Shhh."

Will. She could smell his scent now, of musk and rain and fresh air. The poker fell from her nerveless fingers. He caught it with his boot before it hit the floor, then eased it onto the rug.

Lena's heart hammered along at a clipping pace. Her feet ceased drumming against his ankles and she slumped in his grip, her breasts pressing against his forearm. In the corner, movement caught her eye. A freestanding cheval mirror, showing the pair of them locked together in an illicit embrace. Lena's eyes widened as they met his. He was huge and wet and brooding, the amber spark of his eyes flaring in warning. Spoiling for a fight by the look of him.

Her eyes narrowed. He wasn't the only one who wanted an argument. This was going to be the last time he frightened her.

She bit the fleshy pad of his palm.

"If I let you go are you goin' to behave?"

Lena wriggled furiously.

"I'll assume that means 'no.'" Hauling her toward the bed, he tossed her on it. Before she could even bounce, he'd whipped a silk scarf off the floor and gagged her with it.

Lena's eyes widened further and she kicked at him, making a strangled sound behind the scarf. Will pinned her, his hands driving her wrists into the bed and his legs straddling hers. The nightgown rucked up around her thighs in the struggle and she stilled as his gaze dropped. There was a world of heat in that look.

"Truce?"

Lena nodded warily. As he sat back, kneeling over her, she reached up and tugged the scarf out of her mouth.

"What the devil are you *doing* here?"

He clapped a hand over her mouth. "If Barrons finds me here, we'll be contracted for marriage before we know it." Their eyes met. "Neither of us wants that, do we?"

Her heart pounded uncertainly. Then she gave her head a vehement shake. She'd seen her sister's happiness and good fortune. The only thing worse than a marriage made of duty would be one of unrequited feelings.

Will stared at her for a long moment, his expression hardening. His hand dropped from her mouth, trailing over her cheek before falling to his lap.

"He wouldn't force a contract on us anyway," she murmured. "Leo would probably pretend he'd never seen you here—after escorting you to the door and removing the trellis outside my window."

"Wouldn't stop me." His fingers toyed with the sash of her robe. Then Will realized what he'd said. "If I wanted to get in."

"Stop it." Her hand clapped over his. His palm flattened against her abdomen, devilishly warm. "You're taking entirely too many liberties."

"Wouldn't be the first time it's happened."

Something about his expression warned her. "What do you mean by that?"

A long silence. "Nothin'."

She had the feeling he wasn't talking about the kiss they'd shared. Lena shoved his hand away. "What do you want? What are you doing here anyway?"

Water slicked his hair against his head, dripping down the open collar of his throat. His gaze was hard and flat. He held up a piece of paper and with a start she realized it was the other piece of the letter he'd torn from her.

The last time she'd seen it she'd stuffed it up the

chimney, behind a loose brick where she could take the time to try and decipher it.

"Lookin' for the truth," he said. "Since I ain't likely to get it from you."

"That's mine." Lena snatched at it but his grip was firm. They glared at each other. His shirt clung to his shoulders indecently; the sleeves were rolled up to his elbows and his leather waistcoat sculpted every muscle of his chest. A bead of water hovered in the dip of his lip, another sliding down his roughened cheek. God, she wanted to run her hands over his shoulders, to trace that droplet of water with her tongue.

To sink her hands into the wet mess of his hair and drag his mouth down. To hers.

Taking a deep breath, Lena shivered with unrequited longing. "What are you going to do with it? Decode it?"

"Aye."

Lena licked her lips. "Perhaps it's for the best." She wanted to know what it said just as much as he did. "As long as you don't breathe a word to anyone else about it."

"Afraid Honoria will yell?"

"Afraid she'll lock me in a convent."

"Perhaps you ought to be." The gold color of his eyes was molten.

Lena froze. He'd made it quite clear kissing her had been a mistake. And yet... Her nipples tightened under his burning gaze. The way he was looking at her was almost edible. This mood of his was unpredictable.

She had to get him out of here before she did something foolish.

"Is that everything you came for?" She let go of her end of the piece of paper. "You scared me half to death."

Rain battered the windows as he knelt back onto his knees. He didn't seem in any hurry to leave.

"Will? Whatever this is, you could have waited 'til tomorrow."

Will's expression remained hooded. "You and I need to talk."

"Not tonight. If anyone—"

"Tonight," he growled, and another low peal of thunder rumbled through the room. "I give you enough chances. Tonight I've had enough. I want answers and you're damned well goin' to give 'em to me. All you're goin' to do is answer yes or no, do you understand?"

Lena nodded slowly. Will always kept his temper even and controlled. He didn't dare let it loose. Tonight there was a wildness there that urged for caution.

"Do you know who Mercury is?"

Her breath caught. "I don't... I'm not sure what—"

Will pressed a finger to her lips. "Yes. Or no. Do you know who Mercury is?"

Where had he heard that name? And why would he suspect her of a connection to it? She had to play this right, or who knew how he'd react? Lena nodded hesitantly. "Yes."

He didn't like that, she realized. A frown drew his eyebrows together. "Damn it, Lena. What the devil have you gotten yourself involved in?"

There was no way to answer that with a simple yes or no.

As if realizing her intentions, his eyes narrowed. "Do you have any involvement with the humanists? With Mercury?"

"Yes. And no."

"Lena, the Nighthawks are huntin' Mercury! It won't be long before they find him and anyone connected to him. Today I had to promise Sir Jasper Lynch that I'd keep an eye out for any signs of him. Even as I said the words I knew I were lyin', for I knew you were involved." With a disgusted look, he raked his hands through his hair. "What am I goin' to do with you?"

The question brought to mind a number of answers. But she didn't think he'd approve of any of them.

"Well? Are you goin' to tell me what's goin' on?"

The answer to that was simple enough. Panic flashed through her. "No."

"That's the wrong answer, luv."

"That's the only one you're getting."

"I could make you tell me." He leaned closer, looming over her.

Lena scooted back up the bed until her back hit the headboard. "I hardly think you'd dare. Since you don't want to be found in my chambers any more than I want you found. I'll scream."

The look on his face made her breath shudder.

"You'll try," he said. One large hand latched around her ankle, the obscene heat of his skin branding her. His eyes had gone completely wolfish as he drew her toward him.

Her nightgown slid over the silken sheets, sliding up around her hips. The robe was tumbling from her shoulders. There was a moment where she could have saved it. A moment where sanity intruded. A moment where she remembered the look in his eyes... Was it real? Or had she just imagined it? Did he want her?

Heaven help me, she prayed silently. Then she gave a little shrug and the robe slipped from her shoulders, pooling around her waist.

She had to know.

Will's gaze sharpened. Heat. Hunger. An intensity that scalded her from within. She'd been *right*. It was not disinterest that tightened his expression and tensed the muscles in his forearms.

The realization was heady. She could barely breathe as he reached out and captured her chin in one hand. *Yes, oh God, yes.*

He turned her face to the side, his hot gaze running down her throat. Then to the other side. Lena frowned, capturing his wrist. What was he doing?

Ignoring the delicate scalloped lace neckline of her gown, he caught her wrist and turned it up.

No. Her breath caught and she wrenched her arm to her chest in shock. She knew exactly what he was looking for now.

"Lena." His hand fisted in the bottom of her nightgown.

The amber gleam frightened her. There was no lucidity to it, no sign of Will. Only the predator, his face tight with anger. Clutching his hand, she slid it higher, over the inside of her thigh and the raised scar there.

The ugly reminder of what Colchester had taken from her that day in the alley.

"Is this what you're looking for?" She pushed him away and scrambled for the side of the bed. The hurt was a sharp, stabbing pain in her chest. For a moment, just a moment, she'd thought he was going to kiss her again.

Sliding her robe up over her shoulders, Lena yanked the sash tight and tied it. "How did you know?"

There was no answer.

Lena turned and found him kneeling in the middle of her bed, his head bowed and his hands clenched in her sheets. A tremble ran through his shoulders and his hand jerked. Slowly his head lifted. A shiver ran down her spine as their eyes met.

"Colchester told me." His voice was hoarse. "Told me he'd had you."

A line of heat sprang across her cheeks. *Damn it, not now.* Tilting her head discreetly to the side, she wiped her eyes with her sleeve. "You saw him? Where? I told you not to do anything rash."

"I were at the jewelers. He walked in." A shifting of sheets and then his booted feet came into view. Will knelt in front of her. This close, she could make out the split in his lip and the faint bruise on his cheekbone. Someone had hit him. Colchester, she was sure of it.

"Lena?" The back of his fingers stroked her damp cheek. "What happened?"

His gentleness nearly undid her. She pushed past in a flurry of silk, panic catching her breath in her chest. "I don't want to talk about it."

Three steps before he caught her. She whirled around to push him away and found herself in the circle of his arms. His chest was firm against her cheek, his heat enveloping her. God help her, but she couldn't stop her fingers from curling in his shirt. She felt so safe here in his arms. The fight drained out of her. If only he could hold her like this forever.

If only he wanted to.

"Damn it, what did he do to you?" Will's voice was strangled. "Did he—did he rape you?"

"No," she blurted. "But not for lack of trying." The memory stained her. Colchester, a handsome young dandy in the streets, stopping to smile and charm her. She'd not thought it odd at all, for she'd been used to such flirtation before her father died. She even recognized him as the Duke of Lannister's heir, though she'd been a fool to think for one second that he saw her as anything other than a coal lass. Easy prey.

"He took my blood." Forced her back into the alley. Shoved her hard against the wall. Her pails had spilled everywhere, coal tumbling across the dirty cobbles. She'd tried to say no, unable even then to comprehend what was happening. "I didn't want it. I didn't. But he kept saying I did, that I'd like it."

Warmth burned on her cheeks. As soon as she realized she was crying, a sob overtook her. Colchester had been right. She had liked it, in the end. The chemicals in his saliva had set off some sort of reaction in her body.

Will's hands came up and gently pressed against her back. "Easy now, *mo cridhe*." He rubbed soothing circles against her back. "You're safe now. I've got you."

But she wasn't safe. The tears came harder. Safe

was a world without the Echelon and their grasping blood-suckers in it. Without humanists threatening her family, or Colchester stalking her. Safe was a world where she was loved and happy. Safe was here. In Will's arms.

"And the humanists?"

"I d-didn't mean to get caught up in all of this." But the words were a lie. She'd wanted to find something, anything, to give her a sense of purpose in life.

"Caught up in what?" His voice was lower, huskier. "Lena?" he whispered, stroking the hair off her sticky face. "Tell me."

She pushed out of the comfort of his arms and turned away, shamelessly wiping her face against the shoulder of her nightgown. She knew what he wanted, but she had to explain to him first, to show him that her reasons for all of this hadn't just been some frivolous whim. Maybe then he wouldn't hate her so much if he found out what she was supposed to do. "There was nothing for me in Whitechapel. Honoria had Blade. And Charlie was settling in. We were always so close, but he didn't want to be around me once he became a blue blood. And then—" Her voice broke slightly and she hurried on. "You were gone. And nobody wanted me there.

"I thought that if I returned to society things would change. It was what I'd been raised for. Honoria always had Father and her work, but growing up there was nothing for me but lessons on etiquette and the things a young lady ought to know. When Father died and we were forced to hide in Whitechapel, I was on the cusp of making my debut. It was the happiest time of my life." Her voice trailed off. "I just wanted to go back to it."

Everyone had praised her beauty and charm then, and the glimpse she'd had of the Echelon had only fuelled her excitement to join it. But she had looked at it through innocent eyes. Whitechapel had changed everything about her. She was no longer that naive young girl with stars in her eyes. There was no going back, and it had taken a long time to realize that.

"The rot's not apparent at first," she said. "Leo sponsored my debut and everyone was so charming and elegant. Of course they were. They wanted something from me. I was offered three thrall contracts in the first week. It was terribly exciting."

"You never accepted 'em."

She couldn't turn around and look at him. Crossing her arms over her chest, she shook her head. "One of them—Lord Ramsay—invited me to stroll in the garden with him. I knew what he intended. It's not uncommon for a woman to offer blood before a contract is signed." Her voice dropped. "I couldn't. The more I thought about it, the more it upset me. I couldn't breathe. All I could think about w-was Colchester. In that alley. I was so overwrought that Lord Ramsay slapped me and then Leo was there and he took me home and I-I—"

Warm arms slid around her waist. "Don't cry, Lena. Damn it."

Of course he wouldn't want her crying all over him. She tried to dry her eyes. "I'm sorry. I can't help it. I'm sorry."

"You're not the one who ought to be sorry." Dire

words. A hint of threat underlying them. His hand stroked her hip, her waist. "I hate seein' you cry."

"You do?" she whispered. His hand stroked smooth circles over her hip. So lightly it was almost hypnotic. Somehow she found herself relaxing back into the circle of his arms.

The world upended as he swept her up into his arms. With a gasp she clapped her arms around his shoulders. "Will?"

He was carrying her to the bed. "You're shiverin'."

And she was, she realized, her lips quivering with the chill of the room—and her memories. Tucking her face against his neck, she closed her eyes and breathed in the wet musky scent of him. He eased her under the sheets and then tucked her blankets around her. Then he straightened.

Don't go. She caught his fingertips in mute appeal.

Will hesitated. "It ain't seemly. And I'm wet—"

"I'm so cold," she whispered. "And you're so warm. Please."

"Me shirt's drenched."

"Then take it off."

Something dark and merciless flashed through his gaze. He sucked in a deep breath. Golden eyes burned in the dark of the night. The hunter? Or the hunt*ed*?

"Please," she whispered. "Just for a moment. Just to warm my sheets." If she shivered a little more than was strictly necessary… Well, he would never need to know that.

The moment of indecision stretched out, playing over his face. "Tell me more," he finally said, tugging at his waistcoat. "Tell me what you're involved in."

Lena rolled onto her side, watching him. The light from the gas lamp backlit his broad shoulders. His face was little more than shadow and the burning gleam of those eyes.

Heat coiled through her, warming her from within. Her nipples tightened, the silk of her nightgown abrading them lightly as he reached over his head and dragged his shirt off. She felt like a mess, her face and nose all wet and splotched, but she could no sooner turn her eyes away than submit to a blue blood.

Light gleamed over the wet slickness of his skin, highlighting the play of muscle in his chest and the ripple of his abdomen. He shucked his boots and looked up, his damp hair falling almost to his shoulders.

Far too long and unruly to be fashionable. But, sweet Lord, how she wanted to run her fingers through it. To touch him.

Nervous anticipation ran over her skin. She'd never seen a man half-naked. Gooseflesh sprang up over her body, and she squirmed against the unfamiliar wet heat between her thighs. The bed dipped beneath his weight.

"How did you meet them?"

"Meet them?" She looked up, wondering for a moment who he was talking about. "The humanists?"

Will lay on his back, his head pillowed on his arms as he turned to look at her. "Aye."

Lena slid closer. The first hint of his body heat on the sheets sent a delicious shiver down her spine. She hadn't realized how cold she was. "I already knew one, although I never realized what he was involved in until later. Until I needed it."

"Who?"

"You don't need to know that." She snuggled closer, reaching out with a hesitant hand to stroke his chest.

Will stiffened. But he didn't pull away. Taking it as permission, she tucked herself against his side, laying her head gently on his shoulder. The heat was delicious.

"Lena, I can't protect you unless you tell me everythin'."

The sound of his voice rumbled through his chest. "He saved my life, Will. He was the one who scared Colchester off. Then he brought me in out of the alley and let me sob all over his shoulder." She shook her head. "I won't betray him. I owe him more than you'll ever know."

Will rolled, turning to face her. Her head slipped into the crook of his arm and the position put distance between them. His breath curled over her face. "Mandeville."

"Why would you—"

"I already suspected."

"Please," she whispered. "Don't do anything. I don't want to see him hurt. He gave me a job, Will. He kept me off the streets and looked after me like I was his own."

Something in his eyes darkened. "And where was your bloody sister in all of this?"

"I never told her." As he shifted in protest, she put a finger to his lips. "You don't know what it was like. I couldn't. We were both working our fingers to the bone merely to provide food and shelter, and Charlie was sick with the first signs of the craving. I didn't want to be a burden." Fresh tears sprang forth in her eyes. "And we'd been arguing so much that I didn't feel as if I *could* tell her."

Tears scalded her cheeks. She didn't think she'd had any left, but then this was an old grief, one much covered over and patched. Honoria had made peace with her about the constant arguments they'd had, but she'd never known what had caused the burning resentment. Lena had been so alone, so angry and scared.

Will dragged her close, crushing her against his body. Lena clung to him, burying her face against his neck. "I'm such a mess," she tried to say, but the tears wouldn't stop and the words were distorted. "I'm sorry."

"Ain't you as should be sorry." His voice was dark. "Your bloody sister needs her neck wrung. And as for Colchester—"

She looked up in alarm. "You promised you wouldn't go near him."

"That was before I knew what he done." A nasty little smile curved over his lips. "If it's any consolation, he ain't as pretty as he were."

"Oh, Will, what did you do?"

"Dragged him face-first through a few glass cases."

The thought sent a vindictive thrill through her. Then she shook her head. "You shouldn't have. He'll never forget it. He'll come after you."

There was a light touch against her cheek. "Hope he does." The sound of it was close to her ear.

Realization came slowly. His lips, brushing against

her brow. Lena stilled. Her heart started to race. "Will?" She lifted her head.

His expression was dark, considering. He stroked her face with his hand, cupping her chin. His mouth was dangerously close to hers. "God help me."

Then he leaned forward and kissed her.

His lips were warm and hesitant. Lena sucked in a sharp breath, her heart pounding in her ears. The skin on her cheeks was tight and dry from her tears, but she didn't care. She lay still and quiescent, not daring to breathe for fear that this dream would all go away.

As if sensing her hesitation, he drew back.

"No," she whispered and grabbed a handful of his hair. "Don't you dare."

Fear of losing him broke the barriers of the dam. Her lips found his in the shadows. She pressed herself wantonly against his body, sinking her fingers into his hair.

He gasped as her tongue darted out and caressed his. His hands cupped her bottom, his body coming over hers and grinding her against him. Every hard inch of him was pressed intimately against her. Heat spilled through her, enveloped her. She rolled her hips instinctively, drawing another gasp from him.

Sweet heavens, this is bliss. She wanted more. She wanted him to capture her mouth, take her, right there and then. But his hesitancy lingered in the gentle nips he took at her lips.

If he drew away again...it would kill her. Lena slid her arms around his damp shoulders, her tongue sliding into his mouth. His back arched, enough to press his hips against hers and still kiss her, with the disparity in height. Lena gasped, drinking at his mouth greedily, her hands hungry across the smooth skin of his back.

Will caught her wrists and pressed her flat, tearing his mouth from hers. "No," he gasped.

Lena strained against his grip. "I'm tired of hearing that. Damn it, Will, you know I don't care you're verwulfen. I proved that!"

He shoved away, rearing up on his knees. "That ain't the only problem."

"You don't want me?" She ran her hands over her breasts, feeling the turgid peaks of her nipples through the thin lawn nightgown. "We both know that's a lie."

Will's face darkened and he rolled toward the edge of the bed. Realizing his intention, she wrapped her legs around his hips and rolled with him. Somehow she ended up straddling his hips. When Will looked at her in surprise, she seized the advantage and pushed him flat onto his back.

No force on earth could make him stay if he didn't want to with his strength. She pinned his wrists in a desperate maneuver and then realized that he made no attempt to leave. His gaze was fixed on her chest. Or the missing button that had somehow come off in the struggle, she presumed.

Sliding her hands down over the sculpted muscle of his arms, she sat up, resting them on his chest. His belt buckle dug into the tender flesh of her thigh and she shifted, riding over the hard bulge of his breeches. She knew enough to understand what that meant.

Both of them stilled.

"I could hurt you."

Leaning down, she brushed her mouth against his.

Just lightly. Teasingly. "I don't think you would," she breathed. Licking his lip and then suckling it into her mouth, something coppery burning on her tongue. Blood. His blood. The split in his lip.

His fingers sank into the soft flesh of her thighs and he sucked in a sharp breath. The strain of his erection brushed against her and she stilled, a flare of heat pulsing through her. How delicious a sensation. With a little shiver, she rolled her hips again, rubbing against him.

Will's eyes glazed. "You don't understand." He sucked in a sharp breath, the hiss of it rasping between his teeth. "Can't think. When you do that. Damn it." His hand urged her against him. "Stop it, Lena."

Lena threw her head back, riding over him again. "Why would I want to do that?" She gasped herself, wetness smothering her drawers. It felt so good. So right. And it was driving him wild.

He bared his teeth at her. The whites of his eyes were showing. "I'll hurt you. *I can't.*" His hands, however, told another story. They fisted in the hem of her nightgown, strain tautening the knuckles. "Damn it."

Lena ground against him again. She was wet through, the sensation tearing another gasp from her lips.

The sound of ripping silk opened her eyes. The chill of the room penetrated and she looked down as he tore her nightgown up the center.

"Will!"

He leaned up, biting at her lips, tugging at her arms. This time there was no hesitation as he claimed her mouth roughly, jerking her hips against him. The nightgown hung from her shoulders, trapping her arms against her side. She wanted to touch him, to run her hands over the smooth skin of his biceps, but she couldn't.

Her breasts were bare, the hair on his chest rubbing against the sensitive tips. Sensation exploded through her and she lost time and any sense of propriety. Her careful, practiced kisses gave way to mindless hunger, driving her tongue against his, her body pressed hard to his own. Groaning, she shrugged the nightgown off her arms and then slid them around his neck.

His cock was huge and firm against her. Will bit her lip, then her chin, sliding his mouth down her throat. Lena threw her head back and moaned as he bit his way down her sensitive flesh.

"God, you taste so fuckin' good," he snarled.

Arching her back, she dug her hands into his silky hair. His mouth rasped over her nipple, teeth grazing the sensitive bud. Lena's eyes went wide, her hips jerking involuntarily. It felt so good. Heat speared through her, sinking its claws into her stomach, and lower… She couldn't stop herself. Her body seemed owned by someone else. A creature of need. Of frenzied hungers. Thrusting her breast into his mouth, she raked her nails across his shoulders, through his hair, clenching wet fistfuls of it as his mouth wreaked havoc on her body.

Wild, amber eyes met hers and Will dragged her head back, suckling the tender skin of her throat, his teeth sinking into the smooth curve of her shoulder. The hair on his chest rasped against her breasts and

Lena cried out, grabbing one of his hands, sliding it lower, over her thigh and under her nightgown. She needed him to touch her. Needed…something.

She writhed in a torment of embarrassment and desire as his palm ground between her thighs.

"Don't stop," she whispered, running her hands through his hair. She was so close… To what, she didn't know, but if he stopped right now, she'd kill him.

An enormous clatter of sound broke through her concentration. Will stiffened, his fingers stilling.

Lena dragged his face back to hers, shaking her head. "Just a drone," she whispered, licking at his mouth and tasting blood again. "Just the servants."

"Lena." He caught her wrists, withdrawing his mouth from hers. "*Lena!*"

"Don't go."

"I'm sorry." He looked up at her, his voice hoarse with desire, eyes wild with need. "This were a mistake."

The nervous anticipation faded. Lena caught his wrist as he pushed away from her and sat up. "A what?"

"A mistake," he repeated harshly, forcing her grasping hands away.

He couldn't have struck her a firmer blow. She yanked the ruins of her nightgown to her breasts and stared at him, despair aching in her chest. He couldn't do this to her again.

Taking a step back from the bed, he fumbled for his shirt. "I have to go." That insane gleam was still in his eyes.

"Will," she whispered, clinging to her torn nightgown. "You don't have to go. Nobody would hear us. Nobody would ever know—"

The look he gave her was raw, ragged. "I *have* to go. I'm sorry."

And then he was gone, the wind and the rain tumbling into the room, lightning flashing against the casing.

Fifteen

"ANYTHIN' ON YOUR MIND?" BLADE ASKED.

Will smashed another fist into the punching bag, earning a grunt from Blade. He followed it up with a left-right-left combination, his knuckles burning. "Not a thing," he grunted, unleashing an uppercut that drove the bag—and Blade—back a foot.

"Hold." Blade held up a hand, breathing hard. "Need a moment. You bin at this an 'our. Not all of us 'as the stamina these days."

Will raked a hand through his hair. He was barely winded. And still on edge. The memory of Lena's lithe little body was imprinted on his skin. He'd spent half the night with a cock-stand, unable to keep his mind on his job. Rip had been prowling the rooftops of the rookery with him, keeping an eye on things. Finally, the other man had told him to buy a whore and get his mind back on duty before stalking off in disgust.

No woman. Not for him. He should never have gone to her last night. Never given in to the temptation.

He needed to ease the pressure the only way he knew how. A safe way.

"You want a bout in the ring?"

"Absolutely not." Blade looked up from where he was bent over, his hands on his knees. "Don't know what's set you off this mornin', but I ain't goin' anywhere near those fists today."

Will turned, snatching at his towel. He loosened his collar and dragged the towel over the back of his neck. The urge to ask Blade for advice was nearly overwhelming. But Blade had his own worries, his own concerns. The last thing he needed was Will telling him he'd nearly lost his mind last night and fucked his wife's sister. Or about the curious letter he'd found on Lena and the threat of Colchester.

Neither of them could afford to have Blade drawn into a confrontation with the Echelon.

Blade raked his light brown hair out of his eyes. It seemed to be darkening with every passing day, courtesy of Honoria's vaccinated blood. Will scowled. He'd been the one Blade had turned to when he feared he was close to becoming a vampire; the one who was supposed to kill him before that happened. He could thank Honoria for taking away the burden of that heavy task, but now another problem loomed.

Straightening up, Blade sighed. "Don't look at me with those bloody eyes. Fine. Mebbe a quick bout. Just remember, I ain't whoever's been givin' you grief."

Will kicked off his boots and stepped onto the soft carpeting, tossing his shirt over a nearby chair. Blade stripped down too, rubbing at his knuckles. Though shorter than Will by nearly a foot, he was lean and well-muscled—and dangerously quick. There wasn't a trick he didn't know, and no sign of the knife wound he'd taken. The craving virus had healed it completely.

"Ain't seen much of you this week," Blade said, drawing his fists up.

"Been busy."

Blade stepped forward with a right hook that Will bobbed out of the way to avoid. "Who is she? You've never 'ad a woman as I can recall."

"Not got one now." He ducked a tricky combination and slammed his fist forward, under Blade's guard.

Blade staggered back, grinding his teeth together. "Fine. Let's just pretend you're strung up tighter 'an a lute for no reason. Only thing as leads to that is woman trouble."

Will ducked another right hook and stepped straight into Blade's left fist. The punch snapped his head back, but it lacked the force it once had. Years ago, Blade'd been able to take him down to the mats at nearly every session. Now he was lucky if he could do it once a month.

Will shook his head and dodged a foot that Blade snapped toward his face. He barreled forward, his shoulder driving into Blade's midriff and his arms wrapping around him. Both of them went down hard.

Blade locked his legs around his waist and flipped him. Will took another punch to the face and tasted blood. Kicking Blade off, he rolled to his feet and wiped his mouth.

"You're gettin' slower."

Blade's eyes narrowed and he drove a fist into Will's side. The breath expelled from Will's chest and he grunted, avoiding the next blow by an inch.

"Slow enough?" Blade snarled.

Will looked up, his blood boiling around his ears. "You have to stop drinkin' her blood."

The words fell into the suddenly silent room.

"What the 'ell do you mean by that?" Blade asked, his hands lowering.

Cursing the reckless urge that had made him blurt it out, he shook his head. "Naught."

"Aye, you do. You know exactly what you mean." Blade stared at the back of his hands, stretching out his fingers. "Me skin's gettin' darker. Me hair too. And I'm gettin' weaker. Weak and slow." Barking a laugh, he ran his hands through his hair. "Three years ago I'd 'ave killed to be more human. They says you ought be careful what you wish for." Sucking in a deep breath, he admitted, "I've only bin takin' enough of her blood for her not to be suspicious. The rest I drink cold, out o' the icebox. Honoria thinks me CV levels have reached a plateau." He looked down. "If the Echelon finds out, we're dead."

Will nodded. The Devil of Whitechapel's reputation was the only thing keeping them out of the rookery. If they thought he had a weakness, they'd be on him like a pack of dogs.

"How long 'ave you known?"

"A year. Once I started beatin' you regular-like, I began to wonder," Will replied.

"Shit." Blade turned around and stalked off the mats. "I bin thinkin', maybe I oughta go back to drinkin' normal blood for a bit, get me CV levels up. But 'ow do I tell 'er that? She's obsessed with curin' me."

Will followed him, his muscles still distended. He

wanted more work in the ring before Lena arrived for their lesson—if she arrived—but it was clear Blade was done with it. "The last thing I can offer is advice on women."

Blade barked a laugh. "God's truth." He snatched his shirt up and tugged it over his head. Unlike Will, his skin was dry. A blue blood didn't sweat.

"But you don't need to worry 'bout the Echelon. You ain't the only blue blood we got now. There's Rip and Charlie. And me." Will picked up his towel.

"And what'll the Echelon see? A rogue blue blood with a mech arm, a boy strugglin' to control his blood urges, and a beast that ought to be caged."

It was the truth, but it still rankled. Will slung the towel over his shoulders and hung onto both ends. "Might be true. But remember you ain't alone. They come for you and they've got to go through me first."

"You won't be here forever."

Will stiffened. "Didn't know I were leavin'."

Blade gave him a knowing look. "You need more than this, Will. I think you're just startin' to figure that out yourself."

Will opened his mouth to retort, but Blade's head cocked. Will heard the sound the second after. Skirts. Swishing on the stairs.

"Honoria." Blade looked around guiltily. "She can't know."

"She ain't no fool."

"Not yet," Blade snarled and moved to open the door. "Not 'til I work somethin' out."

Will turned, dragging the towel over his chest. Behind him, the door opened and Honoria's scent bled into the room. With a slight aftertaste of honey-suckle. His gut clenched. Lena. Directly on Honoria's heels. She'd come for the lesson.

A part of him hadn't expected her to show up. Not after last night. With guilt and desire burning a ragged hole in his insides, he wiped the scowl from his face and reached for his shirt.

"Goodness," Honoria murmured to Blade. "Is that blood on your knuckles?"

"Aye. Will forgot to duck."

His gaze went straight past the pair of them. Lena hovered in the doorway, looking every inch the society lady in lemon yellow. Her hair was artfully curled over one shoulder, hiding the bite mark on her neck, and a jaunty little bonnet set off the gleaming highlights in her dark hair.

Lena's gaze dropped, darting over the shirt in his hands and his bare chest before she looked away. A frozen little smile was etched on her full mouth. Her defense, he realized. The way she hid from the world, from her own family even. From him.

Her confession the night before made his chest ache. He'd wanted to go after Colchester with an ax, but the sound of her pain tore something deep inside him. He'd crushed her close, trying to hold the hurt away, but it was bone deep.

Alone. She'd been alone through all of it. Unable to tell her family—to burden her sister. Keeping that pretty little smile fixed in place as if nothing had ever happened when deep inside the wound festered and grew.

He tore his shirt over his head as Honoria lifted

on her toes and pressed her lips affectionately against
Blade's. It was too tempting right now to grab her by
the shoulders and ask her where she'd been when Lena
was lying bleeding in an alley. He knew it wasn't her
fault; circumstances had been what they were then,
but the *fury* in him didn't recognize that. Instinct
fought logic and he'd been too long a wolf at heart not
to go with his gut. He had to get out of here.

"Where are you going, Will?" Honoria asked,
catching his movement out of the corner of her eye.
The smile she wore was almost the same as Lena's, but
far more genuine.

"Got a lesson with Lena."

Lena's head jerked up and crimson infused her
cheeks. She looked him in the eye, her chin tilted with
icy disdain. Cool. Untouchable. Carefree.

With the razor edge of hurt souring her scent.

"Don't you want to know about that letter you
brought me?" Honoria asked. "I've made some progress with the code."

The brief flash of color drained out of Lena's face
and her eyes widened in disbelief.

"Later," he said. "After me lesson."

Honoria murmured something to Blade as he strode
to the door. Lena leaped out of his way as if afraid he'd
actually touch her. *Too late for that, sweetheart.* He'd had
his hands, his lips, his teeth all over her.

And it couldn't happen again.

Her presence drove him right to the edge and
threatened to shove him off. She was too dangerous,
too rousing. Even last night he'd come back from the
fury of passion to see the bite marks and bruises all

over her pale skin. Verwulfen had walked through
fire and lost arms and legs in such a state without even
realizing. The fury, the wild, drove him to actions he
couldn't remember, let alone control.

There would be nothing worse than seeing her
blood on his skin. Or fear in her eyes. As much as
he wanted her—as much as he always had—he could
never trust himself.

And then there was the threat of the loupe itself.

Taking a deep breath, he offered her his arm.
"Comin'?"

This was all he would ever have of her. Stolen
touches, stolen glances. And the desperate, longing
ache in his chest and cock.

"Of course." Resting her gloved fingertips lightly
on his arm, she followed him out the door.

They'd taken barely three steps before Lena
wrenched her hand off his and spun to face him. "You
told her?"

"Not 'ere." Not with Blade's hearing.

Anger stiffened her shoulders. Seizing a fistful of her
skirts, she swept ahead of him. "Where to?"

Considering her question, he placed a hand on
the small of her back and directed her toward the
kitchen. "The yard. Wait for me there. I've somewhat
for you."

Dark eyes glared back over her shoulder in suspicion. "What is it? This is wasting valuable time, Will.
You did well the other night, but there are a few
things I need to go over with you."

"This is important."

After a searching gaze, she threw up her hands and

sighed. "Why not? Go and fetch it then. The sooner we're done, the sooner I can return home. I've got to get ready for the dinner Leo's hosting."

He'd hurt her last night. And done it deliberately. For a moment he wanted to step forward, catch her wrist, and tell her he'd been wrong, that he was sorry. To lift her face to his and kiss her until she was gasping for breath again, her body turning molten under his touch.

But perhaps it were better if she *were* angry with him. For the both of them.

Waiting until she'd turned and departed for the yard, he thundered up the stairs and fetched the small bag he'd left in Blade's sitting room. By the time he arrived in the yard, Lena was pacing, her arms crossed under her breasts and a sad, pensive little look on her face.

When she saw him, the expression melted as if it had never been there. With a disdainful lift of one eyebrow, she glanced at the bag. "I can't accept any personal items. They're not the sort of things a man gives a woman he's not courting." Her tone turned frosty. "We wouldn't want any more *mistakes* of intention, now would we?"

Perhaps giving her a pistol in this mood was tantamount to suicide.

He bit his tongue and dragged a small Hessian sack out of the leather bag. "Bought this for you. I ain't finished tinkerin' with it, but the sooner you learn to use it the better."

"What is it?"

He opened the sack. The pistol gleamed against the

rough cloth, the mother-of-pearl inlay fracturing the weak sunlight into a half-dozen rainbows.

"A pistol?" she said stupidly. "You're giving me a pistol?"

He caught her hand and eased the handgrip into it, closing his fingers around hers. "Small enough to fit in your reticule. You ever fired one?"

"Don't be absurd." Her dark eyes widened. "When on earth would I have ever used a pistol?"

"Honoria knew how to use one."

"Father taught her. He had no time for me."

Will stroked his thumb over her gloved knuckles. "Why?"

"I was never clever enough to understand his work or half of what he said. He was a famous inventor. We had little in common."

"You're clever. All that tinkerin' with clocks."

"A useless hobby." She lowered the pistol. "He wouldn't have been impressed. He would have been able to do it himself in half the time I could. You don't understand."

"Don't I?" The quietness of his words made her look up. "I couldn't do it. I used to watch you playin' on the rug with all them scattered pieces, puttin' them back like they was a puzzle. Baffled me."

"Yes, but you have other talents," she replied. Somehow he didn't think she'd realized that he was still stroking her hand. "You're strong and not afraid of anything. You could kill a man with your bare hands." Something dark came into her eyes. Shadows that made his hackles rise. "You could kill a blue blood. I envy you, you know?"

"With this you can be strong. You can be fearless."

Her rancor faded. She looked at the pistol, seeing it with new eyes. "Do you think I could kill a blue blood with this?"

He tried to ignore the way her words stirred his temper. "When I'm finished with it. I'll modify it like your father done with Honoria's pistol. She taught me how to make them firebolt rounds. I've seen 'em take a blue blood's head off before. Explodes like rotten melon."

Lena shivered. "That sounds dreadful."

"You only have to use it once."

A strange light came into her eyes. She was picturing it. Picturing Colchester's head exploding as the smoke from the pistol cleared. "Teach me," she demanded.

Will faced the yard. It was brick, the walls that enclosed it almost eight feet high. Puss, the enormous mangy cat that considered Blade his servant, strolled along the wall, keeping an ugly green eye on them.

Ivy clung to two of the walls and a scrolled iron gate cut into the brick. Little pots of herbs and flowers gave it a sense of warmth, signs of Esme trying to turn the warren into some semblance of a home.

He rolled a wine barrel up against the far wall, then fetched one of the old milk bottles that Esme had set out for collecting. "Here," he said, setting it on top of the barrel. "We'll practice with this."

"But won't people worry?"

"In the rookery?" He cocked a brow. "People hear gunshot at the warren and they'll turn and walk the other way. Fast. Just in case they get caught up in whatever mess they think's spillin' over."

Lena aimed the pistol wildly in the direction of the barrel. "How do we start?"

"With bullets," he said, unable to take his gaze off her. He'd put that smile on her face. Chased the shadows from her eyes. Reaching into his pocket, he produced a handful. "And by learnin' each part of the pistol's mechanisms."

The wild light in her eyes was intoxicating. He fumbled with the bullets and placed one in her outstretched palm. She was oblivious to his breathlessness, peering at the pistol as though wondering what to do with it. He'd never seen her like this outside of the bedroom last night. So alive. So passionate. Almost exuberant with delight.

Fearless.

He wanted to keep that look in her eyes forever. Colchester had threatened to snuff it out, but he wouldn't let the man. He'd kill him first.

Lena felt his stare and looked up. The glow faded a little. "What is it?"

Not yet forgiven. Perhaps he never would be. Will sucked in a breath and gestured at the pistol. "You're holding it wrong. Here. Let me show you."

He'd protect her. Or teach her to protect herself.

From Colchester.

From the world.

From himself.

～

Honoria swept her skirts to the side and nestled in her husband's lap. Blade leaned back in the armchair, watching her with a knowing look in his eye.

"What 'ave you got planned?" he muttered, a smile curling his lips.

"Nothing," she replied, toying with his collar. Running a finger down his shirt, she tried to look innocent as the texture changed from silk to the rougher velvet of his waistcoat. He'd never outgrown his love of gaudy materials, despite her guiding influence. And she found she quite liked it. Where once the embroidered red waistcoat would have made her lift an eyebrow in sheer bewilderment that someone could truly wear such a thing, now it was as familiar to her as the sight of his face.

And the texture of it, the feel of the velvet and the roughened threads of embroidery against her skin... That was something she'd grown far too fond of.

"Really?" he drawled, snagging her wrist. "I know when that devious little mind's tickin'. I can practic'ly hear the cogs—"

An explosion of sound shattered the silence.

Honoria tumbled into the armchair as Blade leaped for the window, her foot striking the tea service and sending a cup tumbling. It smashed, porcelain shattering across the floor.

"What is it?" she cried, her slippers crunching on the pieces as she sat up. "Are we under attack?"

Blade yanked aside the curtain of her laboratory's window, his face grim and his hand straying to one of the razors he carried at his belt. Then he leaned closer to the glass, a frown dawning. "Bloody 'ell."

Another gunshot sounded. Honoria jerked to her feet and hurried to his side. His stance relaxed, calming the erratic beat of her heart. If Blade wasn't concerned, then neither was she. She trusted his instincts implicitly.

"What?" She lifted on her toes, trying to see. The window ledge hindered her, pressing into her waist. One too many crumpets of late, she suspected. After the months she'd spent starving herself to feed Lena and Charlie, Blade had taken it upon himself to fatten her up, to good effect. He hated the thought that she'd once been one step removed from selling her blood to the Drainers on the street out of sheer desperation.

With an amused smile, he directed her gaze to the yard below. "Your sister's tryin' to murder a milk bottle. I suspect it'll survive some'ow."

Honoria peered closer, pressing her face against the window. She could barely see for Will's broad shoulders. His body was curved around Lena's, his hands on her hips as he showed her the proper stance. Taking her sister by the wrist, he lifted the pistol, staring down the length of Lena's arm. Lena was not watching the target at all, her feelings written all over her face as she stared up at him.

"Oh."

Blade swung her up into his arms with a laugh. "Now where were we?" He swept her back to the armchair and settled her in his lap.

Honoria straddled him in an entirely unladylike manner, her gaze straying to the window. "But—"

"No." He caught her chin and turned her face to his. For once he looked entirely serious. "It were your decision to let them at this for once. She's older now. Old enough to deal with 'er own consequences. And you said you trusted 'im."

"Do you?" she asked bluntly. He knew Will far better than she ever would.

Blade stroked the back of his fingers against her throat. "'E won't ever mean to 'urt 'er."

"But if he does?" She'd never forgive herself.

"We been o'er this." His green eyes met hers. "We tried to separate 'em once and it were disastrous." He paused for a deep breath. "I know she's your sister, luv. But I can't lose 'im. Not again. I'm nearly there. 'E's thawin' to me. Spent more time under this roof in the last week than 'e's done in a month."

"For her lessons," she replied quietly.

"For her." He kissed her cheek. "Don't worry so much, luv. Will's verwulfen. He'd die before 'e ever 'urt someone 'e considered 'is."

"Then why were you so wary about them at the start? Why did you warn him away from her?"

Another light kiss against her lips. She knew him well enough to know when he was trying to distract her. "Blade," she warned, shoving at his chest.

"Ain't nothin' much. Just an ole story I once 'eard."

Honoria gave him her direst look and he held his hands up in defeat.

"It's a Scandinavian law. They says no verwulfen can ever mate with a 'uman. On pain of death."

"That's all you know?"

He nodded.

"What a strange custom," she said. "I wonder why they'd make a law like that?"

"You can ask 'em if you want."

She considered that thought. "I believe I will."

Sixteen

THE HEAT OF HIS BODY IMPRINTED ITSELF ON HER SKIN.
Lena swallowed hard, lifting the pistol and staring
blindly at the target. How on earth did he think she
could focus with him pressed against her like this?
Her bustle was poor defense; even the corset did little
to still the hard feel of his body. Especially when the
memory of that body pressed against hers last night
kept playing over and over in her mind.

*His mouth on her breasts, teeth tugging at her nipples.
Callused hands sliding between her legs and pressing the heel
of his palm to the wetness there.*

"...through the sight like this... Here... Ease your
finger over the trigger..." His breath warmed her ear.

Lena pulled the trigger with a soft groan. Dust
showered off the brick wall.

"Don't worry," Will muttered. "You'll get it."

She wanted to hurl the bloody thing at the milk
bottle. Maybe she'd have better chance of hitting it.

With a growl of disgust—and frustration—she turned
and shoved it at him. "I've had enough. We've been at
this for nearly an hour and my aim's growing worse."

"You'll get it—"

The excitement of the pistol had long since worn off with his nearness. It only served to remind her of last night, and the mistake, as he called it. Her body was flushed with heat and her head had begun to pound. "I think I'm coming down with a chill. And you still haven't explained why you told Honoria about my letter. Don't think I've forgotten about that."

Will's gaze shuttered. "I've no head for codes meself."

"So you involved my sister?" she demanded. "My insatiably curious sister who can't help sticking her nose into other people's business?"

"I didn't have a choice." A hint of anger flared in his eyes. "If you'd told me what you were involved in from the beginnin', I wouldn't have had to resort to drastic measures."

"So this is my fault?"

A strangled sound came from his throat. "I ain't sayin' it's your fault. I just wish you'd told me. Damn it, Lena. I'm tryin' to help you. Do you know what it were like, seein' that message and knowin' you'd got yourself in trouble? That you wouldn't tell me how to deal with it? How to help you?"

"I never asked for your help. I can handle this." Somehow. She crossed her arms over her chest, not quite able to meet his eyes. She'd told him what she could.

"I don't care if you want my bloody help or not, you're gettin' it." He clutched her by the arms, grimly determined. "No matter where you go, I'll be watchin'. I ain't lettin' no one near you. Not Colchester. Not the humanists. Not the Nighthawks."

"Then why are you so determined to teach me how to use a pistol?"

His eyes flickered to the amber-bronze of the wolf and back. "The only reason I won't be there is if I'm dead," he said quietly. "You're the last line of defense. I ain't goin' to leave you without a weapon or the means to use it."

The words were chilling. "No." The thought of him lying at her feet, the warmth drained from his body, was almost enough to undo her. This was exactly what she hadn't wanted. The reason she'd tried to keep him from discovering her secrets. She gripped his shirtsleeves in distress. Damn her resolve to keep a distant attitude today. This was his death he was speaking about. "I wish I'd never told you."

She should have kept lying to him, kept him in the dark. But she'd been vulnerable last night, made so by revealing the secrets of Colchester's attack. The feel of his arms around her had undone her. She'd never been able to share the attack with anyone, or grieve for the hurt it had caused. She'd locked it up deep inside and pretended nothing was amiss.

"Too late now."

Too late... Perhaps. Lena shook her head. She had to find some way to contain this disaster. "If you're going to involve yourself—"

His eyes gleamed. "There ain't no 'if' about it."

"*If*," she repeated, "I let you involve yourself...then you will do so at my command. I mean it, Will. We work together—under my direction—or I'll cut all ties and stop this lunacy in its tracks. That means you don't breathe a word of this to Honoria or Blade. I don't want anyone else involved. It's bad enough that you are. I don't want anyone's blood on my hands."

He scrubbed at the roughened stubble on his chin. No matter how often he shaved, he always seemed to have the shadow of growth along his jaw. "What do you mean by workin' under your direction?"

Lena let out a ragged breath. She hadn't been certain he'd agree. "I make the decisions. You don't go off on your own"—a sure way to get himself killed—"unless I say so. I need to work out what the humanists intend. I didn't fully understand the consequences of what I chose to do. Damn it, Will, I was so angry. I didn't ask enough questions. I don't think I wanted to know. And now I'm involved and I don't know exactly what I'm involved in." She took a deep breath. "I need to work that out before I do anything else. I know what they stand for—the abolition of the blood taxes, equal rights for man, and a voice to vote with. I just don't know how they intend to go about that anymore."

A swift arch of his eyebrows. "Settin' fire to the drainin' factories ain't goin' to achieve that."

Nor would destroying this treaty. "Yes, well, Mr. Mandeville seemed certain it was some sort of guerrilla group within the whole." A slight pause. Just who had threatened her? The legitimate humanists or one of the rebellious ones? "Do you agree to my terms?"

"Aye. I'll do your biddin'," he finally said. "On one condition."

"What type of condition?"

"I'll give you control of this. But if the situation turns nasty or looks dangerous, then you'll shut your pretty little mouth and listen to me." Lena opened her mouth to protest, but he pressed his forefinger against her lips, halting the stream of words. "No," he said firmly. "It ain't up for negotiation. Any sign of danger and I'm in charge, you understand?"

Her breath parted around his finger. Will's gaze dropped as though he felt it in other places and suddenly she did too. The heat of it made her squirm, her insides tying themselves into knots. The thought of tying herself to him, letting him dog her footsteps, was suddenly an unbearable agony.

And a necessary one.

Taking a step back, Lena put herself beyond reach of his hands—those treacherous, tempting hands—and smoothed her skirts. The simple action washed the emotion from her thoughts, and most likely her face. She had no choice in this matter. If she didn't agree he would only find another way to hobble her. At least this way she would be in control. Most of the time. "You're as stubborn as a bull," she muttered. "Fine. I agree."

"If you break your word you'll regret it," he said softly.

Mutiny flared. "I already do."

❧

Three exhausting hours later Will handed her up into the steam carriage she'd arrived in. Lena settled against the plush velvet seats, barely noticing the steady jostle of the engine.

Hovering outside the carriage, he cast a swift glance around at the darkening streets. "Here," he said, tugging a small paper-wrapped package from his waistcoat. "I didn't just buy you the pistol."

Lena stared at the box in her gloved hands. Will wiped his hands on his trousers and shoved them deep into his pockets. The action only strained the material over his thighs, something she tried not to notice.

"What is it?" she asked, rattling the box.

"Open it."

Tugging at the brown string that tied the package, she couldn't ignore his sudden tension. He leaned against the carriage, one hand on the open door as he watched her play with the strings. She had some mind to draw the moment out, to watch his unease grow, but there was no point. Those were the type of games she'd played with him as a foolish young girl.

Tearing apart the paper, she unearthed a small red velvet box. A gold crown was embossed in the material. She knew exactly where it had come from. Most young ladies did. "Will?" she said breathlessly. "I told you I couldn't accept personal items."

His warm hands slid over hers, forcing the box apart. "Consider it practical then."

One last dying ray of sunlight gleamed through a blood red ruby. She almost snapped the box closed. Almost. "I never asked you what you were doing in a jeweler's." She shook her head. "I can't. It's too beautiful. Too expensive."

Will fetched it out, the simple gold band tumbling into his hand. Engraved filigreed thorns wrapped around the ruby, holding it in place. "See here?" He flicked one of the thorns and it sprang out, surprisingly sharp.

She reached out to test it with her finger and he snatched her hand away. "It's a poison ring, Lena. Took me ages to find a jeweler who had one." Leaning close, he glanced at the driver and whispered in her ear. "Full of a hemlock concoction that'll incapacitate a blue blood for a few minutes. How long depends on how old he is, how much the cravin' virus has overtaken him."

He was giving her so much more than a ring. Another weapon. Another means to defend herself. Lena swallowed hard, staring at his face as he demonstrated how the ring would work.

"This must have cost a fortune."

Will shrugged. "I don't spend much. Never 'ave."

"Will, I can't."

He eased the thorn back into its slot, then closed her fingers over it. That stubborn look she was starting to know so well crept over his face. "It ain't open to discussion."

"Is that how you think you're going to stop me from arguing from now on?"

A rare smile softened his lips.

Lena sighed. "Fine. I'll take it." Slipping her glove off, she slid the beautiful ring over her finger. "Thank you."

"Saves me from worryin'."

Lena stared into the ruby's facets. He wouldn't worry if he didn't care, would he? Her blood heated at the thought. *Don't.* She clenched her fist, hiding the ring from sight. *Don't think this is any more than it is.*

Raking a hand through his hair, he looked around. "About last night—"

The warmth drained out of her face. "No," she snapped. "You made it quite clear what last night was about."

"Lena, I need to explain—"

"I don't want to hear it." She turned away, shoulders stiff and face frozen as she smoothed her skirts. "I understand that I made a fool of myself. It won't happen again."

"Lena, you—"

"A gentleman would keep his mouth shut now," she reminded him, falling back on her lecture tone. Anything to hold herself together.

Will stared at her, his gaze an intimate touch she refused to meet. "Very well," he said softly.

"I should be going. It's growing late. And there's that dinner I must attend."

"You're goin' out?"

"Briefly. Then I'll get back to work on Mr. Mandeville's commission. I need to finish the interior clockwork of the transformational. I'm so very close. There's no need for you to check on me tonight. I promise I won't get into any trouble."

He considered her words for a long moment. Then reached inside his pocket again. "I want you to keep this on you at all times," he said, pulling out a whistle. It hung on a fine gold chain and he slipped it over her head, then tucked it into the bodice of her dress as though he barely noticed the shuddering intake of her breath "It makes a sound you won't 'ear, but it'll alert any blue bloods—or me—in the vicinity if you need help." Stepping back, he shut the carriage door and nodded at the driver. "I'll call on you tomorrow before the...the..."

"The balloon launch," she reminded him. "In Hyde Park. With the Scandinavians."

"Right." Will grimaced. "We don't have to go up in one of them?"

"Afraid of heights too?"

"I'm goin' to ignore that." He let go of the carriage and stepped back, shooting her a direct look—and a reminder. "No trouble tonight, Lena."

"Would I get into trouble?"

"You're a bloody magnet for it."

Seventeen

A RUBY. HE'D BOUGHT HER A RUBY.

Lena held her bare hand out. She couldn't stop looking at it, watching the play of light through the polished gem. It was the size of her littlest fingernail. She'd seen bigger. A dozen times over in the Echelon, where they liked to drape their thralls in jewels to indicate the status of their masters. But for Will to have bought her something like this made it more precious than the largest diamond in the world.

Closing her eyes, she leaned her head back against the seat. What was she going to do? How could she keep her heart safely locked away when he did things like this for her? For it was becoming dangerously apparent that her feelings for him were growing.

Dabbing at the perspiration across her brow, she sighed. From the pounding in her head, she was in for a good cup of willow bark tea when she got home.

A sudden jolt threw her across the seat.

Lena snatched at the carriage strap and glanced out the window. They'd stopped. The driver was one of Leo's men, well skilled in the use of the horseless steam-driven carriages. Though they'd barely left Whitechapel behind, the roads weren't bad and nobody would dare attack her this close to Blade's turf. Every man and woman in the rookery knew who the gilded hawk on the carriage belonged to. Blade had declared Leo safe passage to his realm. The cost of crossing his word was death.

"Coachman?" she called as the carriage careened to a halt. "Henry?" There was no sign of the footman riding on back as she glanced out the window. "What's going on?"

Silence greeted her. Considering it was early evening, the streets were frightfully deserted.

From the shadows of a nearby alley, a lambent blue eye suddenly lit up. Lena shrank back into the carriage as a shadow detached itself from the rest. It rose to a height of nearly six feet, then suddenly unfolded itself further until it stood almost eight or nine feet. The eerie gaslit blue of its eye was reminiscent of a metaljacket.

But no metaljacket had ever stood so tall.

Locking the carriage door, she looked around for something—anything—with which to defend herself. Only a few forlorn cushions greeted her gaze. Will had taken the pistol back, determined to improve it for her.

The metal creature stepped out of the alley, moving in large, jerking strides. It *was* a metaljacket, the overlapping plates of its chest and abdomen gleaming with cold steel. The head was square, crowned with a demonic steel helm. A thin slit of glass in its throat was the only sign of any weakness, and behind the glass were a pair of eyes. Human eyes.

Lifting its massive fist, it swung a blow toward her. Lena shrieked and dove across the seat as glass from the window sprayed throughout the carriage. She tore the other door open and fell onto the cobbles, collapsing in a puddle of yellow skirts.

Something tugged in her hair. Reaching up, she found the fine gold chain and followed it to the whistle Will had hung around her neck. Hydraulic hoses hissed behind her and the carriage shuddered. Lena stuck the whistle in her mouth and blew.

There was no sound. Nothing but steel screeching as the carriage slowly tipped on its edge, the monstrous creature trying to turn it over.

Grabbing her skirts, she bolted out of the way. The carriage smashed onto the cobbles, exactly where she'd just been kneeling. Gasping for breath, she darted forward blindly and crashed into something solid and warm.

Hands caught her by the arms. Lena jerked back instinctively and tore free from a man's grip. A leering face came into view. He towered over her, wearing little more than a rough worker's jerkin and tight leather pants. A seeming arsenal of metal hung at his belt. She didn't take the time to look. Instead she turned and bolted back the way she'd come.

Men were everywhere. Ducking under snatching hands, she ran through a gauntlet of ragged, mismatched bandits.

Sound whirred behind her. "I've got 'er."

Lena screamed as something wrapped around her ankles. Pitching forward onto her face, she hit the cobbles hard. Pain tore through her lip and her lungs shrank to a quarter of their size. For a moment she couldn't breathe. There was a great, gaping vacuum in her chest and she sucked and sucked for air but none came. Then suddenly her lungs expanded and she dragged in a huge, rasping breath.

It hurt all the way through her.

The slow step of a pair of boots sounded on the cobbles behind her as someone made their way toward her.

"We oughta hurry, Mendici." A young boy, by the sound of him. "Can't keep the streets clear forever."

"Ain't nobody gonna cry hue, Jeremy." The giant laughed. "Not in these parts."

Lena's gaze fell on the whistle, lying on the ground in front of her. She snatched for it but a boot came out of nowhere and ground it beneath his heel.

The giant smiled at her. "Well, ain't you a pretty little puss?"

She tried to scramble to her hands and knees. Her skirts were wrapped firmly around her ankles by a weighted rope and she got nowhere for her efforts. Behind her a heavy metal boot stepped forward, hydraulics hissing.

"Rollins," the giant gestured. "Pick her up and let's get movin'."

"What'd she mean with that whistle?" A young lad with dirty cheeks came into view, his eyes darting nervously. "Weren't no noise from it." He looked at her. "What'd you mean with that whistle?"

Licking the blood from her split lip, she summoned a smile. She could barely see for the throbbing of her head. "You're in trouble now."

The metal automaton leaned down with a steely hiss, its enormous hand closing around her waist. "Got her," called an echoing voice from within. Then it straightened and she caught a glimpse of the man encased in the metal.

"Trouble?" Mendici looked up at her as she dangled precariously. "From whom? The Devil himself?"

Several men laughed.

"We know how to deal with the bleeders," one called.

"Stick 'em with a shiv coated in hemlock," another called, making a stabbing motion.

"Or a screamer."

"Set Rollins and Percy on 'em," another called.

The laughter swelled.

A shiver of unease ran through her. Far from being the threat it was, these men looked as though they'd relish the idea, and they sounded remarkably well prepared to handle it. If Will had heard the whistle, he'd be walking directly into an ambush. How she wished she'd never blown it.

"Come on, boys." Mendici gave her a wink. "Let's take her to see the master."

※

Will sat at the kitchen counter, watching Esme stir her stew. The smell of it made his mouth water. This was the one place that felt like home to him. He'd spent hours here over the years, dozing lightly in the corner whilst Esme went about her jobs.

When she'd first became Blade's thrall he'd found her presence disconcerting. Until that moment, the warren had been strictly all-male and he'd had little to do with women since his mother sold him to Tom Sturrett.

Esme had been grieving the loss of her husband, desperate straits forcing her to accept Blade's protection. It had been her that taught him to read and fed him good food when his body tried to outgrow him. Her that bandaged his cuts when his first forays into the rookery ended in fights—fights that he'd gone seeking.

He had little recollection of his own mother. Esme was as close as he was ever going to get.

"So," she murmured, tapping the wooden spoon against the pot and turning to face him. "What's going on between you and Lena?"

The question shouldn't have shocked him. There were no secrets in the warren, with four of them owning preternatural hearing. But he couldn't recall ever saying anything that might have given them fodder for rumor. "What d'you mean?"

Esme gave him a look. "William Carver, let's not pretend that I'm in any way stupid. Or blind. You wouldn't want to insult me, would you?"

"Ain't nothin' goin' on between her and I. And that's the way I intend to keep it."

With a speculative look on her face, she wiped her hands on her apron and crossed to sit beside him. "Why?" She slid a warm hand over his. "It's clear you have feelings for her, Will."

He scowled down at the scarred kitchen bench. "I can't, Esme."

"John felt the same, you know," she whispered with a sympathetic look in her green eyes. "He was afraid to hurt me. Afraid he couldn't control himself around me. We took our time, but it's worked for us."

Will rubbed the back of his neck. "Esme, it ain't that simple."

"Oh?"

"Rip's got the cravin'," he said. "Spread through blood to blood contact. The loupe's different. Spread by blood, by a man's seed…"

A knowing light came into her eyes.

"I can't ever be with her," he growled the words out. "I wouldn't subject her to a life like this. And that's if she survived the initial infection."

"Oh, Will—"

The door smashed open.

Will shoved Esme behind him. Rip glowered in the doorway, his gaze following the hand that had pressed her into the corner. A dark light came into his menacing eyes and Will jerked his hands away, holding them up in the air. If it came down to it, he could take Rip and they both knew it. But right now the man wasn't thinking. Ruled by his own personal demons, all he saw was another man touching his wife.

"Just protectin' her, Rip."

"What's wrong, John?" Esme asked.

"Heard a whistle." His gaze darted over the pair of them. "Where's Blade? Anyone missin'?"

Cold touched the back of Will's neck. "Where'd you hear it? How long ago?"

"Outside the wall. Near Old Castle Street. 'Bout ten minutes ago mebbe."

On the way to Aldgate.

Lena. Heat roared through him, blanking his

mind. He was moving before he thought about it, snatching the bladed half gloves off the bench and his hunting knife.

"Who is it?" Rip asked, his voice sounding as though it were distorted through glass.

Esme grabbed Will's arm. "It's Lena, isn't it?"

The next thing he knew, he was hauling himself up onto the gutters of the warren. The rookery stretched out in front of him, a maze of decrepit buildings and lean-tos. Taking a running leap, he headed for the wall that encircled Whitechapel.

Built fifty years ago, during the time of trouble when Blade had first come to the rookery, it stood nearly twenty feet high. More a symbol than a solid edifice, it had been constructed with whatever lay at hand, in order to keep the Echelon out.

Vaulting over the top of it, he dropped down onto a roof far below. Another jump and he was in the street.

People took one look at him and scattered. As he made his way to Old Castle Street, he saw a crowd hovered around something in the street. A glint of gilt caught his eye and his heart leaped into his throat. Shoving through the crowd, ignoring the cries, he staggered to a halt in front of the Caine carriage. It was tipped on its side, glass sprayed across the cobbles. Some enterprising sorts had already started trying to work the gilt free and the curtains were long gone.

Turning, he raked his gaze across the crowd, looking for someone he recognized. Bill the Tanner met his eyes and flinched. Will grabbed him by the collar.

"What happened here?"

"Dunno," Bill muttered, his breath stinking of gin and his mismatched eyes darting independently. "Weren't 'ere, guv. Didn't see nuthin'."

Will drew him up until they were face to face, letting the heat—the Beast—wash through his eyes. "Did you know I can smell it when a man lies? Think carefully, Bill, about whether you saw anythin' here."

"I can't," Bill sobbed. "They'll kill me. Said they'd do it if I breathed a word."

Will's fist tightened until Bill could barely breathe. "What makes you think I won't?"

Clawing at his collar, Bill's eyes boggled. "They got…a monster with 'em… A fire-breathin' monster! I can't. He'll roast me…like a leg o' lamb! Better you than them!"

"They took a young woman with them, didn't they? She's mine, Bill. My woman. And they took her." He forced his fist to open and dropped the man onto the cobbles before he killed him.

The urge to do so was almost overwhelming. The vein in his temple throbbed, his vision blanking at moments. Time and space became odd vignettes of sound and movement. Bill scrambled back across the cobbles and then the world blurred again.

Someone caught his wrist. He barely felt it. Looking down with a snarl, he stopped when he saw the young lad staring up at him with a face as white as a ghost.

"Don't hurt me da," he pleaded. "They went that way." Then he pointed toward the nearest alley, one that ended in a brick wall and a boarded tunnel into the old, abandoned ELU line.

The world came back, narrowing in with crystal precision on the boarded up tunnel. Of course.

"Undertown."

Eighteen

"Where are you taking me?" Lena demanded, as someone tore the blindfold from her eyes.

Blinking against the phosphorescent glare of the smuggler's lanterns they carried, she looked around. Despite the chill to the air, perspiration dampened her hair. Her head felt like it was packed full of cotton stuffing, especially her sinuses.

The tunnels stank of mold and stale air. The men were quiet and moved with confidence; they'd come this way often, she imagined.

A little quiver of fear ticked in her chest. The old abandoned tunnels of the Eastern Line were said to contain the ghosts of all those workers who had died when the tunnels collapsed. Some men had been crushed to death and others trapped in the darkness to slowly suffocate or starve. The ELU had given up on the scheme after it drove them into dun territory and nobody had ever bothered to see it finished. Slowly, year after year, the tunnels had been taken over by those enterprising enough to carve out a living below ground when the rookeries began spilling over.

People trying to hide from the Echelon or the Nighthawks for whatever reason, or those who were simply too poor to be able to rent one of the hovels above ground. She could only imagine how terrified they'd been to live here, with the whisper of ghosts and the very real presence of the Slasher gangs—those who strapped a man down on a gurney and drained him of his blood to sell to the draining factories.

Then three years ago the vampire had taken up residence here, glutting itself on everyone's blood until the tunnels were quiet again and there were even more ghosts to whisper. The vampire was gone, killed by Blade himself it was said, but the grim tunnels terrified her.

"Who are you?"

The man they'd called Mendici waved a hand in her direction. "Shut her up." He struck a flare stick against his leg and the burning phosphorescent glow lit up the pressing darkness. Holding it high, he took a cautious step forward, edging over the rail tracks. The tunnel opened into an enormous cavern, the rail tracks shearing off into nothing. Mendici kicked a rock over the edge and she listened quietly, barely breathing, waiting for it to hit the bottom.

A distant plop echoed up. Water. There was water down there.

Then something thrashed far below. Lena felt the blood run out of her face. "What is that?" A bead of perspiration raced down her throat into her bodice and she shivered.

"The Gatekeeper," the young boy muttered at her side. "Here, you be quiet now. There's other things in the darkness. You don't want to wake 'em now, do you?"

Lena stared at his pale, ghostly face and shook her head.

A steel cable stretched into the darkness. Mendici handed the flare stick to one of his men and pulled something out of his pocket. It looked like a metal rod with a hook on it. Snapping it open, he revealed a pair of handles, then he hung the hook over the cable and latched it tight.

Her gaze went straight to that yawning, gaping pit as she realized his intentions. No way. There was no way she was going over whatever hid in the depths of the waters.

Mendici snapped his fingers at her.

Lena shook her head but two of his men grabbed her by the arm and dragged her forward. Without ceremony, she was shoved against the burly giant's side and his arm slid around her hips.

"Rollins," Mendici called. "You'd best go back. Can't bring Percy over this. Take him home and grease him up. Or whatever you do with that bloody thing."

The gaslit eye of the automaton flared to life. Then it turned, clanking steps echoing back down the hollow tunnel.

"Ready for the ride of your life, luv?" Mendici grinned at her.

"No. I'm not. I won't."

He snatched a handful of her skirts and shoved her toward the chasm. Lena screamed, grabbing for his wrist. Her slippers danced on the edge of the cliff, pebbles crumbling beneath her feet as her horrified gaze met his.

"Choice is yours. You can either swim, or you can go over on this."

Her gaze darted to the tenuous handgrip. "Fine." She licked dry lips. "I'll go over."

Mendici hauled her back against his side. "You hold on tight then. Wouldn't want me to slip." With a nasty chuckle, he dragged her hard against him. Through her corset, she could feel the hard muscle of the man and reluctantly put her arms around his neck. He took back his flare stick and held it between his teeth, then put both hands on the handles. "Rearry?"

"No."

With another laugh, he leaped out into nothingness.

Lena screamed, burying her face in his shoulder as they hurtled toward the far side of the cavern. Air rushed past her ears, cooling her flushed cheeks, and her skirts whipped around her legs. It felt like forever, but within moments he was curling his feet up underneath him and landing with a jolt on a rocky ledge.

"Righto, boys. We're landed," he called.

Lena collapsed onto her hands and knees, her body shaking. She felt like she was going to cast up her accounts, the world still whirling around her.

"Buck up, luv. You're safe. For now." Mendici unsnapped his hanger and tucked it away again. He hauled her to her feet, then peered closer. "Here, you don't look so good."

"I'm not feeling quite myself."

He clutched her chin, then felt her cheeks with the back of his hand. "Christ, you're burnin' up."

"My head's been pounding all afternoon," she admitted. "I believe I'm coming down with a chill."

The flare stick lit his face with an eerie green, high-lighting the dark gleam of his good eye and the steel eye patch. Thought flickered behind his eye. "Aye, well don't come near me men. None of us need to be sick right now."

The young boy, Jeremy, came flying out of the darkness, his face alight with glee. He landed and staggered to a halt, then unsnapped his handle. "I'm done, boys!"

One after the other they came sailing through the darkness until only two remained on the far ledge. Mendici dragged a pocket watch out and checked the time, pacing restlessly on the edge of the ledge. Lena leaned against the cavern wall, too exhausted to do anything. There was no point in trying to escape. They'd run her down in seconds, and the idea of getting lost in these tunnels terrified her. Who knew what else lurked in the darkness, like the Gatekeeper?

A massive roar echoed through the tunnels. Mendici spun on his heel and squinted up into the dark.

"What was that?" the young boy asked. "Mendici?"

Mendici held up a hand to quiet him. Another roar shattered the stillness of the tunnels. The two men on the ledge above raced to hook their hangers onto the cable, glancing over their shoulders. In the tunnel, flares of orange light flickered and died.

"Rollins," Mendici grunted. He cast her a dark look. "Looks like them friends of yours decided to come play in our world. Hope you weren't too fond of 'em?"

Lena drew herself to her feet, leaning hard against the wall. *Will.* The source of that enraged sound was suddenly apparent. "Don't be so sure," she said, staring up. *Please be all right. Please don't be hurt.*

Silence fell. The two men on the ledge glanced over their shoulders, their movements slowing. A relieved smile flickered over one of their faces.

Then one of the men stiffened. He shouted something and jumped for the cable. His body arced out into the air erratically. Barely a second later, the second man made his leap, dropping his flare stick on the ledge behind him.

Lena found herself holding her breath. Could Will truly take on the monstrous Percy and survive? The Greek fire that the Spitfires used could burn through anything, and she'd seen the barrel of the flamethrower attached to Percy's mechanical arm.

A shadow detached itself from the mouth of the tunnel, becoming a man with familiar broad shoulders. Lena let out a shuddering breath. He was alive.

Will stepped up to the ledge, the phosphorescent gleam highlighting his singed shirt. The light cast a play of shadows over the stark bones of his face. There was something in his hand. He held it up; Percy's square head.

Mendici sucked in a breath. "Bring me the girl."

Someone shoved her toward him. He grabbed a handful of her hair and pushed her forward, her slippers teetering on the edge of the ledge. Lena froze, staring up into the darkness. Will had stepped forward too, fury and frustration playing over his features. Only fifty feet separated them, but it might as well be a mile.

"You want 'er?" Mendici roared. "Then come and get 'er."

Lena glanced up at the nasty little smile on his face. "No! Don't, Will! I'll be fine—"

A hand wrapped around her mouth, cutting off her words.

Will wrapped a meaty fist around the cable and swung out, a grim look of determination on his face. Lena's heart leaped into her throat. Damn him. Why wouldn't he listen to her? Her heart hammered against her ribs. If he was hurt trying to save her, she'd never forgive herself.

"Ready, Lowerston?" Mendici asked, watching Will swing hand after hand across the cable.

"Got him," someone muttered behind her.

A thin, tubular shape lifted out of the corner of her eye. Lena turned her head, Mendici's hand sliding from her mouth loosely. Five feet behind her, a man peered through the sight on a rifle.

She didn't think. She'd never reach him in time. Instead, watching his finger caress the trigger, she stepped in front of the rifle.

With a muttered curse he jerked the weapon up, an explosion of sound shooting into the darkened gloom of the cavern's roof. As soon as the bullet hit, it exploded, sparks cascading above like fireworks. A dozen screeching bats flew out of the shadows and a heavy silence fell, marred only by the sinuous stir of water far below.

Lena stared at the man with the rifle, her breath freezing in her chest. What the hell had she just done? If that had hit her, she'd be little more than pieces of flesh and viscera, scattered across the ledge.

"Are you insane?" Mendici roared, ripping her out of the way and shaking her.

Icy dread slithered through her veins. "No," she heard herself say, the words clear and distinct. Her knees gave out and Mendici let her drop to the ground.

"Reload!" he snapped at the rifleman, glancing sharply at Will as if to gauge his distance. "Bloody hell."

Lowerston fumbled for bullets, his fingers shaking. Mendici's nostrils flared. "Looks like I'll have to do this meself."

Dragging something out of his pocket, he held up a small metal cylinder. As his thumb pressed the button on top, she waited for the explosion.

Nothing came.

But Will lost his grip on the cable with one hand, his body jerking almost in pain. He clapped his arm over his ears and face, his body tucking up on itself. The other fist curled around the cable in an iron grip, his knuckles whitening.

"Come on, you bastard." Mendici muttered, staring at him with a glittering eye.

"He can't hold out for long," the young lad piped up. "Nobody's held up against a screamer before."

Will slowly straightened, the muscles in his body rigid. Teeth ground together, his eyes flaring wild, he reached for the cable with the other hand, each movement slow and precise, as if he had to force his body to work properly.

Come on, she whispered silently, her hands clenched at his side. Barely twenty feet away now.

"Bloody 'ell," Lowerston said, sounding slightly awed. "'E's doin' it."

"Not for long," Mendici snarled, snatching an ax off one of his men. He strode toward the edge of the ledge, fist curled around the wooden haft. Not that it would do much good against a verwulfen in the full grip of the battle-fury. "Time to meet the Gatekeeper."

He swung it—not at the heavy iron cable, as she'd expected—but at the timber pulley that held it rigged to the wall.

The timber sheared away, hitting the floor then jerking out into the gaping darkness of the chasm.

"No!" Lena screamed.

Will flew away into the darkness, his white shirt like a wraith. He hit the far side of the cliff, sliding several feet down the cable. Then he shuddered and plunged into the darkness below.

Seconds later—what felt like hours—she heard the splash as he hit the water and the hungry thrashing sound of whatever lurked below.

Nineteen

WILL CRAWLED OUT OF THE WATER WITH A SNARL, HIS
hands coated with grease and blood and a steel tentacle
in his fist. His ears still rang, and the pain in his cheek
told him he might have broken something. Fury
boiled in his blood, along with the creeping lassitude
of the aftermath of a rousing fight. He ignored it.

Forcing himself to his feet, he stared down at the
limp steel tentacle. Whatever the hell that had been,
it was vicious. He'd barely found himself in the
water before it was on him, steel limbs thrashing and
reaching for him.

He couldn't remember much of the fight—he
never could, really, beyond flashing images of sight
and sound—but he could vaguely recall the gaping
maw that sucked in water to fuel its steam-driven
core, and the razor-sharp threshing blades of its
teeth. Smashing his fist straight through the thin steel
sheeting of its body. The burning exhale of steam in
his face as he tore a tentacle off it, using the weakness
of the rivets to his own advantage.

That was where inventors made their fatal flaw with

the metal monsters and automatons they created. For a metaljacket, it was the hinge of their knees and arms; for the steel-squid, it was the segmented join of the tentacles to its body. Tear that apart and all you had was a wounded shell that flopped around like a turtle on its back.

Destroying it hadn't been without cost, however.

Will staggered against a stalactite and pressed a hand to his side. His fingers came away sticky, a result of those iron teeth. Every muscle in his body throbbed with the ache of the fall and the way the smooth surface of the water had felt like he plunged onto heavy cobbles.

He wanted to stumble to the ground and sleep away the hurt. A fatal weakness for his species. Almost unstoppable once they were in a full fury, barely cognizant of injury or pain, verwulfen dropped like stones after the excitement wore off.

Will wiped the blood out of his eyes and staggered forward. Couldn't sleep. Not yet. Lena was out there. He'd heard her scream as he plunged toward the water, heard the soul-shattering loss in her voice as she cried out.

Whoever had her—and he was starting to get an idea of their identity—they were going to wish they'd never dared touch his woman.

∽

They traveled along tunnels worn smooth from feet.

She saw none of it.

The men spoke and laughed amongst themselves, clapping Mendici on the back as though he were a hero.

She heard none of it.

She existed only in a world of dull color and muted sound, seeing Will tumble into the gloomy pit again and again.

He couldn't survive that. Could he? The thought made her feel ill, a heavy weight sitting on her chest until she was afraid she couldn't breathe. Oh God, what had she done? She'd blown that bloody whistle, afraid for her life, knowing that he would come for her and make everything safe for her again. But he hadn't. He wasn't invincible. No matter how quickly he could heal, how strong he was, he was only flesh and bone in the end, the same as she was.

I'll always come for you. But this time she was on her own, for Will was…lost. She couldn't think of the alternative or she'd break, becoming a blind, shivering thing, hovering in her own misery. She had to survive whatever was coming, had to find him, find out if…

She shook the thought away and looked up, trying to focus. Light bloomed ahead. A heavy iron door hung in the shadows, with a man guarding it. She glimpsed cold steel. His hand, a gauntlet of metal, with heavy, slatted plates to his elbow.

Mech work.

Cold etched its way down to her bones, but she felt strangely removed. To endure she'd wrapped away that part that was screaming in grief and forced her mind to work analytically. To examine, understand, find a weakness…

Mech. The word whispered in her head. *A mech.* Bound to the enclaves and forced to work out their contracts to pay for the technology that had given them life or limb. Less than human, the Echelon decreed. Kept out of sight and out of mind.

"Well met, brother," the guard said, stepping forward and clasping Mendici's arm. His curious gaze slid over her. "They're inside. Waiting. You weren't followed?"

"We *were*," Mendici replied. "The Gatekeeper's probably picking the remains of 'im out of 'is teeth."

Another stab to the heart. Lena sucked in a sharp breath. She couldn't go there, to that cold, empty place deep inside. Not yet.

The stranger nodded, running his gaze over the ragged group. "Get yourself something to warm your bellies. I'll take her through."

"I believe I'll come," Mendici announced, tucking his thumbs behind his belt. "I'm wonderin' as to what this is all about."

"Himself's in a curious mood," the stranger warned.

"I've as much a right to be there as 'im. I've as much a right as any free man."

"You can explain that to him. Come." The stranger gestured to her.

Shoving open the iron door revealed a room in the middle of all the tunnels. Crates were stacked floor to ceiling, and candlelight flickered, warming the shadows. Its glow stretched only so far, though. She couldn't see where the walls began. Only an endless maze of crates.

The murmur of voices drew them out of the darkness like a beacon. Mendici rapped at another door, his gaze dropping away. Not as confident as he appeared.

A slit in the door slid open and a single gray eye stared through. Then the slit slammed shut and the clicking of a lock sounded.

"You're late."

The voice was soft, melodic. A man used to the well-toned inflection of command. The door opened and light spilled through, blinding her for a moment.

"Had to take care of a little something," Mendici replied, stepping through.

Lena glared at his back. His dismissive words hurt. Will was more than a *little something*. Brave and strong and stubborn, he had more worth in his little finger than Mendici had in his entire body.

"This her?"

Lena felt the shove from behind as she stepped through the door. Her eyes slowly adjusted to the light. The room beyond held an enormous table ringed with twelve chairs and the remains of a meal. A pair of women looked up from the table, one sprawled with an arrogant grace in her chair and the other rifling through a sheaf of notes. Her hands were stained with ink, her eyes warm and dark with curiosity. She wore a pair of tight men's trousers and a white shirt cinched against her lush curves with a gray tweed waistcoat. A pair of magnifying goggles were pushed back on her coppery hair and her right hand was a metal gauntlet, the fingers moving with a delicate grace Lena had rarely seen. A gold pocket watch drew the eye to her breast, but Lena was certain the effect was unconscious.

Another mech.

The other woman wore a black leather coat, buttoned up the left breast with brass buttons. Gleaming epaulets crowned her shoulders, and her boots encased muscular calves. She flicked the ash on her cheroot, her catlike hazel eyes raking over Lena. One glance

and the cold gaze moved on, lip curling dismissively.
"You wasted all that effort on *this*?"

A man stepped out of the shadows, the same man
who'd answered the door. His hand curled over
the woman's shoulder, slightly possessive. "Patience,
Ingrid. That's no way to treat a guest." The voice
shivered across the skin. A man used to hypnotizing
people with that alone. A showman.

A patchwork coat framed his lean body. At first
glance the coat looked shabby and mean, but Lena
hadn't spent hours grinding her teeth in boredom over
her sewing for nothing. The coat was deceptively fine,
the patches quite deliberately placed, she was certain.
A stained cravat spilled from the open throat of his
shirt, and his black gloves were cut off at the fingers,
revealing the tanned skin of his fingers.

But that was not what drew her eye. A leather
strap held a monocular brass eyepiece over one eye,
his mouth hidden by a brass and leather half mask.
Together they obscured his face so that all she could
see was one piercing gray eye. His hair was the same
dark copper as the first woman's.

"A guest?" Lena demanded, shaking off her dull
wits. "Your hospitality is somewhat lacking. Who are
you? What do you want with me?"

"You wished to see Mercury, did you not?" His
hands spread wide, palms facing her.

The words stole the breath from her lungs.
"Mercury? You're Mercury?"

"And you, my delightful Miss Todd, are a rather
surprising little package." His fingers absently stroked
Ingrid's thick brown hair. "This is one of our little

pigeons," he murmured to his comrade. "A protégé of the resourceful Mr. Mandeville. And quite resourceful herself. She's the mind and hands behind our gift to the Scandinavian embassy."

The way he acted, the slight edge of mocking humor that curled over every word... It made her teeth grate. He'd kidnapped her from the streets when she would have gone willingly. If he'd simply asked, Will would be sitting in the warren, dining with the rest of her family.

Tears sprang into her eyes. The praise was meaningless, the entire *cause* was meaningless. She could summon nothing but grief. "Why the charade? Your men could have asked me to come. One mention of your name and I would have been willing." A dark glare at Mendici. "You've destroyed my guardian's carriage, knocked my footmen unconscious, and...hurt a man I consider a friend. Now you assume I should have some goodwill toward you remaining."

Mercury's fingers froze, the smile faltering. He glanced at Mendici as if in search of explanation.

"Her guardian's a bleeder," Mendici replied with a sneer. "If I could, I'd smash every one of his pretty little carriages. And your so-called friend, my dear, clearly weren't human. Not to have taken on Percy in such a way, or to cross that cable so swiftly." His lip curled. "I don't trust her."

"Yet you expect me to trust you," Lena retorted. "I don't think I want any further part of this. I thought the humanists wished to be equal, but you don't. You want to reverse the social order instead, to grind the Echelon and the blue bloods beneath your heel. To make of them slaves, or little better."

"To make them dead," Mendici snapped back.

"They're not all inhuman," she replied. "I have met some few who I consider trustworthy and heroic. My own brother-in-law is the Devil of Whitechapel and considers his men his family. My guardian is equally kindly and treats his thralls with respect—"

"See?" Mendici snarled to Mercury. "She's a friggin' bleeder lover! I'll bet she's whorin' for 'em. Daresay if we ever locate that man's body we'll find he's into the first cycle of the craving. Certainly didn't like the screamer none—"

Lena turned on him in a rage, her fists clenched. "Will is not a blue blood, you filth. If you had half his courage—"

"Enough!" Mercury roared. He pushed away from the wall and threw a dark glance at Mendici. "I believe I gave orders that you and your men were to seek a warm belly and bed. Why are you here?"

Mendici crossed his arms over his massive chest. "Some of the men are wonderin' about your latest orders. And the lenience you've shown the last batch of blue bloods we caught."

"You're questioning me?" The words were silky soft. Deadly.

"Me and the men, we don't like it none." Mendici scowled. He held up his mech hand. "You promised us revenge, for this. For those hell-spawned enclaves. We didn't risk our lives, lose our friends, to break out of the enclaves for nothing. I want blood. Blue blood. I want to see all their heads on bleedin' spikes." He pointed a finger at her. "Why's she so important?"

"Because she is a set of ears where we have none," Mercury replied.

Another sneer. Mendici took a warning step forward, his hand slipping to his side. When it came up, he was holding a pistol. "There's some as says you're growin' weak. Merciful. We've been talkin', me and the boys—"

A pistol retorted.

A small red hole bloomed in the middle of his forehead and, mouth agape, he slowly toppled backward. The clatter of his steel-plated jerkin as he hit the ground jarred her nerves.

Lena scrambled backward, her spine hitting the wall. The room was still as everyone in it turned tentative gazes toward the woman with the smoking pistol.

Her ink-stained hands didn't so much as shake as she lowered the weapon. Lips thinning, she gestured to Ingrid. "Get rid of him. See that the others understand what we do with those who speak of mutiny here."

The brunette ground her cheroot out and rolled to her feet. Lena hadn't realized until that moment how tall the woman was. Nearly a good inch on Mercury, with broad shoulders tapering to a narrow waist. Only the lush curve of her breasts and hips saved her from a masculine figure.

Wrenching Mendici up by his arm, she threw him over her shoulder with the same amount of effort Will might expend. "You're certain of this, Rosalind?" she asked. "The men liked him."

The petite redhead nodded sharply. "I cannot risk insubordination. Not now, when we're so close. Take him away." She glanced toward the masked figure leaning against the wall. "Leave us," she murmured.

His gaze flickered toward Lena.

"She wants to know if she can trust us," Rosalind replied to the unspoken question. Their gazes met. Held. "Perhaps a show of trust is what she needs."

With a flamboyant shrug of his shoulders, he stepped toward the door. "On your head, so be it. I'll go see if I can help Ingrid find out whose tongues have been flapping. And how far it's gone."

Two steps and he was through the door, with Ingrid on his heels.

It shut behind them and Lena turned to face the woman. They were much of a height and perhaps even age. Or perhaps not. Rosalind's pale skin bore the creaminess of youth and her tip-tilted nose gave her a permanently youthful appearance. Yet the command with which she had spoken was not that of someone untried.

You wished to see Mercury, did you not?

It was only now that Lena realized that the man had never directly referred to himself as such.

"You're Mercury, aren't you?"

Those plump lips pursed. "I'm not going to harm you." Rosalind slid the pistol into a holster at her hip with a dexterity and ease that Lena envied.

"Who was he? The man?"

"My brother, Jack. He is also Mercury. As is Ingrid at times. Mercury has worn many names and faces over the years, the better to hide from the Echelon." Rosalind smiled slightly, gesturing toward a chair. "Sit. Talk with me. We've been very curious about you."

"As am I." Lena dragged out a chair, giving herself plenty of room to move if she needed to. This pretty, pouting young woman seemed friendly enough, but she wouldn't forget the ease with which she'd killed a man. Nor the cool, emotionless look in her eyes as she'd done it.

Rosalind eased into her chair, leaning back with her arms slung across the chair backs next to her. Calculation cooled her brown eyes. "There are very few who know the truth behind Mercury's secret."

"I would never reveal it."

"Even if your sympathies toward the organization are conflicted?"

Lena paused for a moment. "I would not betray you. If I choose to turn my back on this, then I'll walk away and try to forget everything I ever saw."

"Walk away?" Rosalind murmured. "To where? Your life at court? To beg a blue blood to take mercy on you and take you as thrall? How long do you imagine that will last, with your inability to allow a blue blood to feed?"

The only person who knew that was Mr. Mandeville. The betrayal raked her with iron claws.

Rosalind tidied the piles of paper in front of her, then pushed them across the table toward her. "This is everything that we know about you. Compiled carefully in the last year. Jack and Ingrid might think this a risk, telling you of Mercury's secret, but I don't think you'd dare."

A charcoal sketch rested on top. Lena stared down into her own face. The rendering was exquisite, but the expression was slightly disdainful, one eyebrow arched in dismissal. A pretty, hardened flirt.

She lifted it carefully, revealing details about her

and her life. Charlie's name. That made her blood boil. Honoria. Even Blade and Will. The detail went further, examining the minutiae of her life. When she came and went from Caine House. A brief question about why Leo had taken her as his ward, that had been circled in red ink, and daily details about her relationship with him that were shockingly intimate.

No sign of her sharing his bed. Or her blood. I cannot quite fathom the relationship as yet, but I will…

Another page.

They joked of her sister, Honoria, this morning as if he knew her well. Does the relationship go deeper?

And further down.

I find it curious that the Duke of Caine has forgone visiting the house since the arrival of the girl. I've spoken to the servants, the thralls about it. His Grace came regularly each Sunday afternoon to play chess with his son but does so no longer. They have never been close, but one thrall claims that she heard them arguing about Miss Todd. His Grace insisted quite strongly that his son "remove that two-faced snake" from his house but the son refused. Something about this situation strikes me as out of the ordinary. Why would the duke's heir take such a no-account girl as his ward? The duke was once her father's patron, but by all accounts that ended badly, though I don't know why. I will endeavor to find more.

A traitor in Caine House who'd been watching her every move. Icy fingers ran through her. "Mrs. Wade," she whispered, suddenly afraid for Leo. If anyone realized precisely what their relationship was he'd be ruined. Or worse.

"Her loyalty was easy to buy. She has some outstanding debts," Rosalind explained. "You were a potential liability from the start. One with access to a great deal of resources. We took a vote on whether you were too dangerous to use. Ingrid wanted to kill you."

Lena shoved to her feet, the chair squealing on the floor. She couldn't stop shivering. The sweats from earlier had vanished, her body feeling as though someone had turned a faucet from hot to cold. "What do you intend to do with me?"

"If I wanted you dead, you would be. That was never my intention." Rosalind gestured to the side. "Would you like some tea? You've gone white as a ghost."

"I don't want any of your damned tea, thank you very much. And considering recent events I'm not sure I believe you."

"Mendici? That was nothing."

"I'm talking about the humanist who held a damned knife to my throat the other day and threatened my brother!" she snapped.

Rosalind stilled. "I know nothing of this."

Lena licked her lips, uncertain whether to believe her or not. "You want me to break the treaty."

"You told Mr. Mandeville no, that you wanted to meet with us first."

"Then someone wasn't listening," Lena replied. "I

was delivering Mandeville's message to my contact in the Echelon." She tipped her chin up. "Someone accosted me and held a knife to my throat. They said I had to destroy the treaty or they'd hurt my brother. They had one of his toys, from his room. A place nobody should be able to get to. And," she whispered, "they were a blue blood."

The color washed out of Rosalind's face. "You're sure? They didn't follow you there—"

"They knew the humanist codes," Lena replied. "Knew things only someone close to the Council could know. About Will's involvement in the treaty. And where I would be delivering the letter to. It had to be my contact."

"That had nothing to do with us," Rosalind said.

"I thought you were in charge?"

A long, drawn-out moment. "Not everything around here is what it seems," Rosalind murmured. "What if I told you the draining factories were not our doing? That I knew nothing of this threat against you?"

Lena stared her in the eye, forcing herself to be strong. Have courage. Like Will would. *No, don't think of that.* She balled her fists. Choked the pain down. She could fall apart later. "What if I told you I didn't believe you?"

Rosalind grimaced and leaned back in her chair. "What I'm about to tell you must never leave this room." At Lena's nod she continued. "As I'm certain you've realized, there are two factions amongst the humanists. Those that fight for freedom and those that fight for revenge. It wasn't always so, but a year ago we made a daring attack on one of the enclaves and freed a group of mechs. We needed their skills in working metal. Unfortunately, they've not been as cooperative as we'd hoped for. There's a splinter group within the faction, taking matters into their own hands and using our name and information to wreak havoc."

"Why not cut your ties with them?"

Another long look as if wondering whether to trust her. "Come," Rosalind finally said, pushing to her feet. "I have something to show you."

There was no point resisting. And she was starting to grow curious now. "Where are we going?"

"To the cellars."

Pushing into the dark corridor, Rosalind grabbed a lantern from the wall and led her along the tunnel until they finally came to a small door. The smell of chemical lingered in the air. Hanging the lantern from a nail in the wall, Rosalind tugged a key from her shirt and opened the door ahead of them.

Dark shadows waited silently, the faint gleam of lantern light shining off cold steel. Rosalind lifted the lantern and stepped through, spilling light into the enormous cavern and chasing away the shadows. Dozens of enormous automatons sat still and silent, the spark of gaslight absent from their eyes. Dozens more of the metal suits that Rollins had been strapped into. Rows of Percys.

"These are the Cyclops." Pride warmed the other woman's voice and she handed the lantern to Lena. Stepping forward, she ran a hand over the hydraulic hose of the heavy steel arm. The hollow tube of the flamethrower on its arm gleamed.

Leaning under the arm, Rosalind hit a button. With

a hiss, the chest cavity opened and the head slid back revealing a hollow space wide enough to fit a man. Rosalind stepped up on the Cyclops's bent knee and hopped into the cavity. Turning around, she eased back and slid a leather harness around her chest and waist. Two handles rested at arm height. She gripped them, pressing a number of levers and twisting a dial. The steel carapace of the chest slid back into place, a thrumming sound coming from deep within.

"Takes a few minutes to heat the boiler packs," Rosalind explained, her small, heart-shaped face peering over the top of the chest piece. With an expression of concentration, she toyed with something inside and then the hydraulic hoses hissed, the Cyclops straightening to its full height of ten feet. "They're fully mobile, with more flexibility and control than a metaljacket and run on a liter of water a day." With a sudden smile, she forced the arm to lift. "We modeled the flamethrowers on the Spitfires. Burns like buggery when you hit something with it." The fingers on the end of the iron arm gave a wiggle, revealing complete dexterity. "Mech work," Rosalind explained. "The whole thing is mech work."

"That's why you need them."

Rosalind grimaced and the Cyclops sank back down, its engines fading. She slung the steel chest plate open and hopped down. "Aye. The plans were ours." A brief look in her direction. "But the work's theirs." A rusty laugh. "The Echelon forced them into the enclaves to work steel for them and earn out the repayment of their mech enhancements. Not once did they suspect we'd turn their own technology—the skills they taught the mechs—against them. It's the one thing we humans have never been able to counter. We might have been able to over-whelm the blue bloods in France and put them to the guillotine, but our blue bloods are smarter and hide behind automaton armies. Human flesh can't fight metal. So we must even the odds."

"To fight for freedom," Lena said, with a slightly sarcastic lilt. "It sounds remarkably like fighting for revenge."

"Do you think the Echelon are simply going to turn around and give us our rights?" A hint of anger stirred Rosalind's voice. "Perhaps if we ask nicely?"

"People are going to die."

"They already do. Four hundred and thirty men and women took to the streets to protest against the latest hike in the blood taxes. The Echelon mowed them down with the Trojan cavalry, leaving barely a hundred alive."

"They wouldn't have raised the blood taxes if the draining factories hadn't exploded. Now there's a shortage and the Echelon need blood fast. Don't you see? This becomes a cycle of blood and death!"

Rosalind jerked the lantern out of Lena's hands. "I'm disappointed. I thought you would understand. Especially considering where the plans for the Cyclops came from."

"What do you mean by that?"

"Your own father. Sir Artemus Todd, with his brilliant, erratic mind. He spent the last year of his life discovering a blue blood's weaknesses. We use the toxin he created to incapacitate them and his firebolt bullets to kill them. Instead of fleeing from Vickers with you, with his family, he risked his life to place his final plans for the Cyclops in our hands. It cost him everything, but he'll forever be remembered amongst our ranks."

Lena could barely remember the night they'd been forced to flee. Being shaken awake early in the morning and bundled into a carriage. Her father demanding that she look after Charlie, and though she'd seen him speaking with Honoria, pressing a coded diary into her hands, she hadn't caught any of their words.

That night had changed her life forever. Torn from her lessons, her world, her hopes of a future amongst the Echelon, she'd been dragged into the dark, grim confines of the rookeries. All she'd known was that her father's patron Vickers—the duke for whom he performed his brilliant experiments—wanted them dead.

She'd never known why.

"Father was a humanist?" she asked, her voice breaking slightly.

"To the bone."

Another shock on a seemingly never-ending series of them. Lena reached out, trying to find the wall as her knees shook.

"That's why we wanted you," Rosalind continued. "Your sister had betrayed his memory by marrying a blue blood. She could be of no use to us. You, however, showed some skill with clockwork and cogs. You design things that could be useful—"

Lena's mind made the leap. "You think I could

learn to create the Cyclops?" Then there would be
no more need for the mechs. Would Rosalind—or
Mercury rather, for she was starting to see the difference between the two—simply have them killed? The
way she'd done to Mendici? A shiver ran down her
spine. What would Mercury do if Lena said no?

There was nowhere to run. To hide. No allies
remaining. Not even—

No, don't think of him. She squeezed her eyes shut
and took a deep, steadying breath, trying to ignore
the nausea.

Think.

The only way Rosalind could have known of
Lena's skill with clockwork was from Mr. Mandeville.
Suddenly the way he'd always watched over her so
carefully became something far more sinister.

"I design toys," she whispered.

"But you could make a Cyclops." Rosalind took a
step closer. "The transformational clockwork is proof
that you have the skill and the ability to design such
things." Her eyes lit up like warmed chocolate. "You
would be a hero."

A hero. Three weeks ago, she might have still cared
for such things. Recognition, finally, but never from
her father. He had died for the same schemes that lit
this woman's face with excitement.

Everything in her life was a lie. Mrs. Wade spied on
her and Mr. Mandeville too, no doubt. Her father, a
man who'd virtually ignored her as some kind of little
doll, had designed weapons to take the Echelon down.

And Honoria had likely known.

Lena leaned her head back against the wall and

closed her eyes. Who could she trust? There were so many secrets she felt as if her head was going to explode. But then she'd been keeping her own from her family too, hadn't she?

The loneliness hit her like a punch to the gut. No one to trust, no one to tell. Nobody who knew her secrets or had shared their own. Nobody except Will and he was—

Lena lurched to her knees and threw up, her whole body shaking in misery. She'd been trying so hard not to think of him, trying to keep the hurt buried, but it welled up, choking her, forcing her stomach to heave.

Tears burned in her eyes and she wiped her face with her sleeve. Oh God, what was she going to do? How was she going to tell Blade that Will…that he was gone? The thought was inconceivable. He was so large, so full of life and heat and fire, his eyes snapping amber flames whenever she looked at him. She couldn't bear the fist of pain deep inside. She needed to see the body, needed to get him back to her. To bury him properly.

To tell him that if she'd ever suspected he might have kissed her back, then she would never have returned to the Echelon. To this mess.

But first she had to get out of here. She looked up. At the pair of shiny boots in front of her, and the rows of metal drones.

"No," she whispered. "I won't do it."

"Not quite the answer I was hoping for," Rosalind said quietly. The hammer on the pistol drew back. "How disappointing. Come. Get to your feet. I've no further use for you."

Twenty

"I WON'T TELL ANYONE," LENA SAID, STARING AT THE barrel of the pistol. Her father's own design. How ironic. "I want nothing more to do with this. All I want is to go home and forget this whole nightmare."

Rosalind knelt down, the pistol resting on her knee. "Didn't you realize? This isn't a game, Miss Todd. You know too much."

"I won't breathe a word of it—"

"Unfortunately, I'm not sure I believe you."

Bitterness welled. "You were never going to let me go, were you? You're worse than the blue bloods, than the Echelon. You use people, then discard them when they no longer suit your purposes."

A distant look came into the other woman's eyes. Her eyelashes lowered, fluttering against pale cheeks. "It surprises me how innocent you still are." A bitter smile. "I am what I have been made. A weapon. A hunting hawk, finally unleashed from its master's jesses. There can be no mercy, for I expect none."

The gun wavered again.

"Wait," Lena cried desperately. "*Please*. Please don't

do this. I have lost everything today. There is nothing left for me." Tears blurred her vision, made the pistol vanish. She held her breath, her eyes screwed tight, waiting for the retort of the pistol, the pain.

Silence.

With tears sliding down her cheeks, she looked up. Rosalind made a disgusted growl and aimed the pistol at the ceiling.

"It seems there is some small scrap of mercy left in me after all. I know I shall regret this."

Lena let out a shuddering breath, her heart rabbiting behind her ribs. "I promise you won't."

Grabbing her by the arm, Rosalind hauled her to her feet. "Come. I'll blindfold you and have Jack or Ingrid dump you out near the stews."

"Not Ingrid." Lena had a feeling if Ingrid found out about this moment of leniency, she'd take care of the matter quietly.

Rosalind's lips thinned. "You're not in the position to be making demands. Come—"

A scream sounded in the distance.

Both of them froze.

"That had better not be friends of yours." Rosalind's eyes narrowed. She shoved the lantern into Lena's hands and pushed her through the door, holding the pistol against her back. "Or all deals are off."

The sound of steel on steel echoed through the tunnels, then a roar of earth-shattering fury.

It couldn't be... Lena's heart started ticking, her breath catching in her lungs. She wanted to run toward the sound, but something held her back. Rosalind's gauntleted hand on her arm.

Rosalind shoved her against the wall and glanced around a corner. Evidently sighting nothing, she hauled Lena after her. "That's coming from the guard room."

Lena didn't dare hope. He couldn't have survived that fall, could he?

Another roar filled the air and something that sounded like a chair smashing against the wall.

"Get out of the way!" a woman called. "Let me handle this."

Rosalind hissed between her teeth. "Ingrid." She started running, which was precisely what Lena wanted too.

The door ahead of them flew open and a man crashed through it, sliding across the tunnel's smooth floors. Blood matted his hair and he struggled to roll over. Rosalind swore under her breath and knelt down, cradling his chin as she examined him.

The open door revealed chaos. Pieces of chair were scattered like matchsticks, and a booted foot lay motionless, the rest of the person lost to sight.

Will stood in the middle of the mess, breathing hard. His fists were clenched at his sides, his shoulders shaking from barely restrained rage. Blood smeared his wet shirt where it was plastered against his side and his hair hung wetly against his scalp.

Lena sucked in a sharp breath, coming to a halt. "Will," she whispered, her heart swelling within her chest. She stumbled, grabbing onto the wall. *He was alive!* She could barely believe it. Then her eyes narrowed on the blood that stained his side. *Alive and hurt.*

Scalding amber eyes looked up. The shock as their

gazes met swept right through her. His fist curled tight around the shiv he held. "Lena," he growled, and it was a tone she'd never heard from him before.

No time to savor the sweetness of the moment. Through her tears she saw Ingrid come out of nowhere, the leg of a chair held in one hand. She swung it hard and Will caught her wrist with a contemptuous snarl.

It should have been the end of it. But Ingrid moved faster than Lena believed possible and snapped a palm into the joint of his elbow. As Will roared in pain, she followed through with a leg, sweeping his own out from under him.

Will hit the ground hard and Ingrid swung the chair leg at his head. He kicked up, snapping the piece of timber out of her hand and then arched back onto his shoulders and kicked himself to his feet. Snarling with rage, he hit Ingrid around the waist and carried her to the floor.

Lena took a cautious step forward, surveying the room. He'd made a mess of it. Groaning men littered the ground, clutching at broken bones and bruises. Not one of them was dead though.

Yet.

The blur as he and Ingrid fought was too fast to follow. Using his brute strength, he forced the other woman flat to the ground, tearing her shoulder up behind her and kneeling on her. Ingrid snarled, her face ground against the floor and her eyes molten with anger.

Bronze eyes.

Another verwulfen.

Will forced her arm higher. Ingrid's body shook and she winced, her other hand clawing at the ground. His gaze darkened and he set one hand against the joint of her shoulder, his intentions clear.

"No," Lena cried. "Don't do it!"

Leaping forward, she grabbed his arm and tugged ineffectually. Will snarled at her, all wild eyes and teeth and her heart leaped into her throat at the madness she saw there. For a moment she wasn't sure if he would go for her too. She saw it in his eyes, saw the need, the desire to kill glaring back out at her.

"Will," she whispered, sliding her wrist in front of his nose. If he smelt her, recognized her, he would never hurt her.

He eased back on Ingrid's arm. Her hands shaking, Lena gently touched his cheek. "Will, look at me. It's Lena. You know me." Caressing the line of his jaw, she swallowed hard when he turned and gently bit the fleshy pad of her palm.

One bite and her blood would flow, mingling with the blood that stained his fractured cheekbone. One bite and she'd be infected. Quivering violently, she gave a breathy little cry as his tongue rasped over the sensitive flesh. Then he let go, his teeth sliding gently over her skin.

Behind her Rosalind snapped to someone, "As soon as you get a clear shot, take it."

"The girl's in the way. Want me to shoot her?"

Lena froze and glanced over her shoulder. Jack stared down an enormous rifle at her, focusing through the glass monocle.

"If you shoot me," she said, surprised by how calm

her voice sounded, "you'll never stop him." She slid a steadying hand over Will's shoulder. "He came for me. Because of the way Mendici took me. I can stop him."

Rosalind's nostrils flared. Her gaze flickered to Will and back. "He's beyond stopping."

Sliding her body between them, trying to cover as much of Will as she could, Lena shook her head. "He'll listen to me."

Rosalind wavered. Lena could see it in her eyes.

"I'll talk to him," she said. "Calm him down. Then we both walk out of here. I'll keep your secrets."

"Or we could kill you both," Jack said.

Lena's eyes narrowed. "Try it and you'll find out why nobody dares cross a verwulfen. You have to shoot me first and he'll kill her."

"Do it," Ingrid snarled.

"Shut up." Jack lowered the rifle slightly, cold gaze considering. His expression softened slightly as he looked at Ingrid and Lena realized there was some sense of compassion, some weakness within him. "One condition. We want the transformational. Complete the project and deliver it within five days. That's the cost of our cooperation."

Yesterday she might have simply agreed. "Why? What do you intend to do with it?"

"It's a gift. For the Scandinavian ambassador. We've already made contact with them. They're expecting it."

The transformational was only a toy, really. Granted, a very life-sized one by the time she was finished. "I'll never complete it in five days."

The rifle twitched. "You don't have a choice."

Hours of work, soldering steel plate to steel. She'd

finished most of the clockwork mechanism that drove it, but still…

Will's shoulder quivered beneath her touch. Without thinking, she stroked his arm, leaning closer. "Agreed," she said. "I'll contact Mandeville and get him to help. When it's ready I'll have it delivered to his shop."

"You're cautious of us?" Rosalind asked.

"I only make a mistake once."

Their eyes met. Rosalind lowered her pistol and nodded. "Jack."

"Talk him down first." He never took his gaze off Ingrid.

Lena swiveled around. Will was shaking, his eyes clenched tight and his teeth bared as if he fought some internal battle she could never understand. She'd seen him do this before though, knew how he controlled himself.

"I'm safe," she whispered. "I just need you to come back to me, to help me get out of here and go home. Breathe, Will. Deep and slow. That's it." Caressing his face, his jaw, she leaned closer, letting him scent her. "And another one. That's the way." Sliding her hand down his arm, over the rough linen that was rolled up to his elbows, and the sleek bronzed skin of his forearm, she licked her lips. Her hand slid over his, curling between his fingers. "Let her go, Will. Take my hand. I'm here. I've got you."

Sliding her fingers between his, she drew his hand back, knowing that he let her. Ingrid's shoulders relaxed and her eyes shot toward Lena murderously.

"I wouldn't," Lena said. "Even wounded he took

you down easily. I won't be able to talk him out of this again." She slid Will's hand over her knee and pressed it there, then turned for his other one.

Will's fingers quivered over Ingrid's wrist. Lena leaned closer, nuzzling her face against his jaw. His scent filled her nostrils, dark and musky. She wanted to press her lips against his skin, to confirm that he was really here, that he was alive.

Damn it. There were no society rules here and she was beyond caring what anyone else thought. Turning her face, she pressed her lips to his cheek, her hand sliding over his other cheek. Alive. Warm. The pulse pounding in his chest. A cry caught in her throat. So close to losing him... Tears burned in her eyes. Never again.

The rasp of his stubble burned over her too-sensitive lips. Blinking away the tears, she eased his grip away from Ingrid's wrist, her fingers bloody from his cheek. "Come home with me, Will. Take me home."

His hand sprang open. His eyes were still tightly ground together.

Ingrid's body collapsed on the floor and she winced as she drew her injured arm up.

"Don't move," Lena warned her, sliding her arms around his neck. "Stand up, Will." She breathed the words in his ear. "Take me home. Your home."

He looked up then, the madness leeching from his gaze. The beast had not faded completely though. He looked at her with hunger, a madness of its own, and her nipples tightened painfully against the rasp of her linen chemise.

"Yes," she whispered. "When we get home."

"Home." His voice was hoarse. He looked around, realizing he was still kneeling on Ingrid. Then he looked up and something dark flickered through his gaze.

"Put the rifle away," she cried out as Will shoved her behind him.

There was no chance of stopping him if he decided to go for Jack. Not now. Pleading with her eyes, she tried to slide her arms around Will's waist. Anything to slow him, to remind him of his humanity.

Jack slowly lowered the rifle. "Didn't think you could do it." He nodded sharply at her. "Five days."

"Five days," Lena promised, her body relaxing with a sigh of relief.

Jack glanced warily at Will. Whatever he saw on Will's face it made him take a half step back. "You'd best go." Another glance, toward Ingrid. "Because I can't guarantee I can talk *her* off the edge."

❧

The fury that had kept him moving began to fade by the time they reached the surface. His weight was too much for her to bear alone.

"Come on," Lena said in a cheerful tone. "Not much farther." She took a desperate look around. The warren was a good half mile. In these streets, with Will unable to defend himself, it was a dangerous half mile.

Will staggered against a brick wall, the blood on his side drying. He'd never make it all the way to the warren. Lena bit her lip, then glanced toward the small side street where he lived these days. She'd never been inside, but she knew its location.

"This way," she said, wrapping her arms around his

waist and trying to guide him toward the stairs that
led to his door.

A pair of boys smoked cheroots on the base of the
stairs. A year or two younger than Charlie, she didn't
like the way they looked at her.

"Hey there, lady. Why don't you ditch the old man
and come sit with us?" One of them called.

No way past them. Will stiffened as if he'd heard
the insult, and she stroked the lean muscle of his back.
"They're only boys," she whispered. "No danger."

She hoped.

Raising her voice, Lena looked the one who'd
spoke dead in the eye. She'd faced down blue bloods
and humanists. This was only a boy, trying to impress
his friend. "Here now. Care to earn some coin?"

"How 'bout I offer you some tin?" Another smirk.

Lena grabbed Will's shirt. "Don't you dare."
Stepping forward, she kept a wary eye on him. He
might be dangerously close to collapsing, but if the fury
overtook him, it might be enough to rouse him to the
killing edge. "I need a message delivered to my sister."

The other lad tipped his chin up. "Who's your sister?"

"Blade's wife."

Both boys stilled. The one who'd given her grief
paled and leaped to his feet. "Didn't mean naught by
it, miss. What do you want us to say?"

"Tell her Lena's at Will's house. That she needs
to come." Will chose that moment to slump and she
swayed dangerously with him.

The other lad stepped forward to help.

"No!" she cried as a snarl curdled in Will's throat.
The boy froze. "Don't touch him. Don't touch

me. He's not quite himself at the moment. Just run my message."

Whatever they'd seen in Will's face they didn't even question her about the coin. Blade's name carried weight here. Within seconds she was alone, facing the hurdle of the stairs.

Her own body screamed with exhaustion. Lena finally got Will to the top and shoved the door open. He hadn't bothered to lock it. The pair of carved daggers in the door indicated who this house belonged to and not even the bravest thief would dare cross the threshold.

Holding him under the arms, Lena kicked the door shut with her ruined slipper. She'd lost the other in the tunnels and could barely feel that foot for the cold. "Here now," she murmured, guiding him up against the door. Her vision swam. "Stay here whilst I fetch a lantern."

Will slumped. "On the stove."

She saw the outline of the stove against the pale shine of the moon through gauzy curtains. It took a minute to light, then a merry glow lit the room.

Lena looked around. "Goodness, Will. You do realize you can buy furniture?"

There was nothing but a small cot in the corner, draped with a pair of patchwork quilts, a table, and two chairs and the bare necessities of the kitchen. The apartment was small. Almost as small as the one she'd shared with her brother and sister when they first took to hiding in the 'Chapel.

"Surely Blade pays you," she muttered in an appalled tone.

"He pays me." Will took a step toward the bed and swayed dangerously. "Don't have much need...to spend it..."

Lena leaped forward, catching him around the waist. His weight hit her hard and she staggered backward, her knees hitting the cot. They both went down, Will a heavy, crushing weight on top of her.

Her face was buried in his shoulder. Lena wriggled higher so that she could breathe, then collapsed back with a gasp. "Will! You're crushing me!"

No sign of movement in his face. He breathed slowly and she realized he was in that almost unconscious state that followed severe exertion. Shoving at his shoulder, she managed to slither out just enough that his weight was no longer crushing.

Tugging his shirt out of his waistband, she craned her neck to check his wound. A bloody crust covered it. Touching his ribs tenderly, she checked for any signs of injury. By this stage there was little she could do. The virus would congregate in the wound site and do more than she—or even a doctor—ever could.

Satisfied that he wasn't mortally injured, she collapsed back against the pillow. The chill that seemed to pervade her bones was still there. And Will was burning with heat.

Snuggling against his chest, she pressed her cold lips to his neck. The heat from his body made her feel slightly better, though the nausea from earlier had passed, thank goodness. Lena blinked sleepily. She could barely keep her eyes open. The weight of exhaustion hit her hard and she barely had time to wonder if her message would reach Honoria before the blackness took her.

Twenty-one

Morning sunlight streamed through the curtains. Lena blinked, pain stabbing at her too-sensitive eyes. She was so thirsty, her mouth bone dry. "Where am I?"

A shadow moved on the edge of vision. Lena shot to alertness, her heartbeat slowing down when Charlie grinned at her.

"She's awake!"

Honoria materialized, her face white and pale with lack of sleep. Her hand slid over Lena's forehead, deliciously cool. "Charlie," she murmured. "Could you fetch some more water? And something to eat?" The last question was directed at Lena.

She nodded sharply. Her stomach growled at the thought, twisting with emptiness.

Honoria held a glass to her lips. Cool water wet her dry tongue and she gasped greedily at it. The door shut behind Charlie as Honoria settled on the edge of the bed.

"Drink it slowly," Honoria said. "You've been asleep for a long time."

By the time she'd drained the glass she was feeling marginally better. Looking around, she recognized her old room in the warren.

"Will?"

"He's still asleep." Honoria stroked a hand over her damp hair. "Lena, your temperature's abnormally high. You're burning with fever. How do you feel?"

She considered her body. "Hungry?"

Concern flashed through Honoria's dark eyes. "What happened? Can you remember? All Rip could tell us was that he heard a whistle of distress and then Will was gone. We found your carriage turned over in the street, but no sign of either of you. Blade and Rip searched the tunnels but lost Will's scent trail. Someone had sprayed the area with some sort of chemical that obliterated smell."

Everything that had happened flashed through her mind. She opened her mouth. Then shut it. She had sworn that she would speak of the humanists to no one. And she didn't dare get her sister involved.

Tears sprang into her eyes, her emotions strangely raw. "Honor, if I asked you a question, would you answer it?"

"Of course."

Their eyes met. "Was Father a humanist?"

Stillness radiated through her sister's body. "Why would you ask such a thing?"

"It's true then." Lena's voice hardened and she struggled to sit up. "What else did you think was best kept secret from me? Father's work for Vickers? The truth of what he was really doing?"

Honoria stiffened. "Where did you learn of this?"

"It doesn't matter. It's all true, isn't it?"

Something old filled Honoria's eyes. "Yes. I don't know how much you're aware of, but it's true. In the last years of his life Father grew dissatisfied with the way of the world. He started working on a cure for the craving for Vickers, but in his own time he researched a blue blood's weaknesses. He wanted to discover methods of destroying them."

Lena pressed her hands against her face. Everything that Rosalind had told her was correct.

Honoria eased a tentative hand on her shoulder. "Lena? You're not angry at me? I did as I thought best. The information is dangerous. I was only ever trying to protect you both."

"You should have told me." As soon as she said the words she realized how familiar Honoria's statement sounded. They were all excuses she herself had used. A similarity she never thought she'd ever have shared with her sister. They were so different at heart, and yet she couldn't deny that Honoria would risk her own life for her and Charlie without pause. Sliding a hand over her sister's, she squeezed gently.

"Lena, what happened in the tunnels?"

A world she could never reveal. "Someone kidnapped me. I'm not sure who. Will came after them and saved me."

The story was far too brief to appease her sister and they both knew it. But whatever guilt currently flayed Honoria, she didn't dare question the statement.

"Do you think I could see Will?" Lena asked softly.

"He's asleep."

"Just to check on him." She'd thought him lost.

The urge to make sure he was safe and alive was suddenly a crushing need. "Please."

Honoria sighed. "I'll allow it. But only because I understand what you're feeling."

⁓

Honoria eased a hand over her sister's forehead, smoothing her damp curls out of the way. Though she'd left Lena sitting in a chair beside Will's bed, when she'd returned with more water, she'd found her curled up on top of the blankets asleep, her fingers entwined with his.

Blade's arms slid around her waist from behind and he rested a chin on her shoulder. "What's wrong?"

"What do you mean?"

"You're troubled," he said simply.

Pressing a finger against her lips, she led him out of the room and eased the door shut behind her. Though he arched an eyebrow in question, she shook her head and led him upstairs to her workroom.

"What is it, luv?" he asked, frowning as he closed the door behind him.

Nobody would hear them up here. Honoria crossed to her desk and tugged a heavy book down from the shelf. She opened it to the page mark and pressed her finger to the spidery script. "Read it."

Blade squinted at the page, his lips moving slowly. "Don't understand. This is the first stages of the loupe virus and its effects."

"I was studying it in order to try and find Will's cure," she admitted. "The first sign of the loupe is a fever. Headaches, hot and cold flushes, the sweats…"

He understood immediately.

"She's burning up," Honoria whispered. "She shouldn't be that hot, not without severe signs of discomfort, but all she feels is hunger and thirst."

Blade's face paled.

Honoria bit her lip. "There's more. Did you know that the loupe is an extremely virulent disease, and yet there are few verwulfen around?" Heat burned in the back of her eyes and she stroked the page in front of her. She'd come up here to read more as soon as she first suspected what was going on. "Blade, the statistics for surviving the initial fever are extremely poor. Perhaps one in fifteen makes the transition. In Scandinavia and Germany, only the strongest warriors are allowed to be infected. They must prove themselves in a test first, to ensure that they have the strongest chance of surviving." Her vision blurred. "This is why no verwulfen is allowed to mate with a human. Oh God, what have I done?" Her words faded to a whisper, an ache burning in her chest. "I should never have allowed her near him. I should have realized. I should have—"

Strong arms tugged her close, burying her against his chest. "I've a feelin' nothin' we done coulda kept 'em apart." He stroked her hair. "Hush, luv. Ain't your fault. You couldn't a known. There's so little information 'bout the loupe goin' round. And who knows, she might be strong enough."

Honoria hiccupped a sob. "The strongest warriors, Blade. And most of *them* don't survive."

"Then," he said, tipping her chin up toward him, "we need to work out what she needs. How to 'elp 'er."

The thought penetrated where no false comfort ever could. This she could do. She grabbed the book and dashed the tears from her eyes. She hadn't been able to save her brother from the craving virus, but she'd be damned if she'd let her sister's life fade.

"Sit. Read," he said, pushing her into a chair. "I'll fetch a pot of tea and somethin' to eat. Then I'll check on them."

Honoria's eyes were already racing across the lines on the page. "Thank you."

❦

The world beneath her moved. Lena blinked sleepily. Arching her fingers, she dug them into the soft body beneath hers and yawned. Her pillow threatened to dislodge her and she grabbed onto the sheets.

Will rolled onto his side, blinking warily at her. Thick slabs of muscle covered his chest and shoulders, and for a moment, the urge to run her hand through the hair on his chest was almost irresistible.

Grabbing at the sheet to stop it from dropping too far, he stiffened. "We're at the warren." A frown. "What happened?"

"Don't you remember? You collapsed," she said, "and Blade had you brought here. You've slept the day away. How are you feeling?"

His gaze drifted past, toward the water jug.

"Here," Lena said, hopping off the bed in her night-gown and pouring him a glass. She held it out to him, but he grabbed the jug instead and tilted it up. The muscles in his throat worked, rivulets of water pouring down his jaw and into the hollow of his collarbone.

Heat burned between her thighs and she gripped the cool glass hard. Sheer longing was almost a knife to the chest. She had promised herself that she would speak to him if he survived, tell him how she felt, but suddenly she was nervous and tongue-tied again. The way he always made her feel.

She, a woman who could twist a man around her finger with a simple smile if she chose.

A crack appeared in the glass. Then another. Lena looked down in astonishment as the glass shattered, pieces crumbling to the rug. Blood welled from her fingers.

Will lowered the jug, his gaze dropping to the glass. "Bloody hell, Lena." He leaped out of bed, moving with the same economical grace that always drew her eye.

An excess of golden skin. Naked skin. Lena's eyes widened. She had a second's grace to drop her gaze before he swore and jerked the sheet around his waist, tucking the edge in.

Oh my goodness.

Anatomy books could not even come close to picturing the truth. The heat flushed out of her face. She'd caught only a glimpse of his member, half aroused and enormous, bobbing from the thick thatch of dark hair that nested it. The breath caught in her throat. *There was no possible way they could fit together…*

"Here," Will snarled, taking the remains of the glass from her and tearing a piece off the sheet. He dipped it in the water jug and wrung it out, then dabbed tenderly at the cut on her hand. "What happened?"

"It cracked in my hand," Lena said distantly. A

shiver of need swept through her, igniting desires she'd kept under lock and key in her heart.

Will hesitated.

"What is it?"

"There's a piece of glass in there." A frown drew his eyebrows together. "Lena, can you not feel that?" A shivering stroke over something in her hand.

She looked away from the broad, naked expanse of his chest and saw the piece of glass sticking out of her hand. As soon as she saw it she felt the acid bite of pain and bit her lip. "A little. It doesn't hurt very much."

"Lena, look at me."

Into whiskey warm eyes with their impossibly thick lashes. She leaned forward, resting her free hand against his chest, feeling the delicious slide of silky-soft skin beneath her fingertips.

Will sucked in a breath. Then his gaze dropped and pain throbbed through her hand. "Got it," he said. Dabbing at the cut, he examined it for any sign of glass and then tied another strip of sheet around it firmly.

The scent of him, warm and musky, wrapped around her senses. As soon as he let her hand go, she placed it against his stomach, feeling the flinch beneath her fingertips.

"Lena," he warned, in a husky voice. The heat in his eyes contradicted his tone. "We can't."

"Why not?" she whispered, sliding the backs of her knuckles down his rippled abdomen. "You want to. I want to." Tears pricked at her eyes and suddenly her throat was thick. "I thought that I'd lost you. That you were gone. Forever." One hot, salty tear slid down her cheek. She shook her head and looked up fiercely.

"Nothing else matters." A deep breath, her heart pattering madly in her chest. She couldn't quite meet his eyes, but that didn't matter. "I was so scared that I would never have a chance to touch you. To kiss you again. To tell you…"

"Tell me what?" He caught her wrists, thrust them behind her.

Her nipples abraded the linen nightgown. She stared up at him, at the fierce expression on his face. Flickers of warming amber lit his eyes. That was what she wanted to stir. The uncontrollable passion in him. The need. She leaned closer, let her breasts rub against his skin. Sensation shot through her abdomen, clenching white-hot between her thighs.

"Tell me what?" he repeated, more of the amber drowning out the brown of his eyes.

Lena leaned forward and kissed his chest. Will shuddered, his grip on her wrists loosening. "How much I miss you," she whispered. "I played games with you, Will, because I was afraid if I were serious, and you weren't…that I'd…I wanted you to kiss me. I tried to drive you to it, but you would never dare. I thought you didn't want me and it hurt so badly, because I wanted you."

Another shudder of conflicting need within him. He shook his head, his lips parting. "I *can't*." But his hands were easing on her wrists and suddenly it was easy to slip from his grasp.

She slid her hands over his chest and stepped closer. Will backed away, his knees hitting the back of the bed. He tumbled onto the bed, his fist clenching in the blankets. The sheet around his hips threatened to dislodge. Lena knelt on the edge of the bed, slinging her leg over his hips.

His muscles clenched. "Lena, you don't understand."

"Do you want me or not?" A breathless moment as she waited for the answer.

"Of course I do, but—"

She pressed a finger against his lips. The nightgown rode up around her thighs, the lacy edge trailing over her sensitive calves. Licking her lips, she relaxed down onto his lap, gasping at the feel of his rigid member against her wet heat.

So sensitive there. So sweet the feeling. She threw her head back and arched her hips, grinding herself against him.

Fingers clenched in her bottom, almost painfully tight. He urged her against him again and Lena cried out as need tightened within her.

The sheet was trapped between them. She could feel her own body wetting it, the rasp of the linen against the sensitive nub that drove her insane. Suddenly it wasn't enough. She wanted more. Needed more. Sinking her hands into his hair, she fisted it and dragged his mouth up to hers.

Will bit at her lip, suckling it into his mouth. Their tongues clashed and she pressed herself against him, rubbing her breasts, her hips, her quim against his hard body. The taste of his mouth was intoxicating.

The sheet drove her crazy. She slid a hand between them and tugged at the length he'd tucked into the waist of it. Too late he realized her intentions and caught her wrist. Lena held onto the end, feeling it unravel beneath her. She ground her hips against his and this time it was flesh that met hers. Hard, swollen flesh.

"*Can't.*"

She kissed him, not daring to let him go. His cock surged, huge and potent against her and she wet it with her own body, riding along the edge of it. Will made a strangled sound in his throat, his hands digging into her thighs and his eyes glazing. The head of his cock brushed against her, a stretching sensation—

Lena's mouth fell open. Will caught her by the hips and then the pain and stretching was gone and he slammed her back against the bed, hovering over her with a strained growl. His hands pinned her wrists to the bed.

"No." Breathing hard, his back heaving with the strain of it, he looked up and met her gaze. Amber burned desperately.

"You want to."

"I want to," he admitted. Something flashed through his eyes, a sadness that made her heart clench. "I can't, Lena. I promised I'd protect you. Even from myself."

"I trust you," she whispered. "You wouldn't hurt me."

He clenched his eyes shut. "Lena, have you never thought of how the loupe is spread?"

She opened her mouth then froze. Not once had she considered it. "I don't know very much about it." Few people did. Nobody in the Echelon spoke of it. "The craving is spread by blood."

"So is the loupe." His body softened on hers, hips driving her into the bed, need a hard edge in his golden eyes. "And also through a man's seed. Why d'you think I ain't been with a woman?"

Another stunning revelation. "Ever?" she whispered in surprise.

He shook his head, eyes darkening. "Never."

Some fierce sense of possession burned within her. "I didn't know. I thought—" Her mind raced. Not once could she recall seeing him with a woman. She'd never thought of it before, preferring to assume he kept his assignations quiet.

Will's grip eased and he knelt over her, hands on his thighs. His cock bobbed against his stomach, but the dejection in his shoulders told her everything she needed to know. Grabbing the remains of the sheet, he wrapped it around his hips.

"Unless a woman had the loupe already. I couldn't."

Lena shook her head. This couldn't be happening. Just when she had finally admitted to herself the depth of her feelings for him... "Perhaps..." She licked dry lips. "I wouldn't mind. If we could be together—"

"No!" His expression hardened. "You don't know what you're askin'. I've been cut and beaten and even half gutted before, and they're nothin'—*nothin'*—compared to the agony of the loupe when it first hits you. Not everybody survives, Lena." He scrubbed a hand over his face. "I couldn't do that. Not to you."

Tears blurred her vision. The tenuous future she'd begun dreaming of was washed away with the maelstrom of his words.

"Lena," he whispered. A gentle hand brushed the back of her cheek. "Don't cry."

"I'm not," she replied, trying to dry her eyes on her sleeves. Somehow she summoned a weak smile. It faltered. "Yesterday I thought you were dead. I said

I'd do anything to have you back, to have you safe—" The words broke. She couldn't say anymore. Sobs overtook her.

Sheets rustled and then Will dragged her against him. "I never meant to hurt you." He murmured. "I tried to stay away from you."

She nodded, shakily drawing in a breath. "I can see that now." All of the times she'd thought he didn't care for her and he'd only been trying to stop this before it got too far.

He kissed her cheek, his lips wet with her tears. Then her jaw. Her lips. Lena turned her face to his hungrily, wrapping her body hard against him. They kissed desperately, clinging to each other and she almost broke down again, knowing that this was the last time she could ever do this.

Her fingers twined in the silky strands of his hair. Will dragged her closer against him, his cock an emphatic presence against her thigh. His mouth trailed lower, nipping at her chin, then her neck, his tongue tracing the salty rime of her tears.

The shock of his hand against her breast made her suck in a breath. "Will?"

"Just this. Just once." The other hand slid her nightgown higher, his forearm cradling the curve of her bare bottom.

Heat flushed through her. There was never any intention of saying no. If this was all she could have of him… "What are you going to do?"

Will eased her back onto the bed and knelt over her. The rasp of his stubble against her throat arched her off the bed and she dug her nails into his shoulders.

"I've thought of this… Dreamed of this." Teeth grazed the vulnerable column of her throat, a teasing bite that threatened and tempted both. "I want to taste you."

She shivered with longing. He was asking for her surrender. She gave it completely. "Do it."

His lips soothed the ache of the bite. Hands sliding over her nightgown with feverish need, he caught the hem of it and shoved it up.

Cool air stirred against her naked flesh. Lena lifted her hips and shoulders off the bed, letting him remove it. Will tossed the nightgown aside, never taking his eyes off her. They burned like a blacksmith's forge, the heat blistering her soul.

Uncertainty beating in her breast, she lowered her hands against her sides. Her breath lifted her breasts, drawing his gaze to them. Her nipples hardened and she let her gaze rove his face, searching for something, anything.

His expression softened. Still fierce in his desire, the odd hint of longing shaped his mouth. "You're beautiful." Gently he traced her collarbone, his fingers tickling over her skin. They raked lower, drawing gentle concentric circles around her left breast. "Perfect."

"Too small," she whispered.

He leaned against her side, one leg thrown over hers. Capturing her gaze, he slid his rough palm over her breast, cupping it. "Perfect," he growled and lowered his head.

Lips traced the smooth curve of her flesh. She gasped as teeth found her nipple and bit it gently. The hand on her breast slid lower, skating across her quivering stomach. So much sensation. She could barely contain it, especially when his hand delved between her thighs.

A new world. She felt remarkably gauche, untutored. She knew nothing of this, of pleasure. Theory had nothing on practice. Will's fingers found her and she threw her head back, gasping, against the sheets.

"Take your hair out," he whispered, one finger tracing small circles against the wet bud between her thighs.

She could barely move, trapped by the sensation of his hand. "I can't," she gasped, her hips quivering.

Movement ceased. He pressed the heel of his palm against her mound. "Take it out."

Demand filled his voice. Lena lifted her arms over her head and started working on her braid. Her hair tumbled over the sheets in loose waves, thick and dark. Will's expression grew lazy, heavy-lidded. He lowered his mouth to her nipple and suckled it. "That's better."

The coil in her stomach grew. She slid her hands over his shoulders, learning the smooth muscle of his flesh. Then through his hair, fisting in the length of it, unable to string coherent thought or sound together as his lips played with her breast.

A hot tongue swept over her, rasping at her nipple. An inarticulate sound echoed in her throat, harsh and guttural. A wordless plea for more. As if in answer, his fingers danced lightly over her wet flesh, circling the entrance to her body.

"Yes," Lena gasped, back arching obscenely. "Will!"

"Do you like that?" A hint of curiosity gleamed in his eyes. This was new to him too and yet he moved with a confidence that fooled her.

A finger slid deep into her passage and she clenched around it, eyes rolling back in her head. Soft laughter echoed against her flesh, a rumble of pleased satisfaction. So male.

"Yes?"

Her fingers were clenched in his hair so tight he had to feel it. She tried to relax. And failed. "Yes."

Another finger stretched her and she felt the burn deep within as her body eased to accommodate him. Shadows filled his eyes—he wanted it to be his own body—and he bit the soft curve of her breast with a snarl as the amber overtook his irises.

Lena lifted her hips to his hand, silently demanding more. The world narrowed, becoming little more than the sound of shifting sheets and soft sighs and the feel of his fingers pumping within her.

Something beckoned, a sensation she knew she wanted to feel. Tossing her head from side to side, she tried to find it, tried to push harder against his hand. Will's thumb rode over the nub of her flesh and she clenched with a gasp, grabbing at his wrist.

"There," she whispered desperately. "Right there."

"Here?" A thumb pressed hard against her.

She cried out, her hips lifting higher. So close. Almost… The edge threatened to collapse beneath her and his thumb rode her again. There—

Lena screamed as sensation rode through her, blinding her to all else. Nothing but the feel of his body remained, his finger driving deep within her. Claiming her as she wished his body could.

Too much. She cried out and caught his hand, clenching her knees tightly together as she rolled onto her side. Gasping, her face pressed into the sheets, she came back to the world slowly. Will curled around her, his face nuzzling the back of her neck and his shaft pressed against her bottom.

She shifted, driving it between her thighs, her own slickness creating a vacuum. Will sucked in a sharp breath, his hands clutching her tight. "Lena."

Yet his hips pressed against her bottom, the nest of springy hair at the base of his shaft tickling her. His hot flesh rode against her sensitive nub and she gasped again, white lights dancing behind her eyes.

Sinking a fist into her hair, Will dragged her face back, baring her throat. His hips bucked against her again, tearing a new sensation through her.

Teeth sinking into the soft muscle of her trapezium. His fist, a dominating presence in her hair. She couldn't move, trapped by his body. Will ground himself against her again and again, thrusting hard between her thighs. She clenched her knees, her fingers digging into the sheet.

"*Mine*," he growled. "You're mine."

"Always," she cried, her body tipping over that sharp, electric edge again.

His cry echoed hers, hot seed flooding against her stomach. Lena collapsed against the sheets, panting hard. There was no time to relax. Will shoved her onto her back, his eyes wild as he wiped the seed from her skin. Only when the last trace of it was gone did his shoulders relax. He balled the sheet up and threw it away.

Lena reached for him, "Come here."

The muscle strained in his thighs. "I shouldn't." His

gaze drifted to the sheet, voice hoarse. "I shouldn't have risked even that."

Languorous heat settled through her body. She wanted to sleep, desperately. Stretching catlike, she smiled up at him. "That wasn't a question, Will."

He owned her utterly. And yet, when it came down to it, she owned a part of him too.

He came, his body pressing hard on hers, driving her into the mattress. Lena smiled to herself and held him close, rubbing her cheek against his throat.

I love you.

But they were words she didn't dare utter, words that would only cause pain in this moment. She didn't want to cry. Didn't want to see that sleepy satisfaction fade from his eyes. This moment was for them. The last one they could ever have.

The thought made her smile fade slightly but she forced it away. *Mine*, she told herself, sliding her arms around him and holding him tight. The familiar scent of his body flooded her nostrils and she pressed her face into his hair and breathed deep.

No thought of the future. No thought of what couldn't be.

Just the moment.

One she never wanted to let go of.

Twenty-two

A SOFT HAND STROKED HIS CHEST.

Will yawned and struggled to open his eyes. He felt better than he had in years, so relaxed he could barely lift his head off the pillow. The room was dark, the sheets stained with the scent of Lena and the musky scent of—

He froze.

Then caught the hand that stroked his chest.

"Lena," he whispered, lifting his head off the pillow. Starlight glittered through the crack between the curtains.

"Mmph?" She made a sleepy sound and snuggled against him.

She was naked, her leg thrown over his and her head resting on his shoulder. Panic erupted, his heart bursting into a racing staccato. He could feel every inch of impossibly smooth skin, her body slick against his.

The scent of sex. Of his seed, mingled with the delicious scent of her own body.

The loose end of the bandage on her hand tickled

his chest. What had he done? Looking around wildly, he saw the discarded roll of sheet. Memory flooded back in. His fingers, wet within the heat of her body, Lena gasping beneath him, her face twisted with ecstasy. Thrusting hard between her thighs, her knees clamped together like a vise as he spilled his seed against her stomach…

Will's head hit the pillow. Thank God. He hadn't taken her. Hadn't infected her. Relief flooded through him and he caught her hand, squeezing it gently.

The bandage tickled his fingers. He brought her hand to his mouth and kissed her fingertips. Lena barely stirred.

Frowning, he rolled onto his side. She tumbled into his arms like a rag doll, a flush of perspiration on her gleaming, naked skin.

"Lena?" he whispered. Why the devil wasn't she responding?

His side was wet where she'd been lying against him. Will's eyebrows furrowed deeper and he pressed a hand against her forehead.

Perspiration drenched her hair. She moaned slightly, her head lolling as if she sought to remove his hand. He drew it back, mind racing.

She felt hot. Most of the time a human's skin felt cold against his burning heat. Lena always had, her body feeling like cool silk against his. For him to register her skin as hot, she had to be burning up, almost as hot as he himself.

There was only one possible reason for that.

"No," he whispered, turning her chin to peer at her face.

Faint circles of red shadowed her cheeks. Sweat gleamed on her breasts and stained the sheets beneath her. Will rose up onto his knees, his gaze falling on the bandage around her hand.

He yanked it off, lost to any sense of tenderness. Lena whimpered, her head twisting on the pillow and wet strands of hair sticking to her throat. He almost didn't want to look, too afraid to know the truth.

Forcing himself, he opened her curled fingers and stared hard at the palm of her hand.

Smooth pale skin.

Not even a hint of a welt.

"No," he whispered, throwing himself off the bed. Panic churned in his stomach and he raked his hands through his hair, shooting her an incredulous look.

It couldn't be. He'd been so careful with her. No blood, no sex… And he knew saliva was safe or he'd never have kissed her.

Cold dread spiraled through him. "Lena," he whispered, crossing to the bed. "Lena?"

She blinked sleepily, wincing as if her head hurt. "Will?" A soft murmur, her head lolling to the side.

Will caught her chin. "You don't feel well, do you?"

Her pupils looked the size of small marbles. She looked past him, her gaze focusing on nothing. "Just…head aching…"

"How long?" Her eyes started closing again and he grabbed her by the shoulders and shook her gently. "Damn it, Lena. How long have you been feeling poorly?"

Blinking up at him, she caught his hands, her own grip feeble. "Hurts."

"I know." He ground his teeth together and let her go. "I'm sorry. How long has it been hurtin' for?"

"Days?" she whispered, licking at her dry lips. "The morning after you came…to my room."

Will slumped on the edge of the bed. "Days?" he repeated. What the hell had happened that night? He'd kissed her. Tasted her skin. Her breasts. But nothing else. It had to have been blood, but he couldn't remember if he'd been bleeding. He was always so careful. "Was I injured? Did you see any blood on me?"

She shook her head, curling back into the pillow as if her body ached. As it no doubt did. "Don't know." Cupping her hands over her face, she whimpered. "Hurts."

He hovered over her uselessly. "I know." God, how he knew. Joints aching, body burning up, head pounding as if it were fit to split. The insatiable need for water. He stroked her back, light circles to ease the aching he knew she'd be feeling.

"I'll fetch you some water," he said, leaning down and kissing her brow.

"Please."

"Stay here." His heart hammered in his chest as he fetched her nightgown and laid it over her. Anything more would only chafe her skin. Tugging on the pair of trousers he found strewn over the end of the bed, he eased out of the room and shut the door quietly.

A soft whimper echoed from within, stabbing him hard in the chest. Will leaned back against the door, closing his eyes in despair.

What had he done?

The reality of the situation didn't truly hit him until he'd helped her finish a full jug of water. As Lena collapsed back on the sheets into a feverish sleep, he dragged a clean sheet he'd found over her and stood back, staring at her petite figure. She shivered, her skin clammy to the touch.

Will backed away, swallowing hard. *What have I done?* He should never have laid so much as a finger on her.

But years of aching loneliness had their toll. He'd always desired Lena. Too much so. When he first took the letter off her he should have gone straight to Blade. Let him deal with the mess, with Lena's protection. He'd known how much of a temptation she represented for him.

With his feet dragging, he slowly climbed the stairs to the attic. The faint swish of skirts told him who was awake up there.

A murmur of voices greeted him as he lifted his hand to knock. Blade too, then. Guilt choked him but he forced himself to rap at the thick wooden door. There was nothing he could do now. Lena needed her sister.

"Come in, Will," Honoria called.

Light sheared through the darkness as he opened the door. Honoria's usual chignon was a bedraggled mess as she perched in an armchair by the hearth. Blade rifled through the books on the shelves, peering intently at the spines.

Honoria met his gaze, dark circles swallowing her eyes.

She knew.

He faltered in the door, shaking his head, unable to speak.

"Oh, Will," she whispered, coming to her feet. "How is she?"

He opened his mouth but no words came out. Only an inarticulate sound of pain and guilt. The room blurred as heat filled his eyes. "I didn't—I was always so careful. I don't know how—" And then a flash of image swam into his mind. Of the jewelry store. "My lip," he said, touching it. "I had a fight with Colchester and he split my lip." Guilt punched him in the chest. "I kissed her. I didn't think." He'd been more concerned with not bedding her, of fighting away the desire to claim her as his own. He'd forgotten, for a moment, the dangers of his blood. And the wound had been so minor...

Honoria wrapped her arms around his waist and for once he let her. "It's not your fault, Will. No matter what we all said, she would never have stayed away from you." The warmth of her body soaked into his and he rested his chin on the top of her head, holding her awkwardly.

"I should have made her." He drew back and wiped his sleeve across his eyes. "I should never have thought I could do this. I should have come straight to Blade when this all happened. Let him deal with her."

"When all what happened?"

Too many secrets. He shut his mouth and raked his hands through his hair. "What do we do?"

Honoria stared at him for a piercing moment, then let it go. She turned away, gesturing at the half-opened books that littered the room. "I don't know, Will. We've been reading all day—"

"You knew?"

"Her temperature's too hot. It's not human. And I could guess."

He took a step toward her, suddenly angry. "Why the hell didn't you tell me?"

"You were in no condition," she replied simply. "And we knew little about the loupe. I needed to find out more before I could start to treat it."

"Ease up, lad," Blade warned, his eyes darkening. He had his hands shoved into his pockets, but the way he rocked onto the balls of his feet indicated swift movement if needed.

Will turned away, shaking his head. No point getting angry. The only thing that was important now was Lena. "Have you found anythin'? Anythin' at all?"

A slight hesitation. "There's nothing about how to deal with the transition or the first initial stages of the virus. The loupe isn't a very well-documented disease in Britain. I don't think anyone in the Echelon cared whether people survived it. What did they do when you were first infected?"

He stared at the wall. "I don't know. Don't remember much." Just heat, incessant heat. His body aching. Screaming through a newly reknitted throat as his body changed. And the merciful coldness of the cellar as his da' tried to bring his temperature down. "Cold," he said. "The cold helped. Me father put me in the cellar where it were cool." He turned around. "She'll be thirsty. You have to keep her drinkin'." A shrug. "I can't remember anythin' else."

"That's not a lot to go on." Honoria bit her lip.

"I know," he snapped. "I were only five and barely lucid. Do you think I wouldn't mention somethin' if I could remember it?"

"I wasn't accusing you of anything, Will."

Blade had taken a step closer.

Will turned away, fists clenched. "I'm sorry. I'm on edge. I can't believe—" His worst nightmare. Come to life.

A hand slid over his lower back. "We know," Honoria whispered. "Come. We'd best get prepared. I don't think it will be long before her temperature starts spiking. She's already got the rosy cheeks. It's the following fever that will…"

As if realizing what she was about to say, she stopped.

"Hold," Blade said.

They both turned toward him.

"There's nothin' in your books and Will don't remember," he said. "But there's some in London right now who might know how to deal with this."

"The Scandinavians," Honoria whispered. She clapped a hand to her head. "Why didn't I think of them?"

"You're distracted."

"Are they likely to help?" Honoria looked up at Will.

He frowned. "I barely know 'em. But they might."

"You'll have to go," Honoria demanded.

"I'm not leavin' her."

"This is her best chance," she stressed. "Please, Will. You know I'll look after her. I wouldn't let anything happen to her."

He wavered. Honoria would do her best, but he could hardly bear to leave, knowing that Lena might…

Baring his teeth, he nodded. "It's her best chance. I'll fetch one of 'em."

"I wish that didn't sound as if you were goin' to drag 'em 'ere, willin' or not," Blade muttered.

❧

Will pounded on the door of the manor that the Norwegians were leasing for the duration of their stay. Rain dripped incessantly, tangling in his hair and running down his face. The journey into the city had been a mindless one. He could barely remember any of it.

Glancing at his watch every few seconds did little to alleviate the tension riding him. It had taken him twenty minutes. Twenty minutes in which he didn't know what was happening to Lena.

Footsteps finally sounded in the entrance and the door opened on a harried-looking butler. "Yes?"

He pushed forward, into the doorway. "Is the Lady Astrid in?"

"I'm afraid she's not at liberty—"

He had the man by the throat in seconds. "You go and fetch her," he said quietly. "Or I'll rip your heart out through your nostrils, you understand?"

The man went sprawling as Will released him and scrambled back across the marble tiles.

"What's going on here?" someone barked.

The Fenrir stepped out of the shadows of the library, clad in his court attire. The wolf fur was secured around his broad shoulders with a polished bead of amber, and his gray beard and hair had been combed. The menace in his eye nearly threw Will over the edge.

Don't look him in the eye. Deep breath…

"You dare come into my house like this?" the Fenrir asked in a deadly soft voice. "You dare treat my servants like this?"

"Uncle." Astrid's voice. Soothing and calm. She strode to Magnus's side and eased a hand over his arm. "Look at him. He's barely containing himself. Something's set him off." With an appeasing look, she turned to Will. "What is it?"

He took a deep breath, overwhelmed by the scent of too many of his kind. "It's Lena."

"Your woman?" She frowned, then understanding dawned. "She's got the loupe, hasn't she?"

"I were only five. I don't remember how to deal with it, how to help her—"

"May not be any help, lad," Magnus grumbled, subsiding. He stroked his beard. "She's the small girl?"

Both he and Astrid exchanged glances.

"She's strong willed," Will blurted. "She'll fight."

"You should have stayed away from her," Magnus said, lips thinning. "There's a reason we don't mate with humans."

"I ain't touched her."

"It doesn't matter," Astrid said, shooting her uncle a look. "Let me fetch my cloak. I'll come. Whether it helps or not…"

"Thank you."

"Where's your carriage?" she asked.

Will shook his head. "Came on foot. By rooftop."

Astrid stared at him, her pale white skirts swishing around her ankles. Then a blinding smile crept over her lips. "How interesting. Let me change."

Magnus caught her arm as she turned to go. "You're not going alone."

"Everyone's supposed to be at what's-his-name's ball. That hatchet-faced vulture who thinks he's amusing."

"The Duke of Morioch," Magnus replied dryly. "Take Eric. I'm sure he'll relish the opportunity to avoid another night of boredom." He turned his gaze toward Will. "I'm giving you my son and my niece. You bring them back to me or I'll mount your head on a spike, you understand?"

He nodded. A man who spoke his language. "Perfectly."

❧

"The rookeries, eh?" Eric leaped off the rooftop onto the muddy streets below, his fur-lined cloak swirling around him.

Will followed, pushing past to lead the way. The warren came into view and some of the tension went out of his shoulders.

"I expected a manor," Astrid murmured, landing beside them and staring up at the decrepit appearance of the building. "Do you have a cellar? Or ice?"

"You'd be surprised," he muttered, shoving the front door open.

Rip guarded the front door, his hand straying to his belt as the door opened. Charlie and Lark sat on the bottom of the stairs, arguing over who'd won the game of jacks. Charlie's jaw dropped as Astrid followed him in.

She'd changed into a pair of tight leather breeches, with a vest that cinched her waist to a ridiculous span. Her hair had been braided back tightly, leaving her cheekbones bare, and the fur cloak she wore turned her into a barbarian princess. Even Rip's eyebrow rose.

Eric followed. The Norseman smiled, ruffling Lark's hair as if she were a little girl. Charlie looked like he was contemplating a fur cloak and chain mail addition to his wardrobe.

"How is she?"

Charlie blinked, tearing his gaze away from the exotic pair. "Don't know. Honor won't let me in. What's goin' on, Will? I heard Lena crying—"

He shoved past, heading straight up the stairs.

Soft whimpering sounds came from within Lena's room. Rapping softly on the door, he poked his head in.

Lena writhed on the bed, her cheeks burning with fever. Her nightgown clung to her body with sweat, and Honoria hovered by her head with a cool cloth. Blade was trying to keep her still, a glass of water in his hand.

"Did they come?" Honoria asked, strain showing around her mouth.

He couldn't take his eyes off Lena. "How is she?"

Honoria's mouth twisted. "Her temperature's getting higher."

Something shoved him out of the way and Astrid pushed past. She took in the scene at a glance, slinging her cloak over a nearby chair. "You need to cool her. Fast. We'll need ice, and something large enough to put her in."

"A bath?" Blade asked.

"Do you have one?"

"In me rooms," he replied.

"Perfect." She pressed a hand against Lena's temple, closing her eyes. "Very close to the peak, but not there yet. There's time."

"She'll get hotter?" Honoria gasped.

"She dies if she does," Astrid replied bluntly. "Will, fetch me ice. Lots of it."

He spent the next twenty minutes smashing the heavy ice blocks to pieces, then carrying it from the deep cellars to Blade's room. The cellars were freezing; Blade needed a continuous supply of ice in order to keep his blood chilled.

Astrid and Honoria had taken over the bathroom. Astrid filled the bath to the brim with cool water, then poured buckets of ice chips into it.

"Are you certain this is safe?" Honoria asked. "They used to do this to the inmates at the institute I worked at. It was awful."

"It will hurt, yes," Astrid replied, her expression unchanging. She met his gaze, knowing he'd be the one to protest. "Whatever she does, you must not interfere."

"How much will it hurt?" he asked.

"Like fire." She put a hand out to stop him. "This is her only chance. In Norway, we use the snow to quench the fever."

He hovered on the balls of his feet. The worst thing was knowing how much pain Lena was in right now. How much pain would come. He'd spent two days clawing at the dirt in the cellar before the fever broke.

But there was no help for it. "How long?"

Astrid gave him a serious look. "Two or three days. Perhaps one has already passed. She seems halfway through it."

This was her only hope, he reminded himself, though the thought of hurting her made him feel sick. "I'll go fetch her."

Twenty-three

THE MOMENT THEY PUT HER IN THE WATER SHE
started screaming.

Will held her down, despite her weak thrashing, his
teeth clenched and his body tense. Astrid had said the
shock of the cold might kill her, but without it her
temperature would keep rising until she died.

The ice water burned his arms, his fingers eventually numbing. He could only imagine what it felt like
for Lena. And it was all his fault. His eyes blurred with
heat as he held her down, whispering to her that he
was there, that she would be all right.

It didn't take long for her thrashing to subside and
her body to slump into his arms. "What's happening?"
he asked. "Lena?" There was no response. Only the
slight quiver of her lip as she shivered.

"Bring her out," Astrid commanded.

Will cradled her carefully in his arms, icy water
splashing all across the marble floors. They dried her
off, with Astrid monitoring her temperature and the
timepiece Honoria had given her.

"What now?" he asked. "Is she better?"

"Her temperature's dropped a degree," Astrid said, taking the thermometer away. She exchanged a glance with Honoria. "Will, I need more ice."

"More ice?"

"For next time."

He shook his head. Lena lolled in his arms, her skin clammy with cold, yet burning with an inner radiance. "How many times?"

"Each time her temperature goes up. Until the fever breaks."

The hopelessness of the situation hit him. "She's not goin' to make it, is she?"

Astrid stroked the wet strands off Lena's forehead. "You told me she is strong willed, no?"

"Stubborn as rock." Tears burned in his eyes.

"Then bring more ice, Will." Leaning down, she whispered in Lena's ear. "You must fight, little one. Fight for your man, as he fights for you."

The night stretched out, hour after brutal hour. A never-ending vignette as he broke the heavy ice blocks into shards and carried them upstairs, then bathed her in the water. Honoria started crying, silent tears that streaked down her face. He couldn't look at her or he would break. Lena barely stirred when they put her in the bath now.

"Come, *mo cridhe*." He kissed her forehead, wishing there was something, anything that he could do. But there was nothing he could kill here, nothing he could protect her from. His very uselessness battered at him.

Too late…

For so many things. Too late to hold her now. Too late to kiss her, to give himself over to her as he had always feared to do. To tell her that he loved her, as he knew she had longed to hear.

He had held her at arm's bay, for fear of the very thing that was occurring now.

"I will give you the world," he whispered, stroking the hair off her forehead. "I will protect you, I swear. I'll never let you hurt again, I promise. Just come back, Lena. Come back and let me love you."

But she didn't hear him.

Lost to the fever, she didn't hear any of them.

Too late.

⤝⤞

"Her heart's barely beating," Astrid said in a quiet voice.

Morning had broken, sunlight streaming through the window. The room was drenched, as if someone had waged war in the bath. Perhaps, he thought, it *had* been a war of sorts. And now it was becoming apparent that they were losing.

He could hear the thready beat of her heart. Clasping her hand, Will held her close against his chest, waiting numbly for that horrible moment when Astrid would force him to put her back in the bath. He didn't think Lena could take it anymore.

He barely could.

His hands were shriveled and he shivered as he held her wet body in his arms. He could barely see or hear the world around him, his body fighting to sleep, to renew itself.

All he could feel was the body in his arms, the heat of her skin as the fever raged, despite their attempts to contain it. In the last hour, her temperature had increased two degrees. A human would be long dead by now.

Come on. He rocked her, muttering lullabies he could barely remember from his youth. When his mother had not looked at him as if wondering how such a monster could have stolen her son.

Come back to me.

A soft hand touched his shoulder. Astrid. "Will, you must let her go."

No! He snarled and shook her away. If they tried to take her, he would kill them. All of them.

Quiet whispers. "...*too late. He's given himself to her... If she dies, he will pine away...*"

Honoria. Crying.

He forced himself to his feet and staggered toward the bath. It was easier now, for he barely felt a thing. Lowering himself into the bath, he dragged Lena against his chest, her cheek resting on his shoulder. The slow tick of her heartbeat pulsed against his chest. Ice burned across his skin until he was numb all over.

The world faded.

Then hands were dragging him out of the bath, dragging Lena out of his arms. He snarled and flung them away from him, trying to reach for her. Blade's face swam into view. "Easy now, let 'er go, Will. Let 'er go..."

He grabbed Blade by the throat and tossed him aside. Eric was helping Astrid with Lena. He went for them, throwing Eric back into the mirror. It shattered and Astrid stiffened.

"Get out," she cried. "Everybody get out. Leave him to her. Before he kills someone."

Shoving Lena into his arms, she backed away, dragging her cousin with her. The door closed and he was alone, the bathroom a ruined mess.

"Lena," he whispered, curled around her in misery. Why wouldn't she come back? "I'm sorry. Gods, I'm sorry."

The bath was half-empty. He couldn't do it to her anymore. She was shivering as it was, goose flesh pebbled all over her skin.

Dragging himself to his feet, Will lurched toward the bedroom. If she died, then he didn't want her to be cold anymore. Ripping off her nightgown, he laid her down on the sheets of the bed and dried her carefully. Every inch of her was white with cold, her cheeks and chest flushed with a red rash. Every time he touched her, he felt the icy chill of her skin and that burning furnace deep within. A heart of fire buried beneath the ice.

Starting with her feet he began to chafe the heat back into her. No more cold. He couldn't let her die that way. Even now, her heartbeat was a weak echo in his ears.

It took a long time to rub the chill from her skin. Stripping off his wet clothes, he curled up beside her, dragging the blankets over the top of them. He dragged her into his arms, tried to use his own body heat to somehow revive her.

Long hours passed as he felt the heat burning deep within her. It answered his own, rising to the surface until they were both wet with perspiration. "I'm sorry," he whispered, again and again, kissing her damp shoulder.

Sweat broke over her skin, along with a violent attack of shivers. Will buried his face against the back of her neck and breathed in the faint scent of her body. He was so tired. He just wanted to close his eyes and never wake up, but something was struggling against him.

A gasp.

A body wriggling weakly, skin slick with sweat, in his arms.

Opening grainy eyes, he stared in disbelief as Lena whimpered and tried to push him away.

"Hot," she rasped. Her pupils were enormous still, her gaze unfocused.

Will sat up abruptly and she tumbled onto her back, barely able to move. "Lena?"

Dry, cracked lips, her cheeks flushed with red. She'd never been so beautiful. Shoving aside the blankets, she tried to move and sprawled onto the mattress face-first.

Grabbing the blanket, he draped her in it and tried to help her sit up. "Lena?" Grabbing her chin, he held her eyelid up. A ring of bright copper circled her pupils. Incredulous breath expanded his lungs. "You survived." Her forehead was clammy with sweat as he cupped his palm against it, but the intense heat had abated. "The fever's broken."

She pushed at him weakly.

Plumping the pillows under her back, he eased her back against them. "I'll get you some water. Stay here. Don't move." He couldn't stop himself from capturing her face in his hands. She was barely lucid, but the fever had broken. "I love you." He kissed her hard, then drew back when she tried to whimper again. "I'll bring you lots of water."

∽⚬∼

Honoria paced the kitchen, her cheeks scalded with tears and her eyes dry. There was nothing left in her. She'd done all she could and still failed.

Blade dragged her back into his arms. "There's still 'ope. She ain't done in yet or we'd know."

"I feel ill." She pushed him away and leaned against the bench as a fist of nausea threatened to choke her.

She could sense Blade hovering over her, trying to get her to drink a glass of water. He suddenly looked up and she spun toward the door. "What is it?"

The pair of Norwegians waited in the corner, faces tight with strain. She knew as soon as she looked at them that it was Will coming down the stairs.

"Oh, God," she whispered, her knees going out from under her.

Blade caught her, drawing her up so that she was standing when Will came through the door.

Sweat gleamed over his naked body. Wild eyes, wild hair, his muscles burnished with heat. Honoria's jaw dropped and she looked away as he snatched the jug of water off the bench.

"She's thirsty," Will growled, then turned and vanished the way he'd come.

"Thirsty?" Honoria whispered. She spun toward Astrid. "Does that mean...?"

Astrid's eyes were wide. "Goodness," she murmured. "What a shame he's already bound to her..."

Eric punched her lightly in the arm and grinned.

"Put your eyes back in your head, cousin." He stood and clapped Blade on the back. "If she is thirsty, then all is well. The fever must have broken."

Honoria turned toward the door, but Eric caught her wrist and shook his head. "No," he said. "We must trust that he will care for her. Leave them alone or risk having your head handed to you."

Seeing her expression, Astrid smiled. "He is acting *inn matki munr*. Like a newly mated male. He'll be insufferable for days, especially given that he nearly lost her. Leave them alone and give him time to calm down."

Twenty-four

SUNLIGHT SHIMMERED THROUGH GAUZY LACE CURTAINS.

Lena moaned under her breath and tried to cover her eyes. Then she blinked. This wasn't her room. Where was she?

Sitting up sent a shaft of throbbing pain through the base of her skull. Wincing, she cracked her eyelids open and looked around.

Bare timber floor. Rough hewn furniture. A table in the corner with a single chair seated by it. And a pair of boots, attached to long muscular legs.

Will.

She was at Will's flat.

Sunlight caught the coppery tips of his hair and burnished his tanned skin. He dozed, propped up in an old armchair, his arms crossed over his chest and his head nodding forward. Dark circles shadowed his eyes and his jaw bore the signs of several days' rough growth.

The last time she'd seen him he'd been frantic; tucking her into his own cot, muttering that she was safe, that she would be all right now. Telling her again and again that he was sorry.

Lena frowned. When had that happened? She had a vague flashing memory of pain and heat, and then screaming as someone dropped her into what felt like a vat of burning oil. Honoria peering at her worriedly as she tried to give her water. Will snapping at Honoria, driving her from the room as he dragged Lena out of bed and brought her here.

What the devil had happened?

Tossing aside the blankets, she tried to stand up. The world spun and she staggered into the stove, her nightgown tumbling around her ankles. The faint odor of lavender clung to her. Not her usual soap. Someone must have been bathing her.

Will blinked sleepily. "Lena?" He leaped to his feet and caught her, as if she were too fragile to even stand. "What are you doin' out of bed?"

The heat of his body was a welcome sensation. She burrowed her face against his chest and breathed deep. His scent was so familiar, so warm and masculine, but beneath that she caught myriad scents. Starched linen, soap, sweat, a hint of her sister's perfume, even the oil he used to clean the heavy hunting knife he wore strapped to his thigh.

How curious.

"Can you shut the curtains?" she asked. "It's so bright."

His scent changed, became somehow sharper. "It's your eyes. They'll adjust, but it'll take a few days."

"Adjust to what?"

Another pause. His scent became even bitterer. "Lena." He cleared his throat. "Do you remember aught of what happened?"

The seriousness in his face and tone sobered her.

She fought for recollection and failed. "What's wrong? What happened? Is everyone all right?"

"How do you feel?"

An odd question. She considered her body. Now that she was on her feet she felt better, an incredible lightness of being that she couldn't quite explain. "Very thirsty?" And another pressing need she didn't want to admit. Heat flushed through her cheeks. "Do you think I could…use your washroom?"

Will stared at her for a long moment, coppery rings burning around his pupils. He gave a short nod. "O' course."

Herding her to the washroom as if she were an invalid, he started to follow her inside.

"Will!" She tried to shut the door in his face. "What are you doing?"

"Lookin' after you."

"Not in here," she replied firmly. "Out!"

It took a moment, but his lips thinned and he turned on his heel. "I'll fetch you some water to wash with."

He brought water, soap, and a small towel. As soon as he shut the door, she turned to the unmentionable. Perhaps she had been hasty. By the time she washed her hands in the jug of water on his washstand, her knees were shaking. And the water looked damned good. She was half tempted to drink it straight from his shaving jug but forced herself to merely rinse her mouth and scrub her teeth. Using his washrag, she stripped her nightgown off then washed herself with the cloth and soap. Lavender scent assailed her. He'd definitely been bathing her.

Tugging her nightgown over her head, she ignored

her discarded drawers. She wanted clean clothes, something to drink, and a good hot meal.

"Will?" She twisted the knob, but the door sprang open in her grip. Will hovered on the other side with a glass of water for her.

Now that she'd taken care of one need, others were begging for attention. Her gaze went straight past him, to the icebox, just as her stomach gave an embarrassing growl. She took the glass and gulped it down.

"I've mutton stew," he said. "And bread and cheese. It ain't much, but there's lots of it. I had 'em send round as much as Esme could bake."

Stew. Her mouth watered. But there were other more pressing concerns. "Will, why am I here? What's been happening? I can hardly remember the last day."

"It's been four actually."

"*What?*"

Raking a hand through his hair, he turned away from her. "Here. I'll show you." Snatching the small bone-handled mirror off his washstand, he held it close, as if he didn't want her to see.

Sudden dread filled her. What was wrong with her? Her hands flew to her cheeks, but her skin felt normal. Snatching the mirror, she bought it up and stared at her reflection.

"My eyes," she whispered. They stared back at her, the pupils ringed with bright bands of copper. Slowly she lowered the mirror. "But how…? What…?"

Will couldn't meet her gaze. "God, I'm so sorry. I told you I ought never have come near you." He looked up, heat and anger swirling through his eyes. "This is why. I nearly lost you. I nearly killed you!"

He turned on his heel and strode away, hands entwined behind his head. Lena risked another quick glance in the mirror. "I have the loupe?" she asked wonderingly.

He flinched as if she'd hit him.

"Will." Putting the mirror aside, she crossed toward him, but he jerked away, circling the table and chair as if she were hunting him. Taking a slow breath, she put her hands on the back of the chair and leaned on it. "I don't care. I told you I wouldn't mind. If I could be with you—"

"You nearly died!" he snapped, eyes rolling with white.

And she realized then just how close it must have been. His hands clenched and he looked away, tearing his gaze from hers.

"How bad was it?"

"We didn't think you were goin' to make it," he replied hoarsely. "I thought you were dyin', before the fever broke. You don't know what it did to me." He rubbed his chest. "I went a little insane. I threw Blade across the room and brought you here. Honoria comes by every day but I couldn't let her... Not 'til you woke..."

Her heart ached for the pain emblazoned on his face. "I survived."

"Barely."

"It doesn't matter."

His fists clenched and he turned his face away. "Yes, it does. You don't know what this means."

"What this means?" She shoved the chair out of the way. Then the table. It was ridiculously easy. "Is that you don't have any more excuses."

Will backed up against the cot, his hands held in

front of him. "Damn it, Lena," he growled. "I infected you! Your life ain't gonna be the same."

She stalked him. "I certainly hope not."

"You don't understand—"

"I understand perfectly." Stopping in front of him, she pushed on his chest and he stumbled back onto the cot, a look of surprise on his face.

Staring at her hands in wonder, she couldn't stop her smile. "How strong do you think I am now?"

"Why?"

"No reason." *I wonder if I could dangle a certain blue blood off the edge of the Ivory Tower?*

The world had become a different place, full of blazing color, heat, and scents. Dust motes swirled through the shaft of light that lit them. She held her hands up, stirring them about. All her life she felt as though she'd been blind, with the details of the world around her only newly revealed.

"You see this as a curse," she said, sliding onto his lap. The muscles in his thighs tensed. "I don't. I know there shall be limitations. I know my time in the Echelon is done—it was done the moment you carried me out of that ballroom." Seeing his mouth open, she pressed her finger against his lips. "I've been afraid for a very long time, Will. I'm not afraid now. Not even a little. Is that part of it?"

His gaze locked on hers. Mutiny burned there. He didn't believe her.

"There's nothing about my old life that I want to go back to," she whispered, sliding her leg up to straddle his hips. The nightgown slid up around her thighs, and he sucked in a sharp breath, his fingers clenching in the blankets. Lena rocked against his hips, the rasp of the buttons on his trousers riding over her inner thigh.

"I want a new life," she told him. "With you. I know that now." Sliding her hands over his shoulders, she leaned closer, breathing in his delicious musky scent. "I finally know what I want. And I'm not afraid to admit it anymore."

"Lena." His hand curled against her bottom, as if in warning. "You're verwulfen now. A slave in the Echelon's eyes. You might never be able to leave the 'Chapel again."

"Who says I need to?" She brushed her mouth against his. "Who says I ever need to leave this bed?"

Another gasped breath. But his eyes were burning now, turning hot with a flood of amber color.

"You're mine, Will." A smile of victory curled over her lips as soon as she saw the change. "You can't hurt me anymore. You don't have any more excuses. You can hate yourself all you want, but quite frankly, I'm rather impressed with the changes."

As she leaned toward him, he leaned back. Stubborn, stubborn man. Lena followed him, kneeling over him and drinking in the sight of that tempting body.

"Ain't you hungry?"

"Mmm." She kissed at his mouth, licked it. "Yes, I am."

Hands hovered at her sides. Fingers stiff, half reaching for her. "Lena, damn it. You weren't well."

"Anyone would think you a skittish bride on her wedding night." A smoky laugh, her voice lowering. "Now that you can't hurt me, think of all the things you could do to me."

His gaze darkened. "You've just recovered from a fever."

"I feel wonderful." She bit his lower lip, sucking it into her mouth. "I feel better than wonderful." She laughed, dug her nails into his chest. "I feel like I could do some very wicked things to you, right now."

Hands clamped on either side of her hips, and he opened up to her, his mouth chasing hers. "Damn you, I thought I lost you." A shudder ran through him. "I don't have the words to say... I can't fight it anymore," he admitted hoarsely.

"Then don't."

Their mouths met, the taste of him hot and furious, full of denied hunger. It felt so right. She almost shuddered, pressing herself against him, desperate to get closer, skin on skin, to let him sink himself deep within her. Need swamped her. Furious, desperate need.

Grabbing the hem of her nightgown, Will shoved it up. They broke the kiss just long enough to get it over her head, then she was naked against him, the rasp of his shirt abrading her nipples, his hands clenching in the soft flesh of her bottom. Lena wove her fingers through his hair, grabbing fistfuls of the silky strands.

A groan tore through her throat. She threw her head back as his hot mouth closed over the column of her throat. "Yes," she whispered. Her eyes shot wide as his teeth grazed the smooth slope of her breasts.

Her hands half lifted to cover herself, but he caught them and held them wide.

"No," he growled. "You promised me everythin' I could do to you. And I owe you for that bashful bride comment."

The domination in his voice thrilled her.

"Instinct," she replied and threw her head and shoulders back. Light gleamed off her pale skin, her nipples hard and pink. A breathless fist twisted in her stomach at the look in his eyes.

"Do you like them?" she whispered.

Hard lips captured hers. The answer was evident against her thigh, the thick, heavy heat of him branding her intimately. His tongue drove into her mouth even as his hands caught her hips and ground her against him.

It felt so good. Lena whimpered, her hands sliding up through his hair, her nails raking his scalp. The laughter was gone, faded. In its place was a desperate insanity, a hunger, a need to consume. The empty ache between her thighs almost undid her. She scrabbled at his shirt, tearing it over his shoulders until only the briefest scraps of linen hung from his elbows, still buttoned at the wrists.

"Easy," he growled into her mouth, hands capturing her wrists.

"No." She caught the top button of his trousers, but he drew her hands away.

"Plenty of time."

"Now," she demanded.

This time it was his turn to laugh. Caging her in his arms, he crushed her against his chest, his mouth possessing hers. Long, slow, hot kisses. Enough to drive her crazy. She wriggled, wanting more, desperately drinking at his mouth.

"I…" He tumbled her onto her back, his hard body driving her back into the mattress as he pinned her. "Ain't gonna rush this."

"Who said you had a choice?"

Another smile. His special smile. The one that melted her deep inside. "I'm still stronger than you."

Lena stroked her fingers down his abdomen. "And bigger." Definitely bigger. She shivered. Splayed her hands over his chest. "I always wanted to do this."

"Do what?"

"This." She dragged her nails down his stomach, tugging at the waistband of his trousers. "When I was younger, after I first moved into the warren. I wanted to touch you. To taste you. I dreamed of you," she admitted, heat flushing her cheeks.

Will met her eyes, his own sober. "I couldn't."

"I know." She shrugged as if it didn't matter.

"I wanted to." Another devastating smile. "Damn it, Lena, you don't know how much I wanted to. You drove me crazy. I ain't never felt such a thing for a woman before and you were too young… Too… I thought it were only a game for you. I had to leave."

"It wasn't. Not truly." She smiled, latching onto the few words that interested her. "You've never wanted a woman before?"

"Only you."

A warm glow lit her from within. She tugged at his waistband, sliding her finger behind the button. It popped open and Will's eyes narrowed.

"I've had enough wanting. Enough waiting," she said.

"You're impatient."

But he ran the backs of his fingers over the curve of her breast, watching the movement with a rapt fascination. Lena felt that touch in other places. She shivered, writhing beneath him.

"Touch me," she whispered.

"I am."

Wide, slow circles around her breast, drawing ever nearer to her nipple. She arched under his touch, like a cat.

"You're not. You're teasing me."

"Mmm." Warm humor filled his eyes. "I think I know somewhat how that feels."

The devil. She bit her lip and reached for him, but he reared away.

"No. Put your hands on the bed head."

"I don't want to. I want to touch you."

He caught her wrist, forced her fingers around the iron bed head. "I weren't askin'." Taking the other hand, he repeated the motion. "Don't make me tie you down."

Tie her down? The thought sent a shiver of need straight through her. She considered the demand, then relaxed her hands around the iron. "Very well. Just don't take too long."

Will lowered his head, his lips skimming across her collarbone. A soft laugh whispered over her skin. "You're not in the position to be making demands."

"I'm—"

His mouth closed over her nipple, the heat of it scalding her. Her mouth dropped open. "Oh."

"You like this?" He looked up at her, his tongue tracing the hardened bud, a devilish look in his eyes. Since when had he ever been this playful?

She licked her lips. "It's nice. I suppose."

Teeth grazed her soft skin. White heat turned her vision blank. When she could breathe again, he was laughing at her.

"I told you to keep your hands on the rail."

Somehow she'd clenched her fingers in his hair.

"Bet you can't keep 'em there."

Lips firming, she grabbed the bar and curled her fingers around it. "I'll bet I can. What do I win?"

"Hmm." The murmur shivered over her skin. He licked her again, swirling his tongue around her nipple. "If you win… Perhaps I'll let you return the favor."

"Tie you down?" She sucked in a breath. Her arms were quivering. It was increasingly difficult to keep her thoughts straight. "And if I lose?"

"Then for a week you'll do everythin' I say, without even a single argument."

Lena lifted her head off the pillow. "Not a chance."

"Then don't move your hands. No matter what, Lena."

Ducking his head, he kissed his way across to her other breast and lavished the same attention on it. The sensation shot through her like the charged lightning the Echelon used and stored in Leyden jars.

Throughout it all she clung to the bed, her hips arching up, desperately pleading for something, anything more. Her thighs were wet with her own need, the scent of it flavoring the air. He had to know.

"Breathe," he told her, smugly wiping his mouth. "It's about to get better."

"Better?"

His fingers tickled her thigh. His mouth trailed down her stomach and she forgot to breathe. Little white dots danced before her eyes. "Will!"

Nuzzling into the thatch of dark hair between her thighs, he eased them wider. "Heard enough stories 'bout what a woman likes. Might take some practice though. You let me know how I'm doin'."

His mouth closed over her sensitive, wet flesh. Lena's eyes widened. "*Will!*" The word was almost a scream, the shock of it slicing through her in waves of sensation.

Heat seared her as his tongue delved deep inside her. The rasp of his stubble against her oversensitized skin tore another gasp from her throat. Good heavens! What was he doing? How did he know? He nuzzled higher, sucking at the tender nub at the center of the sensation.

Lena lost her bet.

She clung to his shoulders, her hips jerking beneath him as he lathed her delicate flesh. "Don't stop!" She arched her hips up, trying to force herself against his mouth. "Oh, my God! Don't you dare stop!"

Delicious tension stretched and furled deep within her. Head thrown back, she gasped as he lapped at her, suckling her into his mouth. *So close… So close to the edge…*

She screamed as it broke within her. Screamed as he suckled her hard, driving her spasms higher, forcing the sensation through her. Sensation finally ceased as he lifted his head, eyes dark with amusement. He licked his lips and she rolled to the side, involuntary quivers shooting through her body as she sucked in desperate breaths.

Fingertips trailed up her thigh, circling her hip. The muscle jumped beneath his touch. "Lena." Humor flavored his voice. He kissed her hip. "Did you like that?"

"I daresay I liked it rather a lot," she gasped. "But I'm not quite sure at the moment. The world seems to have shifted."

He laughed, his voice dropping to a smoky whisper. "You taste delicious." Another kiss, against the curve of her hip. He crawled up over her, nudging aside her arm and capturing her nipple between his lips.

It was too much, too soon. But she could no sooner have pushed him away now than she ever could have. Rolling onto her back, she slid her legs around his hips with a shudder. "You're still wearing your trousers."

He caught her questing fingers and pressed her flat onto her back. As he captured her mouth, she tasted her own body on his lips. "And you've lost your bet."

Lena lost herself in the taste of his mouth. "You're getting better at this," she whispered, tracing his tongue with her own.

A pinch to her bottom made her jump. "First the blushin' bride, now you question me skill at kissin'?" Grabbing her by the hips, he rolled them until he lay flat on the mattress and she straddled him. "Since you're the one with all the experience, I'll let you lead."

Lena slid her hands over his bare chest. Will cupped his hands behind his head, the very picture of male repose. "I like the fact that you've never kissed another woman before," she protested. "I like being your first. And I intend to be your last." The last few words came out as a low growl.

She slid her hands lower and tugged open the buttons on his trousers. The heavy ridge of his cock strained against the fabric then sprang into her hands with an eager thrust.

He was enormous, her fingers barely closing around the girth of him. A drop of pearly white glistened at the swollen head, thick veins curving around his shaft.

She didn't know what to do. All of the lessons about her flesh rights flew straight out of her head.

"Here," he said, seeing her helpless look. Grabbing her hands, he curled them around his cock. "Like this."

Lena wet her lips, her hands stroking him carefully. His eyes glazed and he threw his head back, lip curled up in a silent snarl as he gripped the end of the bed. Thick muscle strained in his biceps as he squeezed tight.

"You like this?" she whispered, her hands loose as she stroked him.

"Harder."

Tightening her grip, she pumped the silky-slick skin in her hands. She couldn't tear her gaze from his face, watching as the violence of pleasure twisted his features, made him gasp. *She* made him gasp. The thought was heady and with it inspiration struck.

Years ago she'd seen pictures of how to please a man and one thing had always stuck…

Lena bent low and licked at the slit on the throbbing head of his shaft. Will's hips pumped and he cried out wordlessly. It had felt so good for her, so she greedily suckled him into her mouth, tasting the saltiness of his seed on her tongue.

A hand fisted in her hair, driving her lower, his hips thrusting up, filling her mouth, her throat, with his cock. Feral light blazed in Will's eyes and he lifted his head off the bed to watch.

"God, Lena." A gasp. "That feels so fuckin' good." He collapsed back against the bed, his hands urging her away from him. "You have to stop."

"I don't want to." She licked at the thin slit on

the head of him. She'd barely begun to learn what he liked—

The world shifted. He yanked her up, rubbing his shaft between her thighs. "Can't. Have to be inside you. Now." Snarling, he lowered her hips, the tip of his heavy flesh stretching her.

Lena gasped. She could feel the inexorable stretch of her body as he edged deeper. Pain burned. She couldn't do it. He was too big.

As if recognizing her distress, he froze.

Sweat gleamed against his hairline. The muscles in his arms trembled. "I'm tryin'. Tryin' to hold it," he whispered hoarsely.

And he would. He would turn away from this if he thought he was hurting her. Chain whatever turbulence drove him deep inside, force it back into the cage. The hunger gleamed in his eyes, the sheer *need* to possess her, but he would do it.

For her.

Lena shoved down, her mind branded with shock as he filled her. Will hissed, his fingers digging into her hips, even as the pain shot through her.

She gasped, wilting over him, her body so full of him that she didn't know where she began and he ended. The hurt was a pulsing throb where they joined, yet with it came the satisfaction of finally being in his arms, finally sheathing him in her body. She would do anything, pay any price to be his.

Will's hand slid up her back, cupping the back of her neck. "Damn it, Lena. I don't want to hurt you, but you feel so good, so tight."

"It's fading," she whispered, lifting her head a little.

The pain was receding, the loupe healing her. A part of her wanted to own that pain, to brand herself with the proof of his possession.

Will's hips flexed. He groaned, throwing his head back against the pillow. "I'm sorry. I can't—"

She kissed his chest, a shivery sensation spreading through her. "Then don't stop. I want to be yours." Rolling her hips brought another gasp to his lips. She tried again, squeezing him deep within, her body knowing instinctively what her mind didn't.

Will's fingers dug into her bottom. He thrust up, the heat of his body burning her from within.

The pain was gone, chased from her body by a dawning exhilaration. He was hers. He was finally hers, and she was never going to let him go. Lena threw her head back, his hands helping her to find the rhythm that pleased him and taunted her. Each slick glide brought her temptingly close to the edge.

Will curled his back, lifting off the pillow and claiming her mouth. The movement impaled her deeper, her knees driving into the mattress and the base of his shaft rubbing against her slit. Body tightening, she gasped, but there was no escape. From his mouth. From the feel of him, deep inside. From the hands that cupped the base of her skull.

Fingers clenching in her hair, he dragged her head back, his teeth sinking into the soft flesh of her trapezius. Marking her. Claiming her. Driving her over the edge.

Lena cried out as it took her. Her body clenched around his and he groaned, his hips slowing, his thrusts becoming deeper. Crying out, he shuddered violently against her, one hand against the small of her back as he drove her against him.

Long minutes of breathless gasping as she came back to herself. She'd never felt safer, more at peace, than this moment in his arms.

Skin slick with sweat, his heart pounding against hers, she lifted her head slowly. Will shivered. His eyes were bright as copper pennies and fueled with uncertainty. "I didn't hurt you?"

She smiled and nibbled at his ear. Her body ached with the possession of their joining. And she loved it. "No."

"You're so tight, *mo cridhe*." He stroked her face tenderly.

Lena cupped his hand against her face. *Mo cridhe*. Incomprehensible words she could remember him whispering to her in the fever, amongst others. "What does that mean?"

"Little one." He smiled, but the tension lingered in his bronze-warmed eyes.

"I don't think it means that at all."

"No?"

She kissed his palm, looked deep into his eyes. "No."

Will chuckled against her skin and dragged her against his chest as he lay back. His body still nestled within hers. "Go to sleep," he said, with a satisfied yawn. His eyelashes fluttered against his cheeks. "Before I'm tempted to have me wicked way with you again."

❧

He roused sometime later, just long enough to roll her onto her stomach and bite the back of her neck. Lena blinked sleepily as he tugged her hips up and thrust inside her. This time there was no gentleness. Whatever thought spurred him out of sleep, he slaked it on her body, filling her, owning her. Claiming her with such desperation that she collapsed panting on the bed afterward, unable to breathe, her body still tingling with aftershocks.

And again. Barely hours later, with evening darkening the sky. Driving her into the mattress, his eyes gleamed with copper, lost to the feral side of his nature.

It ignited something within her. Urges she'd never felt before. They kissed and bit and thrust at each other, desperate to leave some mark, some shadow of themselves on the other's skin. The darkness within her unfurled and she raked her nails down his back as she screamed her pleasure into the night.

She lost count of how many times he took her. The world faded. Became little more than skin and sweat and seed, the thrust of his body, the acceptance of her own. Sometime before dawn they both collapsed, exhaustion shivering through her body.

Will crept from the bed and fixed a plate of stew for her, warming it on the stove. Her hungers changed and she ate two plates ravenously before collapsing back onto the cot. There was barely room for two, but he curled around her, dragged the blankets over them, and nuzzled into her hair. A part of her liked the fact that the bed wasn't bigger.

"Sleep," he whispered, as if he wasn't the cause of her sleepless night.

She snuggled against him, her eyelashes fluttering heavily against her cheeks. "Only…if you let me…"

She was asleep before she finished her sentence.

Twenty-five

A SHARP RAPPING AT THE DOOR WOKE HER. LENA lifted her head off the warm pillow it rested on—Will's chest—and blinked sleepily. Despite the two bowls of stew she'd consumed, her stomach rumbled as if she'd been starved for a week.

The muscles beneath her tensed. "Stay here."

He rolled out of bed, dragging his trousers on. Lena lazily enjoyed the view, tempted to drag her fingernails over his bare buttocks. She'd once thought him too bulky and coarsely built, but she'd been wrong. He was perfect. All sculpted muscle and bronzed skin. Beside him, the blue bloods paled into insignificance with their padded shoulders and pale skin.

One of the buttons on his trousers was missing, no doubt in her enthusiasm last night. He shot her an exasperated look, then crossed to the door. Lena sat up, searching for her nightgown. Her gaze settled on a pile of abandoned white linen near the door. Dragging the sheet around her body, she tucked it between the crevice of her breasts and tried to comb out the snarls in her hair.

The door thundered beneath the weight of some-one's fury.

"I'm comin'," Will muttered and snatched it open.

Honoria staggered into the room, her face pale and her eyes flashing dark with fury. "You let me in!" she cried. "I've had enough. I want to see her! She's mine too, you kn—" Her gaze lit on Lena and she darted under Will's outstretched arm with a soft cry. Sliding to her knees, she wrapped her arms around Lena and dragged her close.

"I sent you a message," Will muttered.

Lena breathed deeply, filling her lungs with her sister's familiar scent. "I'm all right," she said as Honoria burst into tears.

Blade sauntered inside with a shrug. "You got five days," he said to Will. "That's all I could 'old 'er for."

Will tried to shut the door but it jerked back in his direction and Charlie slid inside with a cheery smile. It faded when he saw her, turning to a puzzled frown. "Why ain't you wearin' any clothes?"

Heat burning in her cheeks, Lena helped Blade collect Honoria. "Give me time to wash up and dress," she murmured. Snatching up her nightgown, she darted into the washroom.

Barely a minute later, Will followed her inside, a harried look on his face.

"Too much of my family?"

His gaze roamed down her naked body and he reached for the washcloth. "Aye. Need a moment. Let me help you."

She squealed under her breath as he slid the washcloth between her thighs. "Will!" Dropping her voice, she tugged it out of his fingers. "Don't you dare!"

Washing swiftly, she dragged her nightgown back over her head. "I don't suppose you thought to bring anything for me to wear with you?"

"I weren't plannin' on keepin' you dressed." He tickled her bottom.

Catching his fingers, she glared at him. "You're in a rare fine mood this morning."

"Aye." He nuzzled closer, his breath sliding over her throat. "Help me wash?"

"That's not going to get us out of here in a hurry," she whispered.

"I know." His hands slid over her hips.

Lowering her voice to a bare whisper, she pushed him away. "Not with my family in the next room, thank you. Wash up and get dressed." Taking her chance, she ducked under his grasping arm and slipped through the door.

Honoria was drying her eyes when she reappeared.

Lena took her hand and led her to the chair. "Sit," she instructed, pushing on Honoria's shoulders. It felt odd to be giving orders, when Honoria had always been the one to issue them. Leaning closer, she kissed her sister's wet cheek. "Cheer up. I'm fine."

"Truly?"

Dragging one of the blankets around her shoulders to cover her thin nightgown, Lena nodded. "I can't remember very much of it at all. I do remember your voice though. Thank you for looking after Will."

Honoria exchanged a glance with Blade. "Not that he allowed much. He virtually kidnapped you."

Blade poured water into a battered old kettle. "You 'as to let 'er go sometime, luv."

Honoria's lips thinned.

"I am all of twenty," Lena reminded her with a smile.

"You're still my little sister."

"And I can beat you in an arm wrestle now."

The reminder didn't sit well with Honoria. Lena laughed and settled on the edge of the cot. Will chose that moment to enter, tugging his shirt into place. Water turned his gold-tipped hair darker, spiking his eyelashes together. Her breath caught. So handsome.

"Urgh," Blade muttered. "Tell me we weren't that bad?"

It took a moment for Charlie to comprehend. His eyes widened. "That's why you're 'ere! You and Will? That's smashing! When did that 'appen?"

"Charlie, don't forget your *h*'s,'" Honoria corrected.

A roll of the eyes. "Yes, ma'am." He punched Will in the shoulder. "How do you like that, eh? Another man in the family. Thank God it ain't one o' them prancing blue bloods from the Echelon. I never thought she'd be sensible enough to choose a decent man."

"Yes, well," Lena said, "I don't believe they'll be having me back anytime soon."

Charlie peered at her eyes. "I like them," he declared.

"Why, thank you." She laughed, then realized that Blade and Honoria were exchanging another of those long glances that spoke volumes. "Why? What is it?"

"Leo's visited three times," Honoria said. "The prince consort wants to know why Will isn't doing his duty and has requested Lena's presence. Leo's trying to placate him."

"They're signin' the treaty tomorrow," Blade said. "If the Norwegians will come to the party."

Will eased a possessive hand over her shoulder. "They can't see Lena. Spreadin' the loupe's punishable by death."

Lena's hand shot to his. "What do you mean?" She looked from him to Blade. "They won't hurt Will, will they?"

"Not if I've anythin' to say 'bout it." Blade sobered. "It's too late to 'ide. The prince consort already knows. I believe the Lady Astrid told him. She probably thought it didn't matter much."

"He wouldn't dare hurt Will," she said, finding her feet and dragging the blanket tighter around her. "He can't risk alienating the Scandinavians until they've signed the treaty. Will, your best chance is to make an appearance tomorrow, force his hand. Make him publicly acknowledge me and what has happened when he must keep face with the Scandinavians."

Will glared down at her. "I ain't takin' you into the heart of the Echelon. Not with the Norwegian's allegiance still in doubt and them pasty-faced maggots swarmin' round us. Not 'til the treaty's signed and you're safe by the law."

"But they won't change the law unless the Norwegians sign," she said softly. "Do you think they will?"

Will's silence was answer enough. "Astrid and Eric helped us. But they ain't the ones in power. And I don't think the Fenrir rules with his heart. I think he knows exactly which way he's gonna play this and why."

"Then we need to convince him otherwise," she said earnestly. "I know you don't want me in danger. But I'm not about to sit and watch when it's *your* head that's on the line!"

"No."

"You promised we'd work together—"

"Unless I thought it were dangerous—"

"For you! Not for me."

"You don't know that," Will snapped. "You've never been spat at or had women hide their children from you. You've never been trapped in a cage, Lena, whilst the blue bloods sneered that that was where you belonged. I tried to tell you. This is a different world and I'm so bloody sorry for that. I'll try to get them to sign the treaty, but I won't risk you. Not again. I couldn't bear to lose you. You know that."

She took a deep breath. Arguing with him was futile. She had to be rational if she had any chance of winning his approval. "You don't know the court. You don't know the dangers to be encountered there. You don't see them because you don't play such games yourself, therefore you don't expect them to be played." He opened his mouth but she hurried on, determined to finish. "It won't be knives or fists or fights in dark alleys, Will. It'll be played with words. You wouldn't even realize the trouble until you were buried in it. You need me. I know this world. I know how to play the game."

"I won't put you in danger."

"If you fail, then you die," she replied bluntly. "And there'll be nobody to protect me. Especially not the law."

He didn't like that. "Damn it, Lena—"

"You know I'm right."

Strain whitened his jaw and his eyes rolled with white. But his shoulders slumped and she knew she had him.

"You don't leave my side. Not even for a moment. If anyone makes a move against you, I *will* kill 'em."

"I believe you," she said softly. Sensing his distress—to let her do this went against every instinct he owned—she stroked his hand. "Thank you."

"Well. Never thought I'd see the day." Blade laughed, then clapped Will on the back. "You know you're in trouble when you been outmaneuvered by a mere slip of a lass."

"Don't you laugh," Honoria warned. "I think it's time we dusted off your court clothes and made an appearance. We can help guard Lena."

Blade winced. "The Echelon's gonna love that."

❧

Lena scraped the last of the soup out of the bowl and peered inside it mournfully. She'd already eaten half a kidney pie, a plate of stew, two slices of bread, and now the bowl of soup. And she still felt hungry.

The others had taken over Blade's sitting room at the warren and were arguing about how to convince the Scandinavians to accept the treaty tomorrow. Will glanced over at her with a frown, then looked down at the bowl. "More?"

She shook her head. "I shouldn't."

Ignoring her, he took the bowl out of her hands and crossed to the soup tureen on the table. "Gotta keep your strength up."

"I'll get plump."

He shrugged and filled the bowl. "It ain't likely, but it wouldn't matter anyway."

The bowl warmed her hands almost as much as his words warmed her heart. Lena peered down into the broth. All her life she'd been nothing more than a pretty face to most men. Her father's princess. A piece of froth to the Echelon.

Only Will saw her as something else. Something more.

A knock sounded at the door and Blade swung around sharply as Esme entered. "Sorry," she murmured with a cheerful smile. "But I've a letter for Lena."

"Lena?" Will straightened.

Lena frowned, accepting the letter. Who would think to find her here? The only one who knew she visited with any great regularity was Leo.

Sliding a thumbnail under the edge of the envelope, she slid it open. It was empty except for a small curl of hair, tied neatly with a ribbon.

Blond hair. Silky fine.

It smelt like Charlie.

Lena froze. "Where did you get this?" she asked hoarsely.

The room stilled as everyone sensed her sudden fear. Esme licked her lips. "There was a man at the door not a few minutes ago. Said he had a letter for you."

Blade crossed to the windows, twitching aside the curtains. "What did he look like?"

As Esme stammered out a vague response, Will took the tuft of hair from her and sniffed at it. He shot a look toward Charlie, then raised a questioning brow at her.

Lena put the soup aside, her appetite destroyed. She knew exactly what it meant. She hadn't been performing as expected. Someone wanted her to destroy this treaty and so far she'd made no headway.

"What is it?" Will asked.

Lena shook her head, pushing herself to her feet. Her throat felt thick. It had to be the person from Crowe Tower. If he could get to Charlie here, get so close as to steal a lock of his hair…

She froze, her hands clenching in her skirts. What could she do? Destroy the treaty and she risked Will's life. But if she didn't…

"Lena?" A warm hand slid over the small of her back. They were all looking at her.

"I…I…"

Will would hate her for this. She thought of his smile, only moments earlier, of the gentle way he stroked her back now.

"It's Charlie's, isn't it?" Honoria asked quietly, her eyes locked on the piece of hair. "What's going on? Lena?"

Tell them and she risked losing Will… But no, that was a selfish thought. Her stomach clenched. Charlie's life was at risk, and so was Will's. This had grown beyond her capabilities to solve.

Her shoulders sank. "It's Charlie's. It's…" One glance toward Will, as if she couldn't help herself. "I couldn't tell you. Somebody threatened me. They had one of Charlie's clockwork soldiers that they'd taken from his room. They said that if I didn't destroy the treaty they'd hurt him." The words wouldn't stop now. "I thought if I did what they said it would be all right. But I couldn't. Not when it meant your freedom…"

Will looked as though she'd struck him. Lena cringed and grabbed his hand. "I'm so sorry. I never meant to do it. I never wanted to…"

He lifted his hand and she flinched. Will froze, then slowly reached out and brushed his fingers under her jaw, tilting her face toward him. "Somebody threatened you?" The words were soft. Dangerous.

Lena trembled. "I told them I didn't want anything more to do with it."

His brows drew together. "Lena, I ain't gonna hurt you." His fingers tightened on her cheeks. "I'm gonna smash someone else's head into a wall, but I would never hurt you."

Relief welled up like a sudden flood. A hot tear leaked down her cheek. "I thought you'd be angry with me—"

"Christ." He grabbed her roughly, enveloping her against his chest. "No more secrets 'tween us. Promise?"

She nodded, breathing in his familiar scent. Her fingers clenched in his shirt.

"You're mine," he murmured. "Foolish plots and all."

Stroking the sticky hair off her face, he lowered his head and brushed his mouth against hers. Lena kissed him desperately, clinging to his shirt.

Behind them someone cleared their throat. "What, precisely, is going on?" Honoria asked.

They were all four staring at her. Blade examined the situation, his eyes narrowed. "Someone came in here, took one of Charlie's toys, didn't they? Took a lock of his hair?"

Charlie clapped a hand to his head, as though searching for the lack.

Will took a deep breath. "Lena? You may as well tell 'em. Blade'll need to know, if we're to keep the boy safe."

Lena slid her hand into his and locked her gaze on Honoria's. "Promise me you won't yell."

Honoria crossed her arms over her chest. "I wouldn't want to make a promise I might break."

This was the price of keeping secrets. Lena squared her shoulders and told them everything.

When she'd finished, everyone was looking at her. Honoria's mouth was a hyphen, but at least she wasn't screaming.

"Humanists," Blade muttered. "Like your father?"

Honoria nodded sharply. "I assume this has something to do with the cipher-text Will wanted me to decode?"

Lena breathed a sigh of relief. "Yes. I thought it was only times and dates for them to meet. Information."

Her hopeful look died when Honoria's gaze skittered away. "I tried an auto key cipher, but I couldn't make heads or tails of it," Honoria said. "So I asked Leo. His colleague, Lord Balfour, has this wonderful machine, based on one of Babbage's uncompleted designs. It's an electro-mechanical rotor cipher machine and—"

"The message," Blade interrupted with a slight smile.

"'Project Firebird aborted. Suspect sabotage from within, holding off and awaiting orders. Mechanists under hand once more. Await further instructions.'"

"What does it mean?" Lena asked.

Honoria shrugged.

"Firebird," Will muttered. "The draining factories?"

"But Ros... Mercury claimed they had nothing to do with that."

"Then she lied," Will said. "Or someone else is sendin' these messages from the humanist faction."

"Bloody politics," Blade muttered.

Honoria frowned. "What I want to know is why you kept all of this to yourself. Why didn't you tell us?"

"I told you," Lena stammered. "I didn't realize—"

"Not you." Her gaze speared Will. "You."

He glanced at Blade, then away. "I thought I could handle it."

Honoria's eyes narrowed. She looked between the two men. "What's going on?"

"Nothin'," Will muttered.

Blade stared at her, his arms crossed defensively over his chest. "Will didn't want me comin' up against the Echelon."

"But you've—"

"I've been drinkin' 'uman blood again," he said suddenly. "It's why me CV results ain't been comin' down more."

Honoria's jaw dropped in surprise. "But...but why? My vaccinated blood was curing you. If we kept going your CV results might almost negate themselves. You might be completely cured. You might be—"

"'Uman," Blade said softly. He looked like a man facing the tumbrel. "It takes away the threat o' the virus, luv, but it takes me strength, me speed." His face screwed up. "It's enough to know I ain't facin' the Fade anymore. I can't afford to be weaker. The

Echelon'd be upon us like a pack o' rabid dogs. Will were tryin' to prevent that from 'appenin'."

Honoria stared at him helplessly, her eyes gleaming with tears. "Why doesn't anyone tell me these things?" Her hot gaze flashed to Lena. "Am I truly so rabid, so fearful, that you're all too scared to tell me? I only want what's best for you. For all of you."

Blade let out a sharp breath, as if he'd feared worse. "It ain't that, luv. I didn't want to disappoint you. You were so set on a cure."

"I'm not irrational," she said.

"You're too rational," Blade said with a tentative smile. He stroked her fingers and she slowly turned her palm toward him, accepting the touch. Relief flooded his expression.

"Well." Honoria let out a sharp breath. "Since we're so set on spilling our secrets today." She pressed her hand to her midriff and blurted, "I think I'm with child."

The color drained out of Blade's face. For a moment he looked as he had three years ago, when he stared the Fade in the face. "Honor?" The whisper was a mix of terror and awe.

Delight swam up inside Lena's chest. "Are you certain?" she asked, taking her sister by the hands.

"I saw the midwife yesterday," Honoria replied, her eyes flooding with tears again.

Lena hugged her close, happiness surging through her. "You deserve it," she whispered. "You're going to be a wonderful mother." She couldn't help a rueful grin. "You've had plenty of practice at mothering all of us."

Esme embraced them both. Over Honoria's shoulder Lena saw Blade stagger against the armchair. Charlie caught him with a grin. Even Will's lips curled in a smile.

"Bloody 'ell," Blade muttered. "That's...that's amazin'."

Then he reached out and dragged Honoria into his arms.

❧

The next day Lena took a deep breath and smoothed the aubergine taffeta over her hips. The girl in the mirror looked like a stranger; corseted and bustled, with elegant feathers in her hair and one of the pretty clockwork brooches she'd designed at her breast. The tiny dragonfly's brass wings fluttered rhythmically and she knew it would draw the focus off her eyes.

Will said they'd change, the coppery ring around her pupils gradually taking over. Lena quite liked them. It was a sign that this pretty girl who stared back at her was no longer powerless. No longer prey.

She smiled and the reflection smiled back at her, teeth slightly bared. Yes. That was better. That was more herself now. She was tired of being afraid, and telling everyone her secrets had taken the last weight off her shoulders. Blade had tightened security on the warren and Charlie was safe and sound now. Nobody would get near him.

All that remained was to bring this treaty to a close.

Her eyes narrowed. She was very much going to enjoy ruining the mysterious assailant's plans.

"Are you ready?" Leo called, rapping at her opened door. He'd insisted that she accompany him. Not only would it help disguise the rumors about her precise relationship with Will, but the weight of his title would offer further protection. If the mysterious assailant made a move toward her, he'd be waiting. Between he and Blade, they'd both resolved to dig out the traitor.

"You've seen Mrs. Wade to the door?"

The first thing she'd insisted upon when she returned to Waverly Place the night before. She'd had enough of being manipulated and betrayed. Mandeville had finished the outer casing of the transformational and picked up the interior this morning, professing his sincere apologies, but she felt it would be a long time before she could trust him again.

"With a reference." Leo's dark expression betrayed his curiosity, but he wouldn't ask. They'd never shared a relationship like that. He'd protected her and guided her through the dangerous waters of the Echelon, but he always held her at a slight distance. Indeed, a distance with which he held the world.

"Thank you," she murmured, stretching up on her toes to press her lips to his cheek. "For everything you've done for me. For taking me in when I didn't know what to do with my life."

A slight pause. Then an enigmatic lift of his brow as he drew away, a rash of heat curving across his cheeks. "I believe what you're saying is good-bye."

She nodded. "I know where I belong now."

"With Will."

"How did you—?"

"Lena," he said dryly, "there are only so many ways the loupe can be spread. I don't even want to imagine how you caught it, since you're my…"

"Your sister," she prompted.

He took a deep breath. "I can never be your brother. Not in public. You know that. This was all I could ever give you."

Always so stiff and distant. She smiled mischievously. "You're going to be an uncle, you know?"

His gaze dropped swiftly to her midriff, then away.

"Not me," she laughed.

An incredulous expression broke over his oh-so-proper countenance. "Good God. He's breeding."

"*He* is your brother-in-law," she reminded him. "With any luck their baby will be just like him."

Horror gave way to a calculated expression. "Yes," Leo murmured. A smile edged over his lips. "*That* would be justice."

He laughed then, the sound of it following them all the way to the carriage.

⤜⤛

Steam carriages disgorged their occupants onto the cobbled courtyard outside the Ivory Tower. Lena gathered her skirts and looked around for Will. The courtyard was a flurry of color, with bright parasols and elegant hats. At a ball, a debutante seeking a protector was expected to wear white. During the day, the vibrant nature of the Echelon sprang to life.

"Where's Will?" she mused.

"I don't see Blade's carriage," Leo murmured. "Perhaps they're not yet here. Traffic in the streets is rather congested."

Her eye caught a conservative group near the stairs. "The Norwegians." Snapping open her parasol, she straightened. "I'm going to speak to them whilst we wait."

"Lena—"

With a blithe smile she turned and stepped into someone. They collided in a tangle of skirts, and Lena grabbed the other woman's arm before she could help herself.

Green eyes widened and Adele looked away sharply. "Pardon," she murmured, attempting to move past.

Lena's fingers tightened. "Don't. Please, Adele."

A pained expression crossed her friend's face. "I can't," she whispered. "My father's on the verge of signing a thrall contract for me with Lord Abagnale."

"That old brute?"

Adele glanced around. "I can't be seen with you. You know what they're like. This is my last chance."

"Adele, there are whispers he beat his last thrall to death!"

Color faded from Adele's smooth cheeks. "You don't think I'm aware of that?" She looked away and Lena's gaze was drawn to the heavy pearl choker that draped her throat.

"Why are you wearing that?"

Adele shook her head. "It doesn't matter."

"Tell me." She reached up, as if to move it, but Adele snatched her fingers and stared at her pleadingly.

"They think I'm anyone's game now. Colchester found me alone—"

"Colchester?" Lena hissed. "What did he do to you?"

"He said since I liked it so much with Cavendish...I couldn't stop him. That's why I need Abagnale. He's rich and he gives his thralls everything they desire."

"That's to make up for the bruises."

"I don't care." Adele's grip tightened. "If he gives me enough, maybe I can pawn it. Maybe I can get enough money to run away. To America. To New York."

Lena's gut clenched. For a thrall to break his or her contract meant execution. "They'll find you."

Adele's shoulders slumped as if hearing the truth had stolen her last hope. "Then I'll stay with Abagnale for as long as…as I can."

It wasn't fair. Lena had found her own sense of freedom, if she could convince the Norwegians to accept the treaty. But Adele hadn't. And neither had any of the young women fanning themselves in the square, putting on airs as they tried desperately to attract a benefactor.

"Don't accept him," she said, tearing her glove off. Grabbing the ruby on her finger, she twisted it off and pressed it into Adele's hand. "It's got a concoction inside it that will incapacitate a blue blood. Here. Like this." She swiftly flicked the tiny thorn out and showed Adele what to do. "It'll give you a chance to get away if any one of them tries to hurt you again."

A fierce light flashed through Adele's eyes. Then faded. "And then what?"

Damn this world. Lena wanted to scream at the injustice of it. "If you need help you can come to me. Or to Leo. Tell him I sent you." Sudden inspiration hit. A way to protect those like her, who didn't have any way to fight back. "That's what I'm going to do," she whispered. "I'm going to open a house. A place for young women in trouble to come to, where no one can hurt them or force them to submit. A place they can stay as long as they want, until we can find a new life for them."

Adele stared at her. "And how do they get away?"

"I'm going to start a new fashion," she declared. "In ruby rings."

Adele looked down, at the gem sparkling on her finger. "I like it," she whispered and a tiny hint of hope returned to her expression.

"Adele!" Mrs. Hamilton snagged her by the other arm, shooting Lena a glance she might have given a stranger. "Come. Lord Abagnale wanted to admire your pretty new necklace."

"Don't make any decisions," Lena pleaded. "Not yet."

Then Adele was swallowed up by the crowd and Lena was left behind, with a new dream smoldering in her heart.

To do such a thing would mean going up against the blue bloods who liked their little game. It also meant surviving the next day. Forcing the prince consort to recognize what Will was doing and hold him to his pledge to change the laws.

Her determined gaze settled on the Norwegians.

They saw her coming, the grizzled old Fenrir's eye narrowing on her. He'd made little concession to the event, still wearing his stark eye patch and wolf fur pinned over his shoulder. The pair of handsome young men at his side had cast off their own furs and wore matching navy uniforms, buttoned up the left breast, with gold frogging and epaulets. She recognized Eric, with his windswept golden hair and the queue of swarming ladies nearby.

Lena nodded to the Fenrir. "My lord."

"So you survived," he growled back.

"Indeed," Lena replied, ignoring his rudeness.

Turning, she greeted the other members of the party. Lady Astrid wore a slight smile, her pale blond hair gleaming against the silvery ruff of fur over her shoulder.

"Considering how ill I was, I'm quite surprised at the swiftness of recovery. I feel in most excellent health," Lena said.

"The initial fever is the only danger," Astrid replied. "Your body's attempts to repel the virus are what threatens you. Once the fever abates, the virus heals you rapidly."

"Fast, furious, and rather violently passionate," Lena mused. "Reminds me of someone I know."

Astrid smiled. "It will take months yet for your full strength to settle in. You will find your moods erratic and yourself prone to emotional outbursts. You must learn to control these, for fear of hurting someone."

"Even a woman suffers from such tempers?"

"Especially a woman," Eric jested.

Astrid turned her quelling gaze on him. "Considering how many times you were dumped in the sea or chained in the cage, you are bold to talk."

"Play nicely." Magnus eased a hand on both their arms. His hungry gaze narrowed on someone. "We are being watched."

The breeze stirred Lena's skirts as she followed his gaze. The Warhammer watched them from across the courtyard. The Duchess of Casavian conversed with him, but that wasn't what caught Lena's attention. On the other side of him, the Duke of Lannister glared at her over a flute of champagne.

Colchester.

She didn't realize she'd taken a step toward him until Astrid caught her arm. The sudden burning rage she felt almost choked her. He had threatened her, hunted her, and almost killed her. And then he'd tried to do the same to Adele. A shimmering red haze settled in her vision.

"You must breathe. Nice and slow," Astrid cautioned her. "This is what I warn you of. This fury. This uncontrollable need. You must let it go."

"I don't want to." With the fury coursing through her she felt powerful, invincible. Without it, she was afraid she would feel like she always had—a timid little mouse, scuttling away whilst Colchester stalked her.

"You would not reach him," Astrid said. "They will cut you down, then turn on us. You know this to be true."

A heavy hand settled on her shoulder. "Breathe," the Fenrir commanded. The weight of his hand calmed her. "Breathe in." As she complied, his hypnotic voice continued. "And as you breathe out, you must let it go."

Colchester tipped his champagne flute toward her in a mocking salute.

Lena's fists clenched. "I hate him. I hate him so much."

"You must let it go," Magnus commanded. "Breathe, Miss Todd. Here is your hotheaded young man." He turned her toward the line of carriages. "What will he do if he sees you so upset?"

Will would rip Colchester to pieces. Lena sucked in a deep breath. She couldn't allow that. "I'm sorry."

"We understand," Magnus replied. "More than most." A brief smile crossed his hard features. "Let it go.

Let your anger and your hate go. Let it wash through you. Like the wind. Cleansing you. Bringing you peace."

Closing her eyes, Lena listened to the soothing timbre of his voice. The muscles in her shoulders relaxed.

"I think you had best take your hand off her," Eric murmured. "Or risk an international incident."

The warmth of his touch was gone. Lena opened her eyes to see Will bearing down on them with Blade and Honoria in tow.

He wore a brown leather waistcoat, the brass buttons riveted to the seam, and a gorgeous velvet long coat that at first glance appeared to be black. Only on close inspection did she realize it was so dark a navy as to look like midnight. The wind ruffled his tangled golden-brown hair as he strode across the yard toward her, scattering ladies and blue bloods alike.

Taking the stairs two at a time, he surged to her side. Lena couldn't stop herself from looking down. Supple leather boots finished just above his knee, with a pair of brass, military-style spurs jangling on the marble tiles.

She couldn't help herself. She had to touch him, brushing the backs of her fingers against his thigh. "Where did you get those from?"

"The boots? They was Blade's little gift to me this mornin'."

"I should have suspected his tastes," she replied, eyeing the rest of him with appreciation. "The coat too?"

"I consider meself lucky its only velvet," Will replied. His eyes were warm with heat and unspoken need.

Lena leaned toward him, then forced herself to stop. They had to behave impeccably today. No matter how much she wanted to grab his lapels and yank his face down to kiss her.

Blade guided Honoria up the stairs with a protective hand on the small of her back. Lena eyed the stark leather coat he wore, and the garish red waistcoat. "You're right." It could have been worse.

Honoria was all charm, greeting the Fenrir and his group with practiced ease. Ignoring their standoffish looks, Blade added his own greetings.

"This is your master?" Astrid murmured, eyeing Blade with open hostility.

Blade snorted. "When it suits 'im. When it don't 'e just tells me to shove off."

"I see," Magnus murmured. "You're not of the Echelon." It wasn't a question.

"Pasty-faced maggots." Blade winked at Magnus and scanned the crowd with a slightly predatory air. "Watch 'em all coo and scuttle about now, like I was a cat thrown in with 'em. Let's just say, me presence weren't expected."

Will leaned down toward her and whispered in her ear, "We've found the girl as took Charlie's clockwork soldier and cut off a bit of his hair. It were one of his blood donors. Said as how a fancy lord paid her for it. Never saw his face though."

Relief flooded through her. "She's no threat?"

His gaze hardened. "Not anymore. Charlie's drinkin' his blood cold from now on and I put the fear of God into her."

"Better that than dead."

"Aye." Taking a deep breath, he turned to the Fenrir. "I've an apology to make. I lost me temper the other night. I should never have forced me way into your home or made such demands of you. I'm sorry."

Magnus stared at him for a long time. "In my homeland, if one of the Fenrisúlfr—this verwulfen that you call us—lost control in such a manner, we would cage him and he would be whipped. It is necessary. To learn to control the *berserkergang,* the fury. The only time we show leniency is during spring rites, when a warrior chooses his mate. Such times are trying. Our instincts overwhelm what we know we must do." He nodded slowly. "You have no apology to make. This once, I grant you leniency, for you yourself suffer such spring madness."

"Once," Eric repeated. "He means this."

"I threw you across the room," Will said, uneasy with the man's good nature. In his place, Will would have been at his throat.

"I should not have reached for your woman." Eric shrugged. "All is well. I am not a man to hold a grudge." Shadows darkened his blue eyes. "And I understand how you feel."

Horns sounded. Conversation lulled as everyone turned toward the tower entrance, prepared for the signing.

"Time to watch this foolery," Magnus growled.

Astrid caught Lena's arm. "Might I have a word, Miss Todd? I should like to speak with you and your man."

The trio of Norwegians froze.

"Astrid?" Magnus arched a brow.

"Go ahead." She waved them toward the door. "I will be only a moment."

❧

Circling the colonnade, Astrid stared out over the rail, the wind whipping her blond curls back like a banner. "My uncle is old," she said suddenly. "A traditionalist. He remembers when we fought the blue bloods and I fear in his heart, he cannot accept this treaty."

Will leaned back against the rail, crossing his arms over his chest. His heart was pounding. Lena could hear it over the beat of her own.

"Why're you tellin' us?" he asked.

"You have a personal stake in this matter," Astrid replied. "But I appreciate your honesty. You have never once tried to manipulate us. I trust this. I trust you. And I need honest answers right now."

Inside, the majority of the Echelon had gathered in the Grand Hall, prepared to watch the historic episode. The prince consort and queen had not yet arrived, but the Council of Dukes was gathering. Will needed to work fast, but Lena knew his answer before he mouthed it.

"You'll have 'em."

He was too loyal, too honest for this work. It was one of the reasons he would not last long in this world alone. And yet she held her breath as Astrid nodded. If he had tried to play them false, would the churlish Norwegians have ever accepted him?

"Can your prince consort be trusted? Can your Council of Dukes?" Astrid asked.

For this he looked to Lena. "I don't trust 'em as a whole. But my opinion against 'em's not wholly rational. Lena knows more."

Lena considered the question. "The prince consort…

No. No, I don't think so. As for the Council, they oppose him in some matters, but not all. He has several of them in his pocket, but each of them has their own agenda. There are some few you can trust. Leo is one. The Duke of Goethe. *Maybe* the Duke of Malloryn. And the Duchess of Casavian's motives are entirely opaque. I don't know what game she's playing, if any."

"The Swedish ambassador intends to accept this treaty. I am trapped in a hard place. If we do not accept, we become caught between two powerful empires. The Swedes have long since wanted to destroy the last of our clans, and with the British on their side, we have no allies. If we do accept, we become the minority in this treaty. To involve us is a gesture, nothing more." Astrid frowned. "I must find an ally for my people. There are none on the Continent. The Hapsburg Empire leash their verwulfen for their armies, and the French are incited with this newfound Illumination cult. The only place I have to search is here. In London."

And if not with the Echelon, then who? Lena's breath caught, her mind taking one of those swift leaps it sometimes did. "You can't trust them!" she blurted.

Both Will and Astrid gave her a look.

"Trust who?" Astrid asked.

"The humanists."

Astrid stilled. "Such talk is treason. Especially when I know whose enemy they truly are."

"I would never betray you to the Echelon." Lena swallowed. "You can trust me, because I was one of them until very recently. I know they intended to approach your delegations, to make their own deals with them."

"We have been approached," Astrid admitted reluctantly.

"They have their own agendas. I was instructed to stop this treaty at all costs. That's what they truly want. They're planning a war, Astrid. They have these enormous metal monsters they strap themselves into. Once they have enough of them to threaten even the Echelon, they'll attack."

"Will they succeed?" Astrid asked.

"I don't think so," Lena replied. "There are factions within the group. One side wishes to wait, to see what the Echelon will do. The others have tried to start a war already. They're killing each other from within."

Astrid released her breath. "Then they can offer me nothing. I need help now." Her fist clenched. "I had hoped…" She shook her head.

Inspiration struck again. Suddenly Lena knew exactly what she had to do. They'd been wrong all along. Magnus might be the one in charge of the Norwegian party, but here was where the power lie.

"You need someone that you can trust." Lena smiled brilliantly. "And we need you to sign our treaty. What if I could guarantee a way to have your voice heard as equal to the Swedish?"

Astrid's eyes narrowed curiously. "And how would you perform this miracle?"

"Well," she admitted. "I shall need a little help."

Twenty-six

"I HOPE THIS WORKS," WILL MUTTERED.

"Trust me." Lena's smile radiated confidence. "I told you I know this world."

The prince consort and his queen swept into the Grand Hall to much fanfare. Towering nearly a foot over Blade and Honoria, Will had a good visual of the room.

The Council waited silently, along with both parties of the Scandinavians. Leo Barrons rested at ease, barely aware of the plot that would soon sweep him up. Astrid needed someone she could trust and Will knew the perfect man. The only blue blood aside from Blade that he'd let at his back.

Crossing his arms over his chest, he allowed himself a tight smile. When he'd thrown up Leo's name as a potential ambassador for the Norwegians to work with, Lena had agreed after a slight hesitation.

"Someone like Leo," she said tightly. "Of course. Someone you can trust. Someone who will hold you in higher regard than the Swedish delegate. Someone even Magnus might accept."

The two women exchanged glances.

"Someone we can trust," Astrid repeated, liking the idea.

The speeches droned on until he swiftly lost interest. He wanted the treaty signed now. Then he could return to Whitechapel, taking Lena along with him.

"Pay attention," she commanded, quivering with heightened tension. "They're about to get to the treaty."

The Swedish ambassador stepped forward with a sly smile and said all of the right things. Behind him, Magnus maneuvered into place beside Leo and whispered something in his ear. Not even Will could hear him over the loud ringing of the Swedish count's voice.

Leo blinked in consideration. After a moment, he nodded and then crossed to the prince regent's side to whisper something.

There was too much to watch. Will applauded as the Swedish count finally finished and the prince regent stepped forward to make his own remarks.

"Ladies and gentleman," he boomed. "An auspicious day for our two empires. As you all know, we are here to sign a treaty with our friends, the Scandinavians. We hope it shall be a long and fruitful union, and to that end, we have decided to announce the appointment of our new ambassador."

Whispers broke out. Several of the dukes exchanged sharp glances. Only Leo seemed at ease, and everyone noticed it. The Duchess of Casavian shot him a narrow-eyed look, then glanced at the prince consort and queen.

"This appointment carries great weight and a great deal of responsibility," the prince consort continued. "We are pleased to announce Mr. William Carver as our new liaison to the verwulfen alliance."

The world dropped out from under him. Heads turned as everyone sought to find him, and the sound of dozens of shocked gasps filled the room.

Will froze, his hands prepared to clap. "This weren't the plan."

"Well, go on!" Lena whispered, a hint of desperate glee in her eyes. "I'm sorry, Will. Leo was a very good suggestion, but there was someone else who was better. You were the only one who couldn't see that."

"I can't be ambassador," he hissed.

Around them, the crowd's clapping started to fade as everyone turned to see what was taking him so long.

"Then the treaty's off," Lena whispered, the smile sliding off her face. "Please. I know you don't like the idea. But think of how much power you could have! Enough to make sure your laws are changed. Enough to offer protection to any verwulfen who needed it. And I'll be there for you. I won't let you do this alone. I'm so sorry, Will. This was the only way I could think to protect you."

He took a deep breath. The room was closing in on him, suddenly far too small. All his life he'd been trapped in the cage, and then in the confines of Whitechapel. It was too much for him.

A hand slid into his and squeezed it tightly.

"You can do this," she whispered, with utmost certainty. "Here is your freedom, Will."

Her hand became an anchor in a world that was swirling around him, a riot of color. Lena was right. Barrons could do this, but he would never have enough loyalty, enough stake in this to truly care. The verwulfen needed someone who would be on their side. And the prince consort needed someone to placate his eastern allies.

But he had other responsibilities. Other debts of honor. Blade met his gaze, his green eyes knowing.

"Go on then," he said softly.

"What about—"

Blade shook his head. "Rip's muscle enough to do me enforcin'. And this'll give you power you ain't 'ad before. Use it," he said ruthlessly. "Times are changin'. Me, a knight o' the realm and you as ambassador?" He laughed. "Gotta adapt."

"Fine." Will looked down at Lena. "I'm gonna be terribly old-fashioned, however, and insist on marriage. I ain't doin' this alone."

A warm light infused her eyes, the copper in them glowing. "How middle-class, Will. Marriage? Truly? Not merely a consort?" With a happy laugh she pushed him toward the center of the crowd. "I accept. Now go."

❧

Lena's heart swelled with pride as she watched him shake the prince consort's hand and bluntly accept the appointment. The whispers in the hall were overpowering. Colchester looked like he was going to explode with fury, his eyes staring daggers at Will.

Suddenly he smiled.

A tremor of premonition edged down her spine. Not Will. He could make any move against her that he wanted. But not Will.

Edging onto her toes, she realized she was suddenly too far away to help if he did something. Knowing it was irrational—Colchester would never dare, not here—she pushed her way past Blade, using her newfound strength to make spaces in the crowd where there were none.

Magnus shook Will's hand with a tight little smile. Allies perhaps, but Magnus would fight for what he thought was best for his people. The Swedish count examined him with a piercing gaze, then took his hand. Will was doing a smashing job despite his unease. He said the right things, even managed a smile.

The prince consort called for the papers. A pair of liveried servants hurried forward, carrying a small signing table with a gold inkwell. Beaming with satisfaction at seeing all of his plots come to fruition, the prince consort made a small gesture to the side.

"And now, a small token of our gratitude!" he called.

A pair of young lads sprang forward, clad in black and gold and dragging a heavy platform into view. The figure stood seven feet tall, draped in a pristine white silk sheet. The crowd clapped as the Swedish ambassador accepted the gift with good grace.

"What is this?" the count asked.

One of the young men grabbed the edge of the sheet and whipped it away with a flourish. A heavy iron-plated man stood on the rolling platform, his arms and chest chiseled, the rough-hewn plating of his face sharp-edged and raw. She'd not bothered to file the rough edges. It suited him—her heavy clockwork rendition of Will.

Lena stilled as the crowd erupted into loud clapping. *What was it doing here?* The last time she'd seen it, she'd given it into Mr. Mandeville's keeping with a good riddance.

The young lads backed away and as they did, she caught a glimpse of one of their faces.

The young boy who'd helped Mendici kidnap her.

The humanists.

Her world slowed, sound draining off at the edges. The Swedish count gestured to Lady Astrid, who stepped forward with a light smile to wind it.

"How lovely," she said, and Lena heard the words as clear as a bell.

Something was wrong. Lena stared at it frantically, recognizing her own artistry. And recognizing, too, the faulty join along the side. Where it had been tampered with.

Astrid turned the handle once. Twice. It strained against her as it never should have. Something was caught near the mainspring or one of the cams. As Astrid released it, the iron man began to quiver, his clockwork cogs sounding like the tick of a clock.

Tick.

Tick.

Tick.

"Will!" she screamed, her voice cutting through the din. Through the haze of her panic, she saw his amber eyes shoot to hers. Pointing at Astrid, she barely started to speak before he took off.

Launching himself across the room, he shoved Astrid to the ground, covering her with his heavy body. People scattered out of the way, confused by his actions, yet recognizing something in his expression that incited fear.

Too many people. Crushed together. Most of the Echelon, including the whole Council and the prince consort. The perfect place to destroy the blue bloods.

"It's going to explode!"

Her cry was taken up, echoed around the chamber. Screams rang out and she found herself shoved aside. The clockwork automaton trembled violently, unable to complete its transformation. Steam hissed out through its vibrating plates.

Catching a glimpse of Will, she saw him shove Astrid into Eric's arms, then turn to look for her. Lena staggered as someone smashed into her, catching his gaze. She shook her head desperately. They were at opposite ends of the room. Safer to go through the opposing doors.

She pointed, then tried frantically to gesture. "Go back!"

A body smashed into her. She was thrown off balance, caught in the whirlpool of pushing and shoving people. The last thing she saw was Will, his face set in a mask of grim determination as he shoved his way toward her through the crowd.

Why was he not going back?

She staggered through the door, swept out of the raging current like a piece of flotsam. Strong arms caught her, wrapping around her body like steel.

"Thank you," she gasped, straining to see Will through the door.

"Oh," said a familiar, silky voice. "I don't think you'll be thanking me at all, my dear."

Lena's blood ran cold as something sharp dug into her spine. "Colchester," she whispered.

Twenty-seven

WILL SHOVED OPEN THE SECOND IRON-BOUND DOOR frantically, the swell of people suddenly surging through. Behind him, the slow, steady tick of the transformational threatened death, steam hissing from it now with teakettle consistency.

Where was she?

He shoved a man out of his way and fought free of the crowd. Lena had been right here, with Colchester's arm around her waist. The look in her eyes as she realized who was standing behind her would fuel his nightmares for months.

Red haze threatened to overwhelm him. He hunted the hallway, but there was no sign of her. Colchester had chosen his moment perfectly. The crowds muddied her scent trail and the bastard could use them to hide.

He had to be somewhere close. Somewhere nearby.

But where?

Suddenly the world went white-hot, flinging him off his feet. He hit the wall and fell hard, pain slashing through his side. Screams filled the air, the sound of cracking plaster tearing through the hall. Inside the Great Hall, flames licked at the furnishings and smoke billowed through the open doors, turning the hallway into a congested nightmare.

He couldn't see. Couldn't smell anything but smoke.

"*Lena*," he whispered, shoving desperately to his feet. She had to be here somewhere.

And that was when he heard it.

Faint sounds of the woman he loved, screaming.

⤜⟡⤛

Colchester shoved her into an antechamber, his sharp bloodletting knife in his fist. Lena stumbled over a chair, tripping on her damned skirts. He'd cut her, the blade slicing through her cheek and flinging fat droplets of blood onto the pale carpets.

The chair splintered beneath her as she fell. Lena pushed herself to her hands and knees and saw the heavy antique leg of the chair beside her. Snatching it up, she scrambled to her feet and turned to face him, brandishing it like a club.

Colchester locked the double doors with a threatening click. Leaning against them, he smiled lazily. "And now, I finally have you alone."

"Not for long," she reminded him. "Will won't be far behind."

"I doubt it." He looked up, toward the floor above them. "That explosion should have ripped most of the Great Hall and the hallway apart. 'Neither fire nor iron told against them,'" he said, repeating the famous quote about verwulfen, "but not even he could survive such a thing. I'm afraid you're on your own."

On her own. A tremble started, deep within her body. "You knew," she said. "You knew it was going to happen."

Colchester's gaze slid toward her. "You will never prove such a thing."

"You smiled. Right before Astrid started winding the transformational. And you very strategically placed yourself nearest the door."

She sidestepped around a small writing table as he stepped toward her. The horror of it shocked her. She'd known that the letters she carried between the Ivory Tower and Mandeville came from someone high within the Echelon, but she had never expected it to be *him*.

"A happy coincidence." Colchester picked up the edge of the table and flipped it aside. "Nowhere to hide, my dear." The small bloodletting blade sliced the air threateningly. Back and forth.

Lena licked dry lips. Where had her courage gone? Her confidence? Where was the surge of invincibility that she'd felt in the yard? She darted behind the sofa into a shaft of sunlight.

Colchester prowled forward, a hunter completely at ease. If she let him, he would kill her, right here, and nobody would ever know who'd done it.

Colchester leaped onto the sofa and over it, his coat flaring around him as he came through the beam of sunlight. She barely had time to think before she swung the chair leg up and smashed him across the face with it.

Dark blood flew, spattering the cream walls. Lena scrambled over the sofa, a surge of excitement running through her veins. Colchester's screams chased her, and he came to his feet, clutching his ruined face. His entire cheekbone caved in, bone gleaming through the torn flesh.

The sight of it excited her in a way it shouldn't have. She felt herself trembling, a sweep of severe cold rushing through her veins. "Come," she said. "I'm not afraid of you anymore."

As she tilted her face up, he suddenly froze.

"You little whore," he whispered. "You filthy beast. You let him *infect you*?"

He hadn't seen her eyes 'til now. Lena hefted the chair leg. "It's the greatest gift any man's ever given me."

The words incited him to a rage she'd never seen before. Ignoring his ruined face, he flipped the sofa up and over, then smashed aside the small reading table. Debris sprayed everywhere as he tore down a bookcase.

Turning on her with a snarl, he held his blade with deadly intent. "I could have given you everything."

"You threatened to take everything I had away. I hated you. I feared you. I don't anymore." Blood was burning in her veins, ice cold. Her heart pounded as she took a step toward him. "You're the monster, Colchester. Will is a greater man than you could ever hope to be. You're nothing beside him. Nothing."

He screamed in rage and launched himself at her. Before, the movement would have been too fast for her to follow, but some part of her had recognized the shifting of his body weight, a precursor to movement. As he leaped, she swung the chair leg, driving it up into his ribs.

The knife scored across her shoulder. It felt like

ice, sizzling once, the pain swiftly fading. Colchester curled over the club she wielded, then drove forward, smashing into her body.

Lena hit the floor hard. The breath smashed from her lungs, his body riding hers to the floor in a tangle of skirts. She could feel his cold breath on her face, his hands tightening around her throat. Maddened eyes glared down at her.

No fear. There was no fear in her, even as her vision narrowed, darkness threatening to loom. Out of the corner of her eye, she saw his knife, discarded on the rug. Groping for it, she caught the handle in her fingertips as Colchester put all his pressure on her throat.

The room darkened. Numbness spread through her until all she could feel was the knife handle. Clenching her fingers around it, she drove it up, straight into his chest.

He screamed, his hands springing from her throat, the short handle of the blade sticking from his chest. Rearing over her, coughing bluish blood, he met her gaze. "Take you…with me." His fingers closed over the knife and he wrenched it from his chest in a surge of fresh blood.

Lena screamed as the blade rose.

The knife never fell. Instead, an explosive sound ripped through the room, fresh blood spattering her.

Colchester roared in pain, his left arm missing from the elbow down. Black flooded into his eyes, a sign that the demon in him had taken control. He'd feel no pain now, barely even notice the blood that poured from the stump of his ruined arm. She must not have hit his heart.

Looking past him, Lena stared at her rescuer in shock.

Smoke curled from the muzzle of a pistol and Rosalind stared at her grimly. She wore black leather from head to toe, men's clothes that somehow suited her, covered over with a long black coat that flared at her hips. A neat little cap covered her distinctive hair and a mask hid the lower half of her face.

Turning, Colchester grabbed the knife from the floor—from the ruined fingers that lay on the carpet—and flung it.

"Look out!" Lena screamed.

Rosalind staggered backward, clutching at the blade in her side. "This wasn't supposed to happen," she whispered, the pistol dropping from nerveless fingers. "We found out, only this morning, what they'd planned. The transformational was gone and so was… so was my younger brother, Jeremy."

Colchester staggered toward her. "You're a humanist," he snarled.

Lena rolled to her feet as Rosalind's knees gave out. "No!" She darted forward, driving her body against Colchester. They both went down.

Colchester grabbed her hair with his remaining hand and yanked her head back. Lena clawed at his face, catching a glimpse of the black soulless misery of his eyes and his shining white teeth as he went for her throat.

"NO!"

The bellow shook the air. Blunt teeth sank into her throat, biting hard enough to tear the flesh. Lena screamed.

Then suddenly rough hands tore Colchester away

from her. Will towered over him in all his fury then turned and flung the duke into the wall.

Colchester dropped to his feet. He met Will halfway, staggering from blood loss but no less dangerous. Lena saw a flash of silver as he tugged a knife from his boot with his remaining hand.

"Will!" she screamed. "He's got a knife!"

Will blocked the swing, his fist straining as he forced the duke's arm back. Slamming him into the wall, he drove the blade toward Colchester's face.

"Let's see how you like the taste of the blade," he snarled and drove it into the duke's throat.

Lena turned away as Colchester made a gurgling groan. The bright scent of hot, fresh blood filled the air and the rasp of the blade as it cut through his windpipe.

The body hit the ground with a meaty thud, the head almost decapitated. Lena looked around, her chest rising with her harsh breath. Will's fist was bloody, the knife clenched in his fingers. A dark, violent expression rode his face and he turned slowly to look at Rosalind's slumped form.

Lena darted between them, holding her hands out. "Will. No."

Bright copper burned in his eyes. He stared at her, lip curled.

"She saved my life," Lena told him. "She shot him."

"She's the person behind the bomb." He took a menacing step forward.

"I came to stop it," Rosalind corrected. With a deep breath, she yanked the blade out of her side and winced. Blood bubbled against her waistcoat. "I was too late. We never wanted this. After the smoke clears, the Echelon will comb the city hunting for whoever did this. We can't afford the scrutiny. Not yet. We're not strong enough."

"Did you find your brother?" Lena asked, helping her to her feet.

"There's no sign of his body upstairs. He must have escaped." Rosalind's voice was flat. "I knew he was fond of Mendici. I allowed it. I should have realized the mechs had poisoned his mind, filled him full of glorious stories. They sent him to deliver the transformational. The bastards sent him to die."

The world was beginning to intrude. Shouting and screams. Footsteps pounding through the corridor outside.

"We have to get going," Lena said, taking Rosalind by the sleeve and looking up at him. "If they find us here over the body, they'll kill us. He's a duke. Nobody can know what happened here."

A violent quiver went through Will's body. His eyelids lowered, a lazy, dangerous look at Rosalind that sent Lena's heart into a paroxysm. "If it weren't for you, he couldn't a grabbed her."

Rosalind bent low, snatching something off the ground. Grabbing Lena around the waist, she hauled her back into her body, shoving the pistol under her chin. The muzzle bit into her soft skin and Lena froze.

"Don't move," Lena warned him. "She's got the same bullets you were making for me."

"Firebolts. Take off an arm or worse," Rosalind snapped.

"Let me go."

"And have him tear my head off?" Rosalind snarled. "Not bloody likely."

"He won't hurt you," Lena said, catching and holding his gaze. "I give you my word that he won't hurt you."

"I'll give her to you," Rosalind said. "But if you make one move toward me, I'll shoot her first. I swear."

Lena staggered into his arms as Rosalind shoved her in the small of her back. She barely had time to think before Will pushed her behind him, using his own body to protect hers.

"Will!" She snatched at his coat, wrapping her arms around his waist. "I promised her you wouldn't hurt her."

"But I didn't," he whispered. "This is twice you've threatened her life—"

"I saved it once," Rosalind replied, pointing the pistol straight at his chest. She licked her lips. "That counts, doesn't it?"

"Barely. You wanted to kill Colchester more than you wanted to save Lena."

"I'm a practical woman. Two boons for the price of one."

"You ever come near her again and I swear I'll rip your head off."

The pistol lowered a fraction. Rosalind clapped a hand over the wound in her side, bending over a little. "I promise. She'll never see me again." A faint grimace. "I have certain things to put in order, it seems."

"How are you going to get out of here?" Lena asked. "Without the guards seeing?"

"Same way I came in." Rosalind crossed to the bookshelf Colchester had half torn from the wall. She swung it open, revealing a hidden staircase. "The whole place is riddled with tunnels. We stole the schematics months ago. Come." She gave Will a wary nod. "I'll get you out without anyone seeing. We can part ways at the bottom. That makes me even, no?"

Lena rubbed the small of his back, coming out from behind him. "Will?" They had to get out of here without anyone seeing them.

He nodded to Rosalind. "You go first. Where I can see you."

Twenty-eight

OPENING THE DOOR TO LEO'S STEAM CARRIAGE, WILL helped Lena into it. Violent shivers shook her body and her eyes were distant. When he'd asked her what was wrong, she'd tried to summon a smile and a shrug. Before he could chase her thoughts down, Blade and Honoria appeared.

Blade and Leo had gotten Honoria out, then Leo had gone back in to help. Smoke poured from the building and the tower guards were frantically trying to assert control.

Time to get out of here. Before people started pointing fingers.

Blade helped Honoria into their own carriage. There was barely room for two more and Will wanted to be alone with Lena for a moment. He hadn't had a single chance since the explosion, and the urge to drag her into his arms, to make sure she was all right, was driving him out of his mind.

Giving swift instructions to the driver, he eased into the carriage and shut the door. It lurched into motion, cutting out of the queue and into the streets. Will jerked the blind closed.

Lena blinked, finally coming out of her reverie. "You do realize this is Leo's carriage?"

"The walk'll do him good," he replied, pushing aside her skirts and easing onto the seat beside her. "Lena." A hesitation. "Are you all right?"

She smiled, but he caught her hand. "No," he said. "Don't give me that smile. I know you're upset." Stroking her dirty gloves, he reminded her, "I can smell it."

Her gaze dropped, her shoulders slumping. "He's finally gone."

"Who?"

"Colchester." Bright tears shone in her eyes. "I feel so overwrought, Will. I've been watching over my shoulder for months, knowing that he'd be there, knowing that even if I was in company I was never safe. When he looked at you and smiled today, it frightened me so much. I thought he was going to do something to you. But it was the explosion. He knew about it. I don't know how. At first I thought he was my contact in the tower, but now I don't think so. He was disgusted when he realized Rosalind was a humanist." She tugged one of her hands from his and wiped her eyes. "I'm glad he's dead," she said fiercely. "But I can't stop shaking. I can't believe we're both safe. That you're safe." Her fist tangled in his shirt. "I nearly lost you…"

Dragging her into his lap, he buried her face against his shoulder. He hated seeing her cry. "He can't ever hurt you again."

"I know," she whispered. Her hands slid over his shoulders, frantic with need. "Touch me, Will. Remind me that you're here. That you're mine."

"Always, *mo cridhe*," he whispered, finding her mouth in the shadows.

Lena kissed him as if she'd never let him go, her mouth hungry and her hands insatiable. Will gathered bunches of her skirts and dragged them out of the way, settling her on his lap. His cock raged behind the flap of his breeches and he ground her against him, tongue clashing with hers. This was heady. This was life. Every hot, sweaty, gasping moment of it.

He bit her throat, tugging on the drawstrings of her drawers. Lena gasped, rocking against his fingers, urging him on.

"Hurry," she whispered.

He dragged them down, but she was straddling him and the material bunched around her thighs. Snarling in frustration, he tore them in two, sinking his fingers into the fleshy curve of her arse.

"God," he groaned. "Have to…taste you."

Tumbling her back onto the seat, he knelt between her thighs. Thick dark hair tumbled over her shoulders and she gasped as he dragged her hips to the edge of the seat, tossing her legs over each of his shoulders. Shoving her skirts up, he cupped her arse and plunged his tongue deep into her quim.

Lena's cry was music to his ears. He wanted to drive away her tears, to claim her as his woman once again. Tasting her, sucking and nibbling at her, he listened to the breathy sounds of her gasps and felt the tension tightening in her body. He wanted to learn every inch of her, to teach himself how to please her best.

Nails raked his shoulders. "Stop!" she gasped. "I want to—"

He tongued her deep, suckling the wet pearl of her clitoris between his teeth. "Want to what?"

Lena shuddered, her knees clamping around his head. Panting with need, she dragged her gaze to his. "I want you," she whispered. "Inside me."

"In a minute."

"*Now.*"

It was the determination in her voice that undid him. He tugged his breeches open and freed his cock, palming it in his hand. Shoving up, he filled her with a single thrust, dragging her closer to the edge of the seat.

So tight. So wet. So hot.

Lena cried out, her thighs clamping around his hips. Clinging to his neck, she dragged his face to hers for a devouring, hungry kiss, no doubt tasting the muskiness of her own body. Will's hips moved of their own accord, plunging into her, his entire body shaking with need. God, she felt so sweet. He wanted to fuck her hard, to drive her down onto the cushions of the carriage and fill her with his cock.

Little urgent gasps broke between them. Lena's body undulated against his, driving him wild with need. He held her against him, grinding the base of his shaft against her. Shudders racked her body, and her inner muscles tightened around him. She liked that, liked what he was doing to her. He could feel the edge of something building within her, feel it in the sudden gasping inattention she gave their kiss. See it in her widening eyes as she cried out silently, her body jerking around his.

A little fist tightened in his chest. His woman. His.

Nobody could take her away from him now and he couldn't hurt her. She could be his forever. Hope swelled in his chest as he ground his teeth together and shuddered. So close. He rode her through the storm, giving himself up to the sensation that streaked through him.

Lena wilted backward, dragging him with her. Will kissed her lips, earning a halfhearted response as his body slid from hers. She made a wordless protest, but he tucked his cock back in his breeches and dragged her into his lap.

His breathing slowed, his heart thundering through his chest. Will buried his face in the warm mahogany lengths of her hair and breathed in the scent of her.

Lena tucked her face against his throat, curling up in his lap. She stroked his chest, splaying her hand over his heart then held it still, as if listening to the beat of it. "What happens now?"

"Now?"

A slight hesitation. "With the treaty?"

He could barely think, his eyelids threatening to shut. But she hadn't been paying attention to anything that had happened since they scrambled out of the cellar. "Blade said they're gonna reschedule it. If the explosion hadn't torn apart half of the blue bloods too, it mighta been a different story. The verwulfen might've blamed the Echelon and likewise. Barrons wants to get to the bottom of it."

"He'll like that," she murmured. "He likes puzzles."

"Are you goin' to tell him?"

"Tell him what?"

"About Rosalind?"

Lena thought about it. "No, I don't think so."

"You don't owe her nothin'," he growled. "They'll cause trouble, you mark me words."

"I can understand how she feels," she replied. "Helpless. Fighting for a lost cause. I won't betray her, Will. Not unless she makes a move against anyone I love."

He stroked a hand over the silk corseted boning covering her back. Her innate sense of loyalty was one of the things he liked most about her. "She makes one wrong move and I'm straight to Leo."

"Thank you." Lena's finger tangled in his shirt collar. She lifted her tearstained face, bright eyes burning with unsaid emotion. "Will...are you angry?"

"Angry? About what?"

"About the trick Astrid and I played? About demanding you as ambassador in exchange for the Norwegians' allegiance."

He thought about it. "It's not somethin' I would have wanted for meself." Sensing the tension in her small frame, he hurried on. "But I'm the only one as can. The thought of change scares me, Lena. I hate the Echelon, hate dealin' with 'em. I were happy bein' Blade's second-in-command, because it meant I never had to leave me safe, little world." He took a deep breath. "You were right. About lettin' 'em make me what I were. Whitechapel were just another little cage that I were allowin' meself to be put into. Can't say I'm thrilled 'bout it, but maybe I need this." He squeezed her tight. "I know I need you."

"You're not mad?" She traced her fingers over his lips.

Will shook his head. "Life were gonna change anyway."

"Oh?"

"You," he admitted. "I couldn't expect you to live with me in that little hovel."

A shy smile touched her lips. "Staying there with you were some of the happiest moments of my life."

The fist in his chest grew tighter. "Me too," he admitted gruffly. Capturing her face, he dragged it to his, forehead to forehead. "You're everythin' to me."

Playing with his collar, she gave him a saucy little smile. "Are you trying to tell me something?"

"Tell you what?"

"How much you adore me?"

Will kissed her cheek. *Maybe.*

"How much…you care for me." Another slightly flirtatious look at him. Her eyes sparkled with mischief as she stroked the rough stubble of his jaw. Then they sobered. She opened her mouth, but he sealed it with a kiss. A way to tell her the answers to the questions she was asking without saying them.

She was breathless by the time he drew back. But not silenced. "How much you love me?" The whisper was a challenge.

He didn't know why she needed to hear the words, when he'd been damned certain he'd shown her exactly how he felt. This was some unknown neediness he hadn't expected to find in her, she with her confident ways.

Will kissed her lips lightly, chasing away the questioning tone. "You know I love you," he said. Her body quivered against his, but he pressed a finger to her lips, stalling her. "I would die for you," he told her. "I'd kill for you. I faced down mechanical squid, rampagin' humanists, and lessons in etiquette for you. I *danced* at a *ball* for you."

The smile on her face warmed his heart. Radiance shone from the center of her being. He didn't care what he had to say to keep that look on her face.

"I love you," he told her sternly. "I always will. You're the only woman I've ever seen. The only woman I ever wanted. I know I ain't much of a catch—"

This time it was her turn to put her finger to his lips. "Don't you dare." Heat flared in her beautiful amber-ringed eyes. "I'm the luckiest woman in London. In the world."

"Aye, mebbe." He slid his arms around her waist. "Are you tryin' to tell me somewhat?"

She laughed. "Look at you, fishing for compliments."

"Not compliments," he warned.

Lena kissed him, cupping his face in her hands. "I love you too," she said quietly. "Oh, Will. I think I've been half in love with you for years."

"It just took me a while to notice."

"How could you not? I gave up the Echelon for you. I faced randy dukes, clockwork bombs, and verwulfen clans. I ruined three sets of gloves."

"Three?" He smiled. "I'll have to replace 'em."

"Yes, you will," she warned. "I won't be showing off my wrists in public ever again."

Possession curled through him. His arms tightened. "No, you won't be. Only I get to see your wrists. Among other things."

Drawing back, Lena toyed with the ribbons of her bodice. "Speaking of… We don't appear to be moving very far with this traffic. I don't suppose that you'll be willing to entertain me…?"

"Entertain?" he drawled, heat sliding through his groin. "Is that what they're callin' it now?"

"Indeed." She tugged the ribbons open. "I believe there are some areas of my education that are lacking. I'll teach you how to belong in this world as long as you teach me something else…how to please you."

The faint swell of her breasts curved over the top of her corset. Will's mouth went dry.

"Trust me, luv," he said, sitting up to help her undress. "You know how to please me."

Epilogue

"WHAT THE HELL HAPPENED HERE?"

The prince consort strode in through the double doors. Cold fury tightened his features and a handful of Coldrush Guards swarmed through the room, ensuring it was safe for him and destroying half of Sir Jasper Lynch's evidence.

Lynch exchanged a telling glance with Barrons. "Don't move," he warned one of the guards. The man froze and Lynch pointed to the bloody footprint he'd been about to step in. "Ruin that and I can't track the owner." He straightened, meeting the prince consort's hard gaze. "Your Grace. It appears the Duke of Lannister has been murdered."

The prince consort peered at the body. Then spun on his heel and broke into a string of invective. "Bloody bombs! The Scandinavians howling for answers and now this! How?"

"Blade to the chest, shot that took off half his arm and near-decapitation. I believe it was the decapitation that killed him, though the shot bothers me,"

Lynch recited. "It's one of those firebolt rounds we've discovered on certain members of the population."

"Humanists," the prince consort spat.

"Perhaps," Lynch replied. He never made a judgment until all of the evidence was in. And there'd been more than one person in this room. He'd managed to track the signs; the strands of hair, splatters of blood, even the scent trails. Four people and a fight, if he wasn't mistaken.

And he was fairly certain he knew who had struck the killing blow. How the others couldn't smell the heavy musk of a verwulfen man—a man Lynch knew well—he'd never know. Perhaps it was all the cologne they wore? Or perhaps, he thought, looking at Barrons's cool gaze, some of them knew precisely who had been here.

"We're uncertain whether the murder was connected to the bombing, or simply an opportunity that someone took advantage of," Barrons said. He paused for a telling moment. "Your Grace, Lynch informs me that one of his humanist informants passed along information about a potential bombing last week. As Colchester was in charge of finding the humanists, Lynch reported the finding directly to him."

The prince consort turned, fury whitening his face. "Are you telling me that Colchester knew about this?"

"Yes," Barrons said softly. "As much as Lynch himself knew."

Waiting for the explosion, Lynch held himself stiffly. "If I'd believed he wouldn't pass it along, I'd have sought an audience with the Council. It was my oversight, Your Grace. And the information spoke only of a possible assassination attempt."

"Why would he keep this information to himself?" the prince consort asked softly. The tone set Lynch's nerves on edge. This was when the consort was at his most dangerous.

Barrons hesitated. "He made no secret of his feelings about this treaty and the Scandinavians. And if you look at the people closest to the bomb—the Council, yourself, even the queen—there was a chance that he might be the most powerful man remaining in the Empire."

Stillness. The prince consort's eyes glittered. "I will see the House of Lannister *destroyed*."

"Such an act would leave the Council unbalanced," Barrons protested.

Casting a harsh look around the room, the prince consort ignored him. "Who was the girl? The one who screamed the warning? I want her found—"

"She's my ward," Barrons said swiftly. "Miss Lena Todd. She creates clockwork toys and jewelry and sells them to a clockmaker in Clerkenwell. She recognized that the automaton had been tampered with and cried the warning."

Lynch said nothing as the young lord settled into silence, but he could read the undercurrents in the room. Barrons was protecting someone. The obvious answer would be his ward, but Lynch often found that taking the obvious path blinded one to the truth.

A scrap of material caught his eye. Black. And stained with blood. It was caught on a stud from the upholstery of a chair.

"You." The prince consort stabbed a finger toward

Barrons. "You're in charge of discovering who tried to assassinate half of my court. And how they got into the heart of the bloody tower itself. And you…"

Lynch straightened.

"Find the humanists." The prince consort spun on his heel, toward the door. "And bring me their heads."

Barrons let out a deep breath as the doors slammed shut behind the prince consort and his men. "Well," he said. "That went well, I thought. He wasn't too concerned about who murdered Colchester."

Lynch knelt down. Touched the piece of fabric. Blood stained his finger and heat swam behind his eyes at the sight of it. "They probably saved him the hassle."

He licked his finger. Taste exploded over his tongue, the ecstasy of a thirst long denied. His mouth went dry and he had to force his body to calm. From the faint scent on the fabric, it had once adorned a woman.

"What have you found?"

Lynch rubbed the smear of blood between his fingertips. The lingering residue of gunpowder caught his nose. "A mystery." He looked up. "There were four people in this room. Colchester, two verwulfen, and this one. A human."

"What's the mystery of that?"

"This one…this one was the humanist," he said. "The one who fired the gun."

And he would find her.

Read on for an early look at

MY LADY QUICKSILVER

Coming soon from Sourcebooks Casablanca

STEAM HISSED AS THE ENORMOUS PISTON ROLLED through its rotation. The woman known as Mercury hurried past, her breath hot and moist against the silk mask over her face and her eyes darting.

Here in the enclaves, hot orange light lit the steel beams of the work sheds and enormous furnaces. The place was riddled with underground tunnels where the workers lived, but above ground the work sheds dominated. It wasn't quite a gaol—mechs earned a half day off a fortnight—but it was close.

Metal ingots glowed cherry red and the air was thick with the smell of coal. Men worked even at night to keep the furnaces hot, silent shadows against the shimmering heat waves. Rosalind slipped past a mech in a pitted leather apron as he shoveled coal into the open mouth of a furnace, the blast of heat leaving a light sheen of perspiration on her skin. Droplets of sweat slid beneath her breasts and wet the insides of her right glove. She couldn't feel the left. Only a phantom ache where the limb used to be and where steel now stood.

Damn it. Rosalind tossed aside the spring-recoil grappling gun and started tugging at her right glove. Her heart wouldn't stop rabbiting in her chest, her body moving with a liquid anticipation she knew well. Foolish to relish such anticipation, but the danger, the edge of her nerves, were a drug she'd long been denied.

She couldn't believe her bad luck. The Nighthawk himself, in the flesh.

A man of shadow and myth. Rosalind hadn't gotten a good look at his face in the darkness, but the intensity of his expression was unmistakable and she'd felt the heavy caress of his gaze like a touch upon the skin. Her most formidable opponent, a man dedicated to capturing her and destroying the humanists. The shock of his arrival had thrown her and Rosalind wasn't a woman who was surprised very often.

She slipped between rows of fan belts with heavy metal automaton limbs on them. The hairs on the back of her neck stood on end. She'd known it was risky, making this one last trip but she didn't have any choice. Martial law had choked the city ever since the bombing of the Ivory Tower and she needed the parts the mechs had promised her.

The bombing had been a mighty blow for the aristocratic Echelon. Every major blue blood lord in the land, including the Prince Consort and his human Queen had been gathered. If the attack had succeeded it would have wiped out nearly all of the parasitic blue bloods, leaving the working classes—the humans—to cast off the yoke of slavery and servitude. No more blood taxes or blood slaves. No more armies of metal-jacket automatons to keep them suppressed.

A bold plan.

If it had succeeded.

For a moment Rosalind almost wished she'd thought of it, but the group of mechs she'd rescued from the steamy enclaves to work steel for her a year ago had gone behind her back. For the past six months she'd urged for patience whilst the mechs had whispered that she was too soft, not merciless enough to lead the humanist movement. In the end they'd taken matters into their own hands. Rosalind tried to stop the bombing attempt before it was too late, to try and save her younger brother, Jeremy. Instead the mechanists had used him, seducing him with grand stories and sending him to deliver the bomb himself.

It had been a catastrophe. The Echelon now understood the threat the humanists posed. Rosalind had been forced to scatter those still under her command as martial law settled its heavy weight over the city and the Echelon put a bounty on their heads. She and her older brother Jack had gone into hiding whilst they tried desperately to discover any word of Jeremy.

Of the mechanists who'd betrayed her and the rest of the movement, there was no sign. All she had left of them was the rancid taste of guilt in her mouth. She knew Jeremy had been fond of their leader, Mendici, and his brother Mordecai, but she hadn't stopped the hero worship. She'd been too busy with the cause and her own personal project to see what was happening within her family.

Steel screamed as it rang against stone. Rosalind spun on her heel and looked around, fists clenched protectively in front of her. Her gaze raked the shadows.

He wouldn't have followed her here, would he? The enclaves were dangerous for a creature of his ilk.

Nothing but stillness greeted her questioning gaze. Sparks sprayed in the distance from a steam-driven welding rig but there was no one in sight.

Didn't mean he wasn't there.

Easing a foot behind her, she stepped back slowly, watching the shadows. The feeling of danger was a familiar one. She'd been a child-spy, an assassin, and years of such work had taught her when she was being watched and when she wasn't.

"You're clever," a cool voice said behind her.

Rosalind spun with her fist raised. The Nighthawk caught her arm in a brutal grip, barely flinching at the blow.

"But I expected that," he murmured, looking down at her from his great height. His fingers locked on her right arm in a cruel grip.

"I'd return the compliment," she snapped breathlessly, forcing her voice lower. Where the hell had he come from? "But I don't think it very clever for a man like you to 'ave ventured 'ere."

She jerked against his grip but it was immoveable. Harsh red light lit his face, highlighting the stark slash of his brows and his hawkish nose. He looked like the Devil's own, his lips hard and cruel and his eyes glaring straight through her. A hard black leather carapace protected his chest; the body armor of the Guild of Nighthawks.

"You and I both know I could kill any number of mechs if they come running." His voice was soft, she noticed, a low gravely pitch that one strained to listen to none the less. He'd be someone who didn't bother to raise it often. Someone who expected his word to be obeyed and wasn't often disappointed.

"Aye," she agreed, curling her middle finger and twisting the tip of it. The thin six inch blade concealed in the knuckle at the base of her hand slid through the glove silently, one of the many enhancements to the joint she'd received. Punch a man like this and she could skewer him. "But I weren't speakin' o' them. This is my world, not yours."

Rosalind stabbed hard, stepping forward with her body to give strength to the thrust. Lynch caught her wrist, jerking to the side so that the blade skittered across his ribs and not through them. Shoving away from her, his fingers came away from his side sticky with black blood. In daylight there would be a faint bluish-red tinge to it—the color gave the blue bloods their name.

He looked up, his pale eyes burning with intensity and the promise of revenge. The blood in Rosalind's veins turned cold at the sight and she snatched the knife from her boot, feeling its familiar weight in her right hand.

Lynch sucked in a sharp breath and looked away from his bloodied fingers. "That wasn't very wise."

Shadows moved. Rosalind shifted, striking up with the knife to where she thought he would come at her. A hand caught hers, thumb digging into the nerve that ran along her thumb.

"Damn you," she swore, as the knife dropped from her suddenly useless hand. She knew a hundred ways to disarm a man. But her arm was yanked hard behind her and as the Nighthawk spun her, shoving her face-first against a brick wall, she realized none of them would matter. For he knew them too.

His strength terrified her, even as it exhilarated. Here was a match, she thought with a shiver. An enemy she just might not be able to vanquish.

Shoving her between the shoulder blades, he jerked her arm up behind her back. Black spots appeared in her vision, but she didn't cry out. Instead she relaxed into it, the pain slowly softening, much like digging a thumb into a hard knot of muscle. She knew pain; it was an old friend and she'd faced far worse than this in her time. Pain didn't scare her. No, indeed she welcomed it. The physical ache was something that she could fight, unlike the gut-wrenching, hopeless fear that assailed her whenever she thought of her missing brother.

Lynch's firm body pressed against her, one knee driving into the back of hers. There was nowhere to move, nowhere to go. He had trapped her quite neatly. But then, she had a surprise up her sleeve, one last ace to play.

Lynch paused. Then he caught her wrist and peeled her mech hand off the wall, examining it. The useless fingers splayed wide as he touched a pressure point in the steel tendons, turning it this way and that. Hatred burned within her.

"Aye," she murmured. "I'm a mech."

His thumb ran over the shiv where it erupted through the glove, revealing just a hint of the gleaming steel of her hand. She hadn't bothered with the synthetic flesh some used to conceal their enhancements. They were never real enough, never the right color or consistency. And she didn't want to conform to the Echelon's demands. Damn them. She was human enough, with all the rights a human should have, no matter what they said about mechs.

Lynch found the catching mechanism and the blade slid back within the steel. "Very clever, lad. No wonder you hit like Molineaux."

"Let me go and I'll give you another."

Silence hung between them. Then Lynch laughed, a short, barking cough of amusement that sounded as if it had been a long time since he'd found anything remotely amusing.

The laughter died as swiftly as it had appeared. His pressure on her arm relaxed and Rosalind slumped against the brickwork as her injured shoulder protested.

"No doubt you would." Grabbing a handful of her coat, he spun her around, one fist clenching in the shirt at her throat. "And perhaps you'd overwhelm me eventually, but I don't care to test the theory. You're bound for Chancery Lane."

The Nighthawk Guild Quarters. Once there, she'd never see the light of day again. Except for a brief view of it on her way to the scaffold.

"I've got a better idea," she said recklessly. The ace up her sleeve… "You and I… We could come at some sort o' arrangement."

Those cold grey eyes met hers. She could see them more clearly now that her sight had adjusted to the hellish red glow but her perception hadn't altered. Lynch would give his mother to the law if she broke it.

There was always a way to manipulate a man

though. Even Lynch had to want something, to desire it... She just had to work out what it was.

"You're trying to bribe the wrong man," he said coldly, shoving her arms out wide.

A cool, impersonal hand ran along each arm, under her armpits and lower, to her hips. His hard fingers found the small pouches attached to her belt—powders and poisons that specifically injured a blue blood. Their eyes met and Lynch jerked hard on her belt buckle. The belt slithered through the belt loops on her breeches with a leathery slap and Rosalind sucked in a sharp breath.

"Every man can be bribed," she said. "What is it you want, Lynch? Money? Power?" She saw the contemptuous answer in his eyes as he discarded her belt with a jerking toss.

"Nothing you can give me. If you move your hands, I'll break them. Even the steel one."

With that, he knelt, sliding his hands down the inside of her legs. His palms were cool and impersonal, but Rosalind jerked at the touch. No man since her husband had touched her there and the feeling unnerved her.

There was another knife in her boot. He took it, tucking it behind his own belt as he started the return journey. Smooth hands slid behind her knees, the pressure just firm enough to make her breath catch. Higher... Higher... Then shying away just before he cupped her arse.

"You missed somewhat," Rosalind forced herself to say as he straightened. To escape she would have to outwit him and for that she needed his senses dulled.

His fingers lingered on her hip. "Where?"

"'Igher," she whispered, tilting her head back to look at him. The smooth leather of his gloves slid over the rough linen of her shirt. "It's me greatest asset."

His thumb splayed over her ribs, beneath her breast. So close. Though she'd wanted to keep her sex a secret, men often underestimated a woman, or were fooled by the flirtatious bat of her eyelashes. She had nothing but contempt for those who'd fallen to her knife for that mistake.

"'Igher," she dared him. Her stomach twisted in anticipation, unexpected heat spearing lower, between her thighs. Rosalind licked dry lips. Don't think about what he is. Use him, use your body.

Lynch's hand slid over the faint, unmistakable curve of her breast, his eyes widening. They were tightly bound, so as not to interfere with her movement, but he was a man. He knew what it meant.

"Surprise," she whispered.

"Bloody hell." He yanked his hand back as if burned. His eyes narrowed but she could see thought racing behind them. "You! You were in the Tower. With the bomb."

One hand curved around her skull and he grabbed a fistful of her hair. Rosalind snatched at his cloak as he dragged her head back, exposing her throat.

Stubble rasped against her cheek and Rosalind's gut turned to ash as his jaw brushed against the smooth skin just below her ear. No! She flailed wildly, her iron fingers wrapping around his wrist, knowing even as she grabbed him that she couldn't stop him. Not if he wanted her blood.

"You are her," he whispered.

And she realized that he was inhaling her scent.

He wasn't going for the vein, after all. Rosalind's body trembled as it relaxed, her stomach quivering. Lord have mercy. She was safe from that particular violation.

Then her mind started racing. "Who?" How had he known that she was in the Ivory Tower the day the mechs had bombed it? The day the Duke of Lannister had died?

Lynch lifted his head, his hand cradling her skull. She saw his eyes and stilled. Dangerous.

He dragged a scrap of leather from his pocket and held it between two fingers. "You left this behind. I could smell you all over the leather. Your scent—and gunpowder."

A perfectly innocuous piece of leather, its absence barely noticed. "And you've been carryin' it around all this time? How touchin'."

"In case I forget the scent."

Rosalind stared into his eyes, her mind making one of those insane leaps of intuition it sometimes did. Lynch wanted her. His own personal obsession, she realized. A mystery—one that appealed to his intellect as well as his desire.

"And now?" she whispered, knowing she had him. This was his weakness, right here. "Ain't there nothin' I can bribe you with now?"

He understood her meaning, his pupils flaring as he jerked away from her. Rosalind tumbled against the bricks, her hand splayed to catch herself. If she were a lesser woman she might have known some prick to her conscience at the rapid rejection. But she'd searched his eyes as she said the words; this wasn't repulsion. For a moment interest had flared there.

"You shot the Duke of Lannister and tried to blow up the Court. If you think I'll make any sort of arrangement with you, you're a fool."

"I shot the duke," she admitted. "A woundin' blow only. 'E was tryin' to strangle an acquaintance of mine."

"You deny being behind the bombing attack?"

"I tried to stop it."

"Do you take me for a fool?"

She dared to take a step toward him. "If I thought it would 'ave worked, then I would 'ave led the action, but this were no plan of mine." No, she'd gone to find Jeremy.

"No?" Lynch loomed closer, his nostrils flaring. "Then what were you doing tonight? Just what are you up to?"

"You tell me." She looked up through the gauze of her mask's eye-slits.

Lynch caught her chin, his finger stroking over the black satin. His thumb slipped beneath the edge of the mask, lifting it over her mouth and higher. "I want to see you."

Her hand caught his. "No." Rosalind took a chance and darted her tongue out, licking the edge of his thumb.

Lynch jerked his hand back, heat smoldering in his gaze. "You disappoint me. Nothing you say or do will change my mind. You're under arrest, petticoats or not."

He reached for her wrist and she twisted, capturing his own. The tendons in his arm tensed, but Rosalind slowly brought his hand up, keeping her gaze locked on his the whole time. She pressed the palm of his hand against her cheek, turning her lips into it. Lynch returned her stare with cool disinterest, but the pulse in his throat had quickened.

Rosalind licked his palm, tracing her tongue slowly across the seam there. "Don't it excite you?" His gaze flickered to hers and she stepped closer, turning his hand over to trace her lips against the tender flesh between the back of his fingers. "You," she whispered. "Me. Two enemies finally come together." Palm out, she pressed her other hand flatly against the rippled abdomen of his body armor and flexed her fingers. The leather was polished with age and use. Impossibly smooth. Like his skin.

The thought took her by surprise. In all her years she'd only ever felt such a curiosity stirring within her once, and that had been for her husband, a man she admired and respected. Lynch was worthy of neither, in her eyes.

Or was he?

She'd learned enough about him in recent months. Testing his weaknesses, discovering what type of man he was—what type of enemy she faced. The answer made her nervous. Cold and implacable, people whispered. Ruthless. Even the Echelon called him Sir Iron Heart, but never to his face.

The man in front of her was hard. She could sense that innately. But the look in his eyes… Oh no, that was not cold. Not cold at all.

"All these months you've been chasin' me, Lynch." The words were a caress, but her mind raced. "And now you've caught me. Ain't you curious? Don't you want just a little taste before you turn me over to the Prince Consort?"

Her own trembling thoughts, used against him.

"No." His head tilted toward her, his breath coming harshly.

Excitement thrilled through her. Anticipation. It was the only time she ever truly felt alive these days. As if she'd been sleepwalking for so long, Lynch's presence was like an icy dash of water to her face. Sliding her hand over each ripple of leather, Rosalind let her fingers pause on the edge of his belt and looked up, beneath her lashes. "Liar."

Furious color flushed the stark edges of his cheekbones. Lynch glared down at her, but the cool disinterest in his eyes had burned away. The blackness of his pupils overwhelmed his irises until she stared into a demon's eyes, his rational thoughts obliterated by hunger, by desire.

She had him.

Rosalind lifted onto her toes, sliding her iron fingers through the inky black strands of his hair. Her lashes half-lowering, she dragged his head down with a fistful of his hair and guided his mouth to hers.

She'd kissed men in the line of duty, seduced them with a flirtatious smile that barely touched the cold, hard ball of emotion within her. It had never meant anything to her. Yet she trembled now, her hand stroking the hard leather-clad body, feeling the buttery soft texture of his armor beneath her gloves. Her words hadn't only seduced him—she felt the truth of them herself. The excitement of something forbidden.

His cool breath brushed against her sensitive lips as

they caressed her own. Lynch resisted. "Take off your mask," he said hoarsely, his own fingers stroking the trembling flesh of her jaw.

"No."

She could feel his body leaning away from her as he fought for his senses. In desperation, she reached up and opened her mouth over his.

A shudder swept through the massive frame enveloping hers. He stiffened in shock and she drank of his mouth, her tongue caressing his with a dare and her hands sliding lower. That hard body melted against her and she felt the moment he stopped fighting his inclinations. Hands cupped her face and he kissed her as if he were a desperate man, passion rising up within him so swiftly that it shocked her. She tasted loneliness in his hunger, and something flared to life within her, something foreign and dangerous. A yearning that ached like a fist in her stomach; an echo.

Rosalind turned her face, gasping into his hair as she sought to pull herself back from that. The moment she could breathe the sensation lessened, but she didn't immediately kiss him again.

His hand cupped her nape and he grabbed a fistful of hair, dragging her head back. Cool lips slid over her chin and lower, across her throat. Rosalind clutched his shoulder, wary of her vulnerability but it didn't return. If she concentrated on the feel of him, on each delicate sensation as he licked at her throat, then she could manage to hold on to herself.

A blue blood. But he felt like a man beneath her questing hands, and he tasted like one as he returned to her lips, his breath sweet with his evening wine. The kiss deepened, his tongue forcing her lips apart, taking no prisoners. Hungry. Her body ached, the throb between her legs so long denied. Eight long years since Nathaniel died and she'd never once regretted not taking a lover. Never found a man who even tempted her. But danger was its own addiction and a part of her thrilled at the man in her arms. The Nighthawk. Her dearest enemy. A shadowy entity she'd taken great pleasure in thwarting for the past six months.

A man she was about to thwart again.

Her back hit the brick wall. Lynch's mouth slid up her throat and claimed her lips again. She barely had time to snatch a breath, or even a fistful of his shirt before his tongue rasped over her teeth. A thousand impressions leeched into her; the chafe of her nipples against the linen that bound them; the taste of his mouth, the drugging scent of him; and the gravely rasp of his knuckles on the brick as he caught her beneath the arse and dragged her legs around his hips.

Rosalind's nails curled into his shoulders, padded only by the single glove she wore. Sweet lord... She was losing herself again... She kissed him, biting at his mouth, drawing his lip between her teeth and nibbling on it. It would be so easy to forget herself, to let herself surrender until she was lost...

No.

Hands caught her own, pinned them to the wall. But she needed them free and she fought him.

Her head spun. "Let me—Let me touch you. I want to touch you."

The words stilled the violence of his passion. Rosalind bit her lip, catching a glimpse of those dark eyes. She wasn't the only one fighting this attraction. And if she let him go—for just a second—then she'd lose him.

Never. Rosalind surrendered, rocking her hips against his, feeling the hard steel of his erection between her thighs. She let her body ride against his, her hands sliding over his shoulders and luring him closer, as she threw her head back and gasped.

Lynch slammed one hand against the wall beside her head, shuddering. "Curse you," he whispered. Then his mouth bit at hers hungrily and he was lost in her again.

Rosalind slid her hands over the corded muscle of his throat, linking them behind his neck. It was a simple matter to tug the glove from her mech hand. Dropping it carelessly, she groaned into his mouth as his hand slid over her arse, tugging her against him hard.

A twist of the knuckle on her mech ring finger and a sharp needle slid from the interior. Rosalind tasted his breath and realized that she was stalling. She slid her hands over his shoulder, the rasp of his stubble scraping her jaw.

Just another moment.

One more…

Her hips rode his and she threw her head back, eyes glazed with passion. "I almost wish…" she gasped, "that I didn't 'ave to do this."

Then she slid the needle into his neck and injected the hemlock straight into his body.

Lynch stiffened, spasms racking him. "No." Slumping against her, he clawed at the wall to hold himself up, his knees giving way.

Rosalind landed lightly on her feet, the hard body pinning her to the wall. It was a good thing, for she wasn't sure her own knees would support her right now. She caught Lynch under the arms as he gurgled something in his throat. Words she probably didn't want to hear.

Laying him on the ground, she stepped back, capping the needle neatly within her metal finger and twisting the knuckle back into place. A sensation almost like guilt licked at her.

A stupid thought. A dangerous one. Sentiment had no part in her world. Nor emotion. Either could get her killed in an instant.

Her knives were tucked behind his belt. Lynch's gaze locked on hers and she realized what he was thinking.

Cut his throat now and there'd be no more night-hawks on her trail, no more martial law. This would be a devastating blow to the Echelon that they might not recover from.

Her fingers slid over the knife hilt as she took it, familiarity molding it into her hand. Rosalind's fingers clenched unconsciously as she stared at him. It wouldn't be the first blue blood she'd ever killed…

Acknowledgments

Huge thanks go to:

My partner, Byron. I could never do this without you and you remind me that there is life outside the computer screen. To my friends and family, especially my local PR manager AKA Byron's mum. There is not a person who has walked in your shop and not seen the book. Thank you all.

To Dakota Harrison, CT Green, and Kylie Griffin: for all the emails, beta reading, hero research, and naming of titles. Unfortunately Buns of Steel did not make the cut. You guys are the best and keep me sane!

To my editor, Leah Hultenschmidt, for helping me tell the best story possible and my agent Jessica Faust, for her enthusiasm and expertise. To Danielle, the PR guru who whipped me through my blog tour and all the staff at Sourcebooks who do all the hard yards.

And to my readers, who picked up this book and plunged into my mad, blood-driven world. None of this could happen without you.

Kiss of Steel

by Bec McMaster

WHEN NOWHERE IS SAFE

Most people avoid the dreaded Whitechapel district. For Honoria Todd, it's the last safe haven. But at what price?

Blade is known as the master of the rookeries—no one dares cross him. It's been said he faced down the Echelon's army single-handedly, that ever since being infected by the blood-craving he's been quicker, stronger, almost immortal.

When Honoria shows up at his door, his tenuous control comes close to snapping.

She's so…innocent. He doesn't see her backbone of steel—or that she could be the very salvation he's been seeking.

"McMaster's wildly inventive plot deftly blends elements of steampunk and vampire romance with brilliantly successful results. Darkly atmospheric and delectably sexy…"—Booklist *Starred Review*

"A leading man as wicked as he is irresistible… Heart-wrenching, redemptive and stirringly passionate…"—RT Book Reviews, *4.5 Stars*

For more Bec McMaster, visit:

www.sourcebooks.com

A Captain and a Corset

by Mary Wine

There's trouble in the skies…

For Sophia Stevenson, there's no going back to the life she knew. She never asked for the powers that make her a precious commodity to the secret society of Illuminists—and their archenemies.

Captain Bion Donkova would give anything to possess the powers that have fallen into Sophia's lap. If only the beautiful, infuriating woman could stay out of trouble, he wouldn't have to keep coming to her rescue…

Bion and Sophia have friction to spare—and nothing fuels a forbidden passion better than danger…

For more Mary Wine, visit:

www.sourcebooks.com

About the Author

Award-winning author Bec McMaster lives in a small town in Australia and grew up with her nose in a book. A member of RWA, she writes sexy, dark paranormals and steampunk romance. When not writing, reading, or poring over travel brochures, she loves spending time with her very own hero or daydreaming about new worlds. Visit www.becmcmaster.com